Judith worked as a legal secretary for many years before she was employed by the Provincial Court of Alberta. Writing, however, was always her dream. So when she retired after 28 years in Provincial Court, she immediately began to write her first book.

This book is dedicated to my husband, Bruce Logan. His steadfast love, undying patience, total support and uncanny ability to decrease my anxieties are appreciated more than I could ever adequately describe.

Judith Logan

NOT ANOTHER WORD!

AUSTIN MACAULEY PUBLISHERS™

LONDON · CAMBRIDGE · NEW YORK · SHARJAH

A CIP catalogue record for this title is available from the British Library.

ISBN 9781788784207 (Paperback)
ISBN 9781788784214 (Hardback)
ISBN 9781788784221 (E-Book)

www.austinmacauley.com

First Published (2019)
Austin Macauley Publishers Ltd
25 Canada Square
Canary Wharf
London
E14 5LQ

I wish to acknowledge my husband, Bruce, and every friend and relative who supported me in my writing. It can't be easy being the spouse/friend/relative of a woman who wanders around in a fog, fictional characters echoing in her head. Thank you all! I love each and every one of you.

Table of Contents

List of Characters

Main Characters

LACEY COLLEEN JORDAN, age 9 (6 days away from age 10) at beginning of story
BRADEN LLOYD JORDAN ('LLOYD'), age 14 at beginning of story
ANNA MARIE JORDAN (Mother, in absentia)
PAUL MARTIN JORDAN (Father, in and out of the picture)
ZACH OLIVIER (Prison friend of Paul/Protector of travelling children)
SERGEANT FRED GABLEHAUS, CONSTABLE PARKER SUTTON and CONSTABLE JILLIAN HAMILTON
JAYSON SILVERMAN and EVELYN BRONSON, British Columbia, child care workers
STELLA FRENCH, Lacey's landlady in Hope, B.C.

Foster parents:

#1 GEORGE and MARTHA SCHMIDT

Foster children: Charlotte Ford (prefers 'Charley' (age 14), Joey (age 10), Lulu (age 5), baby boy (newborn, no name)

#2 HENRY and HARRIET GRESCHNER

Susanna, their biological daughter, age 14,
Foster children: Lloyd (age 14), Lacey (age 10)

#3 SIMON and BERTHA SAVARD

Foster children: Amelia Anderson (age 16), Josh (age 15), Lloyd (age 14), Zoe (age 10), Simon (age 10), Lacey (age 10), two newborn babies, no names

#4 BART and GLADYS BOURKE

First-time foster parents – only Lloyd (age 15) and Lacey (age 11)

#5 PETER and ELSIE PETRIE

Foster children: Annie Barcley (age 16), Lloyd (age 17), Lester (age 15), Lacey (age 13), Twins Peter and Paula (ages 3), one newborn baby, no name

#6 STUMPY and HILDA SOMERS

Foster child – Lacey (age 13)

The Men in Lacey's Life:

PARKER SUTTON, Lacey's husband – married Lacey when he was 28, Lacey was 16

ADAM DRAPER, a butcher, a fill-in truck driver – age 35, Lacey was 17

EVAN SMITHSON – age 54, Manager of Buy-Low Foods, Lacey was nearly 18

MASON OAKLEY – age 46, Inspector, Chilliwack Crime Prevention & Operational Support Unit

Chapter 1
The Search

Lacey Colleen Jordan and her brother, Braden Lloyd Jordan ('Lloyd'), sat on the front steps of their home. Lacey sat placidly as she watched Lloyd study the page. A troubled frown furrowed his forehead. Those forehead wrinkles hadn't diminished since yesterday morning when the envelope arrived. Lacey had found it, lying alone in the mailbox, stark, white and ominous. There was nothing written on the envelope other than the word **LLOYD** and the address, printed in shaky, bold letters. The imprint over the stamp was indistinct, you could not read the origin of the mailing. Since retrieving the envelope from their mailbox, it had not left Lloyd's line of sight.

The early morning air was cold. It would be several hours before the spring sunshine would begin to gently melt the chill that clung stubbornly to the grass and trees.

Lacey thought briefly about putting on her jacket, but it was awfully dirty and wrinkled. It smelled bad. Besides, it seemed like too huge an effort to unclench her cold fingers from the garment. She did not put it on. Instead, she shivered in the darkness. Anxiety made her breathe through her open mouth. She could see her breath coming out in short, nervous puffs before rising lazily upwards.

Lloyd was Lacey's only sibling. He had just turned 14, Lacey would be 10 in 6 days.

For the past 2 weeks, her brother had looked after her, ever since their mother…Lacey shuddered. *Best to keep my mind on the present*, she thought, *but oh! So hard to do*.

Gripping the sheet of paper with both hands, Lloyd stood up and took a deep breath. Trying to smile at his sister, he gently took both of her small hands into one of his larger ones. "It's going to be OK, Lace. Sit here beside me while I think about what to do next." Noticing for the first time that she was shivering, he changed his mind. "We should go back in the house and have a bite of breakfast. Our school bus doesn't get here for an hour yet."

Lacey wasn't buying his stiff upper lip demeanour, not for one single second. A keen sense told her that all was not as it should be.

With yet another sigh, Lloyd folded the letter, placed it carefully back into the envelope, and put it in his shirt pocket. "Come on, baby sister, let's get some breakfast."

Tears threatened. Lacey swallowed hard. Lloyd had told her not to worry. He told her everything would work out. He had taken good care of her so far, she knew he had. Why then was she so worried?

For the past 2 weeks, Lloyd had said the same thing to Lacey every school day, and that was, "Remember Lacey, if anyone asks, everything is fine. Do not, whatever you do, tell anyone that Mom has gone and left us alone. If you tell, they will put us in a foster home, probably in 2 different foster homes, and we won't be together. So, remember, other than saying that things are good, do not say anything else, not another word!"

Once they had boarded their school bus and taken their seats, Lloyd warned her a final time.

Back on the bus at the end of the day, Lloyd leaned back and wearily closed his eyes. As he dozed, Lacey watched her brother. After a busy and active day at school, the kids on the bus were always quieter on the way home, and Lloyd was able to sleep undisturbed.

The bus rumbled along. The deep hum of the motor and the gentle rocking motion should have soothed her, but it did not. Against her will, Lacey's mind insistently drew her back to that first awful Friday, almost exactly one year ago…

Lacey ran up the steps and flung open the back door, yelling, "Hi Mama, I'm home! I had a super day! Just wait till I tell you my news!" Racing into the kitchen, she stopped abruptly.

Her mother and brother were sitting at the kitchen table. Neither said anything, not even hello. Her mother had been crying. Lloyd was deathly pale. He looked over at his mother, powerless to offer any solace as she slumped in her chair, wretched and helpless. She was weeping again.

Lloyd asked, "Should I tell her mom, or do you want to?"

Resolutely trying to pull herself together, his mother gulped, sighed, and said quietly, "I'll tell her, Lloyd. Come here baby, and sit on Mama's knee."…

Even after nearly a year of incessantly demanding further explanations from her mother and her brother, Lacey still found it impossible to believe that her beloved daddy was in gaol and would be there for 9 more years. That was as many years as she had been alive! She didn't understand what embezzlement was, even though Lloyd had told her that it was, quite simply, a sneaky, very bad way of stealing. Lacey knew that any kind of stealing was wrong. She still didn't understand why her daddy would do such a thing, leaving his wife and children alone like that! Every time she thought about it or dreamed about it, Lacey felt sick. Sometimes in the night, she would wake up so angry with her father that her tummy ached and her head hurt. When that happened, she would crawl into bed with her mother, trying not to awaken her. She would lay there for a long time until her breathing slowed down and her tummy quit aching. She would then sneak quietly back into her own bed and finally get back to sleep.

Anna Marie had married Paul Martin Jordan the day after graduating from high school. Because she was already pregnant with Lloyd, and with no work experience other than babysitting as a young teenager, she didn't work. Paul worked as a labourer and went to night school, taking accounting courses. After Lloyd was born, for a while, Anna did housework for several customers, including the laundry and ironing. By the time Lloyd was 3 years old, Anna was pregnant with Lacey. Paul didn't want her to work while the children were small, and so she stayed at home.

This past year had been painfully difficult for Anna and for the children. With her husband in prison and no income to speak of, Anna was forced to go on social assistance. The money she received barely covered the mortgage and utility payments on the house. The small amount left over made for slim pickings with 3 mouths to feed. There were days when she would give the children her share of the meal, saying she was not hungry and would have something later. There was no food to eat later. Anna took in laundry to try to make ends meet, but no matter how many loads of washing and ironing she did, it didn't pay enough to feed all 3 of them.

Anna spent many hours trying to come up with a better solution. When she finally figured out what she thought she must do, her choice was not a good one. It was probably the worst decision of her life, but she was desperate.

One Friday morning, with only one small backpack and her purse, Anna looked around her room one last time. Not stopping to look back, she abruptly left the house before her children returned from school. The last thing she did before getting on the bus was to make sure she still had the envelope containing the letter she had written to her son. She would mail it from a post office once she was far enough away from home that no one could find her.

Glancing out the window, Lacey came abruptly back to the present. She noticed that they were already approaching their bus stop. She grabbed Lloyd's arm and shook him gently. "Lloyd, wake up!" she whispered. "It's our stop."

Still groggy, Lloyd got his books together, stood up and they got off of the bus. Following her brother, but several steps behind, Lacey stopped and stood perfectly still, staring at their house.

"Come on Lace!" Lloyd called. "Let's get inside the house before anyone sees us and asks us where Mom is."

As Lacey began to walk toward the house, she felt a sharp pain in her foot. "I'll be right there Lloyd," she called. "I have a stone in my shoe."

Her brother unlocked the door and went in. Lacey sat on the front steps, struggling with removing the stone. Unbidden, her mind circled back, relentlessly recalling the events of only 2 weeks ago, on yet another Friday. *What the heck was it about Fridays*, she thought to herself. Memories swooped in with a whoosh, as frightening as the fluttering wings on a bat. *Only 2 weeks*, she thought, *it seemed like 2 years!*

She ran up the steps and opened the back door, calling out her usual greeting. "Hi Mama, I'm home. I had a super day. Just wait till you hear my news…"

Something was amiss. Only a deathly stillness greeted her youthful chatter.

"Mama?"

No one was in the kitchen, or the front room. Whatever was going on? Her mother ALWAYS greeted her after school. It was routine, it was part of their family life. They would sit at the kitchen table, and her mother would listen intently to every word as her little girl excitedly chattered about her day. Any change in routine upset young Lacey. This was a definite change in routine! The hair on the back of her neck rose. Her tummy started to hurt. This was not right, this was very wrong! She slowly climbed the stairs. The door to her mother's bedroom was closed. It shouldn't be closed. She knocked, softly at first, then louder, and then frantically she flung open the door.

Lloyd was sitting on the floor in the dark. His face was ashen except for 2 bright red circles in the middle of his cheeks.

"What is it, Lloyd?" Lacey whispered. "Where's Mama?"

He sat stone still. He appeared not to hear her. Finally, she screamed at him, "Stop it! Lloyd, you're scaring me! Lloyd, I said, where's Mama? Where is she? What is wrong with you, anyhow? Where is she? Where's our mother?"

Finally, Lloyd shrugged his shoulders. In his hands, he clutched a small piece of paper. Staring dumbly at his little sister, he shook his head. "I don't know, Lacey, all this note says is that Mom had to go away. I am to look after you for a little while. She will send us a letter very soon. In the meantime, she says we are not to worry. Her letter will explain everything to us."

Lacey could not comprehend what Lloyd was saying. All she fathomed was that her darling mama had disappeared just like her daddy – like the thief in the night that her daddy was. Was she in gaol too? She sunk slowly down onto the carpet beside Lloyd. She started to shake. She gripped her knees between both hands in an attempt to stop the shaking. Teeth chattering, moaning softly, her tears rivered down her cheeks. She was inconsolable. Lloyd helplessly put his arms around his baby sister and rocked her back and forth, not knowing what to say to her. In fact, there was nothing he could say or do, because he knew no more than Lacey did. This dilemma hit them out of the blue, no previous warning, no clues. Not so much as a hint had come from their mother.

Bringing herself back to the present, Lacey went into the house.

It had been 2 full weeks that seemed like 2 long years. It had been 2 weeks full of emotional upheaval, secrets and lies. Now the letter had finally arrived. She wondered aloud if Lloyd was going to read it to her, or if he planned on keeping her in the dark. She HATED being in the dark!

Lacey was small for her age. She looked more like a 7-year-old than a child who was just about to turn 10. After hanging up her jacket, she resolutely marched into the kitchen, placed her little hands on her hips, thrust out her chin and announced, "Lloyd, if you don't read that letter to me right now, I am going to throw a temper tantrum. I will scream so loud that all the neighbours will hear, and then we can't keep our secret any more. I am going to count to 3, just like Mama when she lost patience. One... Two... Two and a little bit... Two and a little bit more… **Threeeeeee!**" She then took a deep breath and let out 3 ear-piercing shrieks, each one impossibly louder than the one before.

The kitchen window was open. Before he could make Lacey stop screaming, the busybody neighbour hollered from the back of her yard, just across the alley, "Everything OK in there, Lloyd? Where's your mother? Haven't seen her in ages. Goodness, but that little sister of yours has a set of lungs on her. What the heck's her problem? You'd think she was being beaten or something! "

Before she could shriek again, Lloyd leaped to his feet and put his hand over Lacey's mouth, hissing. "OK, OK, I'll read it to you, Lacey. Just, for Heaven's sake, shut up!!"

"It's alright, Mrs. Osmond, Lacey is just playing a silly game. She's fine. Mom has gone shopping and then to a movie. I'll tell her you were asking about her. I'm sure she will call you to come for coffee soon. Thanks for asking!" Lloyd hurried to close the window, waving at the old biddy as he did so, grimacing through the glass in what he hoped Mrs. Osmond would perceive to be a friendly smile.

Tempering his annoyance with his little sister, Lloyd waved Lacey into the living room. Sitting down beside her on the sofa, he pulled their mother's letter out of his shirt pocket.

"Lace," Lloyd said, "I will read you the letter. Please just listen as I read it. When I am finished, I will try to answer any questions you may have. I have to say, though, that I probably have as many, or more questions than you. Can you just be quiet and listen? Please? This letter is as surprising to me as it will be to you. Please don't interrupt me, because it will only make it harder for me to read it to you."

Lacey grabbed a cushion from beside her, pressed it hard against her hurting tummy, and obediently nodded. "Okay, Lloyd, I'll be quiet and just listen."

Trying to smooth away the wrinkles from the sheets of paper, Lloyd delayed as much as he could, trying to gather the wherewithal to hold it together, both for Lacey and for himself. Their mother seemed to have been in a hurry when she wrote the letter, because she usually didn't write in such a sloppy fashion. The words were written closely together, some of them were blurred, as if wet by tears. Finally, he cleared his throat and, his voice breaking at times from emotion, he began to read:

Friday, April 3, 1998
My dear Lloyd and my dear Lacey:
I'm sorry for my spelling misteaks. You know that I only finished high school and did not get any more education. You also know that it has been a long time ago that I was in school. I do not have to do much writing when I do laundry and housework for others. I did not pay attention in school so my marks were pore. I goofed around in school instead of learning stuff. Please do not do that. You need education to have a better life than I could ever give you. You seen me strugling to make enough money to pay the bills and buy us groceries since your dad has went to goal. I have been strugling

17

with this letter in my head for the past year, and strugling for the past few weeks to put my feelings and reasons why I left you guys down on paper. I cannot struggle any more. I am all strugled out.

Nothing I tell you in this letter will make what I am doing the right thing, and for that I am truly heartbroke. No matter how long I strugle to make you understand what I have done, I know you will never realy understand. All I can do now is try. I hope you will always love me and forgive me. I don't know what else to do!

With your dad in goal, it has been hard for me to look after the 2 of you the way a mother should. No matter how much laundry I do, I cannot pay the bills. No matter how much housework I do for others, I cannot buy us food, clothes, pay all the bills, little own have any money left over for anything else. After a lot of thinking and praying I seen the way it has to be. I have figgered that all as I can do is to leave you children alone in the house. Family Services will come and take you both to a good home where you can be looked after. I have wrote a letter to them and asked that they put both of you in the same home, and I will mail it from another place, a different town from the one I mailed my letter to you so they can't find me.

Don't worry about me, I will be OK. Love each other, look after each other, study hard and be good children. Know that Mama loves you with everything in my heart. Forgive me, I can't see another way out. Grow up to be good adults. I love you both with all my heart. Remember that I am sorry! God bless you both.

All my love, hugs and kisses, Mama

x o x o x o x o x o

Lacey and Lloyd simply stared at each other in disbelief, sick at heart. After several minutes of silence, Lacey asked Lloyd to read the letter again, and then yet again. No matter how often Lloyd read the words, they made no sense, they didn't sink in. Lloyd crumpled up the sheets of paper into a single ball and threw it across the room. They sat there, staring at the offensive ball for a very long time, absorbing the shock. Eventually, it turned dark outside, yet still they sat.

Finally, like a very old man, Lloyd stood up and woodenly ambled into the kitchen. He opened a cupboard door. All he could find in the cupboard was 2 tins of tuna, 2 tins of soup, a jar of peanut butter and a box of crackers. Looking in the fridge, he stared at a bottle of juice, a loaf of bread and a jar of mayo. The freezer contained a small packet of hamburger. With shaking hands, he managed to toast some bread, put a small amount of peanut butter on it, poured 2 very small glasses of juice. He then called Lacey to come for supper.

"I'm not hungry, Lloyd," she said. "You can eat mine."

"I'm on to you, little sister," Lloyd said. "I know you are as hungry as I am, let's both sit down and eat and then we can think better about what we have to do."

Although they had eaten little in the past 2 weeks, in order to spread the meager food supplies out, and fervently believing with the blind positivity of children that their mother would come home before they ran out of food, they had no appetite. Lloyd nevertheless urged Lacey to eat her tiny meal.

Once they had choked down the food, Lloyd decided it was time for the two of them to make some decisions. "Lacey," he began in an authoritative voice, "we need to make some decisions, together." He waited for some reaction from his sister. Lacey just sat dumbly, staring at Lloyd without comprehension.

"The way it appears to me, we have only 2 choices. We wait for the people Mom contacted to come and get us. We can believe that they will put us in the same foster home and not split us up, but my friend Bobby at school is a foster kid. He hasn't seen his 2 brothers and 2 sisters since they were picked up. They were told that they would all stay together, but they are all in different places. I really don't want that to happen to us, Lace, and so I think our 2nd choice is this. We need to figure out how to get to the prison and see if Dad can somehow help us. He is in there for stealing money. Maybe he has hid some of it where we can get at it and then we can stay in the house until either Mom comes home or Dad gets out."

Lacey's small brow furrowed and Lloyd could tell she was thinking hard. She was a very smart little girl, with a good head on her shoulders for her age. He sat quietly, letting her contemplate his 2 suggestions, simply waiting for her to speak.

After several minutes, Lacey sat up straighter in her chair, looked decisively at Lloyd and firmly stated, "OK, Lloyd, let's do it!"

"Do what?"

"Go and see if Dad can help us," she said, "he's our father, he has to help us!"

"If he can," Lloyd muttered under his breath. Lacey heard him.

"Don't be a 'can't do it' boy, Lloyd," she said, "be a 'I thought I could, I thought I could' guy. Remember the kids' story called *The Little Engine That Could*? That will be us!"

Lloyd stared in wonder at his baby sister. When did she become such a little wise owl?

"I like that idea, Lace," Lloyd said. "Now, I have a plan. Want to hear it?"

Lacey bobbed her head enthusiastically. She said nothing, but it was evident from her expectant expression that she would soon burst if Lloyd didn't quickly tell her his plan!

"I don't think Mom will have had a chance to mail her letter to Family Services yet, but we need to get to the prison and see Dad, soon, before they come looking for us. We will have to go on the bus. I have to call the bus depot and get the exact cost for the 2 of us to get to the prison and back home, and the travel schedule. I am pretty sure I have enough money in my savings account at the bank to cover the cost of the tickets. I have been saving all my lawn-mowing money this summer, as well as my odd-job money. Then, we will buy the tickets and get on the 1st bus heading to Dad. I only hope that the prison will let us in to see him without an adult with us. I don't know if they will, but it is a chance we need to take.

In the meantime, if someone comes to the door, DO NOT answer. Same thing if the phone rings, DO NOT answer it. Above all, DO NOT look out the window. If it is the Family Services people, they will see you and off to foster care we go! Think you can handle this until we can get on the bus?"

Again, Lacey bobbed her head, too excited to do or say anything else.

Lloyd picked up the phone book and looked up the telephone number for the Greyhound Bus Lines. Dialling the number, he motioned for Lacey to bring him a paper and pen.

After several minutes on the phone, he thanked whomever he was speaking with and hung up. Turning to Lacey, he said, "There is a bus that leaves tonight at 11 o'clock and doesn't get to the prison, or rather Agassiz, the closest town to the prison, until 6 o'clock tomorrow morning. That will give us time to eat breakfast. The lady at the bus station was very helpful. She told me that she has been to that prison and it costs $10.00 to get there from the bus station in a taxi. It's about 8 kilometres from downtown Agassiz to the Mountain Institution… "

"What's that?" Lacey interrupted.

"What's what?" Lloyd asked impatiently.

"Mountain Inntapution!" she said.

"Mountain **Institution**. It means Mountain Prison. Don't interrupt me okay? I need to talk this through. Now, after we talk with Dad, we will take a taxi back to the bus station, wait for the next bus home, and then, back home we come. Are you ready to do this?"

"Yes, yes and more yes!" Lacey screeched, so excited that her shrill voice hurt Lloyd's ears.

"Okay kiddo, better have a shower and get prettied up. Dad won't want to see us all grubby. We have lots of time before the bus leaves tonight. First, though, I have to go to the bank and get money out of my account. I am not taking you with me because it might make people at the bank suspicious if I bring my little sister in. Don't want them to think we are a couple of runaways, do we? Just remember, no answering the phone, no answering the door and do not, whatever you do, let yourself be seen through the windows."

"Aye, aye, Captain," Lacey chirped. "Oh, I know what! Lloyd!" she continued. "Let's close all the drapes and blinds and maybe then nobody will think anyone is home, and they will go away."

"Great thinking, Lace! I'll help you do that." Glancing at the clock, he said, "And then I am off to the bank to get the money. Then I think I should walk over to the bus station and get our tickets. That way, when we go to the bus station tonight, we won't attract any suspicion from the ticket guy. At that time of night, he might think we were running away."

"Well," Miss Lacey said practically, "we kinda are running away. Only thing is, we are coming back after we see Dad, right Lloyd?"

Busily closing blinds and drapes, Lloyd muttered, "Right, Lace, you're right."

Minutes later, he had his jacket on, his bus pass in hand, and his bank book firmly stuffed into his shirt pocket. Opening the back door and glancing around to make sure nobody was approaching the house, he whispered to Lacey again that she was not to answer the phone or the door and she was absolutely NOT to peek out the windows!

"Back as soon as I can, Lacey. You'll be OK by yourself for an hour or so. I am not worried about you, I know you can look after yourself. Have your shower and dry your hair. Wear something nice so you look pretty for Dad. By that time, I should be home." With that, he quickly ran out the door and down the street to catch the oncoming bus. Lacey closed the door and went to have her shower.

Lacey looked at the clock. Lloyd had been gone for 2 hours. He was still not back. Lacey tried not to fret, but Lloyd had said he should be back in an hour. She made herself a cracker with peanut butter on it. She knew she shouldn't eat any more because the cupboards were like Old Mother Hubbard's, but she ignored that fact and made herself a 2nd cracker. After that, she cleaned up the kitchen. *I'll just pack my backpack, now*, she thought. *Maybe then Lloyd will be back.*

She ran up the stairs and down the hall to her bedroom. She knew they would not be gone long, so she only packed enough for 1 night and 2 days. She purposefully dragged out the length of time it took her to pack, hoping Lloyd would be home by the time she was done.

The phone rang. She ran to answer it, and then remembered she must not. She let it ring.

Just as she was heading back downstairs, she heard the back door open! She thought for sure she had locked it after Lloyd left. Her heart pounding crazily, she stopped and waited. She heard nothing. Did she imagine it? No! She heard the click of the door closing softly but nothing else. She shut her eyes and held her breath. She was certain that whoever the intruder was, he would hear her heart beating loudly in her chest.

Just as she was starting to panic, Lloyd came around the corner. She screamed even though she had already opened her eyes.

Lloyd was as spooked as his sister. "For heaven's sake, Lace!" he hollered, "It's me! Stop that yelling!" Suddenly realizing that he was yelling too, he closed his mouth.

Lacey rushed down the remaining stairs and flung herself at her brother. "Oh, Lloyd, why were you so long? I was getting so worried. Then you snuck in the back door without calling out to me, and I thought the people had come to take me away, and you would never find me, and I didn't know what I would do then, and I waited, and I waited, and I waited!"

When she finally paused to catch her breath, Lloyd hugged her and sat down on the stairs. Pulling her down beside him, he gently wiped the tears off her cheeks, then he told her what happened and why he was gone so long. He said that when he got to the bank, there was a policeman at the door, and another policeman in the lineup in front of the teller's cage. Fearful, perhaps irrationally, but not knowing what else to do, he left the bank and wandered around for a bit. He returned twice more, but the policemen were still there. The 3rd time he returned, Lloyd said, he simply took a deep breath, said "Good morning, sir" to the police officer at the door, and then went to stand in line just as the 2nd officer finally finished with his banking business. By the time the 2 policemen had left the bank, more than an hour had passed since Lloyd first arrived. Next in line, Lloyd finally approached the teller. He told Lacey that when he asked for most of his money to be taken from his account, the woman cheerily chattered, "Aah! Finally saved enough money for that new bicycle, did we?"

Lloyd told Lacey that he had stared right at her, crossed his fingers behind his back, and lied with a simple, "Yup!"

Lloyd continued, "Even though I knew that you would be frantic with worry, I took the time to run to the bus station and purchase 2 return tickets. Before Lacey could ask him what a return ticket was, he clarified, "to take us to Agassiz, and then back home."

"So, Lace," Lloyd said, "after buying our tickets, we have only $20.00 for the 2 taxi rides, and $20.00 left for our meals. We will take some crackers and peanut butter with us and a bottle of water each, but we could be pretty hungry by the time we get back home."

"I'm not worried, Lloyd," Lacey asserted, "I'm little and a little eater too, so if you get really hungry, you can eat my crackers!"

Lloyd couldn't speak around the curious lump that had formed in the back of his throat. A couple minutes passed before he quietly suggested she pack her things for the trip.

"Already done!"

"Wow, Lace!" Lloyd said, "Way to go! Guess I better do the same. Then all we have to do is wait until about 10 o'clock tonight and head for the bus station. In the meantime, the same rules still apply – no answering the phone, no answering the door, and no standing in front of the windows. Maybe just read a book or do some homework, but whatever you do, you have to be quiet."

"Okey dokey, Captain! Quiet and invisible here, Boss!" With a final titter, Lacey then saucily ran up the stairs to her room.

The balance of the day and early evening dragged. The telephone rang 3 times, the children let it ring. The doorbell rang twice, the children ignored it (although Lloyd snuck a peek out of the upstairs hall window and saw that it was just Mrs. Osmond.) She was probably getting a little suspicious. Lacey whispered hoarsely to Lloyd that it could be hard to sneak out to the bus with Mrs. Osmond on the lookout.

"Nah," Lloyd reassured Lacey, "we will go out through the front man-door of the garage. Mrs. Osmond can't see us from there."

Finally, it was time to leave for the bus depot. Double checking everything to make sure all was in order before they left, Lacey and Lloyd put their backpacks on, quietly went out the front without turning on any lights, locked the garage man-door behind them, and headed down the block. Rather than have the city bus driver wonder why 2 kids were taking the bus downtown this late at night, they decided to walk to the bus station.

They walked quickly down the street. Luck was with them. No one approached them, and no vehicles passed them. They reached the bus depot with time to spare. Lacey and Lloyd sat quietly in the far corner, waiting for their bus to begin loading.

"It's kinda scary here, Lloyd," Lacey whispered loudly, "there is a man over there that keeps looking at us!"

Lloyd casually glanced over in the direction Lacey indicated. The man she was talking about looked away quickly when he saw Lloyd glancing at him, putting his newspaper up to cover his face. Middle-aged, he wore a red plaid long-sleeved shirt under a black leather vest, faded blue jeans, and scuffed cowboy boots that were very worn down at the heels. He carried a backpack. The man had dark, shifty, glittering eyes, and stringy hair. Well, what little hair he had was stringy, and looked like it hadn't been washed in quite some time. He was fine-boned and scrawny. Lloyd couldn't tell how short or tall he was because he was sitting down in the corner, trying unsuccessfully to hide behind the newspaper. A sticker on his backpack proclaimed 'Born to Ride!' but gave no indication of what it was that he was born to ride. Even though he held the newspaper in front of his face, Lacey paid close attention to the parts of him that she could see. She noticed tattoos on each finger and another tattoo between his thumb and forefinger on his right hand. Because of the distance between Lacey and the stranger, she couldn't tell what they were, or what they said.

Soon it was time to climb on the bus. Lloyd helped Lacey up the steps and herded her quickly down the aisle and into a seat close to the back.

"Can I sit by the window?" she asked Lloyd. "I'm not sleepy yet, and I like to look out."

"Sure, Lacey, sit by the window," Lloyd replied, "but be very quiet, and don't talk to anyone. If someone tries to talk to us, we will just pretend to be asleep, OK? Keep your backpack with you."

Sitting down, Lloyd watched the other passengers settling into their seats. It looked like it was going to be a full busload. He looked for the man with the 'Born to Ride' sticker, but couldn't see him without standing and taking an obvious good look around.

"Do you see him?" Lacey asked in the world's loudest stage whisper, "did the Sticker Man get on our bus?"

"No, I don't see him. Don't worry about him, Lacey, he's not going to bother us. He was probably just bored while waiting for the bus. I noticed he was looking at lots of people, not just you and me."

After several more minutes, the bus driver came down the aisle. Lloyd handed him their tickets.

"Thank you, young man," the driver said. Starting to move on, he suddenly backed up! Looking carefully at both children, he asked, "Is someone meeting the 2 of you at your destination?"

Before either Lloyd or Lacey could reply, the 'Born to Ride' sticker man popped up from 3 rows ahead, "They are with me, driver, I am taking them to their destination."

"Oh, OK, then," said the bus driver. He returned to the front of the bus. Sitting in the driver's seat, he merrily whistled as he backed the bus out of the terminal. At last they were on their way.

Lacey was staring out the window of the bus, singing quietly to herself, in her own little world, concentrating on making up lyrics about the bus ride and going to see her daddy in prison. Fortunately, she had neither seen nor heard the 'Sticker Man' speaking with the bus driver.

Lloyd sat glumly, wondering what in the world he was going to do when they reached Agassiz if he couldn't figure something out before then. Thinking hard, Lloyd vaguely recalled that, when the man stood up, there didn't appear to be anyone in the seat beside him. The 'Sticker Man' had 2 seats to himself. Lloyd decided that once Lacey fell asleep, he would walk up and confront the man. Hopefully, he could explain himself to Lloyd's satisfaction. If not, it was going to be a long and stressful ride.

Lacey showed no signs of being tired and falling asleep any time soon. She was bopping along to the music blaring out of her headphones. Sometimes, she would forget herself and start belting out the tune she was listening to. Fellow passengers would notice her from time to time, and smile.

Lloyd sat still, waiting, waiting and waiting for his little sister to fall asleep.

FINALLY! Lloyd whispered something softly to Lacey. She didn't reply. A tiny little snore. Once again Lloyd whispered to her, but louder. Still no reply. Lloyd took a small blanket out of her backpack and covered her with it. Painfully, he forced himself to sit still for another 10 minutes. Finally convinced that she was asleep, Lloyd rose out of his aisle seat and started forward.

He stood still in the aisle immediately behind the 'Sticker Man'. The man was not asleep, he was staring quietly out of the window at the darkness. Taking a deep, calming breath, Lloyd approached the man. "Excuse me, sir," he said. "May I have a seat beside you for a few minutes? I have some questions to ask you."

The 'Sticker Man' patted the empty seat. "Take a load off, son," he said. "Tell me what's on your mind."

Lloyd's knees wobbled. Gratefully, he sank into the seat and immediately asked the 'Sticker Man', "Why were you watching my sister and me in the bus depot? You frightened my little sister. But more, no, REALLY disturbing, is you told the bus driver that we were with you! Who are you? Where do you think we are going? Who do you think we are, and why do you care?"

"Whoa there, sonny boy," the 'Sticker Man' said. "That's a ton of questions. I'll answer all of them, but slow down, just slow down!"

Lloyd waited as patiently as he could for the man to explain himself. He could see that the 'Sticker Man' was trying to get his thoughts together, and so he sat still, saying nothing. In a couple of minutes, he turned to face Lloyd.

"I'm sure sorry I caused you to be frightened. I didn't know how to approach you in the bus depot without you sounding the alarm, and so I figured the best way was to just wait for the bus to leave. You couldn't jump off a moving bus, and I thought it was safer to talk with you once we were well underway. You, though, have beaten me to the punch, so to speak."

The 'Sticker Man' continued, "My name is Zach Olivier, not the 'Sticker Man' as I heard your young sis call me. I was in prison with your father."

At this point, Lloyd interrupted. "Who's our dad?"

Zach replied, "His name is Paul Martin Jordan, your mama's name is Anna Marie Jordan, your sister's name is Lacey Colleen Jordan, and your name is Braden Lloyd Jordan, although you prefer to be called Lloyd."

Stretching painfully in his seat, Zach cracked each of his tattooed knuckles, then continued once again. "Your mother wrote a letter to your father, telling him that she was going to leave you kids alone until someone would come and put you in a foster home. I have to tell you, your pop was some upset. Refusing to believe that Anna could actually abandon the kids, he nevertheless raised holy hell around that prison, trying to get the guards to talk to the warden and have him do something. The guards just figured he was losing it and paid him no mind."

"Paul and I shared a cell. I was just released last week. Your dad asked me to track you down, make sure you and your sister were OK. When I sent word to him that you 2 were on your own, that I could find no sign of your mama anywhere, he figured you might try to come and see him.

"I have been following you since yesterday morning when you went to the bank and then bought the tickets to go see your dad. I sure admire your plan, Lloyd, but you see, you couldn't have made it alone. First, the bus driver was suspicious and figured you to be runaways. That was your 1st hurdle. Lucky for you 2, I was able to convince the bus driver to change his mind."

"Your next big problem would have been at the prison. They wouldn't have let the 2 of you in to see your dad without an adult present. That's where I come in. You can come in to the visitors' area with me and then you can see your dad."

"How do I know we can trust you?" Lloyd asked.

"I guess you don't, Lloyd. It's a chance you have to take, though, if you expect to see your dad." Reaching into his back pocket, Zach withdrew a crumpled piece of paper. "Would you recognize your dad's writing?"

"Sure!" Lloyd said.

Zach handed the boy the piece of paper. Lloyd unfolded it and carefully read the short note:

Hey Lloyd, hey Lacey. Don't be afraid. Zach is one of the good guys.
He will bring you to me. See you soon. Luv ya! Dad

Lloyd suddenly felt like a lot of the weight on his shoulders had slithered off. He recognized his father's writing and trusted his dad completely. If Paul said Zach was a good guy, Lloyd believed him.

Standing up suddenly, Lloyd excused himself, saying he had to check on Lacey. If she awoke and he wasn't sitting beside her, she would panic.

"No worries, kid," Zach said. "Once you check on her, if you want, come on back, and we'll chew the fat. I can't sleep, and I suspect neither can you."

A minute or so later, Lloyd returned. Slumping down in the empty seat with a sigh, he leaned his head back and tried to think of something polite to ask Zach. He had a million questions for him, but they were probably too personal or downright rude to ask, seeing as they had barely met.

As if reading his thoughts, Zach said quietly, "Ask away, Lloyd. If I don't want to answer, or can't answer, I'll let you know." He turned sideways in his seat, leaning the back of his head against the window.

"Okay, sir," Lloyd began, "will you tell me why you were in prison, how long were you there, and when did you get out?"

"First of all, Lloyd," Zach said, "you can dump the 'sir'. I'm just Zach." Struggling to get more comfortable, or perhaps simply to clarify his thoughts, he continued, "I was in prison because I got stinking drunk one night. So drunk, they kicked me out of the bar. I refused to let somebody else drive. When they tried to take the keys away from me, I took a swing at a cop. Hit him right in the nose, followed by a blow to his cheek bone, and then a final blow to his mouth before they got me down and put cuffs and shackles on me. I was stupid, blind drunk, but that is no excuse for what I did. I hurt that guy bad, broke his nose, broke his cheek bone and knocked out 4 of his teeth." Zach sat pensively for several minutes before continuing with his story. "I got 5 years in prison for aggravated assault on a police officer. I'm just lucky that's all I got. The judge took into consideration that I didn't have a record and let me off easy. I haven't had a drink since, and have no intention of having one, ever again." Glancing over at Lloyd, Zach said, shamefacedly, "That cop was a young fella with a family. I took away his earning power and caused him and his family a lot of hardship. The demon rum got me in trouble many, many times. I took my 1st drink when I was only 12 years old, and never quit drinking until I went into prison. I swear, I am done with the drink. I will go to AA, do whatever it takes, but I will never hurt another person or his family, ever again."

After a minute, Lloyd spoke up, "I noticed, sir, Zach – that you have a tattoo between your thumb and pointer finger. What does it mean, if you don't mind me asking?"

Holding out his hand, Zach showed Lloyd the tattoo. It consisted of 5 dots, 4 around the outside of a 5th one in the center. It looked to Lloyd like a dice representing the number 5.

"And what do the dots mean, Zach?" Lloyd asked.

"This can mean many things depending on which prison you were in. I picked it to mean the 4 walls of the prison, with me in the middle. I wanted something to remind me every single day of where I was and where I am now. I figure that if I find myself looking for trouble, that tattoo should remind me that being locked up is not a hell of a lot of fun."

"What about the ones on your fingers?"

"It's 2 words," said Zach. He stretched out his left hand, fingers pointed towards Lloyd, so that Lloyd could take a closer look. He then placed his right hand beside his left one. Lloyd carefully studied the elaborate looking letters. Beginning with Zach's pinky finger on his right hand, each finger bearing one letter, he read the word 'H-A-T-E'. His gaze moving on to the left hand, the letters formed the word 'L-O-V-E'. Lloyd glanced up at Zach. "What's the meaning of those tattoos?"

"No real significance," Zach said. "I saw the tattoos in a movie once, a long time ago when I was just a boy. It was called *Night of the Hunter*. Starred Robert Mitchum and Shelley Winters. You won't know those names, they were movie stars when I was a kid. Mighty fine actors they were, I always loved any movie that they starred in. *Night of the Hunter* always stuck with me, and when I finally got the chance, I took it and had the Hate and Love words tattooed above my knuckles. LOVE is tattooed on my left hand, because it is the hand closest to my heart, and I am reminded, every time I look at my hands, of where I have been and where I do not want to go again."

"How long ago was that movie?" Lloyd queried.

"It was 1955, Lloyd, long before you were born, long ago and far away. I just never forgot that movie. It was a film noir… "

"Zach," Lloyd interrupted, "what's a film noir?"

"After I saw the movie, I had to look that up," Zach explained. "The complicated meaning is 'a film marked by a mood of pessimism, fatalism and menace.' In simple words, I take it to mean a film about something not pleasant. A film noir deals with unhappy things. Doesn't leave you feeling happy, but usually you learn a lot about the dark side of human nature. I watched then, and still do, a ton of those kind of movies. I always try to learn something from them, so that I can make a better, happier life for myself than the people in those movies always do."

"Back to my questions please, Zach. How did you meet my dad, and when did you get out of prison?"

"Met your pop in the laundry room. I had just been transferred to the Mountain Institution from another prison. Your dad and me, we were both assigned to laundry duties. Liked each other right off. Neither one of us cared to participate in any shenanigans the other prisoners were up to, just wanted to do our time and get on with life, so we had that in common. Your dad spent a lot of time talking about you kids and your mama. Because my sentence was a lot shorter than his, he made me promise that when I got out, I would check on you. And I just got out of prison last week after serving my full 5-year term. First thing I did, I kept my promise to your dad, I checked on you. Found you and your little sis, but haven't spotted your mama – is she OK?"

Lloyd felt tears welling up behind his eyelids. He quickly closed his eyes so Zach wouldn't see. "I don't know, Zach," he quietly said. Reaching into his jeans pocket, he brought forth the letter from his mother and handed it to Zach. A few minutes later, after Zach handed the letter back to Lloyd, Zach said, "Well, I'll be damned! What kind of a broad would do something like that – abandon her own kids?" Quickly he added, "You don't have to answer that, Lloyd. Nobody could possibly answer that."

"Thanks for checking on us, Zach. I need to try to sleep now. See you when we get to Agassiz, okay?"

"You bet, kid, sleep well. Tomorrow you will see your pop and hopefully, he will have some ideas about what to do with you. Good night for now." Zach turned his back to Lloyd, leaned against the window and closed his eyes.

Lloyd went back to his own seat. Lacey was still sleeping soundly. He pulled the blanket tighter around her, leaned back in his seat and closed his eyes.

After what seemed to Lacey like only minutes, she sat up. Rubbing her eyes, she stared over to her left and right up into the face of the 'Sticker Man'! With a startled squeak, she poked Lloyd in the ribs. "Wake up, Lloyd! Wake up!" Lloyd groaned, and shoved her hand away. "Leave me alone, Lacey, I'm sleeping."

Lacey continued to poke her brother in the ribs, all the while staring into the face of the 'Sticker Man'. Lloyd finally straightened up, snarling at Lacey as he did so, "What the heck is wrong with you, Lace? I told you to leave me alone." Hanging on to Lloyd's shirtsleeve for dear life, she silently pointed upward. Lloyd looked to his left. "Aah! Good morning, Zach," Lloyd said. "I'd like for you to meet my little sister, Lacey. Lace, say hi to the man who is going to get us into the prison to see Dad. If you hadn't been such a sleepyhead, I would have told you about Zach sooner."

Zach grinned at Lacey. "Pleasure to meet you, little missy. You 2 better get your gear together. We'll be at the bus station in Agassiz in about 10 minutes. We'll have a bite of breakfast, and I'll fill you in on procedures at the prison."

The 3 travellers walked to Jack's, a restaurant not far from the bus depot. Lacey looked at Lloyd and whispered (loudly!) "How much money do we have again, Lloyd? I don't want to order something too ''spensive'." Zach looked at her across the table and smiled. "You can order whatever you want, little missy, I'm buying this meal. I bet you haven't had a lot to eat since your mama left, and you are probably mighty hungry! Their breakfast specials are pretty good here, and they are large portions." They all ordered the special. Their meals arrived and the children ate every single bite. Zach, watching them attack their food, signalled the waitress and ordered more toast and hot chocolate.

Finally, Lacey leaned back against the booth. "I'm stuffed, Mr. Zach, just stuffed! Thank you for breakfast, it was delicious!"

"Yes, thank you sir – Zach – it is very kind of you to buy us breakfast."

Zach grinned. "It's my pleasure, kids. Nice to have company for a meal."

"Do you have kids?" Lacey asked Zach.

"Hush! Lacey!" Lloyd admonished. "That's too personal a question!"

Zach glanced pensively out the window. He then turned and looked at Lacey. "I do have kids, a boy and a girl, Alexander and Loretta. Alex is 9 and Loretta is 6. They live with their mother on the west coast. My wife divorced me when I got sent to prison. The kids live with her." He sighed deeply. "I don't blame her. I put her through hell and back with my drinking long before I went to prison. Yet another reason to stay out of trouble, and definitely out of prison. I sure do miss those babies, though."

Lloyd gritted his teeth and said bitterly, "What a shame. You have kids that you want, and can't see them, we have a mother we want, but she deserted us, so we can't see her. Life is pretty ugly, isn't it, Zach?"

Zach stared long and hard at Lloyd. "Listen to me, kid, life is what you make it. I screwed mine up big-time. I would give my right arm to go back in time and not do what I did. Simple fact is, I can't. What's done is done, it can't be undone."

"Now, the way I see it, I have 2 choices I can make from this time on. First choice, sit around and feel sorry for myself, the old 'woe is me' routine, start drinking again, don't look for work, just waste the rest of my life. Second choice, I can find whatever job I can find and as an ex-con it might be difficult, but I can get a job, do my best, and live my life in a way that will benefit me and everyone around me." He held Lloyd and Lacey's attention with an intense gaze. "Which way do you think I should go? Which way do you think I will go?"

Lacey suddenly crawled underneath the table and popped up and on to the booth on Zach's side of the table. Putting her arms around his neck, she hugged Zach fiercely, but said nothing. She sat down beside him. Zach swallowed hard. "Want to guess which way I'm going, Lacey?" Zach asked her.

Lloyd gulped, took a deep breath, and interrupted. "You're a good man, Zach, and you will make the right choice. Thanks for telling us that. We hope you'll keep in touch and let us know how you're doing from time to time." He stopped and waited as the waitress came and cleared the empty plates off their table.

When she left, Lloyd added one more thing. "Oh yeah, and for your information," he said, "some of my bitterness just went away with those dishes. I won't forget how kind you have been to my sister and me and just so you know, we will make the right choices, too."

Zach cleared his throat noisily. He blew his nose into a napkin, excused himself and went to the washroom. He came out, paid the bill, called a cab, and motioned to the children to come with him.

Standing outside while they waited for the cab to arrive, Zach quickly briefed the children on what to expect at the Mountain Institution. "Normally, you would have had to fill out an application form in order to visit an inmate." He grinned wryly. "One good thing about not getting in trouble while I was in the joint, I knew a guard. He owed me a favour. Voila! No delay with filling out the application!"

Zach continued, "When we get in there, we'll all have to sign the visitors' log. From there, we will be searched... "

"Searched? For what? We don't have anything." Lloyd looked distressed.

"Just gaol house procedure. Everyone gets searched. Don't worry, it won't take long," Zach said. He continued, "Then we will be shown to the visitors' lounge. It's a big room, bright and sunny. Unlike what you see in the movies, your pop will be allowed to sit with you at a table and chairs, you won't have to talk from one side of a plexiglass window. You can visit for as long as you like, being the children of Paul. I figure about an hour should do it for the 1st visit. I'll just say hi to Paul, then I'll leave you to visit with him by yourselves. When the visit is over, I will come back into the lounge and get you, make sure you get on the bus, and then I'll be on my way."

Lacey was alarmed! "But, Zach," she whined, "you have no place to go. You need to come home with us!"

Saved by the cab. "Let's go see your pop, little missy," Zach said, changing the subject somewhat. "He's waiting to see you."

Chapter 2
The Trap

Once they entered the building, a guard stood in the centre of the entryway. Zach introduced the kids to Gary, the guard.

Gary was very kind, even going so far as to squat down to bring himself to Lacey's eye level as he questioned her about her reasons for attending at the prison. Rising, he asked Lloyd the same questions, in the same compassionate tone of voice. He then walked over to Zach and shook his hand. "Good to see you, Zach. Are you keeping out of trouble?"

Zach grinned at the guard. "You know it, Gary! I ain't never coming back here, except maybe as a visitor."

"I'm very happy to hear that, Zach." Turning towards Lacey, Gary said, "Let's get this register signed, shall we, so you can see your dad. He has been waiting anxiously all morning for you to arrive."

After the register had been signed by all 3 visitors, they followed Gary down the hallway towards the visitors' room.

Zach sat and waited with them at a table for 4, while Gary went to instruct another guard to bring Paul to the visitors' centre. Looking over at Zach, Lloyd remarked that he seemed awful fidgety, was something wrong? Zach said, "Aw, it ain't nothing. Just being back at the prison is making me squirrelly, that's all."

Suddenly, a door on the far side of the room opened up and a bearded man walked into the room, followed closely by another prison guard. The man stood hesitantly just inside the doorway as if unsure whether to walk forward or turn around and run. Although his mouth moved, no words came out of it.

Zach broke the awkward silence. He stood up and walked toward the man. "Hello there, Paul," he said. "I told you I would take care of getting the kids here to see you."

At last, Paul seemed to find his tongue. He walked towards the table where Lloyd and Lacey were sitting. When he reached the table, he just stood there and stared at them for several moments. Finally, he asked, "May I sit down with you?" Lloyd said nothing, just nodded, and pointed to one of the 4 chairs.

Zach stood up. Paul, immediately, his voice filled with panic, said, "Don't go, Zach, please! Stay! We have things to discuss."

Zach joined the group, sitting down on the edge of his chair. He kept glancing surreptitiously towards the entrance door from time to time, wondering how soon he could escape from the tension in this room. Just when the silence around the table was growing unbearable, Lloyd said, "So, Dad, I see you've grown a beard. I didn't recognize you for a minute."

More silence.

Lacey got out of her chair and stood shyly behind her brother, stared at her father, but said nothing. Her father smiled tremulously at her. He took a deep breath and said, "Lacey, don't you know me?" She simply continued to stare at him.

With a deep sigh, Paul looked towards his son. "Lloyd, I know you have a million questions. Ask away. If I can answer, I will."

His throat clogged with bitterness, Lloyd said, "Do you really expect us to be excited to see you after what you did? You taught us right from wrong, walloped our butt if we didn't do the right thing, but you – what you did is beyond my understanding. You're a thief! You left us! You left Mom with no money and no way to take care of us. Now she has disappeared, and we are totally alone. Dad, I'm 14, but I'm just a kid! You robbed me, as well as the company you worked for. You robbed me of my childhood, you left me with adult responsibilities! I have really struggled, every single day, to unravel my feelings about this. I know I need to forgive you, but how? How am I supposed to forgive both my parents when my dad is a thief, and my mother abandoned her family?" His voice hitched on the last few words and he unsuccessfully blinked away the tears that formed in the corners of his eyes.

Paul was dumbfounded. He croaked, "What do you mean, your mother has disappeared?" Glaring over at Zach, he said, "Zach, you didn't tell me that she really did it! What the hell?"

Zach shrugged his shoulders and responded, "Hey man, I didn't have a chance. I just found out late last night myself. That doesn't mean that I have given up on finding Anna, it just means I had to get your kids here to see you before I try and find your wife. Actually, I really thought she might have been in contact with you by now, but apparently not."

"Look, I'm going out to have a chin wag with Gary. The kids came to see you. Spend some quality time with them." Zach got up off the chair and exited the room.

Paul swallowed hard, and then began, quietly, "It's a long, long story, kids…" He stopped.

"We've got nothing but time, Dad," Lloyd insolently muttered. "We came all this way to hear it, didn't we Lacey?" His little sister chewed on her thumbnail, and nodded.

Finally, she whispered, "Yes, Daddy, we want to hear."

With a smile that was more of a grimace, Paul asked her if she would sit beside him. Lacey shook her head 'no' and went and sat in a chair at the opposite side of the table. Folding her hands on the table in front of her, she appeared to be years older than 9 as she watched her father struggle for words.

"You don't know anything about life yet, kids. You don't know what it is like to work day after day, night after night, even every weekend, just to make ends meet. I worked for this accounting firm for 15 years, gave my boss all that

I had in me. I went to night school to get my accounting papers, gave up a lot of family time to get that degree. I got no recognition for my efforts and not even enough of a pay raise to pay the bills."

"I watched that bast... sorry, I mean, I watched my boss raking in the dough and not sharing a nickel of it. He got rich on the backs and brains of his employees. We got nothing."

"I was at my wit's end. Falling further and further behind after paying for night school and having to quit my weekend job so I could study, I finally had enough. I was the bookkeeper. I went through all the firm's books with a fine-toothed comb and figured out a way to skim something off the top every month. The boss never checked the books. The accounting firm had just filed the corporate tax return. I figured I would have any funds I 'borrowed' repaid by the time the next year's taxes were due. Oh, I had it all planned, down to the last nickel. I would 'borrow' just enough to get ahead of the game, pay off my outstanding debts, and then pay back the firm. But it seemed so easy that my withdrawals got larger and larger, and nothing was being paid back. Next thing I know, it's tax time again. Sure enough, the accounting firm discovered the deficit."

"The boss called everyone to a special meeting in the library, to meet with the accountants. The entire staff showed up.

"The absolute very first thing, the boss came right out and asked who was at fault for the missing funds. I just sat there. Everyone looked at everyone else. You could cut the tension with a knife it was so thick in that library. Every single person in that room looked guilty and felt guilty. Some faces were pale, some were red and sweating, everyone silently accusing everyone else. The old bast... boss just sat at the head of the table, arms folded, waiting."

"After what seemed like forever but was likely only a few minutes, the boss stood up and told us that even if we had to sit there for a month, no one was leaving until this got sorted out. He then plopped his fat a... sorry, 'bottom', back down onto his chair and folded his arms again, waiting."

"One of the girls from the office said she had a sitter, and she had to get home at the regular end of the workday so the sitter could leave. The boss said it was too bad, he guessed she would have to confess before then, or somebody else would have to confess. He told all of us that he was dead serious. Nobody could leave until someone confessed. He sat down abruptly and continued to wait, his beady little eyes going from person to person around the room, burning a hole in each of us as he waited some more. He waited. He waited. Still, he waited.

"After a couple of hours, I couldn't stand it another second. I stood up, looked the boss in the eye, and said, "All right you cheap bast... boss, you win. I did it. Let the others go home."

"But, Dad," Lloyd began, "why didn't you say something? I saved some money. You could have had it anytime if I knew you needed it! Why did you have to steal? That's what I don't get."

Paul, ashamed and red-faced, said, "You didn't have enough money to make a dent in what I owed, Lloyd. Anyway, what kind of a father would I have been to take your savings?"

"A better father than a thief," Lloyd said. "I suppose you don't have any of that money stashed away someplace where Lacey and I could get it, would you? It would be real nice to have a bit of cash to buy some groceries!"

"There's not a cent, son," Paul shamefacedly said. He quickly changed the subject. "Now, tell me about your mama. Do you have any idea where she might have gone?"

Lloyd reached into his pocket and pulled out the letter from Anna. Unfolding it with utmost care, he handed it to his father, without a word. Paul scanned the contents, then handed it back to his son. "Guess I couldn't have screwed up any more if I tried," he said.

Suddenly, there was a soft commotion behind the kids. Looking around, they saw a man and a woman approaching. There was something officious looking about the pair as they approached the table.

Suddenly, Lloyd stood up. "You bastard!" he roared at his father. "Those are child welfare workers, aren't they? What have you done, Dad, what have you done?" Grabbing Lacey, he shoved her behind his back, holding tightly to her hand as he waited for the inevitable.

The woman spoke first. "You must be Lloyd," she said. Peeking around him, she said softly, "And you must be Lacey. Your mama wrote to us and asked that we look after you until she is in a position for you to move back home with her. We have a wonderful couple just waiting for you and Lloyd to come and stay with them."

"I'm not coming with you, I'm not!" wailed Lacey. Whirling around, she glared at her father. "You did this, didn't you? You told them where to find us!" She stopped for a moment, horrified beyond further words.

"Nah, he didn't, Lacey," said Lloyd. "That bastard Zach turned us in. Why did we trust him? I should have known better. He couldn't just leave well enough alone. He promised Dad he would check on us, and then that asshole ratted us out."

Paul had enough. He stood up, pointed his finger at Lloyd, and said in a stern tone, "Watch your mouth!" He continued, "You're partly right. Zach did call the Family Services people, but at my request. You have tried to look after things at home. It is impossible. You know it, I know it, Family Services know it, and your mother knows it best of all. Until I am out of prison, or your mother returns, you are going to be looked after, have enough to eat, and a place to sleep. Now buck up and go with these nice people. I will keep in touch with the department, and with the 2 of you."

Softening his tone, he told his children, "It's not going to be forever. Make the best of a bad situation and learn from your parents' mistakes. Look at it this way, at least you will both be in the same foster home." With a choked sob, Paul turned away from his children and shuffled back to the prisoners' entrance door, his shoulders slouched forward so he was almost doubled over, looking for all the world like a 90-year-old man.

Chapter 3
George and Martha Schmidt

Lloyd stood up, straightened his shoulders, and took Lacey by the hand. "Come on, Lace," he coaxed. "You heard what Dad said." Not another word was spoken as they walked over to the social workers, who stood patiently waiting for the children.

The man was very tall and thin. Lloyd thought he was probably about 30 or so years of age. He wore black dress pants, a white shirt, black shoes, no jacket or tie. His hair was red, his face full of freckles. He wore black-framed eyeglasses.

Looking Lloyd directly in the eye, the man spoke. "My name is Jayson Silverman, Lloyd. I will be the child care worker in charge of your case. Any questions or concerns you may have while you are in the care of Family Services can be directed to me, if your foster family can't answer them for you." Reaching into his shirt pocket, he withdrew a business card and handed it to Lloyd. "Both my office number and my mobile phone number are on this card. Feel free to call me at any hour of the day or night."

The woman was short, plump. She looked quite a bit older than Jayson Silverman. She was short enough that she didn't have to squat down to look Lacey in the eye, but tall enough that she did have to look down to speak with the child. She wore a navy skirt with matching blazer, and a navy and red-printed blouse. Red high-heeled shoes completed the outfit. Her straight hair was turning gray and was cut short. Her eyes were a brilliant blue. She did not wear glasses.

Looking down at Lacey, the woman spoke. "My name is Evelyn Bronson, Lacey. Like Mr. Silverman, I am also a child care worker, and I am in charge of your case. What Mr. Silverman said to Lloyd, is the same for you, except you would call me instead of Mr. Silverman. Here is my business card containing my office number and my mobile number. If it is important, and if you can't get answers from your foster family, you can call me, any time. Put this card in a safe place and don't lose it. You never know when you might need to call me."

Lacey thought to herself, *That was very strange. Why would she need to call her anyway? Surely her mama would be home before she would need to call Mrs. Bronson about anything.*

Following the 2 adults, Lloyd and Lacey left the prison building and headed towards the parking lot. Approaching a small silver car that looked like it had seen better days, Jayson Silverman unlocked it. He opened the trunk, directed the kids to put their backpacks in it. They then crawled into the back seat and put on their seatbelts.

"I'm really hungry, Lloyd," Lacey whispered loudly. "Breakfast was so long ago that my tummy is growling!"

Evelyn Bronson overheard the little girl. Turning to her partner, she asked Jayson if he would stop at McDonald's on their way back to the office. With a grin and a wink, he agreed that was a great idea.

While waiting in the lineup at the drive-through, Mr. Silverman took food orders from Mrs. Bronson. Looking at the children through the rear-view mirror, he asked them what they would like to eat. With a little encouragement, he got the orders from both children.

Reaching into his pocket, Lloyd tried to hand him a 10-dollar bill over the seat. "Put your money away, Lloyd," Mr. Silverman said. "The government can pay the shot today. Now, are you sure that is all you want to eat? How about a milkshake to go with your burgers and fries, and how about an apple pie? I don't know about you guys, but I am always hungry and right now I am starving!" Approaching the drive-through window, he gave the cashier their order, and then drove up to the pick-up window to wait for their lunch.

"We're only a few blocks from our office, so I think we should take our food and eat it at the office while we fill out the paperwork," Mrs. Bronson said to Jayson. "Once that is done, we will talk with Lloyd and Lacey about their foster home."

"Okay, boss lady," said Jayson smartly. "Driving to the office here, boss lady!" Winking again at the back-seat passengers, he retrieved their orders from the cashier, handed the bags to Mrs. Bronson, and then proceeded to drive to the office.

A short time later, they were all seated in the coffee room of the Family Services offices. Lacey and Lloyd ate ravenously, leaving not a crumb or a drop when they had finished their lunch.

Once everyone was finished eating, Mrs. Bronson clasped her hands in front of her primly, resting her elbows on the table. She looked first at Lacey, then at Lloyd. Then she spoke. "I am sure you must both be feeling very confused and worried. Let me try to put some of your uneasiness aside. First of all, you are NOT being taken away from your own home and parents and being placed for immediate adoption. For the time being, we just want to see that you are kept warm and fed and cared for in the absence of your mother and father."

"Authorities are now searching vigorously for your mother. Hopefully, she will be found soon. If she is physically healthy and otherwise able, you will be going home with her. If she can't be found or is unwell, you will stay in the system until your father gets out of prison. If he has been a model prisoner and can prove to us that he is able to support you both financially and emotionally, has been to all of the mental health sessions and rehabilitation sessions offered to him at the Mountain Institution, you, in all likelihood, will be able to go home with him. Of course, that could be quite a while in the future unless he is able to get out of prison early for good behaviour. That, of course, is still several years away."

As Mrs. Bronson rose to refill her coffee cup, Jayson Silverman took over. "I know you are wondering about the foster care family we are taking you to. Let me tell you about them. Their names are George and Martha Schmidt. They have been foster parents over many years, for many children. In fact, in this area, they have fostered more children than any of the other active foster parents that we have in our files.

"At any one time, they have up to 6 children in their care, ranging in age from newborn babies to 17 years of age. The babies, generally, are adopted within a short time of their birth. The older children, not so quickly.

"However, as Mrs. Bronson just told you, adoption is NOT in the immediate future for you 2. You will probably be lucky, going back to your own home in the not too distant future, depending on whether or not, sorry, strike that, depending on WHEN the authorities are able to find your mother.

"Mr. and Mrs. Schmidt live in Alberta, in a small town not far from the British Columbia border, only about an hour or so away from your home city. They have a large 6-bedroom house. At times, you may have a room to yourself, at other times, you may have to share a bedroom with up to 3 other children. Every effort is made to keep like ages together, however, that depends, naturally, on the ages of the foster children in the home at any one time."

He paused, and looked expectantly at Lloyd and Lacey. "I'm sure you must have questions?"

Lloyd said, "No, sir. I'm just happy that Lacey and I are able to be in the same foster home. I know they will find our mother very soon. We will both do the best we can while waiting for her to come home. I realize this is just temporary. We are getting used to waiting."

Lloyd leaned back in his chair and sat pensively. Suddenly, he leaned forward. "Yes, I guess I do have just one question. If we are going to a foster home in Alberta and the 2 of you are British Columbia child care workers, why don't we have Alberta social workers taking our files?"

"Hey, man, that is an excellent question," Mr. Silverman said. "The fact is, no one knows where your mother is at the moment. She could be anywhere, in any province, or even out of the country. Your father is incarcerated in the Province of British Columbia, and in order to keep in touch with him regarding where you 2 will be fostered, it is simply easier and more economical to use B.C. workers. In addition, Alberta is overworked and underpaid, so we try to help them out whenever possible. If, in the unlikely event that you require immediate assistance, we would contact an Alberta social worker to take charge until we could get to you."

Jayson Silverman looked over at Lacey, who sat at the edge of her chair, visibly upset. "Well?" he asked her. She stared at him, saying nothing.

Lloyd leaned over and put his hand on his little sister's shoulder. "Answer him, Lace," he whispered to her. "He wants to know if you have any questions."

Lacey sat up straighter, looked Mr. Silverman in the eye and stated resolutely, "No sir, I don't have any questions at this time, BUT, my mama will be back for us before I even have any questions!" Despite the firmness in her tone, 2 large tears trickled down her cheeks.

"OK, then," Jayson said, "Mrs. Bronson and I will drive you to the Schmidt's house first thing in the morning. It is too far to drive there this late in the day. For tonight, Mrs. Bronson has made up places at her home for you to sleep. I will pick all 3 of you up tomorrow morning at 8 o'clock, sharp!"

A half hour later, Mrs. Bronson and the 2 children were standing in the middle of the small living room on the 3rd floor of a 4-storey apartment building. "I'm sorry, but I have only 1 spare bedroom, and this pull-out sofa. Lloyd, you would probably be more comfortable in the spare room. The bed is larger. Lacey, this evening we will make up the pull-out for you to sleep on.

"It's only 3 o'clock. I have some paperwork to do. The television, I don't think, has much on in the afternoon that is of interest to children, or anyone else for that matter. You will notice, however, that I have a whole shelf full of movies, and another shelf full of books that you might be interested in. Please, make yourselves at home. I will be working at the kitchen table if you need anything." She turned and walked into the small kitchen and immediately spread out her files.

Lloyd and Lacey sat on the sofa, staring at each other. "What do you want to do, Lacey?" asked Lloyd. Lacey replied, "Well, Lloyd, what I really, really want, is to go home. But I know, I know…" She said this rapidly, before Lloyd could admonish her.

She got up, walked over to the window and looked outside. Immediately across the street, in full view of Mrs. Bronson's apartment, was a lovely park. Even this early in the spring, the trees were exhibiting signs of the warmer weather to come, branches plumping up, the odd bud swollen enough to be visible even from this distance. There were a few park benches scattered haphazardly through the small park. Carefully tended flower gardens lay, stark and bare, awaiting the planting by town workers of shrubs and seeds which the sun and the rain would gently push, coaxing the beauty sleeping beneath the soil out into the open. Lacey imagined she could smell the blossoms in the air once everything was in full bloom. One corner of the park housed playground equipment, swings, slides, a merry-go-round, and a set of monkey bars.

As Lacey continued to stare longingly out the window, the sun appeared from behind a cloud. She turned to her brother and said, "I really, really, really want to go to the park. Do you think she will let us?"

Lloyd said, "I doubt it, Lace, but ask her and see."

Not realizing that in the small apartment it was impossible not to eavesdrop, purposely or not, Mrs. Bronson suddenly appeared. "It is probably against my better judgement," she said, "but if you both can promise me, and by that, I mean the 'cross-my-heart-and-hope-to-die' kind of promise, that you will not leave the park except to come back here, then I see no harm in you going to the park. Just know, I will be watching you and will hold you to your promises."

With a happy screech, Lacey turned and hugged a surprised Mrs. Bronson. "We promise! We promise we won't go anywhere but the park and then back here! Where's my coat, I can't wait! Come on, Lloyd, let's go!"

A couple of hours later, Lacey and Lloyd returned to the apartment, their flushed complexions rosy from both the fresh air and the escape from stress for that short period of time.

"Thanks for honouring your promises, children," said Mrs. Bronson. "Supper is nearly ready. Hope you like spaghetti and meatballs. Wash up and come to the table."

Within a few minutes, both children were sitting at the table, eating Mrs. Bronson's excellent spaghetti dinner. For dessert, there was ice cream and chocolate sauce. Once again, Lloyd and Lacey ate, and ate, and ate. Finally satiated, Lloyd leaned back in his chair, grinning. "That was terrific, Mrs. Bronson," he said, "Best meal we've had since our dad… " Here he stopped and swallowed hard. "Well, you know," he said quietly. "Thank you for a great dinner."

Mrs. Bronson smiled understandingly. "I am glad you enjoyed it, Lloyd. It was very nice to have company for a meal. My husband passed away from a heart attack nearly a year ago. We had no children, and so it has been pretty lonesome in this apartment ever since he died."

Lacey spoke up. "Oh, I'm very sorry, Mrs. Bronson. I know how terrible it is to be lonesome, and so does Lloyd. Thank you for supper. Spaghetti is our very favourite."

Clearing his throat roughly, Lloyd stood up. "Mrs. Bronson, Lacey and I will do the dishes so you can watch the news on TV. Then, do you think we could pick either a program or a movie we would all like, and watch it before bedtime? I know we will be leaving early in the morning, so we should really do this before it gets too late." He looked at her, waiting her reply. It took a minute or two for Evelyn Bronson to answer through the lump at the back of her throat. "Thank you," she whispered and quickly disappeared into the living room. Almost immediately, a news broadcast echoed from the living room through into the kitchen.

As soon as the children finished the dishes, they went into the living room. Suddenly they were riveted to the television screen. On the screen was a picture of their mother! A policeman was attempting to answer questions from a crowd of reporters, but they were shouting their questions all at once, their voices overlapping one another so that no one question could be distinguished from another. The officer stood patiently, waiting for the reporters to settle down. Finally, he held up his hands and shouted in order to be heard above the crowd. "Enough!" he bellowed. "If you want to hear what I have to say, be quiet! Otherwise, this news release is over." He straightened up to full height and waited until the noise died away.

"That's more like it everyone. Now, listen to what I have to say and then I will take your questions, one at a time."

"We are searching for Anna Marie Jordan. Mrs. Jordan is 32 years of age. She is approximately 168 centimetres tall and weighs approximately 52 kilograms. She has chin-length, naturally curly, dark brown hair and brown eyes. Her picture is being shown on all television newscasts for the next few days. My assistant has copies of the photo available for you should you wish to pick one up at the end of this news release."

The questioning began, almost immediately building up to the previous frenzy, until the officer held up his hands. He pointed 1st to a female reporter in the back of the throng. "Why are you looking for Ms. Jordan? Is she wanted in relation to a crime?"

"Mrs. Jordan appears to be missing. She has never gone missing before, and her family is, quite simply, most anxious to find her," replied the policeman, skilfully avoiding any reference to crime.

He pointed next to a male reporter in the front row. "What kind of vehicle was she driving when she left home?" he asked. "She left on foot, no vehicle," the officer responded. "It is believed that she took a Greyhound bus, but where she went, or even which direction she went, is unknown at this time. We have no leads. We are hoping that someone who sees her photograph on television, or in the newspaper, will remember seeing this woman somewhere, and will contact our detachment."

After answering a couple more questions, he said, "You now have all the information that we have. There is nothing more I can tell you. If and when we hear anything more, we will issue another release. In the meantime, please pass on the information. Thank you for your attention." He turned around and, ignoring the melee behind him, got into his police vehicle and drove away, leaving his assistant to deal with passing around the photo of the missing woman.

The television announcer placed the picture of Anna Marie up on the screen again, and relayed the telephone number, fax number, and street address of the local R.C.M.P. detachment, once again stressing that if anyone spots this missing woman, or knows where she is, to contact the police at the earliest possible time.

Lacey had been kneeling in front of the television screen, her hands touching the photo of her beloved mama, sobbing quietly as she listened and watched the report. Rising up off the floor, she emphatically said to Lloyd and to Mrs. Bronson, "They are going to find her, I just know it. Everything is going to be okay. I really need to sleep now. Please, I don't want to watch any more TV."

"We all need to sleep now," Evelyn Bronson said. "We have a long drive ahead of us and an early start in the morning. Good night, children. I will call you when my alarm rings tomorrow morning."

After the tumultuous day that had passed, it was no time before everyone was sound asleep.

When the alarm rang, it felt like it had only been minutes since they fell into bed, but it was 7 a.m. Mrs. Bronson was already up and cooking breakfast. Lacey went into the bathroom and put on a clean pair of jeans and T-shirt, washed her face, attempted to brush her hair and teeth, and then left the bathroom for Lloyd to use and to clean. She went into the front room and struggled to fold up the sheets and the quilt.

By 7:30, all 3 were sitting at the kitchen table, enjoying French toast, bacon and hot chocolate. By 5 minutes to 8, the dishes were done, the children's meager possessions in order, and they were ready for Mr. Silverman to pick them up.

Although the trip wasn't as long by car as it was by the bus, which had stopped at every little pimple on the map when they took the trip to Agassiz, it was still a long drive. The children dozed in the back seat as Jayson and Evelyn chatted quietly in the front.

After a quick stop for lunch and a bathroom break, they were once again on the road. Apprehensive because they were going to a strange town, a strange house, and strangers in the house, Lloyd and Lacey said little the entire trip. From time to time, Lacey grabbed on to Lloyd's hand and squeezed it tightly.

It was late afternoon when Jayson drove into the Schmidt's gravel driveway. Lacey stared at the house. It was a tall, 2-storey house. It had an attached 2-car garage. A covered veranda ran the length of the house. A wicker rocking chair sat next to the front door. Several other lawn chairs were scattered on various parts of the veranda. The house itself was a pale yellow with white trim. It badly needed painting, as did the attached garage.

Two tricycles lay tipped over, left neglected on the lawn. The flower beds, which ran along both sides of the driveway and across the length of the veranda, appeared to be quite weedy. Being early spring, it was pretty much impossible to tell what had been growing in them. On the right-hand side of the lawn, there was an old swing set, a slide, and a set of monkey bars. A covered sandbox completed the play area.

The 4 walked up to the front door. Lacey stood behind Lloyd, hanging on to the back of his belt so tightly that her fingers cramped. Mr. Silverman rang the doorbell. Mrs. Bronson gently unwrapped Lacey's fingers from Lloyd's belt and then pulled her forward to stand beside her as they waited for someone to answer the door.

After ringing a couple of times, they heard someone approaching. The door opened a crack and a diminutive child stuck her dirty face and runny nose out of the crack. Staring at the group on the veranda, the little one hollered, in an amazingly loud voice, "Mrs. Martha, they're here!"

"Ask them in, Lulu. I'll be right there, as soon as I change this little one's diaper."

Staring at the visitors, Lulu opened the door a touch more. "She said for you to come in, so come in."

"Thank you, Lulu," Mrs. Bronson said. "Could you show us where to sit?"

"OK, come on and sit in the front room. It's for guests." She turned and glared at Lloyd and Lacey. "Kids aren't allowed in the front room."

"These children are allowed, just this once, Lulu," said Mrs. Bronson, in a voice that left no doubt that Lulu would have to let the children into the living room.

"Mrs. Martha won't like it, and neither will Mr. George," the little girl grumbled. "But I guess it will be OK, just this once."

The living room looked like a shrine. Lloyd wondered why it wasn't roped off! The furniture was old, but immaculate. The carpet had no worn spots anywhere, the fireplace looked like it had never held a fire. Elaborate doilies covered the backs of the sofa and chairs, the draperies were closed so that the room was dreary and dark. The coffee table and matching end tables gleamed brightly. Nothing sat on top of the tables, not even a lamp. Lloyd, Mrs. Bronson and Mr. Silverman perched on the edge of their seats as if afraid to rumple the upholstery. Lacey chose to stand beside Lloyd.

Just as it was beginning to be uncomfortable, a large woman wearing a frazzled expression, a faded pair of blue jeans, a grungy white shirt, and carrying a very new baby, came to the doorway. "Sorry I didn't answer the door. This little munchkin decided to crap his drawers, just as you drove up. Here, Lulu, take the baby and put him in his crib, will you." Turning to the visitors, she suggested they all traipse into the kitchen and have something to drink at the kitchen table. She spun around and everyone followed her down the hallway and into the kitchen, dodging toys scattered in every direction.

Mrs. Bronson accepted a cup of coffee. Mr. Silverman turned down the offer. Lloyd and Lacey were offered a glass of water, which they accepted, but only to be polite.

"Now," Martha Schmidt began, "I expect you kids to call me Mrs. Martha. My husband, George, who is at work right now, expects to be called Mr. George. Counting you 2, (and here she pointed an arthritic finger at Lacey and Lloyd) we are full up. One newborn, a 14-year-old girl, 10-year-old boy, a 5-year-old girl, and you 2.

"We have strict rules in this house. We have to, in order to keep track of what goes on from day to day. Most days are uneventful. Some days are pure pandemonium!" Here Martha Schmidt grinned, shook her head and rolled her eyes, her salt and pepper hair falling forward over her eyes. Impatiently, she swatted the offending hair out of the way before continuing. "You 2 won't be with us very long. Only until a more permanent set of foster parents can take you. Mr. George and I take in temporary placements, often newborns, with the occasional older children like you 2.

"All the older children are given chores to do. We expect you to do your chores with no complaining or dilly-dallying. These chores are rotated every Sunday evening, so you will be doing different chores each week. If you are here longer than 2 weeks, you will be enrolled in school. You will be expected to study hard, obey the teachers, and still do your chores when you come home. Any questions?"

"No, ma'am," said Lloyd. "No," said Lacey.

"Well, folks, I have a lot to do. I can't just sit here gabbing all day long. You 2 kids go out to the car and bring in your stuff. These social workers have a long drive back. When you come back in the house, I'll show you where your stuff goes."

Outside, beside Mr. Silverman's car, Mrs. Bronson hugged both Lloyd and Lacey. "I have grown very fond of both of you in just over a day," she said. "I think you will like it here, but remember, you will probably be moved again in the not too distant future. So just be good, be nice to everyone, do your chores, and you will get along just fine. Good luck to both of you. Maybe we will see each other again." Choked up, she turned and got into the front passenger's seat, quickly closing the car door behind her.

Mr. Silverman handed them their backpacks, mumbled something about being good and to remember it was not permanent. He then climbed into his car and quickly backed out of the driveway, leaving Lloyd and Lacey glumly staring at the car as it disappeared down the road.

"Well, Lace," Lloyd said quietly, "time to go inside and see where our rooms are. At least, we are in the same foster home. Let's try hard to do what we are told to do, and then maybe the time will pass by quickly. Maybe they will find Mom in a few days and we can go back home again."

They went into the house and stood in the entryway, not sure of what to do next. Lulu was sitting on the steps leading to the upstairs. She opened her mouth and hollered, "Mrs. Martha, they're back!"

Martha Schmidt came out of the kitchen, yelling, "How many times do I have to tell you, Lulu, don't holler!"

Looking at Lloyd and Lacey's backpacks she said, "Well, you 2 sure travel light. Won't take up much room in the already crowded bedrooms. Come on upstairs and I'll show you where you'll bunk. Once you've unpacked, come back to the kitchen and we'll discuss your chores."

At the top of the stairs they stopped so that Mrs. Martha could catch her breath. "Got to quit smoking," she stated matter-of-factly. "Now, you first, Lloyd. Follow me." She shuffled down the hallway to the left and opened the 2nd door on the right. Inside were 2 sets of bunk beds with colourful comforters displaying pictures of model cars on them, a 4-drawer chest of drawers, and a small desk. Above the desk were bookshelves, attached to the wall.

A redheaded, freckle-faced imp popped up and leaned over the edge of his top bunk. "Hi, I'm Joey, I'm 10," he said. "What's your name, and how old are you?"

"I'm Lloyd, and I'm 14," he said. Turning to Mrs. Martha, he asked her which drawer he should use, and which bunk he should sleep in. "No matter," she replied. "Any empty bed and any empty drawer will do. Once your stuff is on the bed, and in the dresser drawer, they're yours. No one else will use them. You can also use any empty book shelf. As you can see, there are 4 beds, 4 drawers, and 4 bookshelves, so there is one for everyone using this room. Now, you just settle in, and I'll show your sister where she sleeps. Don't forget to come to the kitchen when you're done."

Mrs. Martha stopped at the far door on the opposite end of the hall. Tapping gently on the door, she opened it. This room was exactly the same setup as Lloyd's room, other than the comforters sported bright yellow happy faces.

Sitting at the desk was a sullen girl with long blond hair streaked with brilliant pink stripes, wearing a ton of makeup.

"Lacey, this is Charlotte, but she prefers to be called Charley. She'll tell you which bunk and which dresser drawer you can use. You can also use one of the bookshelves above the desk. Now, you get settled and then come to the kitchen." Mrs. Martha turned, went out of the room, silently closing the bedroom door behind her.

Lacey stood patiently in the centre of the room, waiting for Charlotte/Charley to give her directions. Without saying a word, Charley pointed to the bottom bunk across from hers. She silently pointed to the bottom drawer of the dresser and the bottom shelf of the bookshelves. She then turned her back on Lacey and, pointedly, continued flipping through the magazine she was holding.

With a shrug of her shoulders, Lacey began to unpack her things. She then left the room. She got to the head of the stairs before Charley screamed, "Hey, kid! You find a door closed, you leave it closed, got it? Get the hell back here and shut the damned door!"

Startled, Lacey went back to their room, grabbed hold of the door knob, and slammed the door. *Well! That's not exactly what I call a fine start*, she thought to herself as she headed downstairs and towards the kitchen.

Back in the kitchen, Lloyd was already sitting at the table. When Lacey arrived, Mrs. Martha asked if either one of them knew how to cook.

"Not much, ma'am," said Lloyd. "I can pour cereal and make toast," Lacey announced somewhat proudly.

"Well," said Mrs. Martha. "Guess that means that you, Miss Lacey, can be the table setter and the dish dryer. You, Mr. Lloyd, can be the table clearer and the dish washer. Charlotte will sweep and wash the floor, and Joey will take out the garbage. Lulu will clean the bathrooms. She's only 5, but she is learning quickly how to clean. As I said before, if you are still here in a week, the chore rotation will change."

"The rest of the rules are short and simple. Mr. George will tell you about them at supper time. Now, you have an hour before Mr. George gets home and you have to set the table. You can play in your rooms, or you can go outside for some air, but you can't leave the yard. I'll see you in one hour." She immediately turned her back and began peeling potatoes for supper.

Lacey looked at Lloyd. "Wanna go outside and sit on the veranda?"

"Yeah, I guess so," Lloyd said, and immediately began walking toward the front door.

Mrs. Martha spoke up. "No, no, no! Only visitors come to the front door. You are no longer a visitor." She pointed to the far side of the kitchen. Through the doorway was a covered porch, with a door to the outside. Upon entering the porch, the children stopped and took a quick look around. Coat hooks were screwed into the drywall on the longest wall, in 2 rows. Lloyd guessed, correctly as it turned out, that the lower ones were there so the smaller children were able to hang up their own coats. To the left of the door there was a long boot rack, divided into 8 sections. There was a window on the end wall, with a simple wooden bench beneath the window.

Once their quick once-over was completed, Lloyd opened the back door and they stepped outside. The 4 wooden steps ended at the edge of a fairly large cement patio. Other than a barbeque and a half-dozen cheap lawn chairs haphazardly scattered on to the cement, the back yard was empty. Closing the door behind him, he took Lacey's hand, and looked around.

The yard was very uninviting. No flower beds, no lawn, no trees, just rocks and bare dirt. The only structure was a dilapidated old shed about the size of a single garage. Peeking through the dirty window, Lloyd saw a lawn mower, some gas cans, a workbench cluttered with tools, but not much else. Looking to their right, they saw 3 houses strung out along the road. It appeared that Mr. George and Mrs. Martha lived at the extreme edge of a very small town. Straight across from the back of the house was a cultivated field. As far as they could look in that direction, only the empty field was in sight. No trees there either, and no farmhouse.

Lloyd and Lacey finally just sat dejectedly in 2 of the lawn chairs, and waited for the hour to be up.

Hearing a vehicle on the driveway, Lloyd and Lacey went back in to the house. There was no one in the kitchen. They heard Mrs. Martha speaking with a man. They presumed it was Mr. George. Not knowing what to do next, they simply stood in the kitchen, waiting.

In a few minutes, a large man stood in the doorway. He had sparse grey hair which he had moved over to the right side of his head in a comb-over. He stood very erect, was well over 186 centimetres tall. He probably weighed 122 kilograms or more. Lacey looked scared to death until the man smiled at her and spoke in a very gentle voice. He said, "Welcome children, to my home. I hope you will be comfortable here. I'm Mr. George to you. As long as you obey the rules and finish your chores in a timely fashion, with no grumbling, you and I will get along just fine. Now, the numero uno rule in my house is this: every day when I get home from work, I need to sit and read my paper quietly, in the family room, while supper is being prepared. Other than the newborns, of course, everyone else is to be quiet. If the baby starts to squawk, if you are not on table-setting duty, you are expected to try and settle the baby down upstairs, where I can't hear you.

"Once I am done reading the paper, we will have our meal." He stared intently at Lacey. "You, young lady, look like the table setter to me. Get on with it, but quietly!"

He then turned and walked into a family room, located across the hallway from the 'sacred' living room. Mrs. Martha scuttled after him, a cocktail of some sort in each hand. Going into the family room, she placed the 2 drinks on a coffee table. She immediately left the room, closing the door behind her.

Back in the kitchen, she quietly showed Lacey where all the dishes were located, admonishing her when she made too loud a noise shutting cupboard doors and drawers. The whole atmosphere made Lacey so nervous she could barely manage to set the table. Lloyd, feeling sorry for his sister, helped her with the table setting.

After what seemed like a very long time, Mr. George came out of the family room and sat down at the head of the table. Mrs. Martha told Lacey to go quickly and call Charley, Lulu, and Joey, to come for supper, and make sure they knew that Mr. George was at the table, waiting for his food. Lacey just stood and stared at her. Mrs. Martha clapped her hands together and said, "Go now, girl! Hurry up! Mr. George doesn't like to be kept waiting. Now run!"

Lacey ran.

Lulu and Joey came downstairs on the run. Charley sauntered down the stairs with an insolent look on her face. She was the last one at the table. Mr. George looked at her, saying not a word, then suddenly slammed his fist down on the table. "Miss Charlotte, go back to your room. If you can't obey, you don't eat. Simple as that. Pass the potatoes please."

"I'm sorry, Mr. George. It won't happen again. I am very hungry," Charley said in a subdued tone of voice.

"Too bad. You should have thought of that before you disobeyed the command to come to the table. Now get!"

Angry tears running down her cheeks, Charley pushed away from the table and stomped back up the stairs.

The rest of the meal was eaten in complete and utter silence. Not until Mr. George pushed his chair back from the table and left to go back into the family room to watch television, did anyone else dare to leave the table. Mrs. Martha rustled after her husband with 2 mugs of coffee, joining him in the family room, leaving all the children to complete their various chores.

Once Lacey was sure that there were at least a few minutes before either of the adults would return to the kitchen, she quickly made a sandwich from the table leftovers and snuck it upstairs to Charley. "Here, Charley," she whispered, "I brought you something to eat."

Charley gasped. "Kid, you don't know what you are doing! If you get caught you will be in huge trouble. Thank you, though, you have more guts than brains." She quickly started to eat the sandwich, making sure not to leave any telltale crumbs on the desktop. Turning around, she said to Lacey, "Kid, you better get back down to the kitchen and dry those dishes. As soon as the news is over on the TV, Mrs. Martha will be back in the kitchen to inspect everything. Go!"

Lacey went.

After drying the last plate, Lacey was worried. With Charley confined to her room, what happened to the sweeping and washing of the kitchen floor? Lloyd told her not to worry, between Lacey and himself, they could get the floor done in no time.

Sure enough, as soon as the news, weather, and sports were over on TV, Mrs. Martha came back in to the kitchen to inspect. She could find no fault with anything either Lacey or Lloyd had done. Oddly, she almost seemed disappointed, but managed to commend the 2 on their chores. She must have noticed the floor was washed, but she said nothing about it.

"Now," Mrs. Martha said, "you spend the rest of the evening until you go to sleep, in your rooms. You can read or play games with the other children, but you cannot leave your rooms except to have your shower before bedtime. You have to be showered, your teeth brushed, and be in your beds by 9 o'clock. Mr. George will be around to check on you. Believe me when I tell you, don't be late for 9 o'clock bedtime or none of us will sleep tonight."

With not another word, she turned and went to look after the newborn baby. Lloyd looked at Lacey, shrugged his shoulders, and headed up the stairs. Lacey was right behind him. At the top of the stairs Lloyd stopped and turned around, giving Lacey a fierce hug. "Good night, Lacey. Don't forget to say your prayers. Pray that Mom comes home soon so we can get out of here!"

"Good night, Lloyd. Don't worry, I pray hard every night that Mama will soon be home. See you tomorrow morning."

Precisely at 9 p.m., Mr. George stuck his head into the boys' room. Satisfied that both Joey and Lloyd were in bed, he simply said good night and shut the door.

Tapping on the girls' bedroom door, he immediately entered the room, without waiting for a response to his knock. With barely a glance at Charley, he sat down on Lacey's bed. Putting his beefy hand on her middle, he seemingly casually rubbed her belly, on top of the covers. Trying to divert her attention from what he was doing, he asked her how she liked it at his house so far. Wiggling out from under his hand, Lacey rolled back against the wall and said, "It's OK, thank you." He reached over in an attempt to pull her back towards him. She whimpered, "Don't do that! Please, Mr. George, I don't like it!"

Charley had enough. She flew out of her bed, screaming, "Leave her alone you sick pervert! Leave her the fuck alone! She's just a little girl and you are a big, fat prick!"

Mr. George turned towards Charley, his hands curled into fists.

"Run, Lacey, go to the bathroom and lock the door – go now, run! Don't come back until you hear me call out that it's safe!" Charley stood between Mr. George and Lacey, pushing her urgently towards the door.

The second she was gone, Mr. George shut the door, locked it, and walked back towards Charley.

After what seemed like hours, there was a knock on the bathroom door. Lacey huddled in the corner between the tub and the toilet. She sat totally still, and quiet. There was another knock. "Lacey, it's OK, it's me, Charley. Open the door, please." Lacey made a soft mewling noise, but she crawled to the bathroom door and opened it. Charley stood outside. As soon as the door opened she came in and re-locked the bathroom door.

Looking at Charley, Lacey gasped. Her nose was bloody and her pyjamas were torn. She shook so badly that her teeth were chattering. Reaching around Lacey, she turned the shower on.

"Please don't leave this bathroom, Lacey. Wait for me, OK? Don't open this door for any reason. I need to shower."

Lacey nodded in agreement, then slid down the wall and sat with her head on her bent knees.

Charley's shower took a long time. Only when the hot water ran out and the icy cold water hit her sore and battered body, did Charley come out of the shower. As she gently dried herself, she grimaced as the towel touched her ribs which were already bruising. Weeping silently, she got an aspirin out of the medicine cabinet and swallowed it with a glass of water. Then she reached for Lacey's hand and drew her gently into the hallway and back to their bedroom.

She immediately yanked the bottom sheet off of her bunk and stuffed it into the waste paper basket under the desk. Once back in their beds, Charley continued to weep. Lacey didn't know what to do for her. Finally, she got out of her bed, got some Kleenex and sat on Charley's bunk. "What can I do? How can I help you?" she asked as she handed the tissues to Charley.

Charley reached for Lacey's hand. "You can help me by NEVER, EVER being alone with Mr. George. If there is nobody around, make sure you find the others and stay where they are. If there is no one else around, except Mr. George, run outside and hide until someone else comes back to the house. Believe me, you don't want to be alone with that awful man."

"Well, why don't we tell Mrs. Martha? She can tell Mr. George not to be so mean, can't she?"

"No, Lacey, we can't tell Mrs. Martha. It would make her too sad. Mr. George is a very evil, mean guy. If he found out we told Mrs. Martha about him, he would kill us. We can't tell anyone about this. We just can't." Rolling over to face the wall, she mumbled something indistinct.

Lacey sat on the bed for another minute, and then crawled back into her own bunk. She lay there awake for a long time, listening to Charley crying softly into her pillow.

Suddenly Lacey bolted upright in her bunk. "Charley, where's Lulu?"

Between sobs, Charley said, "She's on newborn duty."

"What's newborn duty?"

"The person on newborn duty sleeps in the nursery on a cot next to the baby's crib so that if he wakes up in the night, the duty person has to keep the baby quiet so he doesn't wake up Mr. George or Mrs. Martha. Sometimes that means taking the baby into the back entry if he doesn't quiet down. The nursery is across the hall from Mr. George and Mrs. Martha's bedroom. That's where Lulu is tonight."

The next morning, Charley was still asleep when Lacey crawled out of bed. Quietly, so as not to awaken her, Lacey went to the bathroom to get dressed. She then went downstairs and set the table for breakfast. When Mrs. Martha came into the kitchen, the table was set, bowls of cereal were filled and sitting at each place. Mrs. Martha smiled at Lacey and patted her on the head. "Good girl," she said, "good job."

Mr. George came into the kitchen. Behind his wife's back, he held his pointer finger up to his lips. She understood his pantomime perfectly. She nodded at him and then ignored him.

Charley didn't come down for breakfast. Mrs. Martha asked Lacey to go and get her for breakfast. Lacey replied that Charley had a flu bug and had been awake most of the night. She was still asleep. Mrs. Martha said they should just let her sleep then. Sleep was the best cure for the flu.

"Yes, ma'am," said Lacey. The rest of the meal was eaten in silence.

Immediately after breakfast, Mr. George gave his wife a peck on the cheek, grabbed his coat, and left for work. The air in the kitchen lightened considerably after he left.

Once the chores were done, the balance of the day stretched ahead. Whatever would they do for the entire day until suppertime chores were required? Lloyd broached the subject with Mrs. Martha, who said, "Oh for pity's sake, you're a big boy. Figure something out!" She then stomped out of the kitchen and into the family room, where she plopped herself down in front of the TV, hollering to Lulu that she was to look after the newborn. Soon, sounds of some soap opera could be heard through the closed family room door.

"Want to go for a walk, Lace?" Lloyd inquired.

"Okay, but first I want to check on Charley. I'll meet you in the back yard in a couple of minutes."

When Lacey opened the bedroom door, Charley was up and dressed. "Is he gone?" she asked Lacey. Lacey nodded, "Yes."

"Thank God," Charley breathed. "Listen, Lacey, thank you! It was nice sharing this room with you. I'm sorry that I was so rude when you first arrived. Now, listen. I'm leaving here. Please don't tell anyone that you know I planned to run away. In fact, if anyone bothers to ask you, just tell them you don't know anything, OK? And, whatever you do, don't let that pig Mr. George near you! I can't protect you because I'm leaving, so you have to look after yourself. If possible, get the hell out of here!"

"But, where are you going? You're just a teenager. Who'll look after you?"

"Don't worry about it, kid," Charley said. "Any life will be better than my life in this house of horrors. I'll be OK." With that, she gave Lacey a quick hug. In an instant, she was gone.

Swallowing hard, Lacey watched out of the window. Charley came into view briefly, running down the road, and glancing frantically over her shoulder to make sure she wasn't being followed. Before she was out of Lacey's line of sight, a brightly coloured truck pulled over. It reminded Lacey of a giant pumpkin, orange with black and green letters on the door. The last thing she saw, was Charley climbing into the pumpkin, and then heading on down the road.

In the back yard, she couldn't sit still. Lloyd looked at her curiously. "What's up, Lacey? You seem very upset." Lacey said nothing, but chewed her thumb nail nervously.

"Tell you what, Lace, let's go for a walk. It will feel good to get away from this house for a bit. I'll poke my head into the family room and let Mrs. Martha know we won't be long." He ran up the back steps. In a flash, he was back. "She doesn't care. Just said don't bother her and make sure we are home in time for chores. Let's go exploring." He looked at her worriedly. "Which direction, Lace?" Wordlessly, she pointed at the field across from the back yard.

Following the field in the direction of the tiny hamlet (it was too small to be called a town), they walked in silence for a time. Just past the houses that were closest to the Schmidt' house, a meager line of poplar trees rimmed the edge of a small creek. The water level was so low that they could easily cross it on the rocks sticking out of the water. Once on the other side, they turned to their left, following the creek bank until they could no longer see the houses. At this point, a very large, very flat rock jutted out over the water. The land had dropped off dramatically here. The children sat down on the rock and swung their legs above the small ravine below the edge of the rock. The spring sun felt warm on their faces. Lacey lay down on her stomach and looked over the edge. Lloyd held on to her feet so she wouldn't fall. With the sunshine beating down on them, Lacey put her head on her arms and soon fell asleep. Lloyd continued to sit with his legs dangling, keeping one hand at the ready should Lacey roll over in her sleep and fall.

Nearly an hour later, she awoke with a start and a sharp cry from the edge of a troubled dream. For a minute, she didn't know where she was. Then she remembered and her spirit sank.

Lloyd said, "Look, sleepyhead, look to the right as far as you can. See that old tree stump? I think there is something in it. Do you see something white? At the back of the hole, near the bottom of the stump." He pointed in the general direction of what he thought he was seeing.

"I think so!" she said. "This walk is turning into an adventure. Let's go check it out!" She backed up from the edge of the rock before she stood up and ran towards the stump. Peering into the hole she did, indeed, spy a small white object. "I think it's a piece of paper, Lloyd," she called.

"Hang on a minute, Lace," he said. Kneeling beside her he then lay flat on his side and looked into the hole. He tried to reach the object but his hand was too large. "I can reach it," Lacey said assuredly. "Let me!"

"OK, but be very careful not to rip it. It could be nothing, but just in case, let's be cautious okay?"

Lacey stood up, holding a tightly crumpled up piece of paper triumphantly on her small palm. She looked around for some place to sit and smooth out the paper. Nothing closer than the flat rock. They quickly ran back and sat down.

Lloyd carefully smoothed out the paper. "There's something written on here, Lacey," he said.

"Read it! Read it!" Jumping up and down in her barely suppressed excitement she nearly tumbled off the rock.

"What the heck? There's writing on this note."

"So, read it to me already, Lloyd."

"OK, OK, hang on to your horses. I'm trying to read it but it's not easy. Some little kid printed this. The ink is pretty faded. Just keep quiet for a sec, OK?" Frowning, he squinted at the paper. After a couple of minutes he straightened up. "OK, it says: *'If you find this note I will be gone. Call the police. Kids are not safe at the Schmidt house. The Schmidts are bad people. Do not let kids stay there.'*

"Who wrote it?"

"It doesn't have a name on it, Lace. Guess it was just some bored kid trying to find something to do. Kind of like a note in a bottle only the kid obviously didn't have a bottle." Lloyd pulled his arm back, prepared to throw the note into the creek.

"**DON'T!**" Lacey screamed. "It's not fake, don't throw it away!"

"What the heck? What are you blithering on about? I told you, it's just some crazy kid's game."

By this time, Lacey was crying so hard she couldn't speak for a minute. She grabbed onto Lloyd's arm. He hung onto the paper with his right hand and patted his sister's back with his left one. Once she had calmed down some, he stared sternly at her and said, "Lacey, you need to explain yourself. What's going on?"

Lacey told him everything. How Mr. George had rubbed her belly, how she didn't like it and asked him to stop. How he didn't. How Charley protected her, screaming at her to run out of the bedroom to the bathroom. How Charley came to the bathroom, bleeding. How Charlie stuffed her sheet into the waste paper basket. How Charley ran away, getting into the 'orange pumpkin truck' and driving away. Finally, how Mr. George had put his pointer finger to his lips, in that way warning her to say nothing.

When she finished, Lloyd was pacing back and forth, his hands fisted. Unaware that he was crying, he just kept repeating, "Lace, I'm sorry, I'm so, so sorry. You should have come to me right away. I am supposed to protect you!" He sat back down on the rock and held his head between his hands.

"What can you do Lloyd, you're just a kid too. No one will believe us anyway."

He thought for several minutes. Finally, he removed his head from his hands and looked at Lacey. "I've got it Lacey. I will phone Mr. Silverman. He'll know what to do. Come on, we have to get back to the house while Mrs. Martha is still watching television. I'll get Mr. Silverman's card and call him from the phone in the kitchen. We have to hurry though, we probably don't have much time."

So, the 2 of them retraced their route and scurried back to the Schmidt house.

"You keep watch, Lace. If you hear Mrs. Martha coming out, talk to her in a really loud voice so I can hear you."

"What should I say to her?"

"Doesn't matter! Just delay her as long as you can to give me time to put the phone back. Now, go stand outside the door to the family room. But stand still, and be quiet so she doesn't come out to check on any noises."

Lacey went.

Lloyd dug in his back pocket and pulled out Mr. Silverman's card. He dialled the mobile number he had been given. It went straight to answering machine. Afraid to leave a message in case Mr. Silverman tried to call back when the Schmidts were around, he simply hung up the phone.

He went to the hallway and crooked his finger at Lacey to come to him. "Where's the card that Mrs. Bronson gave you? I need to try and call her."

"What about Mr. Silverman?"

"His phone went straight to his answering machine. It isn't safe to leave a message. Please, give me Mrs. Bronson's card!"

Lacey took it out of a pocket in her jeans. She handed him the card.

Lloyd went to the back-porch room and dialled the mobile number Mrs. Bronson had given to Lacey. The phone was answered on the 3rd ring.

"Evelyn Bronson speaking. Who is this, please?"

Lloyd told her. "Mrs. Bronson, I don't have much time. Please just listen to me and then tell me what to do." He relayed all of the information his sister had given him as fast as he possibly could and still be understood. When he finished, there was silence on the other end.

"Mrs. Bronson? Are you still there?"

More silence.

"Mrs. Bronson, please! I haven't much time, what should we do?"

Finally, she spoke. "Tell Lacey to get the sheet out of the waste paper basket, and hide it and the note someplace where you know it is safe. Wrap it up, or put it in a plastic bag. Then phone me back and say only one word, 'DONE'. Can you do that?"

"Yes, ma'am, if the garbage hasn't been emptied we can do it."

"Can you get us out of this house? I know it is a temporary placement, but we need to get out, now!"

Mrs. Bronson said, "I'm working on it, Lloyd. It won't be long. In the meantime, keep an eye on Lacey. Be strong. I will get you out of there."

"What will happen to the Schmidts?"

Silence.

Lloyd asked again, "What will happen to the Schmidts?"

With a heavy sigh, she said, "I don't know, Lloyd. That will be up to the Alberta Social Services workers to decide. I will let them know what you told me, but that's all I can do."

Before he could say anything more, Mrs. Bronson hung up.

Lloyd replaced the kitchen telephone and then looked for a plastic bag. Finding a grocery bag, he motioned for Lacey to come to the kitchen. He told her what Mrs. Bronson had requested. He told her to go fast and stuff the sheet into the grocery bag. He would then put the note in with the sheet and run back to the flat rock and push the bag as far back into the opening in the tree stump as he could. It would be a tight squeeze, but he was sure it could be done. He would push it in with a stick, if his hands wouldn't fit.

Lacey ran upstairs. In a couple of minutes, she ran back down and handed Lloyd the plastic bag. "Got it! Joey hadn't emptied the basket yet."

"Okay, Lace, you stay here and start setting the table for supper. That way you will be ahead of the game. If Mrs. Martha wants to know where I am, just tell her I'm still outside, but I promised to be back in time for supper. That's if she even bothers to ask where I am."

"What if Mr. George comes back?"

"He won't bother you before bedtime. You'll be OK. Just don't get close to him. Mrs. Bronson is trying to get us out of here really quickly, so we just have to be patient and be careful. Think you can do it?"

"Of course, I can, Lloyd, I'm not a baby! Now go hide the bag, but hurry back!"

Lloyd took off on the run.

Lacey started to set the table for 6 people instead of 7. She really missed Charley, worried about her. Not wanting the Schmidts to question her about Charley, she set the 7th place.

Lulu came down the stairs. "What are ya doin'? It's not supper time yet."

"No, it's not," said Lacey, "but I have nothing else to do."

Lacey paused. She said, "Hey, Lulu, are you still on newborn duty? You're pretty little to look after a baby all night."

Lulu puffed up, not unlike a young peacock. She grinned, "I'm little, but I'm mighty," she boasted. "'Sides, I like babies. I also like sleeping in the baby's room. No one comes in there at night."

"What are you talking about, Lulu? Does someone come into your room at night?"

"Just Mr. George," she said matter-of-factly. "He hugs me and says goodnight to me and Charley. Where is Charley, anyhow?"

Lacey felt sick. "I don't know, Lulu," she replied. "I guess she's gone to a different foster home."

Quickly changing the subject, she said, "Listen, Lulu, you should ask Mrs. Martha if you can stay on night time baby duty. You're really good at it."

"Yeah! I will." Lulu said, "It's my favouritest duty." She skipped out of the room, humming a little tune as she left.

Lloyd managed to race back into the house just before Mrs. Martha came out of the family room. He ran up the stairs to his bedroom so he wouldn't have to face questions about why he was puffing and sweating.

Martha Schmidt walked into the kitchen, looked at the already-set table, but said nothing. She went to the pantry cupboard and got out what she needed to begin to cook supper.

Mr. George would soon be home. She painted on her busy, happy face, adapting her personality for Mr. George.

The phone rang. Mrs. Martha asked Lloyd to answer it because her hands were wet. He picked up the phone. He answered as he had been told to answer, "Hello, Schmidt residence."

"Lloyd? Don't say anything. It's me, Mrs. Bronson. Just so you know, I have found you 2 a new foster home. You will be picked up tomorrow. Don't let on that you know, just put Mrs. Schmidt on the line, please."

"The phone's for you, Mrs. Martha. I don't know who it is." (This last sentence spoken with his fingers crossed behind his back!).

Mrs. Martha took the phone from Lloyd. When she heard who was on the other end, she motioned for the kids to go into the hallway where (she assumed) they couldn't hear her conversation. She was on the line for several minutes before she hung up.

"Well, well," she chirped in a falsely cheery tone. "You and your sister are being placed in another foster home. A worker will be picking you up tomorrow morning at 9 o'clock. A pretty short stay, huh?"

The front door opened, and Mr. George stepped in. Mrs. Martha scuttled over to him, kissed him on the cheek as he took off his coat.

"Well, Mr. George," Mrs. Martha said, "Tomorrow, Lloyd and Lacey are being placed in a new foster home. Money will be short this month if we don't get replacement kids right away," she whined.

"Don't worry about it, Martha. We'll manage, we always do. Just have to cut down on the portions of food you feed the kids. Now, woman, where's my cocktail?"

"Oh, sorry! I'm sorry. The social worker called just as I was starting to prepare your drinks. I'll get them right away. Just you get comfortable and I'll be there in a minute!"

"See that you hurry it up, woman!" he growled. "I'm thirsty."

At the supper table, Lulu asked if she could keep on being the newborn's nighttime caregiver. Mrs. Martha agreed that she could. The balance of the meal was eaten in total silence.

At bedtime, Lacey gave Lloyd a fervent squeeze. "We're leaving, Lloyd! Tomorrow! Everything will be okay now. Have a good night and be ready in the morning. We are really leaving this terrible house."

Lloyd gave her a high-5 and went into his room and closed the door.

That night, Mr. George did not go into either of the bedrooms to say goodnight to the children.

Chapter 4
Henry and Harriet Greschner

By 6 o'clock the next morning, Lacey had made her bed and was washed, dressed and packed. She was sitting on the stairs waiting for Lloyd and for 9 o'clock to come. Her brother wasn't far behind. By 6:30, he joined her on the stairway. Quietly, so as not to disturb the rest of the household, they tiptoed into the kitchen.

Lloyd helped Lacey set the table for breakfast. He suggested that they put on their jackets and wait outside in the back yard until Mrs. Martha got up. That way they could talk in a normal tone of voice and there was little to no chance they would be overheard.

Sitting in the lawn chairs, Lacey could not contain her excitement. "Lloyd, this is gonna be so great! No place could be as bad as this place. I don't even care if the new place is a teeney-weeney tent. I just wanna get out of here. And guess what? Mama will be home in 2 more days 'cause that's my birthday and she won't miss my birthday when I'm gonna be 10!"

Despite a now-seemingly permanent, painful, anxious knot in the pit of his stomach, Lloyd managed to smile weakly at his optimistic baby sister.

"Lacey, listen to me. This is important." He leaned over and picked up his backpack. From an inside pocket, he withdrew a sheet of paper. "This is a map that I have drawn, showing where the flat rock is and where the tree stump is. If, for some reason, we get separated, we can use that as our drop spot. You can leave me a note in there and tell me where you are, or ask for help from me. I will check that tree stump as often as I can. Also, if you find yourself in a foster home that is as bad as this one, you can get hold of Mrs. Bronson and find out how to give her the map with the directions on it."

Lacey's mouth puckered and then her jaw dropped.

"What do you mean, if we get separated, Lloyd? We will always be together in foster homes, or at home when Mama gets back. I don't get what you mean."

"It's just an emergency plan, Lace. We will probably never need to use it, but it is always a good idea to have one, especially because you and I are on our own. Do you agree?"

"Yeeessss?" she replied uncertainly, the end of the word a question more than an affirmation. Then she straightened up in her chair and nodded emphatically, "Yes, you are right as always, Lloyd. We have a plan!"

Lloyd said, "We need to come up with a word to call the rock and the stump, like a code word. Any ideas?"

"Sure!" Lacey bounced up and down in the flimsy lawn chair. Lloyd grabbed it before she toppled over. "How about 'the Mailbox'?"

Lloyd pondered for only a minute. "Lacey! You're brilliant! Nobody would ever guess that 'the Mailbox' is in a tree stump, by a flat rock over a creek, in the country. They would naturally assume that it was a real mailbox! You should be a detective. You've the mind for it. Always thinking, aren't you, kiddo?"

Lacey beamed.

"You know, Lace, that this is probably the biggest secret we will ever have to keep in our whole lives, don't you? No matter where we end up living or working, no matter how many years pass by, we can never, ever, tell anyone the code word for the rock and hiding place. Just imagine if Mr. George or Mrs. Martha heard us talking and they went to the tree stump. They would take that bedsheet, and that note, and destroy it. Then everyone would think we are liars. We need to pinkie-swear that we will never tell anyone about that hiding place. It will be our secret forever, because we need to be able to contact each other if we ever get separated, like we talked about."

Lacey held up her hand, her little finger crooked and ready to swear. Lloyd did the same. Once their ceremonial swearing had taken place, they both felt much better.

"Breakfast's ready!" They both jumped as Mrs. Martha's loud bellow assaulted their ears.

"Do you think she heard us, Lloyd?" Lacey whispered anxiously.

"Nah," Lloyd responded, "she was too busy crashing around. Besides, she has no interest in kids' talk anyhow. Let's get in there and eat. It'll soon be 9 o'clock."

Mr. George came to the table. When Mrs. Martha had her back to him, he glared at Lacey. Using his pointer finger, he made a slashing motion across his throat, then put his pointer finger to his lips. Lacey got the message loud and clear. She nodded her head in agreement. She did not look at him again. He left for work immediately after breakfast, without saying a word to anyone, not even his wife.

Mrs. Martha seemed determined to get as much work out of the 2 children as she could before they left. Not only did she have them do the dishes, and clean the kitchen, she had them sweep, and then mop, the kitchen floor, the hallway, and the back-entry floors. Without complaining, they put their noses to the grindstone and were completely finished by 10 minutes to 9.

Precisely at 9 o'clock, the doorbell rang. Mrs. Martha put a phony smile on her face, and opened the door.

Surprise! Jayson Silverman and Evelyn Bronson stood on the veranda. Lacey squealed with delight and launched herself into Mrs. Bronson's waiting arms. Mr. Silverman shook Lloyd's hand. "How you doing, Lloyd?" he asked rhetorically. He knew they weren't doing well at all.

"Grab your things and let's get going. We don't have far to drive, but Mrs. Bronson and I have to go back to British Columbia today, so we can't dawdle."

With a withering look at Mrs. Martha, he and Lloyd went to the car and put their belongings in the trunk.

Mrs. Bronson stared at Mrs. Martha. "If I have my way," she said, "you will never get any more foster children in this house for as long as you live." Mrs. Martha blanched, swallowed, finally turned around and headed into the house. She didn't even close the door.

Evelyn Bronson gently shut the door, took Lacey by the hand, and led her to the car.

Once they were all seated in the vehicle, she asked Lacey and Lloyd if it would be possible to get the bedsheet and note before they headed to their new foster home. Lacey looked frightened, glancing over at Lloyd for reassurance.

"Yeah, I can get it. Will you wait in the car until I get back?"

"Of course," said Mrs. Bronson, "but we can drive you there."

Lloyd replied, "Actually there is no road. If you can park away from here, where Mrs. Martha won't spot me, I'll hurry and get them."

"No problem," said Mr. Silverman. "Where should I park?"

"Just go back about 3 blocks. There's a service station there. It won't take me more than 15 minutes to run and get the bedsheet and note and be back at the car from there. I'll hurry."

Once parked, Mrs. Bronson asked Lloyd if he was sure he didn't want Mr. Silverman to go with him. Lloyd responded that it would be faster if he went by himself. He got out of the car and took off on the run before they could question him further. It wasn't that Lloyd didn't trust the social workers, but he and Lacey had pinky-swore never to divulge the location of the Mailbox, and he intended to honor that pledge. Just to be sure that they couldn't see which direction he was headed, he circled the block and hid out of sight for a couple of minutes. He couldn't see the car from where he was hiding, so he finally felt safe enough. He began to run.

Because of his previous deviations attempting to get to the Mailbox unseen, he was closer to 25 minutes getting back to the car. Sweating and panting, Lloyd bent over and put his hands on his knees while he tried to catch his breath. "Sorry! It took me a little longer than I remembered. Here's the stuff." Reaching into the car, he handed the plastic grocery bag to Mrs. Bronson.

Mr. Silverman held out his hand. "It's OK, Evelyn. I'll take this and put it in the trunk. It will be safe there." She handed the bag to him.

Back in the car, they headed out of town, towards the next foster home.

It was only a short drive, probably half an hour. Mr. Silverman exited the main highway and drove up a winding road. Stopping near the top of the hill, he motioned for them to get out of the car and admire the view.

It was a bright, clear morning. To the west, the Rocky Mountains shimmered in the distance. Mr. Silverman said those particular Rocky Mountains were in British Columbia. Looking down over the edge of the road, a small lake sparkled. It was surrounded by evergreen trees. It looked as if there were a lot of birds swimming in the water. So peaceful, so beautiful. Standing still and admiring the view, they could hear squirrels and chipmunks in the trees below.

Pointing to his left, Mr. Silverman indicated a large log home about 100 metres away. A circular driveway in front made for an easy turnaround. The road ended at the house. A wrap-around, covered veranda beckoned invitingly. Unlike the last foster home, this one needed no repairs. The yard was lovingly tended and even this early in the spring, small green shoots were pushing their way up through the well-rototilled flower beds.

Hearing the car approach, the front door opened and a man and a woman came out. They appeared to be about the same age as Lloyd and Lacey's parents, mid-to-late 30's. The man was tall and muscular. He looked like a hard worker. The lady was lovely. Tall and slim, her blond hair was tied back in a ponytail. They both wore warm smiles as they descended the steps and walked towards their guests. Only when they reached the driveway did they notice a girl standing shyly behind the woman.

Mrs. Bronson introduced the children to Henry and Harriet Greschner, who in turn introduced them to their 14-year-old daughter, Susanna. She was the spitting image of her mother. Lloyd's eyes lit up and his face turned a bashful red when he heard they were the same age.

Inviting Mr. Silverman and Mrs. Bronson in for tea, the pair regretfully declined. They had a long drive back and still had some office work to do when they got there.

"We understand," Mrs. Greschner said softly. Her voice was as pretty as she was. "I am sure that Lacey and Lloyd will fit right in with our little family. Have a safe trip home." She then retreated tactfully so that they could say their goodbyes to the kids.

"Don't worry," Mrs. Bronson whispered, first to Lacey, and then again to Lloyd, as she hugged each of them farewell. "We will make sure that the grocery bag and its contents get into the right hands. The Schmidts will never have another chance to hurt another child. Now, I am pretty sure you are going to love it here. Neither mine nor Jayson's phone numbers have changed. Feel free to call us at any time, not just if you have a problem." With one last hug, she got into the car, her eyes suspiciously moist.

Jayson Silverman swallowed hard, shook both Lloyd's and Lacey's hands, folded his tall thin body into his small vehicle, and drove away

Waving until they were out of sight, Lloyd and Lacey turned towards the veranda.

Harriet Greschner said, "Come on up and have a seat. It's close to lunchtime, so we have prepared some lunch. It's an unusually warm spring day and for once, there is no wind. Susanna and I decided it would be a perfect day to have lunch outside on the veranda."

Mr. Greschner chuckled. "Well, Lloyd, I'm mighty happy to have another man around this house! Even the dogs are females. I can see that you and I are going to have to stick up for each other, in this house full of women!"

Sitting on the veranda, and eating Mrs. Greschner's and Susanna's delicious lunch, the atmosphere was so relaxed, that by the end of the meal, both Lacey and Lloyd felt like they had been there forever. Gone was the tension of the last foster home. They both found themselves very happy.

Mr. Greschner asked Lacey how old she was. "I'll be 10 the day after tomorrow," she said bashfully.

"You'll be 10!" Mr. Greschner exclaimed. "Well, Mother, we'll have to do something about that, won't we?"

"We certainly will," Mrs. Greschner replied. "What is your favourite kind of cake?"

Lacey perked up, no longer bashful. "Carrot cake with lots and lots of cream cheese icing!"

"Well, young Lacey, Mrs. Greschner just happens to make the world's best carrot cake, in my humble opinion." Putting his arm around his wife, Henry Greschner gave her a gentle squeeze, and a peck on the cheek.

Harriet Greschner said, "The only thing is, Lacey, you're lucky you're the birthday girl. It means you get the 1st piece of cake. Lucky thing, too, or else my husband would eat it all up!"

"Now, how about we show you around the house, and then you can unpack your things. You will each have your own bedroom, with an attached bathroom. The only thing that we ask is that you please keep your rooms and your bathrooms clean and tidy. Otherwise, the rooms are yours to decorate as you wish."

"Are we the only foster kids here?" Lloyd quietly asked.

"Yup," Mr. Greschner responded. "Susanna is an only child. We couldn't have any more after she was born. She's getting pretty spoiled and bored living with 2 old folks like her mom and pop." Here he winked and hugged his daughter, who smiled lovingly up at her father before he continued, "So, we figured the next best way to get her some siblings was to take in a couple of awesome foster children. You 2 sure seem to fit the bill. Welcome, both of you, to our humble abode! You are now part of the family."

Lacey turned pale and emitted an audible gulp.

"What is it, sweetie?" asked Mrs. Greschner, in a very concerned tone.

"Well, Mrs. Greschner, it is really nice here, and you are really nice, and Mr. Greschner is really nice, and Susanna is really nice, but we have a mother and a father, and so we can only visit here. When our mama comes back, we will be going home with her. I'm sure she will be back for my birthday." She stopped her blithering and looked down at her shoes, miserable and embarrassed for seeming so ungrateful.

Suddenly she was swooped up in Mr. Greschner's arms. Looking straight into her startled eyes, he quietly said, "We know, young lady. But just until your mama comes back, do you think you would like living here? When your mama returns, we know you will be going back home, but we would sure be honoured if you would stay with us until that happens. In the meantime, you can 'unspoil' Susanna for us, OK? Until your mama comes, we'll have a lot of fun. There's a lovely little lake at the bottom of this hill where we can swim, picnic, canoe, and watch the Trumpeter swans. They nest there, and it is really interesting to watch them sit on their eggs, waiting for the cygnets to hatch. They come back every year, and are so used to us, they don't fly away if we canoe quietly on their lake."

Lacey appeared to be thinking, hard. Finally, she put both her arms around Mr. Greschner's neck, squeezing him tightly. "I think this will be the best place in the world to wait for our mama to come back, Mr. Greschner. Thank you, and I'm sorry if I was rude."

Henry coughed and turned his head, his eyes brighter and shinier than usual. "Not a problem, little one. You weren't rude at all, you just told it like it is."

Harriet took Lacey by the hand. Turning to Lloyd, she said, "Come with us, Lloyd, we'll give you the grand tour." Shyly, he nodded and followed them into the house.

The inside of the large log home was even more spectacular than the outside. A large country kitchen/dining room housed an oak table that could easily seat up to 18 people. The kitchen looked into a very large living/family room. A gigantic wood-burning fireplace, made from river stones, filled an entire wall. Still on the main floor, the master bedroom, at the back of the home, was huge, as was the en suite. The veranda, that they had seen when they first arrived, encircled the house. You could access the veranda through patio doors from every room on the main floor. A powder room for guests completed the ground level.

A curved, floating staircase elegantly wound its way up to the 2nd floor. The railing along the top overlooked the main floor.

The ceilings on the 2nd floor were as high as the ceilings on the main level. Upstairs, there were 4 bedrooms, each with its own full bath. Susanna showed them her bedroom at the end of the hall. Lloyd and Lacey were told they could each have their pick of the remaining 3 bedrooms.

They were overwhelmed.

Peeking in to each room before they made a decision, Lloyd immediately knew which room he wanted. It was a large, comfy room, furnished with beautiful western maple furniture. The entire end wall was a combination bookcase/television stand/storage unit. It contained doors, drawers and shelves, perfect for any kind of storage. One entire shelf was filled with books and VHS movies that would appeal to a teenage boy. Lloyd wondered aloud how much space he needed for one backpack that was far from stuffed. A gas fireplace occupied the corner beside the entrance to the bathroom. The curtains and the thick comforter matched. The beautiful autumn colours in the fabric were so soothing, Lloyd felt he could cocoon himself in that room for a very long time.

Lacey picked the room right next to Lloyd. She liked knowing that he was so close by, in case she needed him.

The room she picked was the same layout as Lloyd's. In fact, all of the bedrooms had the same design and furnishings. The only difference was that Lacey's room (as she already was calling it) had curtains and bedspread fabric perfect for a young girl. The bed skirt was patterned with horses, kittens, and dogs. The fluffy down comforter was a dusty rose background with rainbows appliqued all over. Several large, stuffed teddy bears sat upright against the pillows on the bed. This room also had a corner gas fireplace. One shelf in the bookcase was filled with books and VHS movies suitable for girls ages 10 and older. The wooden rocking chair in front of the fireplace held a beautiful china doll. A cozy, rainbow-coloured afghan was draped over the back of the chair.

Lloyd turned to Mrs. Greschner, who was standing in the doorway of now-Lacey's room, and quietly asked, "This is too much. Are you sure you want us to use these beautiful rooms?"

She smiled. "Of course, we do, that is unless you want to sleep outside on the veranda? It's pretty cold out there this early in the spring. Or..." she pretended to ponder. "Or, you could sleep in the doghouse. It's pretty big." She burst out laughing. Lloyd looked uncomfortable.

"I'm sorry, Lloyd," she said. "I'm just pulling your leg. Yes, we are absolutely, unequivocally certain that we want you to stay in these rooms. We have been anxiously waiting for you to get here ever since we learned yesterday that we were lucky enough to be having a brother and a sister come and live with us. Now, why don't you 2 get settled, and then rest for a bit. I need to get supper started."

It took them no more than a few minutes to unpack their belongings. Lacey showed up at Lloyd's door when she was done. "Let's see if Mrs. Greschner will let us go outside, OK, Lloyd?"

"Sure, let's go ask her."

Mrs. Greschner was in the kitchen, busily stirring something in a pot. It smelled delicious. She looked up, smiling. "All settled in?"

Lacey nodded shyly. Lloyd saw Susanna standing beside her mother, and he became speechless.

"We are wondering, Mrs. Greschner, if we could go outside and explore for a bit before supper. It's so pretty here." Lloyd waited for her to reply, all the while praying that Susanna would be able to come outside with them, and show them around.

Harriet Greschner said, "Of course, you can. If there is something you can help with, I'll call you. In the meantime, Susanna, would you like to go and show them around?"

"Sure, Mom," Susanna said. "Come on guys, let's go explore."

Besides the house, there was a triple-car, attached garage. To the side of the house, back amongst some beautiful, tall, blue spruce trees, a cedar log building sat. Susanna opened the door. Her father was inside, wearing a carpenter's apron, and busily sanding a large dresser. "Hey, guys, checking out the place, huh? Susanna, you make sure they get the grand tour." Looking over at Lloyd, he asked, "Are you interested in woodworking, Lloyd?"

"I don't know, sir, I've never tried it. It looks interesting, though. I might like it."

"Well, I would welcome some male company when you are finished your tour. I built this house, the outbuildings, and almost all the furniture in the house. Once I finished with our house, word got around that I wasn't a half-bad carpenter. Now, I keep busy building furniture for other people. Would you mind giving me a hand with some things that need more than 2 hands to handle, from time to time?"

"I'd like that," Lloyd said, his eyes lighting up.

Lloyd followed the girls out of the shop. They continued the tour.

Behind the house, just out of sight, in another forest of evergreens, was a beautiful little girl's playhouse.

Susanna said to Lacey, "I used to spend most of my waking hours in that playhouse that my dad built for me. I'm kinda old for it now, so I guess you can take it over. Only thing is, we are in the bush here and so you can't go wandering out of sight of the house by yourself. The dogs keep away most of the wild animals, but occasionally, the odd bear ends up in the yard, especially if we have barbequed meat and haven't cleaned off the grill properly. The dogs will chase it away, and then we can go outside again."

"I haven't seen any dogs," Lacey said. "I love dogs!"

"We have 3 dogs," Susanna said. "They're probably off chasing squirrels or chipmunks. You'll meet the moochers soon enough."

"What kind of dogs, and what's their names?" Lloyd asked.

"Oh, here they come!" Lacey said excitedly. She knelt down and waited for the 3 animals to sniff her thoroughly before licking her cheeks hello.

"This large old girl is our 1st German Shepherd. Her name is Boomer. She's 12 years old. This next wiggle worm is also a German Shepherd, but she thinks she's a people! Her name is Miss Maggie and she's 3 years old. Last, but not least, this big, black, barking dog is a New Zealand Huntaway. He's 3 also, and his name is Crow. They are supposed to be guard dogs, but they are more likely to lick you to death than anything else. They do take their guard dog duties seriously, though. So, if you hear any barking at night, don't worry. They are just keeping the wild animals away from the house."

The only other building on the property was a good-sized machine shed, located right behind Mr. Greschner's shop. This building held a landscape tractor and various attachments, such as a snow blower, a mower, and a rake. Gardening tools hung on the wall, in perfect alignment. Spotlessly clean and organized, you could have eaten off the floor.

"And that's the so-called grand tour," Susanna said. She smiled at Lloyd and said, "Want to sit on the veranda and have a Coke? I can tell you about the school you will be going to with me. We will be in the same class. The school is pretty small by city standards, and there is only one Grade IX class. Lacey, if you want, you can sit with us, or play in the playhouse."

"Can the dogs come in the playhouse too?" Lacey asked.

"Yup, but you will have to keep the playhouse clean, so, if they make a mess of any kind, like muddy feet, or their fur is full of leaves, you have to sweep it out."

"No problem, I can do that. At our last foster home, I learned to sweep the floor and to wash it." Off she ran, calling to the dogs to follow her, which they happily did.

When suppertime arrived, they sat at the big dining room table. It was so relaxed. Everyone talked about what they had done during the day, what they planned to do the next day. All 3 Greschners made sure to include Lloyd and Lacey in their conversation and planning. Bashful at first, they soon joined in. It seemed incredible that they could feel so at home in less than a day.

Lacey said, "Mr. Greschner, one of your dogs is a boy dog."

"I guess you are right, Lacey! You're a smart little chick, aren't you? Thanks for reminding me. Sorry, Lloyd, I guess with you and me and Crow, there are 3 boys and 5 girls in the household now." He chuckled.

"Now," Mr. Greschner said gently, "my wife and daughter and I were talking. We feel that 'Mr. Greschner and Mrs. Greschner' just seems too formal for 2 children who are already part of our family. How about if you call us 'Uncle Henry' and 'Aunt Harriet' while you are here?"

"Sure," Lloyd and Lacey replied in unison.

"Another thing," Uncle Henry said. "I know you are waiting for your mother to come, but until she does, you will have to go to school. You can take the rest of the week off to get used to us, but come next Monday morning you will have to get on the school bus with Susanna, OK?"

"That's fine," said Lloyd.

Lacey's lower lip stuck out, but she managed to say, in a trembling voice, "OK, but only if Mama hasn't come back yet."

The next morning, Lacey sleepily headed down the stairs as soon as she heard Aunt Harriet in the kitchen.

"Good morning, sleepyhead!" Aunt Harriet said cheerfully. "Did you sleep well?"

Lacey nodded. She took a deep breath and said, "Aunt Harriet, we don't have any more clean clothes. We thought we were just going to visit our daddy and then go right home, so we only took 2 changes of clothes, besides the ones we wore on the bus. We wore everything for more than one day, but we've run out of clean stuff."

"That's no problem, my dear. You just gather your things together, and Lloyd's, as well. Bring them down here, and I will get your laundry done right away. In the meantime, you can have a pyjama day. How does that sound?"

"OK, Aunt Harriet," she said, "but it's gonna be a lot of washing every couple of days. Of course, Mama should be here tomorrow, so it might be the only day you will have to wash our stuff." She was standing with her back to the family room and, fortunately, missed the look that passed between the Greschners. Henry had come in behind Lacey, unseen and unheard.

"Tell you what, Miss Lacey, you run on up and get the laundry, and I'll make chocolate chip pancakes for breakfast. Maybe rap on Susanna's, and on Lloyd's bedroom doors. I don't know about you 2, but Susanna does love my chocolate chip pancakes. It's about the only way I know to get her butt out of bed on a non-school day!"

As Lacey turned around to run upstairs, Uncle Henry held up his hands, "Whoa there, young lady! I have a question to ask you before you run off! What do you think about us all going down the hill to the lake on somebody's birthday tomorrow? We can go canoeing. It's too chilly yet to swim in the lake, but we can certainly spend some time there in the canoes."

Lacey stood quietly, and then asked, "Can my Mama come too?"

Again, 'the look' passed above Lacey's head between Henry and Harriet.

Harriet said, "Of course she can, Lacey. If your mama is here tomorrow, she is most welcome to come with us to the lake to celebrate your birthday."

With an ear-to-ear grin, Lacey raced up the stairs, yelling to Lloyd and to Susanna as she ran.

"Slow down!" Uncle Henry called. "Don't want you killing yourself before you are 10 years old!"

Lacey giggled, but she did slow down.

The morning of Lacey's 10th birthday dawned clear and crisp. The forecast was for a sunny day. Everyone chipped in and they packed a big enough picnic basket for a dozen people. Lloyd helped Uncle Henry put both canoes up on the roof of the truck, and Lloyd learned the proper way of securing the canoes so they wouldn't get damaged.

Although the lake was very close to the Greschner property as the crow flies (or rather, as the mountain goat climbs!), it was not possible to physically walk or climb down the long, steep bank. It was a fair drive to get there by road. Even though the lake already had a name, "Island Lake," they wanted to have their own name for it. As they rode, they held a contest. All 5 suggested names for the lake. Because it was Lacey's birthday, she got to be the judge, to choose the name that she liked the best. She chose the name that she, herself, had come up with, 'Mountain Goat Lake', because of the steep bank from the lake to the house. "Fix, fix!" shouted Lloyd and Susanna in unison, laughing heartily.

Mountain Goat Lake became a favourite place for all of them to unwind, relax, and just be.

Being so early in the spring, despite the warmth of the sun, there were no other people at the lake when they arrived. They had their choice of where to set up their picnic area. Arriving in the fresh air at lunchtime, everyone was hungry.

Aunt Harriet had outdone herself. There was cold fried chicken, potato salad, pasta salad, freshly baked buns, fresh lemonade, home-baked chocolate chip cookies, and the most delicious looking 3-layer birthday carrot cake, loaded with cream cheese icing, complete with 10 birthday candles, and 10 birthday, light-up sparklers.

Once they had finished eating, Aunt Harriet asked Lacey whether she would prefer to open her gifts at the lake, or after they got back home. Lacey thought it would be fun to open them back at the house because the 3 dogs could see her opening her gifts.

"All right!" Uncle Henry then asked Lloyd and Lacey if they had ever been canoeing. Neither had. So, right there on the slightly sandy (but mostly rocky) beach, he had them sit in the canoe and he patiently showed them the basics.

"OK, Mom!" he said to Harriet, "I'll go in the red canoe with Lloyd, and you ladies can take the green one. The way I see it, Mom, you and I can just sit back and relax in our canoes, while the youngsters do all the work." He laughed.

They loved it, and by the time the afternoon sun was starting to disappear, both Lloyd and Lacey had a good understanding of the basics. They were becoming very good at paddling. They wanted to race, but Uncle Henry said they should wait until they had a little more practice paddling before they got too ambitious.

Not a large lake, Mountain Goat Lake nevertheless was big enough to have its own island near the back 3rd of the water. The small island was covered with dense shrubs, and tall poplar and spruce trees. They paddled the entire length of the lake, around the island and back, so many times that Uncle Henry joked that he was getting dizzy.

Finally, Aunt Harriet said it was time to pack up. She had a roast in the oven for supper, and they should head on home.

Once everything was unpacked from the truck and put away, they all sat on the veranda to watch Lacey open her gifts. Boomer, Miss Maggie, and Crow, pushed and shoved each other until all 3 dogs had her surrounded as they lay down beside, in front of, and behind her.

Unbeknownst to Lacey, Lloyd had bought her a birthday card and a cheap, but pretty, beaded bracelet the same day as he bought their bus tickets. He had carried the small, gift-wrapped parcel hidden in the bottom of his backpack, awaiting her birthday.

Aunt Harriet, Uncle Henry, and Susanna, gave her a new pair of pyjamas and matching slippers, some books, and a journal. Susanna said it was so she could record the happenings in her life to show her mother when she returned.

There was even a parcel from the dogs. It contained a pretty pair of pierced earrings in the shape of a pony.

Even as Lacey was opening her gifts, and exclaiming over each and every one, her eyes kept drifting towards the road. Of course, her darling mama was nowhere to be seen. She swallowed her disappointment, but later on when she was in bed, she cried herself to sleep.

The next morning, a loud clanging noise made the kids all sit up in their beds! Groggily, all 3 children staggered to the top of the stairs. Henry stood at the bottom of the stairs, happily and noisily ringing a cow bell!

"Time to get ready for school, kids! I already spoke with the principal, and with your teachers. They are expecting you. The school bus will be here in a half hour, so hop to it. Breakfast will be ready before you are."

Harriet was bent over, clutching her stomach. The pain was excruciating. Hearing her husband approaching, she quickly stood up straight, but she was pale and sweating. Unaware, Henry walked into the kitchen and gave his wife a big hug and a smooch. Winking at her, he whispered lasciviously, "We have the house to ourselves today, darling, that is, if we keep the dogs out!"

Harriet blushed and shoved her husband gently towards the table. "Oh, hush," she said, but she was pleased.

Lloyd and Lacey took no time at all to settle in to the new school. Naturally friendly and outgoing, they fit right in with the other students. They liked their teachers, and they studied hard.

On the weekend, the Greschners took the children to a small city about an hour and a half away, and bought them each a full new wardrobe.

Harriet experienced severe stomach pains from time to time but managed to keep them from Henry and the children.

Time passed. Before anyone knew it, an entire year had gone by. Lloyd and Susanna were both now 15. Lacey turned 11.

The Greschners prepared a special celebratory meal on the 1st anniversary of Lloyd and Lacey's arrival into their home. They made a point of telling the children that, if they didn't already have parents of their own, Uncle Henry and Aunt Harriet would gladly adopt them! The children felt very special and loved in this foster home.

Although Lacey still prayed for her mama to come and get them, she was beginning to lose hope. "At least, Lloyd," she told her brother one evening, "we have a very special place here."

"You're right, Lace," Lloyd said gently. "We have a great home here. And at least we won't have to go to another foster home until Mom comes back, or Dad gets out of gaol and we can go home, OK? We can be grateful for that."

Within a month, the time arrived when Harriet could no longer hide her discomfort from Henry.

One day, Susanna, Lloyd, and Lacey, arrived home from school. The house seemed very empty. Susanna went over to a chalk board that hung on the side of the refrigerator. There was a note written on the board, in Henry's neat handwriting:

"Mom had a medical appointment today. If we are not there when you get home from school, we won't be long. Have a snack, do your homework, and we will bring pizza for supper."

Thinking nothing of it, the kids did as they were instructed. "Anything for pizza, right, Lloyd?" Susanna teased.

"Yeah, Lloyd, anything for pizza, you're a pizza nut!" Lacey joked.

Pretending to be annoyed, but secretly flattered, Lloyd said, "You girls don't know what you're talking about. It's you 2 who are the pizza nuts. Although," he added cheerfully, "I won't turn down a pizza for supper! Now, let's get our homework done so we can set the table. That way, the pizza won't get cold waiting for us to get going."

They finished their homework, they set the table, and they fed the dogs. Susanna made a salad. Still the Greschners weren't home.

It was nearly dark when the truck drove into the yard. Stopping at the front veranda, Henry climbed out of the vehicle. Picking his wife up and carrying her into the house, despite her protests that she could walk, he lay her gently onto the sofa in the family room. He turned to call the kids, startled when he saw them standing at his heels.

"What's going on?" Susanna asked. "We were getting worried! Where's the pizza?"

"Have a seat, children," Harriet said weakly. "We have something to tell you."

"For quite a while now, I have been feeling unwell. I tried to hide it from all of you, and apparently I succeeded, by the shocked looks on your faces. Anyway, we finally got in to see the doctor today. There was an Oncologist, a cancer specialist, there from the city, making rounds with my doctor. They did some tests while we were there. They wanted me to stay in the hospital once the results became clear, but I needed to come home."

At this point, Harriet paused to catch her breath, and gathered up her courage for the hardest part, telling the children the results. Henry sat down beside her and put his arm around her shoulders. His eyes were red and watery. His hands were shaking. Seeing that his wife was unable to continue, Henry spoke, his voice ragged.

"Harriet has pancreatic cancer, Stage IV, the most advanced stage. There is nothing that can be done. They cannot cure this disease, all they can do is make her comfortable with painkillers."

Susanna flew over to the sofa and knelt in front of her parents. "There has to be something they can do," she cried wildly. "There has to be!"

Pulling their daughter up onto the sofa between them, they simply hung on. What more was there to say?

Lloyd felt that they shouldn't be in the room, intruding on the family's private grief. He motioned to Lacey, and they soundlessly tiptoed up the stairs to Lacey's room.

Some time later, there was a tap on the bedroom door. Lacey called softly, "Come in." Henry stood in the doorway, mute, unable to move. Finally, choked with emotion, he held out his arms and both Lacey and Lloyd flew into his welcoming hug.

"Kids," Henry finally said, "this is the hardest thing I will ever have to do in my life, but I have to tell you that I called Mrs. Bronson. With all that will be going on here in the next few short weeks, I simply cannot look after 3 children. Harriet has only a month or less to live, according to the doctors. I need every bit of strength that I have to make sure that her last weeks are as comfortable as possible, and to help Susannah through this. We love you both as if you were our own, but how could we have foreseen this tragedy?"

"I'm apparently not as strong as I look. I'm so, so sad for you both, but Mrs. Bronson is coming to get you tomorrow morning. Please be sure all your things are packed, including the new clothes that Harriet bought you, before Mrs. Bronson arrives." He turned and barely made it through the door before he broke down completely.

The children couldn't move. Lacey stared at Lloyd. A sour lump formed in the back of her throat. She thought she was going to throw up.

After quite a few minutes, Lloyd stood up and said, "Well, we better get packed, Lace." Because he knew they wouldn't be able to fit their new clothes into the packs, he went to the kitchen and got 2 large green garbage bags, one for Lacey, and one for himself. Then, he went to his own room to pack his things.

Nobody had any appetite, but nevertheless, when suppertime came, Susanna called Lloyd and Lacey to come down for pizza. All 5 sat at the large table and tried to choke down the food.

When they ate as much as they were able, Harriet held out her arms to Lacey and Lloyd. They went over to her. She hugged them as tightly as she could manage, muttering into their hair, "I love you both." That slight emotional effort cost her. She pushed her chair away from the table and, nodding at Henry to help her, she went to her bedroom, tears running down her cheeks.

Once Henry had Harriet settled in their room, he spoke quietly to Susanna. "Can you stay with Mom for a bit, Susie? I want to take Lloyd and Lacey to the lake one last time. They love it there, so much."

"Of course, Dad," she said. "That's a really good idea. Take your time. Mom and I will use the alone time. I'll lay down beside her and, hopefully, she can sleep."

Henry turned to Lloyd and Lacey. "Get your jackets, kids. We are going for one last canoe ride together."

Although it was dark, a bright moon shone over the waters of Mountain Goat Lake, causing the ripples on the water to shimmer like diamonds. The nesting pair of Trumpeters ruffled their feathers, their dark eyes momentarily startled, but then, the pen settled silently back onto her eggs, as if she was somehow aware of the calming effect that her presence, and that of the cob, meant to the sorrowful 3 humans in the canoe.

Lloyd, Lacey, and Henry, floated aimlessly for an hour, then they paddled back to where they had left the truck.

Sitting on the wooden jetty, and dangling her bare feet in the chilly water while the guys loaded the canoe, Lacey breathed deeply, trying to memorize the feeling of peace and solitude at the lake. She would never forget this place. It would always hold a special place deep in her heart, no matter how the rest of her life turned out. She was sorry that they would not be around to see the cygnets when they hatched. She silently blew a kiss in the direction of the swans. She got into the truck.

Back at the house, they simply stared at Henry. "Thank you, sir," said Lloyd. "That was special. Knowing your grief, we appreciate it more than we know how to tell you." Lacey said nothing, she just walked over to Henry and held out her arms. He hugged her silently, then turned and went into his shop, closing the door behind him.

Chapter 5
Simon and Bertha Savard

It was a little after one o'clock by the time a vehicle drove up the hill and stopped in front of the Greschners' house. It was not a familiar vehicle, but the 2 people who stepped from the dark grey Jeep Cherokee certainly were.

Despite her sadness, Lacey yelled, and nearly fell off the veranda steps rushing to greet both Mrs. Bronson and Mr. Silverman. Clinging tightly to Evelyn, Lacey hauled her up the steps to where Uncle Henry was standing.

Gently peeling the girl from her waist, Evelyn Bronson held out her hand towards Henry, shaking it gently and murmuring her sadness at learning of Harriet's illness.

"I'm just sorry she is not out here to greet you," Henry said. His complexion was pale, the skin on his cheeks sagged. His eyes were lifeless and bloodshot. He needed badly to shave. "This has been a very rough time. She is resting. It took a toll, telling the children. It has taken another toll, not being able to keep Lacey and Lloyd. We love them as much as we love our own daughter, Susanna."

Lloyd appeared in the doorway, lugging both backpacks and the 2 large, very full, green garbage bags. He dragged them over to the jeep and waited for Mr. Silverman to open up the back and help him load. He then climbed silently into the back seat, refusing to look at anyone. Susanna waved at him, crying softly. He did not acknowledge her.

After another round of goodbyes, Lacey had one foot in the back seat already, before she screamed, "Wait! Wait! Uncle Henry, will you be sure to get hold of Mrs. Bronson when Mama comes looking for us? Please?"

Lacey hadn't mentioned her mother in a long time. Henry thought she had given up on the notion that her mother would come to take her home. Staring resolutely above Lacey's head to avoid further tears, Henry replied, "You know I will. Now, you take care, and be good for your next family. We will miss you both desperately, but this is how it has to be."

"I know," Lacey said, "I know." Giving Susanna a very hard squeeze, she then climbed into the back seat of Mr. Silverman's jeep.

Without further ado, the jeep encircled the drive and headed down the hill. No one looked back. No one saw Susanna and Henry, with their arms around each other, crying bitterly and waving weakly at the departing children, long after the vehicle had disappeared from their sight.

After about 15 minutes, Mrs. Bronson flipped down her sun visor on the pretext of fixing her hair. She noted that, although both Lacey and Lloyd still had tears in their eyes, the bout of heavy weeping had ceased. Closing the visor, she asked, "Do you want to know about your next foster family?"

Lloyd shrugged his shoulders. "I guess," he said in a soft and sad tone.

Lacey, mimicking her brother, shrugged her shoulders. "I guess," she said, in the same soft, sad tone.

Twisting around in her seat so she could see the children's reactions, Evelyn said, "The good news first. You do not have to change schools. Your next family lives in a tiny hamlet about 25 minutes east of where the Schmidts live. There is no school there, so you will be bussed to your existing school. Hopefully, that will make your transition easier. You can continue to see your friends.

"Once again, you will be in a temporary foster home. I am sorry, but understandably, we received little to no warning that you would have to be placed in another home. The only place we could put you on such short notice is with Simon and Bertha Savard. They already have 6 foster children in their home. You 2 will bring that number up to 8. However, 2 are newborn babies and they will be going to adoptive homes within the next couple of weeks. Unusual as it is for one family to house so many children at any one time, special consideration has been given in your case, because of the unusual circumstances. Believe it or not, Mr. Silverman and I worked very hard so that you could at least be with your friends."

Nothing was heard from the back seats. With a deep sigh, Evelyn Bronson turned and faced the front, leaving the kids alone in their grief, for the time being.

Suddenly, there was a loud holler from the back seat. "Pull over!" Lloyd hollered. "Quick!"

Immediately, Jayson Silverman pulled the car to the side of the road and stopped. "What the – are you OK, Lloyd? Are you ill?"

"Look!" Lloyd pointed to the house across the street. It was George and Martha Schmidt's place. In the side yard, where the playground equipment was, 4 small children were playing, being watched by a teenage girl.

"I thought you said they would never look after children again," Lloyd was nearly yelling.

"Yeah, that's what you said!" This came from Lacey, who **was** yelling. "That place is bad. We told you that, and you said, you said ..." At this point, Lacey began to stutter. Lloyd placed his hand on his sister's to try to calm her down.

Jayson and Evelyn stared at each other, their expressions unreadable. Finally, Evelyn spoke.

"I gave the bag to Mr. Silverman and he gave it to the Alberta authorities. A brief pause, and then Mrs. Bronson said, "Didn't you, Jayson?" She gave him a deep and unwavering stare. He said nothing. Mrs. Bronson repeated, "Didn't you, Jayson?"

"Of course I did, but as the old saying goes, *the wheels of justice turn slowly*."

"That makes no sense," Lloyd said. "Those kids shouldn't be there! Even if an investigation is going on, they aren't safe."

"Don't worry about it, kid," said Jayson. "I'll check up on the status as soon as I'm back at my office. Everything will be OK."

Evelyn Bronson looked as upset as the children, but she said nothing more.

Lloyd sat in the back, quiet and sullen. Lacey held her tummy. It was hurting like it did when they had stayed at the Schmidts' house.

In approximately 20 minutes more, Mr. Silverman wheeled his jeep into a gravel driveway.

"This is your new foster home, but probably for no more than a few weeks, or maybe a month," said Evelyn. "Our foster parent numbers are way down, but we do what we can."

Getting slowly out of the vehicle, Lloyd and Lacey looked around.

The house in front of them looked pretty tiny to house 2 adults and 8 children, even if 2 of them were newborns. It was a bungalow, grey stucco with black trim. The trim was peeling and badly in need of more paint. This house had no attached garage, in fact, there was no garage at all. A sagging old wooden shed peeked out from behind the house, looking as if it would fall down any minute. A few scattered toys littered the postage stamp-sized lawn, but there was no playground equipment, not even a swing. A mud puddle contained a toy dump truck and a shovel. The puddle appeared to be the closest thing to a sandbox that there was.

Walking up to the front door, Mrs. Bronson rang the bell. Nothing was heard. It appeared as if the doorbell was broken, so she knocked loudly. There was a lot of noise emanating from the interior of the house. Mr. Silverman then reached over and banged on the door for several seconds.

Finally, the door opened. A distracted woman peeked out. "Oh, it's you!" she said grumpily. "Come on in to the zoo." The woman led them into the smallest front room Lacey had ever seen. Shoving a grey cat off of the sofa, she motioned for Mr. Silverman and Mrs. Bronson to take a seat. Pointing at a small wooden footstool, she told Lloyd and Lacey they would have to share. Lloyd sat down. Lacey sat on the floor beside him.

The woman herself sat down in the only easy chair in the room. It faced a small TV, which sat on a grubby wooden TV tray in the corner.

She did not offer refreshments.

"This doesn't seem like the best time, Mrs. Savard," Evelyn Bronson said. "I'm sorry we have to impose this way, but as I explained to you on the phone, it is a bit of an emergency situation."

"Can't be helped," said Mrs. Savard. "Anyway, I can use their help. Got my hands full with 8 in the house at once, as you can imagine." She looked over at Lacey and Lloyd and smiled. She was missing an eye tooth on the top, and a bottom tooth right in the middle. Lacey thought she looked just like a witch.

"You know, kiddies, I might have my hands full, but I do really love children, so does Mr. Savard. You'll meet him later, when he gets home from work."

Mrs. Savard heaved herself out of the easy chair, emitting a loud 'OOMPH' as she did so. "Got a bad hip," she explained.

"Well, you best be on your way," she said to the 2 social workers. "I have a busy day, and I'm sure you do also. The kids will be fine with me. I'm not worried if it takes a while to place them somewhere else. Lord knows, we can sure use the extra money."

Evelyn Bronson bent over and whispered in Lacey's ear, "Do you still have my card?" Lacey nodded and hugged her tight.

As soon as they left, practically before they were even out of the driveway, Mrs. Savard stood with her hands on her hips and surveyed the 2 children in front of her. "Names!" she barked, "What's your names and how old are you?"

"Lacey," Lacey squeaked. "I'm 11 years old."

Lloyd stood tall and looked Mrs. Savard in the eyes. "Lloyd," he said firmly. "I'm 15 years old."

"Well, you 2, better bring your stuff down the hall here. Not much storage space, so you best leave your things in those green bags. You can store them under your beds, digging out what you need as you need it." She limped down the small hallway, stopping at a small bedroom closest to the kitchen. Opening the door, they saw 2 bunk beds. Each bed had a single mattress on the top and a double mattress on the bottom. There was no room for any other furniture in the room. Each bed was covered with sheets and a single, faded pink blanket. No quilt, no bedspread. A single pillow on each of the top bunks, 2 pillows on each of the bottom ones. "This here's the girls' room," Mrs. Savard said. She pointed to the top bunk on her left. That's Zoe's bunk. She's 10." A skinny little girl with matted, dirty-blond hair, grinned down at Lacey. Mrs. Savard continued. "The bottom bunk on the left is Amelia's. She's 16." A very pretty girl, with long auburn hair tied back in a ponytail, sat on that bunk, reading a movie magazine. She smiled and winked at Lacey.

Mrs. Savard said, "So, young Lacey, that leaves you a choice, top right bunk or bottom right bunk. Of course, if we get more emergencies here, you will have to share your bottom bunk with a new girl, if you choose that bed. As you can see, it's a double bed size. The top single bunk would be yours as long as you are here. You wouldn't have to share." Quirking her bushy eyebrows inquiringly at Lacey, Lacey pointed at the top bunk.

"All right, then. The bathroom is at the end of the hall. You have to share it with the boys. Rule is, no fighting over the bathroom, and no hogging it neither. Get in, do your business, wash up, clean it up, and then get out. Got it?" Lacey nodded. "OK, then, make yourself at home. Don't care where you put your things as long as they aren't in the way so's people will trip over them."

Mrs. Savard turned to Lloyd, who was standing outside the door in the hallway.

"Next room down, right beside the girls, is the boys' bedroom. Same size, same layout. Tapping politely on the door, Mrs. Savard waited until a very young voice said, "Enter at your own risk!"

With a broad grin, Mrs. Savard entered the room. Lloyd followed.

"The little rapscallion in the top bunk," said Mrs. Savard, pointing to her left and upward, "is Simon. He's 10, and full of tricks. Watch out for him!" Mrs. Savard chuckled. Lloyd decided then and there that, although she might look like a witch, she was certainly a good witch, with a kind heart.

"Here in the bottom left bunk is Josh. He's 15, same as you. Hopefully you 2 will become friends, right, Josh?" She stared pointedly at a gangly young man with dark brown hair and numerous red zits on his face. "We'll try," he said in a vaguely smart-aleck tone of voice.

He looked at Lloyd. "Howdy. What's your name again?"

"I'm Lloyd," Lloyd said in a non-interested way.

Mrs. Savard continued. "So, as you probably heard me tell your sis, if you pick the top right bunk it will be yours alone while you are here. If, however, you pick the bottom right bunk, and we get another guy in here, you will have to share it."

"I'll take the top bunk," Lloyd said quickly.

"One last thing. Mr. Savard and I sleep in the room at the far end of the hall. At night, we push the bassinettes out into the hallway just outside our door. If you hear a baby cry, don't worry about it, unless you really love babies and want to pick it up. If not, be quiet if you get up and go to the bathroom, so as not to wake the newborns. Or anyone else, for that matter."

She turned and limped out into the hallway. "Make yourself at home. Don't leave things on the floor where someone can trip over them. (Lloyd thought to himself, *yah, yah, yah, you already told me that.*) When supper is ready, I ring a dinner bell. That means come running. No dilly-dallying. See you at supper." She closed the door and went back to the kitchen.

Lloyd finished unpacking. Already tired of Simon's silly, 10-year-old's chatter, he looked over at Josh. Josh buried his nose in an automobile magazine, pretending to be deeply absorbed. Shrugging his shoulders, Lloyd left the room and tapped on the girls' bedroom door.

Lacey peeked out. "Oh, Lloyd, I was just going to come looking for you. Should we go outside and check things out in the yard?"

"Sure," he said. We'll just stop in the kitchen and make sure it is OK with Mrs. Savard. She didn't say anything about chores, but we'll check anyway."

Mrs. Savard was busy with one of the newborns. Hearing Lloyd's request, she abstractedly waved her hands towards the back door. "Go on, then, but don't leave the yard. Mr. Savard will be home soon and he'll wanna meet you right away."

Out in the back yard, which was about the same size as the tiny living room, they surveyed their new home. At least, there was grass at this house, albeit weedy and in need of mowing. The old wooden storage shed was the size of a single car garage, but close up, it looked even more precarious than from a distance. A peek through the dusty, cracked window, revealed it was for storage. Crammed full. No wonder, with 8 kids and 2 adults elbow-to-elbow in that tiny house! A primitive wooden picnic table, made out of 4 sawhorses and a sheet of rough lumber, sat against the house, just off of the lawn. A couple of wooden benches sat on the long side of the table, front and back. A pair of ragged, plastic lawn chairs sat at either end.

Lloyd noticed a rusty electric lawnmower leaning against the picnic table. He plugged it into the wall. It started, so he began to mow the lawn. It was something to do. He didn't mind mowing, in fact, he enjoyed yardwork. It only took about 15 minutes to mow the entire back yard, side yard, and front yard. Pretty tiny.

No sooner did he finish, when a growly, loud voice behind him made him jump.

A skinny man stood, looking at Lloyd. He had salt and pepper hair, tired brown eyes, and a face full of more wrinkles than a man that age should have. He wore a pair of gray coveralls, too large for him, and grease-stained. He carried an old-fashioned metal lunch box. He looked desperately tired, but seemed friendly enough, despite his rough voice.

"Well, well, a kid with some ambition! Nice change around here. Young man, you are…?"

"I'm Lloyd, sir. Are you Mr. Savard?"

"In the flesh, young man, in the flesh." Looking over at Lacey, he raised his eyebrows and waited.

Lacey looked terrified. Taking pity on her, Lloyd answered for her. "That's my sister Lacey, sir. She's 11 years old. I'm 15, sir."

"Welcome to our humble abode, kids. Now if you'll excuse me, I have to get changed. Supper will be ready in about 10 minutes, so you should stand in line at the bathroom door and get washed up when it's your turn."

"Oh, thanks for mowing the lawn, Lloyd. Appreciated." Mr. Savard turned around and walked into the house. He walked like he was carrying a dump truck full of gravel on his shoulders. Watching him, Lloyd was glad that he had been able to help out by mowing the lawn for this exhausted man.

Following the lead of the other children, they got in line, Once they were washed and ready for supper, Lloyd and Lacey walked to the kitchen. Mrs. Savard handed each child one hotdog, a small handful of chips, and a glass of very watery powdered milk. No ketchup, no mustard, no butter. Just a dry bun and a wiener, plain chips, and watery milk. They were told to take it outside and eat at the picnic table.

Lloyd looked over at the tiny kitchen table. A pair of dinner plates full of mashed potatoes, gravy, roast beef, and corn on the cob, sat on the table. Fresh buns lay in a basket, with a dish of butter beside it. A large piece of chocolate cake sat to the right of each of the 2 plates.

Mrs. Savard caught Lloyd looking. "Listen, kid," she said to Lloyd, "Social Services doesn't pay us enough to feed 8 kids and 2 adults. Seeing as the Mister and I do all the work, we need that food for energy. So just take your plate outside and eat. No complaining, hear me?"

"In this house," she explained, "once you're done eating, you wash your own dishes and put them away. Then you do your homework. Bedtime lights out at 9 o'clock."

"The school bus gets here at 7:30 in the morning. The alarm goes off at 6 a.m. because it takes a while for 6 children, using one bathroom, to get ready, and then eat. Your breakfast will be on the table. Eat it outside, or standing in the hall. Table's not big enough for everyone to sit, so no one sits. Your lunch will be at the front door. Grab it on your way out."

Sitting outside at the picnic table, Lacey noticed that everyone was taking teeny tiny bites, chewing for a long time. Amelia made a face. Looking at Lloyd and Lacey, she explained, "This is all we get to eat until breakfast. We find that if we eat it very slowly, chew small bites, it seems like more food. We can't have 2nd helpings, so we try and make it last."

Lacey and Lloyd had already done their homework before they came to the Savard house. The evening stretched ahead, with nothing for them to do.

Josh, the young man with the spotty face, took pity on Lloyd. He handed him an automobile magazine to look at until lights out. Lloyd appreciated the gesture, but he had zero interest in either cars or mechanics.

In the girls' room, Amelia was reading another movie magazine. Lacey noticed it was inside the cover of a school binder. Amelia winked and said, "Just in case one of the Savard patrols check to see how the homework is coming along."

Zoe grinned down at Lacey. "Wanna play a game? I've got some cards."

"No. Thanks, Zoe," Lacey said politely, "but I'm pretty tired. I think I'll take my shower and then go to sleep early. Maybe another day, OK?" Although Zoe looked disappointed, and opened her mouth as if to protest, she decided against it. She simply closed her mouth and nodded.

The next morning, when the alarm rang, the household became what could only be described as 'orderly pandemonium'. Within a half hour, all 6 school children were washed, backpacks organized, and ready for breakfast. The smell of bacon hovered tantalizingly. The children all sniffed the air like hungry puppies.

Lloyd couldn't believe it. Each child got one single piece of toasted white bread, with such a minimal amount of peanut butter spread on it that you could hardly tell there was anything at all on the bread. A small glass of the same watery, powdered milk completed the breakfast.

Lacey was so hungry, that she ventured, in a small voice, "Mrs. Savard, may I have another piece of toast, please?"

"No, you may not, Lacey," Mrs. Savard said in a kindly, but firm fashion. "I don't have money to waste on 2nd helpings. I told you yesterday, Social Services doesn't pay us enough. Now, don't forget to grab your lunch as you head out to the bus. See you after school."

She abruptly turned her back to Lacey, and dished up bacon and eggs, toast and jam, and fried potatoes for her husband.

"Goodbye, have a great day!" said Mrs. Savard to the children. Mr. Savard simply waved cheerily as the children filed past him. His mouth, momentarily, too full to speak. Swallowing, he said,

"See you at supper."

At the front door, again following the lead of the other children, Lloyd and Lacey picked up their backpacks. On the hall table sat 6 withered apples, and 6 cookies. That was lunch!

Lloyd looked questioningly at Amelia. She softly said, "Get used to it. We won't get any more food than what you saw."

Lacey couldn't believe it. "I'm gonna tell my teacher about this," she said firmly. "This has to be against the law, 'cause you can't starve kids." She looked anxiously at Lloyd. "Can ya?"

On the school bus, Lacey asked Lloyd if he thought that Susanna would be at school today. He shrugged his shoulders, he didn't know. Stomach growling, grouchy from hunger, and the events of yesterday and this morning, he stared silently out the window.

Lacey soon became bored. Looking around, she saw Zoe sitting by herself. Lacey walked up the aisle to sit beside her.

"Sit down while the bus is moving, young lady," the bus driver hollered from the front. "You know better than that, don't ya? I know you know better, 'cause you used to be on Pete's bus. Well, you're not a new kid on a bus ride. This ain't your 1st rodeo, so sit down!"

Her cheeks flaming, Lacey slunk down and returned to her seat beside her brother. Despite his grumpiness, he reached over and gave Lacey's hand a pat. She wiped her streaming eyes, straightened up in her seat, and murmured to herself, almost under her breath, *"Oh, Mama, where are you? We really need you more than ever."* Lloyd heard her. She still believed. He did not.

It was a bit longer bus ride than when they took the bus from the Greschners' place, but they eventually arrived at their school.

Lloyd looked around for Susanna, but he didn't see her. They were in the same class, though, so she might be in the classroom already. He hoped so.

Lacey ran ahead. Her teacher was in the classroom, marking some papers at her desk. She looked up when Lacey entered the room. "Good morning, Lacey," she said. "You know you aren't supposed to be in the classroom until the bell goes."

"I know. I'm sorry, Miss Sampson, but I need to tell you something. My brother and I need your help."

Miss Sampson looked at the earnest little girl, waited for her to continue. She motioned for Lacey to sit down at a front desk. She rose and closed the door to the classroom.

Lacey explained how Harriett Greschner was dying, and so they had to move because Mr. Greschner was too sad to look after 3 kids. She explained that they were now in a new foster home that was so tiny the kids had to eat outside or eat standing up in the hallway, if the weather was too bad to eat outside. She explained how hungry she was, what the kids had for supper and breakfast, what Mr. and Mrs. Savard had to eat for supper, and for breakfast. She told Miss Sampson that she didn't know what to do. She asked her teacher to tell her what to do.

After a full minute of silence, Miss Sampson asked the little girl, "Are they physically mean to you?"

"Noooo," drawled Lacey. "We're just hungry."

Miss Sampson stood up, "Well, Lacey, if they are not physically harming you in any way, there is nothing I can do. You are getting fed. You have a place to sleep, other children to keep you company, and 2 adults to care for you. I think you are doing just fine. You're much better off than a lot of the children in this school. You have a very active imagination. You need to settle down and settle in to your new foster home, make the best of things. Give yourself a chance, and you will find that things are not as bad as they seem this morning.

"Now, go outside with the other children until the bell goes." She put her head down and continued marking the papers in front of her.

Susanna was not at school. Lloyd was so disappointed. He and Susanna had become very close. He wanted to be there for her as she underwent the stress of her mother being so ill. *Oh well*, he thought, *maybe she'll be here tomorrow.*

By the time they climbed back on the bus at the end of the school day, Lloyd had a headache from hunger. He leaned his head back and tried to doze, hoping to quell some of the growling hunger pangs.

The school bus stopped and all 6 kids got off. They walked slowly towards the house, reluctant to be crowded into the tiny place any sooner than they had to.

Suppertime consisted of 3 tiny meatballs, a tablespoon or so of Kraft dinner (one box was split among the 6 children), a teaspoon of peas, a half a piece of bread (dry, no butter) and a juice glass size of the same watered down powdered milk. Not enough to completely kill the hunger, but a bit more than last night.

Even though she tried to eat as slowly as the other kids, Lacey still finished before anyone else.

Mr. and Mrs. Savard were eating ham and scalloped potatoes, fresh bread and butter, peas and carrots, salad, and pie for dessert. They didn't even look the least bit guilty when they saw Lacey glaring at them as she washed her plate and glass. Mr. Savard told her to hurry up, he was sure she had homework to do. She put her dishes away and then stomped noisily through the hallway on the way to her room.

Lloyd was next to enter the kitchen. Glancing indifferently at the Savards, he quickly washed his dishes, and then went towards his room to do his homework.

Lacey was sitting on the floor, her back against the boys' bedroom door, waiting for Lloyd.

"You know, Lloyd, I talked to Miss Sampson today about us being so hungry and all."

Lloyd asked, nonchalantly, "What did she have to say?"

"Nothing to help us. She didn't believe me."

Lloyd shrugged his shoulders. The shrugging was becoming a regular part of him. Lacey found it annoying. He didn't seem to care enough to try to do something. Without another word, she turned and went to the girls' bedroom.

The weeks passed. No word came regarding a more permanent foster home for Lacey and Lloyd.

The newborn babies were adopted, and 2 more newborns arrived the same day.

The food supply became even more scant. All of the foster children were growing painfully thin.

Susanna still wasn't at school. Lloyd's teacher said she was studying at home so she could spend more time with her mother.

Lacey became a sounding board for Amelia. She would sit quietly in the bedroom while Amelia would tell her about how she was going to become a model, or a movie star. Once she was certain that whatever she told Lacey would go no further, she shared with her the fact that she was going to run away. Lacey cried and tried to convince her that she wasn't old enough to live on her own, and how everyone would miss her if she left. No amount of pleading on Lacey's part could change Amelia's mind. She tried to get Amelia to tell her exactly when she was leaving, but all Amelia said was that she would let Lacey know.

One morning, just as the sun was struggling to rise, casting a soft pink glow behind the cotton candy clouds softly lounging in the sky, Amelia shook Lacey, putting her hand over Lacey's mouth so she couldn't cry out.

"Sssh! Hush now, Lacey, and I'll take my hand away. I just want you to know that I am outta here. I also want you to know that if I didn't have plans, and if I could choose a sister of my very own, I would pick you."

With her back pack slung over her shoulder, Amelia whispered goodbye and left by the back door. Lacey went to the window to watch Amelia until she was out of her sight. Within a minute, Amelia was on the road. She turned and waved in Lacey's general direction, blowing her a kiss before she turned to run down the road. Before she was out of Lacey's sight, however, a brightly coloured truck pulled over. Orange, with black and green letters on the door, something about the truck niggled at the back of Lacey's brain. She watched Amelia climb up into the cab. She watched until it was gone from her sight. Déjà vu. Shades of Charley.

It was easy getting ready for school the next morning without the Savards noticing Amelia was missing. That morning, Mr. Savard ate before the children and left early for work. Mrs. Savard was so busy with the newborns that she did not come to the door to say goodbye.

When Lloyd noticed that Amelia wasn't there, he asked Lacey if Amelia was OK. Josh looked at her with suspicion. Zoe and Simon didn't pay any attention. Lacey whispered quietly, to both Lloyd and Josh, that Amelia was gone, but she didn't know where. That much was the truth.

Lloyd's teacher pulled him aside just before classes started to tell him that Harriet Greschner had passed away. Stricken, he asked for details of the funeral. None were yet available, but his teacher said she would let him know, as soon as she heard anything.

Deciding not to tell Lacey until after school, Lloyd's mind and heart were with Susanna and her father. Although he didn't say anything aloud, Lloyd missed the Greschners so much, that he felt like he had a hole in his heart.

He wondered if Mr. Savard would drive them to the funeral, and he wondered what he could do to help Henry Greschner and his daughter. If Lloyd felt this bad, Heaven only knew how Henry and Susanna could manage!

On the school bus on the way home, Lloyd quietly told Lacey about Harriet Greschner. She cried so heartbrokenly that Lloyd wished he had waited to tell her when they were off the bus.

Running into the house, Lacey tore into the bathroom and slammed the door shut.

Mrs. Savard belatedly called out, "No running in the house!" She then asked Lloyd what the problem was. He told her.

Lloyd asked if there was some way that he and Lacey could go to the funeral, when they found out when it was.

"No! I am a firm believer that children shouldn't go to funerals. Gives 'em nightmares. Just remember her the way she was. Besides, it costs money for gas, which we don't have."

Lloyd felt a coal-hard lump forming inside of him. Silently cursing his father and his mother for placing them in this situation, Lloyd began to give serious consideration to the rest of his own life. Even though he was only 15, being on his own couldn't be more difficult than this.

Pausing to think, Lloyd knew, however, that he couldn't abandon Lacey and leave her to fend for herself. She was pretty mature for an 11 year old, but she wandered around with her heart on her sleeve. It would be simple for someone to prey upon his little sister. He would just have to tough it out, but he didn't have to like it!

For supper that night, each child was given a peanut butter sandwich and a small glass of the now-familiar watery powdered milk. Mr. and Mrs. Savard ate like royalty. They did not even notice that Amelia was not eating with the rest of the brood. They were too busy discussing how many days it was until the government foster parent cheques arrived.

Right after supper, Lacey went to her room and crawled into bed, but not before she bunched up the sheets and blanket on Amelia's bed, with her pillow underneath so that it looked like a person was asleep, as if snuggled in the middle of the mass. When Mrs. Savard poked her head in at lights out, Lacey put her forefinger against her lips. "Sound asleep," she stage-whispered to Mrs. Savard. Her foster parent nodded, and quietly shut the door. Lacey lay down on her bunk and cried herself to sleep. She had done her best to give Amelia time to get away. She was not sorry about that, but she missed the older girl fiercely.

Before the Savards could ask about Amelia the next morning, the phone rang. After several minutes, Mrs. Savard hung up. "Lacey and Lloyd, looks like they have found you another foster home. Someone will pick you up when you get home from school today. You seem to have a magic aura around you. The new foster family is within this general area. You won't have to change schools. Hurry off the bus. You will have to pack your things before the social worker comes to get you."

"By the way, have either of you seen Amelia this morning?" Not waiting for a reply, she shooed them off before they missed the bus.

Chapter 6
Bart and Gladys Bourke

Seated on the bus on their way to school, Lloyd quietly whispered to Lacey, "Get on the bus as fast as you can after school, Lace."

Lacey sighed. "Yeah, yeah, Lloyd, I know. We are moving, AGAIN. I don't have to like it, though."

Lloyd whispered again, "We need to get off the bus and run like crazy to the Mailbox. I just need to be sure you remember where it is. You lead the way, and I will follow behind you, just to make sure, OK? We won't have much time, because Mrs. Savard will be wondering where we are. I already packed so it will save time."

"What will you tell her when we're late?"

"I'll just tell her the bus was late. That's if she even notices. Also, Josh says he'll cover for us, if she asks. He will tell her we just went for a quick walk because we were going to miss this place." He gave a wry grimace. "As if!"

"Oh, she'll notice! The other kids will be there. I'll hurry, Lloyd," Lacey said. "I already packed my stuff too, so I won't keep anyone waiting."

After school, everything went according to plan. They tore off the bus, and began running. Lacey had no problem finding the Mailbox. It was a little bit closer to the Savard's house than it was to the Schmidt's. She almost wished they would find another note, because maybe then somebody would believe it was real. Lacey certainly believed.

The Mailbox was empty.

Running as hard as they could, they reached the Savard house in record time. Pausing out of sight of the kitchen window to catch their breath, Lloyd spoke raggedly to his sister. "Just," he panted, "just in case Mrs. Savard should ask, just tell her we went for a run before we have to sit in the car. Just tell her that. Nothing else. We did go for a run. We do have to sit in a car, so we're not lying. Got it?"

Lacey nodded. "I'm ready," she said, "Let's go in."

They quickly went into the house and quietly went to their rooms to bring their belongings to the front door. When Mrs. Savard hollered for them, they were sitting on the front step, waiting for their ride.

Mrs. Savard stood in the doorway, glaring at the 2. Hands on her hips, she asked, "Well, were you even going to say goodbye?"

"Yes," said Lacey meekly.

"Of course," said Lloyd sullenly.

Just then, a vehicle drove up. Not one they recognized. It was a burgundy Ford SUV. The driver's door opened and Evelyn Bronson stepped out. Lacey raced over to her, nearly bowling her over with her enthusiastic hug!

"Where's Mr. Silverman?" asked Lloyd.

"He's away on a bit of a working vacation," said Mrs. Bronson. "He won't be back in the office until late next week. However, I gather from talking with your teacher, Lacey, that things aren't that great at this home either, so I decided to come by myself. Are your things all together?"

Walking up to the front door, she spoke briefly with Mrs. Savard. Lloyd and Lacey had already said goodbye to the other kids. They knew it was rude, but they were hoping not to have to say goodbye to the old skinflints, namely Mr. and Mrs. Savard. They waved at Mrs. Savard from beside the car, almost, but not quite rudely, muttered 'Thanks' and 'Goodbye'.

"Lloyd, do you want to sit in the front?" Mrs. Bronson asked.

"Yes," said Lloyd.

"I wanna!" Lacey pouted.

Lloyd stared at her. "Lace, I need to talk to Mrs. Bronson about us going to Aunt Harriet's funeral. It's a lot easier sitting beside her than yelling from the back seat."

Lacey, pacified, crawled into the back. Lloyd put their green garbage bags containing all their belongings into the back of the SUV. He then folded his awkward, skinny frame into the front passenger seat.

"I heard that Harriet Greschner passed," Mrs. Bronson said quietly. "Such a sad, sad thing. I know you children were fond of her."

Lloyd offered the first comment. "Mrs. Savard said she doesn't believe in kids going to funerals. 'Gives 'em nightmares,' she said." Tears threatened behind his eyes and he blinked rapidly to clear them before they could roll down his face.

"Well, I don't believe that for a single minute," Evelyn Bronson said in a firm tone. "Harriet's funeral is tomorrow. I am staying over at your new foster parents' place so that I can take you both, if you want to go."

Lloyd lost his battle with control, tears streamed down his cheeks. "Thank you, Mrs. Bronson," he said, in a husky whisper. "Thank you so much."

Lacey bounced up and down, restrained by her seatbelt or she would surely have climbed over the seat and onto Evelyn's lap. "Yes, yes, yes! Thank you, thank you, thank you!"

This new foster home, (*Number 4, but who's counting*, Lloyd thought to himself), was halfway between the Schmidt's and the Savard's, not that either Lloyd or Lacey would ever darken those doorways again, if they had anything to say about it.

Lucky break! It was the closest home to the secret Mailbox yet.

Bart and Gladys Bourke lived on a farm, just off the main road, and on the same side of the road as the Mailbox. As they drove into the farmyard, Lacey could barely contain her awe. "Look, Lloyd, horses and cows, and ducks and geese and turkeys, and dogs and cats, and even pigs!" Pausing for breath, she said, "Mrs. Bronson, look, a trampoline! Stop! Stop the car, I need to get out!"

"Just hold on to your horses, young lady," Mrs. Bronson said. "You will have plenty of time for that. First, we need to introduce you to your new foster parents."

She pulled the car up in front of a very pretty, 2-storey farmhouse. A dark gray siding was brightened up with white trim around all of the windows. Each of the windows on the upper floor held a flower box full of red geraniums. The veranda that ran across the width of the house was sparkling clean. No paint chips, no weeds, no lawn needed mowing.

Conspicuous in its absence, though, other than the trampoline, there was no playground equipment, not even a swing. Lacey loved to swing. The lack of a swing was a disappointment to the young girl.

All of the outbuildings sported the same dark gray siding with white trim. Everything was so antiseptically clean that Lacey wondered if the animals were given a bath. As if he could read her mind, Bart Bourke appeared in the doorway of the barn, a hose held in his hand. Wrapping the hose onto a hose reel beside the barn door, he soon was walking towards the group.

He reached Mrs. Branson's car just as his wife opened the front door.

"I'm Bart Bourke." Looking at Lacey and Lloyd, he said, "You can call me 'Mr. B'. Everyone does. The woman that just came out the door is my wife, Gladys."

Mrs. Bourke hurried over, smiling brightly. "I'm Gladys Bourke. Happy to meet you."

She continued, "Evelyn, it is so good to see you again. We are thrilled that you are spending the night with us. Come on in, everyone. We will get the children's things put away."

Mr. B interrupted his wife. "The young lad and I have chores to do right now, Gladys. We'll be along shortly, after I show him around and let him know what I expect from him in the way of chores." Putting his arm around Lloyd's shoulder, they walked towards the outbuildings.

With a shrug, Gladys Bourke grabbed Lloyd's things. Mrs. Bronson picked up her own overnight bag, and also helped Lacey with her possessions as they headed towards the house.

"Normally, we don't use the front door 'cept if there's guests. Evelyn, since you are a guest, I'm sure Mr. B won't mind us using the front door. I'll show you the back door later, Lacey. For now, let's just get you settled in. Supper's in the oven. Mr. B sure does like his supper as soon as he's washed up from chores. Your room is this way, just follow me. Evelyn, your room is up here also. Come on up." Mrs. Bourke led the way up the stairs.

Once upstairs, Gladys Bourke explained that there were 3 bedrooms and 2 bathrooms. Hers and Mr. B's room was at the far-left end of the hall. The other 2 bedrooms were at the opposite end of the hall separated by a bathroom. She opened the door closest to the end of the hallway. "This is the guest room. Evelyn, you will sleep in here."

The room was small. It contained a double bed, covered with a home-made, crocheted afghan, in soft colours of silvery gray and blue. A dressing table, with a mirror above it, was placed on the wall to the left of the bed. A small closet, with no door, completed the room. Looking out the window, Evelyn could see both her car and the road. She noticed that the gate from the main road into the farmyard was now closed.

"This is very lovely, Gladys. Thank you." Mrs. Bronson put her overnight bag on the chair that sat in front of the dressing table.

"Make yourself at home," Mrs. Bourke said. "Once you've unpacked, come on downstairs and we'll chat while I finish getting supper ready. Come with me now, Lacey. Let's have a look at your room."

To Lacey, the room looked as small as the bathroom that adjoined her bedroom in the Greschner house. It was set up identical to the guest bedroom, except there was a comforter on the bed, pink and white in colour.

The bathroom was a full bath, complete with a tub/shower combination.

"Where's Lloyd's room?" Lacey asked.

"Oh," said Mrs. Bourke, "there's a bed for him downstairs, just off the mudroom. That way, Lloyd will be able to get up and get the milking done before his breakfast, and before he leaves for school." She continued, "Unfortunately, there is no door on that room. Mr. B hasn't got around to putting it on. Don't think he will, he says it will make the room too small if you install a door that opens in, and take up too much room in the mudroom if it opens outwards. Your brother will use your bathroom. Just make sure you both leave it as clean as you find it. Mr. B is real fussy that way."

The main floor consisted only of a small front entryway, with a coat closet to the right of the door, a small sitting room, and a large country kitchen, which served as both kitchen and dining area. A large wooden table looked like it could seat about 8 people. Lacey could see a mudroom just off the kitchen. A large laundry sink, washer and dryer, a boot rack, and hooks on the wall for outside clothing, completed the fair-sized room. A doorway, minus a door, took up only a small part of the mudroom. Looking suspiciously like a closet, it held only a single bed. There were 3 shelves attached to the wall above the bed, plus 3 hooks on the wall beside the bed. These would have to suffice for Lloyd's things. A tattered plaid blanket, instead of a bedspread, and a very thin and tattered duvet that didn't look like it would be warm, lay across the bed. Lacey felt her heart sink.

Nowhere in this house did she see a television set.

Returning to the kitchen, Mrs. Bourke asked Lacey if she knew how to set a table.

"Yes, ma'am," Lacey said. "It was one of my chores at the Schmidt house, and I used to help Aunt Harriet at the Greschner's."

"Great!" gushed Mrs. Bourke. "Just look in all the cupboards and set the table for 5, please. Make sure Mr. B's place is at the head of the table." Turning to Evelyn, she asked her if she would like a cup of tea.

Once Lacey had completed setting the table, she sat down and waited. She was not sure for what.

Gathering her courage, she asked Mrs. Bourke where the television was.

"Oh, my dear, we don't have time to watch television," she said. "We are busy from first light until dark. By then, we are so pooped out we just go straight to bed."

"Oh," said Lacey weakly.

"How come you don't have any playground equipment for kids here? I really like to swing, but I don't see a swing. The trampoline looks like fun though," she proffered hopefully.

"Oh, the trampoline is strictly off-limits!" said Mrs. Bourke. "There was a bad accident on that trampoline 2 years ago. A little one jumped too close to the edge, fell and hit his head. Got a bad concussion out of it. He recovered, but it took a while. We got sued, and it cost us a potful of money."

"Hmm," Lacey said. "Why don't you take it down then?"

"Mr. B won't hear of it. He says it is a good reminder that foolish play leads to hurt. Unless he is working, Mr. B thinks everything is a waste of time. To him, work is the only thing worth anything in this life." She stopped, horrified. "Please, forget I said all that. Mr. B is really a very good man, he just doesn't know how to enjoy himself."

Lacey was beginning to worry for Lloyd. Looking over at Mrs. Bronson, she couldn't read the expression on the social worker's face.

Mrs. Bourke smiled. "You, my dear child, might be able to convince him to make you a swing out of an old tire and tie it on a big branch of that American elm tree over beside the house. He has a tire that would be just the right size. In fact, he was commenting just the other day that it was too bad that we didn't have a child around who would like to have a tire swing. You'd have an even better chance of Mr. B building it for you, if you offered to help him."

"OK," Lacey said. "I'll do that after we are back from Aunt Harriet's funeral."

Mrs. Bourke looked at the table. "Fine job, young lady, that is just fine. Thank you very much. You are going to be a great help around here, I can tell that right off!"

Why did Lacey feel that there was something very dark behind that compliment? Giving her head a shake, she figured it was just because Aunt Harriet had died, and they were in yet another new foster home. She should be happy. Mrs. Bronson had come all the way from British Columbia to move them and she was staying over to take them to the funeral. Lacey and Lloyd had nothing to worry about. Or did they?

Restless, and not remotely interested in the conversation that the ladies were having, Lacey got up and went outside (via the back door!) A couple of the farm dogs approached her. She held out her hand, letting them sniff her. Once their tails started wagging, she sat down on the lawn and paid them the serious attention that those 2 dogs felt they deserved.

A full half-hour passed as Lacey sat on the grass, deep in contemplation.

A gruff voice jolted her out of her reverie. "Idleness is the devil's tool!" Mr. B's voice was deep, loud, and harsh!

"I, I, I'm sorry, Mr. B. What should I be doing? I set the table for supper already. I just wanted to play with the dogs while waiting for supper."

"There is always something to do, gal. If you can't see something that needs doing, then ask. There will be no idle time on this farm. Now, scoot on back to the kitchen and tell my wife that we'll be ready to eat in 10 minutes."

"Yes, sir," Lacey quavered, "I will."

Behind Mr. B's back, Lloyd rolled his eyes. Lacey gave a weak smile and ran towards the back door of the house.

Exactly 10 minutes later, everyone was seated at the table, enjoying an excellent meal of stew and dumplings. No problem with 2nds in this foster home. They could eat until they were full. Mr. B said to 'fuel up', that it was hard to work effectively on an empty stomach. There was no further conversation until Mr. B pushed his chair back from the table, sipping his coffee, and waiting for dessert.

Mrs. Bronson asked, "So, Bart, tell me, because I, of course, am not the official Alberta social worker for Lacey and Lloyd, why you want to be a foster parent?"

"Got no young'uns of our own, and need the help and the money," he stated simply. "Gladys needs help in the house." He continued. "Figured this would be the best way. Now, to be honest, we ain't never had much to do with children, so we will all of us have lots to learn. Gladys and I will need to figure out how to deal with kids, the kids will need to learn how to work hard and work well."

Mr. B yawned. "Well, young Lloyd, we need to be up at 4 in the mornin' to get the cows milked. Early to bed in this house. You'll need to learn how to attach the milking machine to the cows, how to disengage it, and what to do with the milk in the pails once you're done. I'll show you tomorrow. After that, you will do it yourself. Now, off to bed with us. Evelyne, what time do you have to leave for that funeral?"

"It starts at 11," she replied. "We'll have to leave here by 9:45, as I am sure the school gymnasium will be packed. Are you not coming? They are, after all, country neighbours."

"Too much to do," Mr. B responded.

"Well, Gladys," Evelyn turned to her friend. "I would be happy to have you come with us."

Gladys Bourke looked over at her husband expectantly.

Mr. B spoke for his wife, "Nope, laundry day. She ain't got no time to go gallavantin' around the country when there's work to be done. If these here kids hadn't lived with the Greschners, they wouldn't have time neither. Please give our regards, though. Now, off to bed. See you in the morning, Lloyd." He left the table.

Lloyd looked over at Mrs. Bourke. "Where am I to sleep, ma'am?" he questioned.

Lacey jumped up. "I'll show you, Lloyd."

Lloyd stared, dumbfounded, at the closet. "You've got to be kidding me! What the hell? Where's the bathroom?"

Lacey took him upstairs, showed him the bathroom, and relayed Mrs. Bourke's message that Mr. B expected the bathroom to be as clean as they saw it, every time they used it. Lloyd simply muttered, "Good night, Lace, see you in time to leave for the funeral." He turned on his heel and went back downstairs, muttering under his breath, "Is every foster parent in the world an asshole?", momentarily forgetting that the Greschners had been excellent foster parents. He crawled into the bed and pulled the solitary blanket up around his ears.

Long before Lloyd was ready, it was 4 a.m. He was rudely awakened by Mr. B roughly shaking his shoulder. "Come on, boy, them cows are already bellerin' to get their udders emptied out. Don't worry about washing up, you can do that after milking's done."

Lloyd, half asleep, crawled out of bed, threw on his jeans and flannel shirt. He had to run to catch up to Mr. B, who was already nearly at the barn.

The early morning air was crisp. It was dark, not even a hint of daylight. Lloyd decided he would need to dig out a warmer shirt and jacket if he was expected to get up every morning and go outside and over to the barn. He did notice, though, that there was a lot of heat coming off the cows. It was actually quite warm inside the barn. He paid careful attention to what Mr. B was showing him. The cows stared gratefully at Mr. B as the electric milkers began to do their job and the tension from the udders relaxed.

Mr. B was patient, and a thorough teacher. Lloyd watched, and listened carefully, and learned quickly. Other than the ungodly hour, Lloyd decided that, overall, it might not be so bad, this milking of the cows.

Shovelling down a hot breakfast of oatmeal with warm, fresh milk, fruit, toast and juice, Lloyd would have given everything he owned for another couple of hours of sleep. However, he went upstairs and had a shower, then dug out what he figured would be adequate funeral clothing, from his suitcase. He didn't have much in the way of dress clothing, but he put on a pair of khaki pants and a navy shirt. He was happy that the Greschners had given both him and Lacey luggage for Christmas. At least, there was room for his clothes to be folded neatly and, therefore, they were not too badly wrinkled.

Mrs. Bronson and Lacey came downstairs, dressed and ready to leave. Lloyd asked the social worker if he should run up and clean the bathroom. Evelyn replied that she had cleaned it, but thank you anyway.

Lacey sat in the front seat this trip. Lloyd didn't mind. As they approached their school, they were amazed at the number of vehicles that were already there. They filled the entire parking lot and both sides of the road. Lloyd estimated there were at least a couple of hundred vehicles, mostly farm trucks.

A lineup formed just outside the gym doors. A young woman at the door handed them a card containing the order of service and a summary of Harriet Greschner's life. Once inside, they looked around for 3 chairs together.

Before they could find a place, though, Susanna spied them and waved them up to the front.

"We've saved you seats beside us," Susanna said when they reached her. "Mom would have wanted this." She hugged Lacey and took Lloyd's hand. "Thank you so much for coming!"

"Where's Uncle Henry?" Lacey asked.

"He is speaking with people. He'll be right back. Oh! Here he comes now." Susanna used this opportunity to slide closer to Lloyd.

Uncle Henry sat down. "Thanks for coming, kids. We'll talk more later."

It was a large gymnasium and it was filled to capacity. Extra chairs were brought in, and when the supply ran out, people stood at the ends of each row of chairs.

Neither Lloyd nor Lacey had ever attended a funeral before. They didn't know what to expect.

At the front of the gym, directly in front of them, a decorative urn sat on a wooden table that was covered with an embroidered tablecloth. A picture of Harriet Greschner stood beside the urn.

"What's the urn for?" Lacey whispered to Mrs. Bronson. "It's Harriet's ashes," Evelyn whispered back.

"Oh!"

Bouquets of flowers adorned every surface at the front of the gym.

A stereo system had been set up, with numerous speakers placed around the circumference of the gymnasium, so that everyone present would have no trouble hearing.

Sitting quietly, Lacey and Lloyd tried to quell the emotions that threatened to overflow. Lacey's stomach burned. Lloyd clung tightly to Susanna's hand.

A woman sat patiently on a piano bench. At an unseen nod from someone just outside the doors, she began to play the piano. The community choir, clad in their choir robes, entered the gym. Singing their way to the front, they turned to face the full house, and continued to sing *'Church in the Wildwood'*.

A man in his early 40's stood at the front. Lloyd presumed that he was the minister, although he wore no vestments of any sort, simply a pair of grey dress pants, a white dress shirt, and a somber tie. Nodding solemnly towards the Greschner family, he began. "For the few of you in this auditorium that may not know me, I am Pastor Luke. I have been in the company of the Greschners for the past trying weeks. I trust that I was able to make Harriet's untimely passing more peaceful."

Pastor Luke read:

"In my Father's house are many mansions. If it were not so I would have told you. I go to prepare a place for you."

He paused before continuing, "We are here today to celebrate the life of Harriet Greschner, a loving wife and mother, a good friend and neighbour to us all.

"Harriet was always willing to lend a helping hand to anyone and everyone, no matter how difficult or menial the request."

"Her life was cut short far too early. There is, however, no questioning the Will of Our Lord. He takes His people Home when He knows it is their time."

"Henry Greschner assures me that, although they are not a church-going family, they are, indeed, a family of faith, that, although their mourning is bone-cutting in its depth and scope, they do not question the Why of Our Lord. They do not ask, 'Why?' for there is no answer forthcoming. They do not ask, 'Why us? Why not someone else's wife and mother?' for there is no answer forthcoming."

"Henry assures me that with only one look at the beauty of their land, you cannot deny God's presence. Having spent a lot of time there in the past weeks, I can fully agree. The Hand of the Lord certainly must have created that beauty, restfulness, and tranquility, that the Greschners carved out of that property."

"Henry tells me that Harriet spent many, many hours trying to comfort families who lost their loved ones. Shortly before she passed, Harriet asked me, 'Please, Pastor, help my family through this trying time. They will need your help. It is my time. I will be out of pain, and I will be at peace, knowing that Henry and Susanna will have you to help comfort them.' Be assured that I intend to keep my promise to her."

"Now, please listen as our wonderful choir sings *'How Great Thou Art'*."

The gymnasium filled with the power of the voices of the choir, which numbered 40 strong, musical voices. You could have heard a pin drop when they finished.

Pastor Luke rose and thanked the choir. He then said, "Now, please, welcome our brother, Henry Greschner. He has chosen to personally give his wife's eulogy and apologizes in advance for any breakdown he may suffer during this most difficult, but loving, gesture on his part." Nodding towards Henry, Pastor Luke took a seat.

Henry rose. Turning towards the pianist, he nodded. She quietly played a soft accompaniment of *'Shall We Gather at the River'* as he cleared his throat and started to speak:

"Harriet would be overwhelmed to see all of you dear people here to help us with her celebration of life. Thank you for coming."

"So many memories! I scarcely know where to begin, but here I go."

"Harriet and I were childhood sweethearts. We married young. I was 20, she was only 18. Neither of us had any living family when we married. We were each other's world."

"We couldn't wait to start a family, but for several years it wasn't meant to be. Four miscarriages later, my beautiful wife gave birth to Susanna. We were so filled with joy. It was so easy to welcome her into our little family circle. For several more years, we hoped we could expand our family, but it was not to be."

"We bought the piece of land where our home now stands and began the hard, but satisfying, work of creating a home in the wilderness. It is not wilderness any more, although we are still at the end of the road. Every log in our home, every stick of furniture, was handmade with love."

89

"Once completed, Susanna was already in school. Deciding, after a full family discussion, that it would be good for Susanna to have siblings, we took in 2 wonderful foster children, Lacey and Lloyd Jordan. We were truly blessed with their presence. The toughest day of our lives was feeling that we were not able to keep them once Harriet became so terribly ill."

Looking over at Lacey and Lloyd, he said directly to them, "Never feel that it was your fault, that you were lacking something that would make Susanna and I want you to stay. It is nothing you did, it was a lack of strength on my part. Although I cannot raise 3 children on my own, always remember how much we love you."

Clearing his throat, Henry continued, "A lot of the trees around our home are natural, that is they were growing on the land when we purchased it. However, Harriet decided we should have more evergreens. Unbeknownst to me, she ordered a dozen blue spruce from the County. She waited until I was off somewhere one day, and started digging holes to plant the trees in. She wanted to surprise me when I got back. After nearly a full day of literally leaping and jumping on the shovel, she managed to dig the holes, soak them with water and plant the little trees, which were only less than a metre tall at the time. Well, what a surprise I had when I returned home."

"Harriet was sitting on the front veranda, hot and exhausted, but beaming from ear to ear. Those little trees, planted with so much love, and tended to thereafter as carefully as one would care for a newborn baby, have grown into real beauties, now standing over 6 metres tall. Today they stand proudly, as beautiful and strong as my beloved wife throughout her lifetime."

Clearing his throat, he stared at Susanna. She gave him a thumbs-up and smiled, enabling him to continue:

"As I said, so many wonderful memories, so little time shared with those we love and admire. No one was more caring, more astute, or as good at coming to the rescue of those in need, than my wife."

He related several more memories, and then ended by saying, "If all of us were half as caring and loving as Harriet was, the world would be a much better place. As a tribute to Harriet, please take the time from your busy lives to tell those closest to you how much you love, care for, and appreciate them. Life is short, tell them daily. Do a good deed for a fellow friend or neighbour, without being asked, and always be willing to listen. In that way, we can begin to become the type of person Harriet Greschner was, and in that way, she will always remain in our hearts, never to be forgotten."

"My beloved, Harriet, I release you to our Lord's loving care. Thank you for the years we had together. I will always love and miss you."

Henry sat down and lowered his head, tears dripping onto his knees.

Susanna then rose, walked to the front, and turned to face the crowd. "My mother asked me to read this to you. It was her favourite:

'Had I not friends, then life would be a barren thing,
A desert where no flowers would spring, a road where tragedy would
sting
At all its bends.
Were there no eyes to smile upon me now and then,
Or firm handclasp of honest women and men,
I think I'd never ask again for suns to rise.
Were there no feet to tread by mine, no hands to soothe the wounds of
strife,
Or tender words to cheer me,
Life would be unsweet.
But I have friends! I count far more than gold or land
Their friendly smile and lifted hand!
Because of them life can be grand – until it ends!'

Silent tears. A soft thank you. Susanna sat down and leaned her head on her father's shoulder, in silent comfort.

Pastor Luke stood up. "Our choir will sing their closing hymn. It is marked in your hymnals if you would care to sing along. The hymn is *'The Old Rugged Cross'*."

"Henry and Susanna have asked that you please stay here in the gymnasium and join them, at the conclusion of this service, for lunch and reminiscing."

At the conclusion of *The Old Rugged Cross*, the choir immediately began the recessional song, *'When I Get to Where I'm Going.'*

Mrs. Bronson spoke to the children. "We can stay for a short time. Eat some lunch. In half an hour, we will have to leave. I promised Mr. B that I would have Lloyd back in time for more chores. In the meantime, speak with your Uncle Henry, and with Susanna. I see several people here that I need to speak with. I will find you when it is time to go."

Lining up at the lunch tables, which seemed to have appeared out of nowhere and magically filled with a ton of food, Lacey suddenly gasped, "Lloyd, it's Mr. George and Mrs. Martha! What do we do?"

"Nothing," said Lloyd. "Just try to avoid them. I doubt they want to talk to us any more than we want to talk with them!" He filled his plate with enough food for 2, and went and sat down next to Susanna. Although Susanna had no appetite, she nonetheless made a gallant effort, pleased that Lloyd had thought of her.

All too soon, Mrs. Bronson appeared. "Time to go," she said.

Lloyd gave Susanna a hug. He then found Uncle Henry and shook his hand. "Great eulogy, Uncle Henry. That was a very heroic thing to do."

Uncle Henry said, "Hardest thing ever, but I just spoke from my heart. Guess Harriet was guiding me from above, because I didn't break down."

"No, sir, you sure did not."

"Where are you living now, Lloyd?" Uncle Henry asked.

"At Bart and Gladys Bourke's farm. Just got there yesterday afternoon, so don't know how it will work out."

"Do your best, Lloyd. Keep in touch through Susanna. Maybe sometime later, we can go to the lake and do some canoeing." He patted Lloyd on the shoulder and then turned to speak with someone else, who was waiting his turn.

In the car on their way back to the farm, Lacey asked, "Mrs. Bronson, is that what all funerals are like? I mean, I feel like everyone there was a friend of the Greschners, that even if they had never met her, they would know her now. Do you know what I mean?"

"I know exactly what you mean, Lacey. Not all funerals are as personal as this one. I can tell you for certain that I have never before attended a funeral where the spouse gave the eulogy! I so admire Henry Greschner, that was not an easy feat, and he pulled it off admirably. And Susanna! What a tribute to her mother. They are extraordinary. So strong, so loving."

"They are one of a kind, that's for sure," said Lloyd. "Too bad there weren't more foster parents like them."

Detecting the underlying bitterness, Evelyn glanced at Lloyd in the rear-view mirror. "Just hang in there, Lloyd, it won't be forever."

"By the way, I spoke to the warden at the Mountain Institution. Your dad has a hearing coming up in 3 months. He is applying to get out early for good behaviour. I will keep you posted on the outcome."

"Any word on our mother?" Lloyd queried.

"Unfortunately, no." Mrs. Bronson's lip quivered as she reported the sad fact.

They reached the Bourke farm. Evelyn stopped at the side of the house. Mrs. Bourke came out and asked Evelyn if she would like to have coffee before she left. Evelyn told her that, unfortunately, she had to get on the road. She had a long drive and wanted to get back before it got too dark.

With a glint in her eye that looked suspiciously like held-back tears, Evelyn Bronson quickly hugged both Lacey and Lloyd, got in her vehicle, and drove quickly away.

"Lloyd!" Mr. B hollered from the pig shed door. "Close and lock the gate, and then come on over and I'll teach ya about feeding pigs."

Lloyd waved an assent. He ran down to the gate and closed and locked it, wondering all the while why the gate needed to be locked.

Back at the pig shed, he asked Mr. B about it.

"See that black and white billy over there? Well, that little troublemaking goat figured out how to open the gate the very first day we got him. Had to make sure there was nothing he could climb on and get out, either over or under the danged fence."

"Well, Mr. B, if he's that much trouble, why do you keep him?"

"Kinda got a soft spot for the little critter. Figure anything as smart as him deserves a good home. 'Sides, he keeps me on my toes. Now, enough dilly-dally for one day. Let's talk pigs."

A couple of months went by. Although Lloyd was a fast learner, and liked animals well enough, he found it very hard to get up at 4 o'clock every single morning, do his chores (which were many!), sit through school all day, come home to more chores (both before and after supper), and still find both the time and energy to keep up with his schoolwork.

When he tried to talk to Mr. B about it, the matter was just waved off. Mr. B told him he was young and smart, and he should dang well be able to keep up!

When Lloyd tried to talk to Mrs. Bourke about it, while Mr. B was upstairs having a shower, she got a worried look on her face. "Did you ask Mr. B about it?"

Lloyd responded glumly that he had, indeed, tried to talk to him about it, but didn't get anywhere. "I thought maybe you could talk to him, Mrs. Bourke. He's your husband and you know how to approach him about things, I imagine?"

"Oh, my goodness! My dear you must learn that what Mr. B says, goes. He is the owner and the boss of the farm and all its inhabitants. That includes me. Now, so long as you do your chores without any complaint, and you learn what he teaches you, you'll have no problem with Mr. B. If you can't manage your schoolwork and the farm chores at the same time, well, you're 15 now and legally, you can quit school if you want to. Maybe that's the answer. You can always go back to school when you are older."

Lloyd literally stared at Mrs. Bourke with his mouth hanging open. "Are you serious! Quit school? Not on your life. I am not quitting school. Nothing good ever happened to our mother by not furthering her education, and I don't intend to follow in her shoes. Forget it, Mrs. Bourke, just forget I ever tried to talk to you."

Lloyd went to his closet and pulled out his homework. He was tired, so very tired. Tired of trying to balance chores and school, tired of wondering how his dad was doing, and what his dad was going to do, if, and when, he was granted parole, tired of wondering what his mother was thinking when she disappeared, tired of wondering where the hell she was, tired of having to be the wise, older brother. Lloyd was tired, just so damn tired.

Later, when Lacey peeked in on her brother to say goodnight, he was laying on his bed, fully clothed, his math textbook in his hand. She covered him up, took his book away, turned out the light, and let him sleep.

Other than helping Mrs. Bourke set the table and doing the dishes, there was not much for Lacey to do. Mrs. Bourke was a very organized woman. She needed little help.

Bored, Lacey wandered over to the barn and approached Mr. B. "Mr. B, could you teach me to do chores? That way I can help my brother. We will get things done twice as fast and Lloyd will have more time for his schoolwork. I love the animals. I might be small, but I'm strong. Please, could you teach me too?"

She stood there quietly until Mr. B's unspoken scrutiny made her nervous. "Well, Mr. B, what do you think? I'm ready to learn, just say the word."

"This is men's work, little lady. Your job is to help Gladys, with the housework and the flower gardens. You're busy enough, I reckon."

"But, but…" she stammered, "there shouldn't be men's work and women's work. We should all work together and get things done. That's what my Mama always said. Couldn't we please just try letting me help with the chores? If I don't work out, at least you let me try!"

"Not another word, young lady. Now, you just march your pretty little self back to the house and see what Gladys has for you to do. Come on Lloyd, give me a hand here." He turned his back to Lacey, ignoring her completely.

She stomped on back to the house, sputtering all the way. Mrs. Bourke asked her what was wrong. When Lacey told her, Mrs. Bourke said quietly, "Mr. B is right, you know. He's always right." Lacey thought she detected a tone of despair and bitterness in Mrs. Bourke's tone, but she ignored it.

"Well, can't you at least give me something to do? How about teaching me how to cook something other than toast? How about teaching me how to sew? I'm going crazy, here, Mrs. Bourke, just plain nuts!"

"And, by the way," she flung over her shoulder, "that tire swing never got hung in the elm tree neither!" She flounced out of the kitchen, slamming the back door on her way outside.

The old elm tree, aside from having a perfect branch from which to hang a tire swing, was an easy climb. The leaves formed a protective screen around Lacey as she climbed. Leaning against the trunk about halfway up the giant tree, she could observe most of the farmyard and she could certainly see if anyone came in to the yard. Of course, that was rare. The few times that someone did stop by for a visit, Mr. B was always too busy to stop. If Mrs. Bourke tried to invite them to stay for coffee, a black glare from her husband made the visitors uncomfortable and they left without a visit.

Spring became early summer, early summer became late summer, late summer turned to early autumn. The leaves on the elm tree and the other trees and shrubs around the farm reflected brilliant autumnal colours. What a shame that nature's beauty didn't receive the rapt attention that only Lacey had the time, or the inclination, to bestow.

Both Lacey's 12th birthday and Lloyd's 16th birthday had come and gone, remembered only by the siblings. A brief mention to Mrs. Bourke had yielded only the comment, "Mr. B thinks birthday celebrations are a foolish waste of time when he could be working outside."

Evelyn Bronson had called the farm to let Lloyd and Lacey know that their father's probation application had been denied. Mrs. Bourke asked her husband, "When would be a good time to tell the children? His reply was, "When they ask." Lloyd had been in the back entry at the time and overheard their conversation. He didn't need to, so he didn't bother to give Mr. B the satisfaction of asking.

At school, Lloyd's marks dropped dramatically because he had so little time to concentrate on schoolwork.

Lacey's dropped because she was bored. Her attention span was short and although her memory was excellent, she lost interest when things were too easy. She caused a fair amount of disruption in her classroom. Had her teacher thought about the reasoning behind Lacey's disruptive behaviour, she might have bumped her up a grade, which would no doubt have solved the problem to a certain extent.

Christmas came. No tree, no decorations. Mr. B said the true meaning of Christmas could be celebrated without any trimmings. Christmas dinner was a roast chicken, because Mr. B said roasting a huge turkey would just be a waste with only 4 people to eat it.

Both Lloyd and Lacey had to turn down parts in the Christmas play because Mr. B would not 'waste the money on gas attending a frivolous Christmas pageant.' Rehearsals were held right after school, but the kids had to get home on the bus right after school so Lloyd could do his chores. There was no possible way that Mrs. Bourke could pick them up, Mr. B absolutely forbade her leaving the farm without him.

The farm was pretty much self-sustaining. Mr. B butchered his own beef, pork, or chicken when the freezer was low on meat. An excellent shot, he hunted in the fall for moose, elk, and deer. If he spied game he aimed, he shot, he killed. No waste of ammunition.

The few staples they couldn't produce on their own were stored in a cold room. When the staples became low, Mr. B would drive his wife to the general store in the nearby village, wait for her in the truck while she shopped, and then drive back to the farm. Very occasionally, they would have lunch in the quaint little restaurant located at the back of the store. Rarely were they gone from home more than a couple of hours.

He made the children stay home. They were supposed to use this precious time alone to catch up on schoolwork. They did, but often studied high in the comfort of the enfolding branches of the old elm tree. Much of their time in the tree was spent discussing their father, their missing mother, their missing foster sisters, Charley and Amelia. Charley would now be 16, Amelia would be 17 by now. No one at school knew where they were, in fact, most of the students barely remembered the missing girls. Lloyd and Lacey remembered them though, and thought about them nearly every single day.

These trips to the village happened about every 3 months. Other than these quick trips to the store, the Bourkes never left the farm. Other than school, the children never left the farm.

The more exhausted Lloyd became, the grumpier he got. One day, when Mr. B was particularly demanding, Lloyd shouted at him, throwing down his shovel. It barely missed hitting Mr. B. Lloyd was so fed up he didn't even apologize for almost hitting the man. In fact, he almost wished he hadn't missed. There was a side of himself emerging that Lloyd did not like, but he couldn't seem to help himself.

Lacey dearly missed the company of girls her own age. Most of her friends from school were having sleepovers on the weekends, pyjama parties where they listened to records, danced, giggled, tried on makeup, watched movies on television. Lacey was invited to every sleepover, but she had to decline each and every time. After a while, they quit inviting her. Lacey spent a lot of time crying into her pillow at night.

After nearly 2 years on the Bourke place, Mr. B and Mrs. Bourke called the children into the house for a meeting.

Mrs. Bourke's eyes were bloodshot, watery. She had been crying. Lloyd and Lacey couldn't figure out what was wrong. Why this meeting?

Mr. B cleared his throat, began to speak. "I got a call from a feller, an old classmate of mine from the area where I grew up. His wife just passed and he is looking for a change. He's a farmer, just like me. I hired him."

Lloyd's eyes lit up. "Wow! That will sure help us with the chore load won't it Mr. B! That is really good news."

Lacey said nothing. She figured there was more to this than that simple announcement. She was right.

"Well, see," Mr. B said, "It's not so easy as that. We took you 2 kids on as our first foster kids. We didn't know nothing about rearin' children. It was an experiment. Figured with the money Social Services would pay us for you, and the work I could get out of you, we would come out ahead of things. Turns out, we haven't. Come out ahead, that is."

"The government don't pay enough to feed 2 growing children, let alone clothe 'em. And Lloyd, even though you worked hard, the farmer will be more help to me than a kid."

"Also, the only place for the new guy to stay is in Lacey's room. Don't have a cabin or a trailer on the place for him to live. So, guess what I am trying to tell you is, we let Social Services know that we don't want to keep foster kids any more. A social worker will be coming to get you tomorrow, right after school. Already have another foster family to keep you. Just like when you come here, you won't have to go to a different school. These new foster people live just down from the Schmidt's place, first house past their place."

Lloyd thought he was going to throw up, right on the kitchen table. *Dear God,* he thought, *of all the places not to be, anywhere near the Schmidt's place was top of the list. What next!*

Lacey clutched her stomach. She had to bend over, the pain was so bad.

"Cut the phony drama," Mr. B said. He pushed himself away from the table. "Come on, Lloyd, might as well get some more work out of you while you're still here."

"Screw you," Lloyd muttered under his breath.

"WHAT did you say!!!" Mr. B shouted. Mrs. Bourke cowered in her chair.

He grabbed Lloyd by the ear and shoved him out the door.

"Get to that barn and get busy, or I'll take a whip to you, boy." Lacey and Mrs. Bourke could hear him yelling at Lloyd all the way to the barn.

By this time, Mrs. Bourke was crying pitifully. Lacey just gave her a withering glance. She had no respect for the woman. None whatsoever.

Lacey went up to her room and began to pack her things. Once she finished there, she went into Lloyd's closet and packed up his things for him. Knowing Mr. B, Lloyd would have no time for packing. Between evening chores and morning milking, Mr. B would get every last scrap of help out of Lloyd that he could.

Once finished, Lacey went outside. Walking over to the barn, she stuck her ear to the closed barn door. At least Mr. B had quit shouting. She then ran to her beloved elm tree, climbed high into its branches. Only then did she break down.

Near dark, she heard Mrs. Bourke calling her. She ignored it.

A few minutes later, Lacey was startled to see the face of Mrs. Bourke. She was sitting on a large branch just below Lacey.

"You know, Lacey," said Mrs. Bourke, "this is my favourite spot on the farm. I often climb this tree when I need to think about things, just like I know you do too."

"Mr. B don't mean nothin' by what he said at the table. He never had no brothers and sisters, never had no children of his own. He does the best he knows how. He learned hard work growing up, he works hard now. Doesn't know any different."

"I also know you think I'm hard done by, living out here on the farm, rarely leaving the place. Fact is, Mr. B is very good to me. I love the farm. I don't miss not going here and there and everywhere. I know it's tough on you young people, but you see, I've been a lot of places in my earlier life. I don't feel the need to travel anymore. I can tell you one thing for sure, though, Miss Lacey. I'm going to miss both you and your brother somethin' awful."

"Now, want to come in and have some hot chocolate before bedtime? We'll make enough for Lloyd and Mr. B too." She climbed down and waited on the ground for Lacey to climb down.

Mrs. Bourke put her arm around the dejected young girl, and they walked back to the house.

Chapter 7
Peter and Elsie Petrie

As Lloyd and Lacey alighted from their bus the following afternoon, a familiar jeep drove into the driveway.

"Hey, you 2! I've come to take you to your new place. Sure is great to see you again!"

Jayson Silverman shook Lloyd's hand, and gave Lacey a brief hug.

Lloyd started to speak, Mr. Silverman shushed him. "We can talk in the jeep on the way," he said. "For now, let's just get your stuff and say goodbye."

Mr. B and Mrs. Bourke helped bring the children's belongings out to the jeep. Lacey went over to Mrs. Bourke and gave her a small hug. "Thanks," Lacey said simply.

She then turned to Mr. B. She didn't feel that he had done anything for her in the past 2 years. She simply looked at him and said goodbye before climbing into the back seat of Mr. Silverman's jeep.

Lloyd looked at Mrs. Bourke. "Thank you," he said. He then walked over to Mr. B and held out his hand. Mr. B cleared his throat awkwardly and shook it. "Thanks, Lloyd, you were far more of a help than I ever imagined a young kid could be. Sorry we ended yesterday on such a sour note. Good luck at your new place."

With not another word, Lloyd got into the front passenger's seat of the jeep. He didn't look at the couple as Mr. Silverman backed out of the drive and turned to drive away in the same direction that he had come from.

"Where's Mrs. Bronson?" Lacey asked.

"She's on vacation. She hasn't had a vacation for well over 2 years and she needed a break. She works much too hard. It was long overdue."

"Oh," Lacey said. She settled back in her seat and watched the passing scenery.

Jayson glanced over at Lloyd. "Wanna talk about it, Lloyd?" he asked.

With a gesture that was becoming very familiar to Lacey, Lloyd bitterly shrugged his shoulders, his jaw clenched so tightly it hurt. He took a deep, calming breath, then simply said, "We didn't mean anything to those people. We were just a pair of work horses. We are far more worried about going to this new foster home, though, because it is so close to the Schmidt place. We know that Mr. George and Mrs. Martha still have foster kids there. I can't believe that the Social Services people would allow that, after what happened when we were there."

Mr. Silverman said quickly, "I passed on the information you gave me, but because this is Alberta, and I work out of British Columbia, they won't tell me what they did with it. I suggest that you stay as far away from that place as you can. If you run into any problems, well, I am hoping you still have my card?" He looked inquiringly at Lloyd.

"Yes, sir, I do," Lloyd said resignedly.

Changing the subject, Lloyd said, "Our father should be out of prison now. We heard that his parole application was denied 2 years ago, however, he has served 2/3 of his sentence and so?" Here he stopped and looked over at Jayson Silverman, waiting for his response.

Jayson took a deep breath. "Yes, Lloyd, he is out of prison. He got out 3 months ago, however, no one knows where he went. His probation officer asked me to speak with you and your sister, to see if you had heard anything from him. I told the PO that you would know nothing, because your father has never contacted either me or Mrs. Bronson to find out where you were. Am I right? You haven't heard from him?"

For an entire minute, Lloyd was mute. A brilliant red haze clouded his vision as a debilitating rage swept through him. His fists were clenched so tightly that his nails dug into the palms of each hand. His chest burned, his breath hitched painfully. He heard Lacey crying in the back seat, but for the life of him, he was unable to speak. He remained motionless in his seat, waiting for the rage to pass. He finally noticed that Jayson Silverman had pulled the jeep to the side of the road. Stopped. He got out and came around to Lloyd's side, opened the door, pulled Lloyd from the vehicle, and clumsily put his arms around him. He held on to him until he felt it was safe to let him go.

"Lloyd, Lacey, I know you haven't heard from him, but it's my job to ask."

Lacey flew at Jayson, pounded him with her fists, spitting words at him. "You said our father got out of prison 3 months ago! Why are you just telling us now? We might be just kids to you but we had to grow up fast – darn you anyway, Jayson Silverman! No," she corrected herself, "DAMN you!"

Lloyd, now slightly more under control, said quietly, "Mr. Silverman, surely you know that if we had been told sooner, or if you had told our dad where we were before he got out, we would probably be able to tell you where he is, right? In fact, he might not even have taken off. If he knew where we were, he would have come and taken us home."

What could Jayson say to that logic?

He knew Lloyd was right. He had no excuse. Both he and Evelyn Bronson had become caught up in their British Columbian jobs, and that vital piece of info had slipped through the cracks. As sorry as he was for the oversight, he knew that neither Lloyd nor Lacey were in any frame of mind to accept his apology.

He drove on, passing the Schmidt house and stopping at the next house up the road. Although it was probably a half a kilometre from the Schmidt's, it was still within sight. Not ideal, but the Bourkes needed their space. The Petries were willing to take the kids immediately.

At first glance, the Petrie home was nothing like the Schmidt's. This place, although old, was as shiny and well-groomed as a Granny dressed up for church. Nothing needed paint or fixing. The lawn was mowed and neatly trimmed, the veranda swept clean, the furniture neatly arranged. The flower beds were well tended. Bright, multi-coloured flowers nodded cheerily at the visitors as they walked past.

A goodly amount of children's play equipment was set up to the right of the home. It was also well cared for. There was even a deck box for children's outdoor games equipment, sitting next to a bicycle rack, so, rather than the careless handling of children's toys and bikes, the people in this house obviously cared enough to teach the children to look after their possessions.

On closer inspection, though, Lacey remarked that the Petrie home was the same design as the Schmidt's. She fervently hoped that the inside was different. It was.

Mrs. Petrie answered the doorbell, holding a sleepy newborn in her arms. Her voice jiggled a little as she rocked the baby. "Come in, please come in and have a seat. I'll be with you as soon as I put the baby in her crib. Make yourself at home."

Both Lacey and Lloyd looked around with interest. There was nothing inside this house to remind them of the Schmidt place. It had obviously been renovated completely. The entire main floor was all one big room, except for a bathroom near the back mudroom. At the far end of the main room was the kitchen.

A large, rectangular dining table served as a divider between the kitchen and family room. A teenage boy and a teenage girl were seated at the table, playing a game of cards.

A shelving unit was built along an entire wall. In the centre of the unit was a large TV set. On each side of the television, a huge variety of books filled the shelves. Both were avid readers, and Lloyd and Lacey eagerly scanned the contents on each shelf. There was everything from beginner readers all the way up to an exquisite, real leather-bound volume of *War and Peace*.

Jayson Silverman sat down on a comfortable sofa. He appeared to be enjoying their enthusiasm. It was a certainly a change from the dressing down he received from them when he had to pass on the news about their father.

In a few minutes, Elsie Petrie reappeared. "Sorry about that," she said. She sat down in an upholstered rocking chair and waited patiently for Lloyd and Lacey to notice her. Finally, she cleared her throat.

"Oh!" said Lacey. "I'm sorry, I didn't hear you come in. Your book collection is like a library, you have so many books. It's wonderful."

Mrs. Petrie smiled and nodded. "You are most welcome to read any of the books on the shelves, once your chores and homework are done. We only ask that you respect them, no bending of pages or cracking the spines."

"Oh! I would never!" Lacey responded. "Thank you! I can't wait to dive in."

"You will also note that the books are placed in categories, alphabetical within each category. When you remove a book, we expect you to return it exactly as you found it, in the same place that you found it. More about that later, for now, some introductions."

Mrs. Petrie turned towards 2 toddlers, obviously twins, who appeared from upstairs, the little boy holding a blanket, the little girl holding a baby doll. They sat down on the floor by Elsie Petrie's feet, sucking their thumbs.

She said, "These little ones are twins. They are Peter and Paula. How old are you, children?"

Peter hid his face in his blanket. Paula smiled shyly and held up 3 fingers.

"That's right, Paula, very good! You are 3 years old."

Glancing over at the table, she motioned for the 2 teenagers to come over and be introduced.

"So," she said, "say hello to Annie. She's 16 years old. And say hello to Lester. Lester is 15. We also have a newborn baby girl, who doesn't have a name yet. I expect she will be gone within a week. Her adoptive parents will give her a name."

"Now, you are?" She stared at the new kids, once again waiting. She kind of reminded Lloyd of a cat staring at a mouse, just waiting for the mouse to make a mistake and then it would pounce.

"I'm Lloyd. I just turned 17," he said.

"I'm Lacey and I'm 13," she said.

"Well," Mrs. Petrie said, "I'm Elsie Petrie. You can call me Mrs. Petrie. My husband, Peter, will be home from work soon. You can call him Mr. Petrie.

"Annie, please take Lacey upstairs and show her your shared bedroom.

"Lloyd, Lester will show you your room. You will have to share a bedroom, and the 4 of you will have to share the bathroom. We expect that to be a peaceful process, and we also expect that you keep it as clean as you find it. Now, off you go, I need to discuss some things with Mr. Silverman."

Upstairs, Lacey surveyed her new bedroom. As immaculate as the rest of the place, there were 2 twin beds against a long wall, separated by a tall chest of drawers. A large clothes closet was split in half, each half a mirror image of the other, obviously meant to be equally shared. Beside each bed was a good-sized night table that would double as a small desk. Down comforters adorned each bed. Very pretty pastel colours. Matching curtains brightened the room. Each bed held an array of toss cushions. Immediately outside the window was a very large old American elm tree, its branches close enough to the bedroom window that Lacey was pretty sure she could climb from the window into the tree. It would be a great refuge.

Annie noticed her scrutiny. "It's easy," she volunteered shyly. "I can get all the way to the ground. Mr. and Mrs. Petrie's bedroom window faces the other side of the house. They haven't caught on."

"They seem, well, Mrs. Petrie at least, seems pretty nice," Lacey said.

Annie gave a wry smile. "You'll find out," she said. "All is not as it seems in this foster home! What I can warn you about is this: make sure you keep everything as you find it, as neat, as tidy, as clean. God help us all if something is not as it was, or as it should be."

"What do you mean?" asked Lacey.

"You'll find out," Annie repeated. "Believe me, we'll all find out."

Leaving the bedroom to go back downstairs, Lacey bumped into Lloyd, literally. "Whoops! Watch it there, sis!" Lloyd grabbed her before she could tumble down the stairs. "What's the hurry?"

"No hurry," Lacey said. "I just need to watch where I'm going."

As soon as Lacey and Lloyd got back downstairs, Mr. Silverman stood up, saying he had to get going, he had a long drive home. Lacey and Lloyd followed him out to his car. Mrs. Petrie hovered just outside the front door, too far away to hear clearly as the children said goodbye to the social worker.

"Well, kids," Jayson Silverman said, "we are running out of foster homes for you, so, take it easy on these guys, huh?" A glare from both Lloyd and Lacey had him quickly adding, "Just kidding for Pete's sake. Just kidding!"

With a quick wave, he hopped in the jeep and took off, gravel spinning slightly as he stepped on the gas.

Turning to go back to the house, they spied Mrs. Petrie puttering on the veranda, pretending she hadn't been trying to eavesdrop.

The pair stood in front of her, waiting for instructions of some kind.

As if possessed, Mrs. Petrie's face turned dark. Her eyes sparked dangerously. Her entire demeanour portrayed someone entirely different from the sweet and friendly woman who had greeted them earlier.

"Sit down!" she suddenly barked. "I'll let you know the rules around here."

Before she could lay down the rules, her face undertook an amazing transformation. Glancing behind them, they noticed a black truck driving up the road. It turned in as the garage door automatically opened. Getting out of the car, an immaculately dressed, tall, slim man walked towards them.

Mrs. Petrie simpered, "Hello darling, how was your day? Come and meet our newest wards. This is Lloyd. He's 17, so he won't be with us for long. This little blondie is Lacey. She's only 13. Aren't they just the sweetest children we've had yet? So good looking."

Lloyd got the impression that Mr. Petrie wanted to roll his eyes but didn't dare. He tentatively held out his hand, wasn't sure whether or not to shake Lloyd's so he let it drop back to his side. "Hello Lloyd, nice to meet you. Welcome to our home." He repeated his greeting to Lacey, then went into the house to change before supper. Lloyd and Lacey made a move to follow him into the house.

"I said, **SIT DOWN!**" Mrs. Petrie hissed. "I'm not done with you yet. Now quickly, before Mr. Petrie comes out, here is my rule. My one and only rule is: **WHAT I SAY, GOES**. I expect you to jump up and say how high when I give you a chore, without any whining or questions. This house and this yard don't look the way they do by accident. They look that way because the foster children in this house keep it this way. If I find something not done, or not done **EXACTLY** as I show you, there will be consequences. I expect nothing less from any foster kids than perfection. If you expect to catch the school bus every day, you will have to hustle before going to school, to make sure everything is in order. If it is not, you will not be going to school that day. You will be scrubbing the floors on your hands and knees. Not only that, the rest of the kids in this house will pay for your slovenly workmanship as well as you will. Got it?"

Startled, Lloyd tried to recall whether or not he had ever heard anyone speak in such bold, underlined tones before. Terrified, Lacey simply nodded at her foster parent. Lloyd stared Mrs. Petrie down. Clearly frustrated and unwilling, she blinked first.

Hearing Mr. Petrie coming towards the front of the house, Mrs. Petrie whispered, "Ssh! Not a word to Mr. Petrie or you will find out how difficult it can be in this house. If it gets difficult, it is your own fault. Now, shut up and behave."

Again, a transformation took place as Mrs. Petrie turned towards the doorway. "Now, darling, come and sit on the porch and tell me about your day. Lloyd, here, will get you a nice cold beer from the refrigerator."

She turned to Lloyd, "Well, Lloyd, please grab a couple of beers from the fridge and bring them out here. Then, you 2, go get unpacked while Mr. Petrie and I catch up on our day. Thank you, sweetie, there's a good boy."

Behind her back, Lloyd made a gagging gesture. It was irreverent and rude, but funny. Lacey didn't feel like laughing.

Squeezing past Mrs. Petrie, the Jekyll and Hyde personality surreptitiously and viciously pinched Lacey's arm as she went by.

"OUCH!" Lacey yelped.

"What's wrong Lacey?" Mr. Petrie asked.

Mrs. Petrie, who was standing behind Lacey, out of sight of her husband, pinched her again, harder this time. Cluing in, Lacey said quietly, "Nothing, Mr. Petrie, something just bit me, probably a mosquito. Sorry I yelled." Quickly she opened the front door and went inside.

Once she was finished unpacking, she sat down on her bed. She bent over, clutching her stomach. *Great,* she thought, *not even here a day and the old stomach pains are back.*

A couple of minutes later, the bedroom door opened. Annie came in. She sat down on her own bed and looked intently at her new roommate for a minute. "Well, Lacey," she said quietly, "do you have a bit of an idea of what goes on in this place already? The woman is totally psycho. She has 2 personalities, one for Mr. Petrie and any visitors, and one for us kids."

Lacey said bitterly, "Seems as if Lloyd and I are doomed to living in the worst foster families in the entire system!" She then gave Annie a short but descriptive version of the various foster homes she and Lloyd had lived in.

Changing the subject slightly, she asked, "What about Mr. Petrie? He seems nice."

"He is nice, when Mrs. Petrie is not around, which is very seldom, by the way. When she's here, he pretty much ignores us. I think he's afraid of her too. Don't know how he could miss seeing her split personality, even though she tries to hide it when he's home. Just a heads up: if you are given a chore, you better do it as well as she expects, otherwise, we all suffer. She's an evil, menopausal old bitch, and I'm getting out of here as soon as I can."

"Oh!" was all Lacey could think of to say.

Glancing at the clock on the wall, Annie jumped up. "Come on, help me set the table. The old biddy will nearly be finished their cocktail hour by now. If the table's not set by the time she comes back into the house, we're in for it, tomorrow, after Mr. Petrie leaves for work."

As they set the table, Annie continued informing Lacey about their foster mother's expectations. "Mrs. Petrie has no tolerance for anything sloppy, dirty, dusty, or out of place," Annie informed her. "In actual fact, she has no tolerance for anything. She will even measure with her thumbs to make sure the cutlery is all the same distance from the edge of the table and the edge of the plates. Once, one place setting was a little out of whack. She took every single dish and put them all away in the cupboards. Mr. Petrie wasn't home, he was away on business. None of us got any supper that night."

"Not even the little ones?"

"Nope! She made us all stand in the kitchen and watch her eat until she was done, then we had to clean up her dishes. The twins cried most of the night because they were hungry. Mrs. Petrie said it was our fault, that if we hadn't been so careless and slovenly, everyone would have eaten. She made Lester and me stay in the twins' room and keep them quiet so that she could get her sleep!"

"I don't think Lloyd will put up with that stuff. He's pretty protective of me, and will be protective of the rest of you guys too. He's 17, and bigger than her. I don't think she can do anything to hurt him."

Annie laughed, but it was not a happy laugh. She sounded desperate and infinitely sad. "Don't bank on it, Lacey. She might not hurt Lloyd, but she'll make the rest of us pay if he doesn't toe the line. I'm thinking you should fill him in as soon as you can. Otherwise, we'll all suffer."

At the supper table, it was heartbreaking to watch the twins. They sat like little wooden soldiers, very much afraid of spilling something. What should have been a chance for everyone to talk about their day was never to be. There was no talking at the table. Even though Mr. Petrie tried to instigate a discussion, a swift and painful kick from Mrs. Petrie under the table to the shin of whoever was handy, halted any ideas of contributing to the conversation. Finally, Mr. Petrie gave up. He finished his meal and then retired to the front veranda with his newspaper.

Once he was out of sight and hearing, Mrs. Petrie began again, "All right, everyone. Get busy! Lloyd and Lacey, do the dishes, mop the kitchen floor, and then into the living room with you. Dust everything in that room, including the books. You can use a Swiffer duster today, because it is a weekday. On weekends, you need to use a damp cloth and clean things properly. Once you have finished, let me know. I will inspect your work. If all is in order, you can retire to your bedrooms, finish your homework, or study if you don't have any homework. Then get ready for bed. Remember, though, if you don't do your chores properly, you won't be going to school tomorrow, you'll be home doing what you should have done correctly today."

Mrs. Petrie then turned to Annie and the little ones. "Flower bed detail for the 3 of you. Off you go, little ones, and help Annie."

"Lester, you are on vehicle cleaning duty. Dust Mr. Petrie's truck, inside and out. Clean the windows on the truck, inside and out, and then mow the lawn."

"Lloyd, you will do the same to my car. Once you're done that, vacuum the garage floor and window sills to get rid of the dust from the vehicles. Then, up you go to your rooms. We expect excellent marks from our wards. If you don't get them, there will be consequences for not only yourself, but for the rest of the children in this household."

She went outside to join her husband on the veranda, leaving the kids to their respective chores.

It was 2 hours later that all the children finally completed their assignments. Annie went to the front door and let Mrs. Petrie know that everything was finished.

The woman actually came into the house and donned a pair of white gloves! Marching purposefully around the house, she passed her gloved hand over every piece of furniture and window ledge she passed by. She found nothing untoward. Lacey let out the breath she had been subconsciously holding during the inspection.

Mrs. Petrie said, "Not bad for the 1st time. I expect you'll improve daily, as you learn what's expected of you when you do your chores.

"Now, goodnight everyone. The school bus comes early, so, off to your rooms."

Lying in bed, Lacey waited a few minutes. She then asked Annie what happened to all the kids when someone didn't do what was expected.

In a most bitter tone, Annie replied, "All sorts of terrible, ridiculous things. However, the worst thing is the fridge."

"The fridge?" Lacey queried. She waited for Annie's explanation.

"Yeah," she said. "It's in the garage, at the very back right-hand corner. It's painted black so if someone peeks in the window they don't even notice it. It has a very heavy chain wrapped around it. When someone gets in trouble by disrespecting Mrs. Petrie, they are dragged out to the garage and put in that fridge. The longest I remember anyone in there was 2 entire days and nights. Of course, Mr. Petrie was away on business. She wouldn't dare do that if he was home."

Horrified, Lacey asked, "How can anyone breathe in there?"

"Oh, there's some air comes in, because once the kid is put in there, Mrs. Petrie puts the lock on the door, but keeps a large stick to place in the door. It prevents the door from shutting completely, but doesn't leave enough space so you can wiggle out, no matter how little you are. The end that is inside the fridge is sharpened to a very fine point. If you try and move, it really hurts!

"It's hell," Annie continued. "I was put in there once. I can tell you, I never sassed anyone in this house again!

"Here's a tip. If you get put in there, try and control your breathing, to save as much oxygen as you can. If you panic, it gets really hard to breathe."

"Dear God!" Lacey breathed. "What else does she do? Nothing could be worse than that!"

"She has a wooden paddle. It's smooth on one side and bumpy on the other. Depending on what you did, you get hit with one side of the paddle or the other. If she decides you have done something wrong, she has you bend over the footstool in the living room. She never hits anyone where a bruise might show. She usually sticks to walloping your butt. As much as it hurts, the humiliation is worse, because she makes you take down your pants so she can hit you on the bare bum. Worse yet, all the rest of the kids are made to stand and watch. If anyone looks away, she adds 5 more hits. Again, this never happens when Mr. Petrie is around."

"Why doesn't someone tell him?" Lacey asked.

Annie laughed, a twisted, strangled sound that made Lacey's skin crawl. "I tried once," she said. "He didn't believe me! The next day he left before the school bus came. The old she-bitch kept every one of us home from school. She made us scrub the floors in every room on our hands and knees. When we finished, she inspected them, threw the trash on the kitchen floor, mud on the other floors, and made us do all the floors over again. The only reason we got to stop and she didn't make us wash them again, was that it got close to when Mr. Petrie should be coming home from work. You saw how her demeanour changes when Mr. Petrie is around."

"There must be something that we can do!" Lacey pleaded. "There's got to be."

"Who's gonna believe a foster kid? To foster parents, all we are is money. You can almost see the dollar signs in her eyes every time she looks at you."

"Well," Lacey commented, "the food is good here, and there is as much of it as we want. When Lloyd and I were fostered at the Savard's place... " She then told Annie about how hungry they were, and how they watched Mr. and Mrs. Savard eat like a king and queen, while the children were nearly starving.

Annie told her, "Yeah, well, it was kind of like that here too, but one of the teachers at the school finally noticed that all the Petrie fosters were getting skinnier and skinnier, appeared weak, and were unable to concentrate on their school work. One of the kids even stole somebody's lunch. He got caught. The teacher coaxed him to talk. That teacher then called Social Services. An investigation happened. We did get good food since then."

"Why didn't that kid tell the teacher about the punishments?"

"Because Mrs. Petrie threatened to cut off the hand of the 1st kid who squealed."

"Oh, God!" Lacey moaned, "Would she really do that?"

"I don't know, Lacey. However, do you want to chance it? Sometimes, instead of punishing the offender, she will punish the youngest child. Believe me, that is worse than taking the beating yourself. As far as I can see, the only escape is to run away. I've been delaying it because I've grown very fond of the twins. I know she will take it out on them once I'm gone, but I'm at the end of my rope. I have to get out of here."

After a minute, Lacey told her about Charley and Amelia running away.

"Did they catch them and take them back?" Annie asked.

"No," Lacey said. "The police put up a few posters, the television news put their pictures on the TV a couple of times. Then, nothing. Neither the police nor Social Services seemed to worry a whole lot about a missing foster kid, especially at ages 14 and 16. Guess they figured the runaways would either sink or swim. I really liked both of those girls, and I miss them. I just pray every day that they are OK. Now, if you run away too, I will really feel alone."

Annie asked, "Have you heard anything from either of them?"

"Nope," Lacey said. "Not a thing."

"Any idea where they went? They never gave you a hint before they ran? How did they get away from here? Did they have bus money, 'cause that's the only transportation out of this small place, other than hitchhiking."

"**NO**, to your 1st question, and **NO** to your 2nd question." Lacey then told Annie about watching the girls run away, and about them hitching a ride.

Annie watched Lacey's eyes widen as something niggled in her brain.

"What?" Annie asked.

"I think the girls were picked up by the same truck driver!" Lacey said. "They ran away from different foster homes, and at different times, so I didn't make the connection until now, but the truck that picked them up was unusual. It reminded me of a pumpkin. It was orange, with black and green lettering on the side. I was too far away to read the logo. I was just so happy they got a ride so quickly, that I didn't think anything of the truck at the time."

Lacey turned on her lamp and sat straight up in her bed. "Promise me something, Annie, please. Promise me that you will tell me when you are ready to run away. I'll come outside and wait with you, but I'll be behind you in the ditch, hidden by the side of the highway. When you get picked up, I'll write down a description of the vehicle that picks you up, and also the licence plate number. That way, if I don't hear further from you, I will have something to take to the police."

Annie said nothing for several minutes. Lacey thought she must have fallen asleep, and she turned out her light.

Suddenly, Annie's voice emerged from the darkness. "Don't worry about me, Lacey," she said. "I know what I'm doing. I'm 16 years old, almost an adult."

She continued, "I can't promise you that I'll let you know when I'm going, because if you don't know anything, Mrs. Petrie can't punish you for what you don't know. I will promise you, though, that I will be very careful when I am hitching a ride. If I don't like the looks of the driver, I won't get in. I also promise you that I will somehow get word to you about where I am, what I'm doing, and that I'm OK. In fact, Susanna Greschner is my best friend. She knows I will be leaving here. She gave me her mailing address. I will send word to Susanna, and she can show you my letter when you're at school. I can't send word to you here because Mrs. Petrie reads everyone's mail. She decides if and when you get any mail addressed to you."

"Well, I don't have to worry about that, because I don't know anyone who would send me mail."

Lacey figured that plan would have to do. She rolled over and tried to sleep, vowing to keep a very sharp eye on Annie for the next few days. Either Annie would tell her that she was running, or as soon as Annie looked like she was ready to run, Lacey would follow her and get the plate number from any vehicle that picked Annie up on the highway. Assuring herself that her plan would work, Lacey fell asleep.

The next morning, after breakfast, Lloyd, Lester, Annie, and Lacey, went outside to wait for the school bus.

Wanting to let Lloyd in on the plan, Lacey started to speak but was stopped by Annie's glare.

"Look behind you, Lacey," Annie hissed at her. Glancing over her shoulder, she saw Mrs. Petrie standing at the mailbox, an easy listening distance from where the students waited for the bus.

"Oh!" Lacey covered her mouth, horrified with herself. She could have given away Annie's escape plan. "Sorry!" she whispered to Annie. "I'm so sorry!"

"Just be careful," Annie whispered back. "You'll get used to Mrs. Petrie's snooping soon enough. A trip to either the fridge or the footstool and you'll never forget again."

The garage door opened. All 4 of the kids turned and waved goodbye to Mr. Petrie as he left for work.

When the school bus arrived, Lloyd, Lester, and Annie, climbed into the bus. Just as Lacey got her foot on the bottom step, Mrs. Petrie called to her. "Lacey! You aren't going to school today. I need help with the twins and the newborn. Get back here. Tell the driver you're sick."

Lacey did as she was instructed. She tried to catch Lloyd's eye, but he was busy talking with Lester. He didn't see her get down off the step.

Standing beside Mrs. Petrie, Lacey said, (*politely,* she thought) "Mrs. Petrie, I have a math exam today. It's worth 20% of my final mark."

"Are you sassing me, girl?" snapped Mrs. Petrie in a truly terrible voice. "I said, are you sassing me?"

"No, ma'am," Lacey quavered. "I am just letting you know. You have no way of knowing my school schedule. I am just telling you."

Roaring even louder, Lacey thought that Mrs. Petrie truly resembled a dragon, both in sound and looks. Grabbing Lacey by the hair, Mrs. Petrie shouted, "You will tell me NOTHING, do you understand me, NOTHING! I do not tolerate insolence of any sort in my home. Come with me, girl, you are about to find out what happens when you disrespect me!"

Still hanging on to Lacey by her hair, Mrs. Petrie dragged her towards the garage. Pushing the young girl into the building via the man-door at the back of the garage, she opened the door to the fridge. "Get in there, girl, you need a lesson in civility."

Lacey whimpered, "Mrs. Petrie, I'm sorry! I didn't intend to sound disrespectful, I really didn't. Please, don't put me in there, please!"

"If you don't shut up, girl, you're going to be there even longer. Now, this is your first time, so, if you keep quiet, I'll let you out after lunch. If you keep on jawing at me, you won't get out until tomorrow. What's it going to be?" She put her hands on her hips, set her jaw, narrowed her eyes and waited. "And one more thing, missy, if you try to call out to the mailman or anyone else, you'll be in there for a full week. Mr. Petrie has gone out of town on business for the next 10 days, so watch it!"

With not another word, Lacey stepped shakily into the fridge. Mrs. Petrie re-wrapped the chain more tightly around the appliance. Putting a sharp stick between the door frame and the outside of the fridge, she nearly speared Lacey in the eye as she did so. She locked the fridge door with a large padlock. She then turned around and left the garage, whistling as she walked.

Whimpering softly, Lacey tried to put her small hand outside the fridge door. She could only insert her baby finger. Breathing hard, she tried to calm down. Remembering Annie's instructions, she practiced deep, slow breaths.

Lacey was still small for her age. Very carefully she tried to stand up. The top of the fridge brushed the top of her head but she was able to stand. When she tired, she squatted down or sat with her back leaning against the side. In this position, however, she had to draw her knees right up past her chin. At least, she was able to change positions. Annie was a much larger girl and Lacey was pretty sure that she had not been so 'lucky' when she was in the fridge. As well, it was daylight. A dusky glimpse of sunlight forced its way through the crack in the fridge door. It produced a twilight effect, not bright enough to read by, but certainly bright enough that Lacey did not panic in total darkness.

Lacey spent the hours in the fridge shifting positions and thinking about the years since she and Lloyd had first been left alone, abandoned by their mother. So much had gone on, so little had been accomplished. Nothing had worked out according to any particular plans they may have tried to implement. She wondered what they could ever have done to warrant their mother leaving and later on, their father disappearing without a trace. Now they would never be able to go home with their dad. He would be put back in prison, once they found him. For breaching probation, he would have to serve the rest of his sentence. Whatever had he been thinking when he took off like that. Exhausted by her panic and by her recollections, she dozed off and on, for a few minutes at a time.

She heard a vehicle stop at the mail box. About to disregard Mrs. Petrie's stern instructions to be quiet, she opened her mouth to holler for help. Before she could utter a sound, she heard Mrs. Petrie's voice, right outside the garage. "Hello, John!" she chirped to the mailman. I see you have some government cheques for me today. You are a dear, aren't you?"

Once the mailman had driven away, Mrs. Petrie entered the garage. "Good girl," she said. "You followed my instructions and didn't say a word. Just for that, I will let you out."

Gratefully, Lacey waited for the lock to come off. Despite being able to change positions, she still felt stiff and sore. Stretching and bending, she gradually worked the kinks out.

Her stomach growled loudly.

Mrs. Petrie smiled, an evil smile. "Hungry, are we? Too bad. You missed lunch and will now have to wait for supper. I suggest you go to your room and study until I say you can come out."

"Yes, ma'am," Lacey said meekly. "I can do that." She hurried to the bathroom, and then lay down on her bed and cried herself to sleep.

A few hours later, she awoke with a start. She sat up. Where was she? Where were the rest of the kids? Oh yes, the fridge. Her stomach growled angrily. Right, no lunch.

Hearing a motor outside, she went to the window. The school bus stopped outside the yard. Lloyd, Lester, and Annie, got off and started up the driveway.

When Lloyd came running up the stairs, Lacey ambushed him outside her bedroom door. Grabbing him by the arm she hissed at him in a hoarse whisper to be quiet. She pulled him into her room, closing the door.

"What the hell, Lacey!" Lloyd exclaimed. "What's going on? Why weren't you at school? You had your big math test today, did you forget?" Worriedly, he stared at Lacey.

She filled him in, quickly and to the point.

Before Lloyd could ask her anything else, they heard Mrs. Petrie hollering. "Lacey! Get down here. Just because Mr. Petrie is away doesn't mean you don't have to follow my schedule. Bring me a beer, and I'll drink it on the veranda. In the meantime, get the table set. Your chores today are no different than yesterday."

Silence. Then, "**EVERY ONE OF YOU LITTLE SNOTHEADS! GET AT YOUR CHORES!**"

They heard Mrs. Petrie stomping out to the veranda. Everyone scattered. Everyone knew what they had to do, even the twins.

Mr. Petrie was away for 10 whole days. They were 10 days of hell for the foster children.

They heard the newborn crying in her crib but they didn't dare stop their chores to tend to her. There was work to be done, and done properly.

Much later that evening, Lacey was nearly asleep. Annie's voice broke the silence. Although speaking softly, her words penetrated the darkness.

"You know, Lacey, I need to get out of here. But, I will make you a promise. I promise not to run until Mr. Petrie gets back from his 10-day business trip. All the rest of you kids will have a better chance of avoiding extreme punishment as long as Mrs. Petrie doesn't know for sure when her husband will come home. Sometimes, he comes home early. I have often wondered if he suspects something and is trying to catch her at it. So far, we aren't that lucky. Anyhow, I will be ready to go the night he gets back. The old cow will be so busy trying to impress him that they won't have time to notice I'm gone."

In the dark, Lacey breathed a sigh of relief. "Thank you, Annie," she said. "Good night. See you in the morning."

The next morning at school, her math teacher asked her why she missed her math exam. Lacey told her that she wasn't well. Something in the way she said it caused her teacher to look at her more carefully.

"Are you better now, Lacey?" she asked. Trying to hold back the tears, Lacey responded, "Yes, ma'am, for the time being, I am."

"Is there anything you want to tell me?"

Her voice muffled by swallowed tears, Lacey said, "No ma'am. I guess I will just have to work harder to make up for the 20% I lost by missing my exam." She rose, and was almost to the door, when her teacher's voice stopped her.

"Lacey, I have a pretty good idea of what is going on, but unless you talk to me about it, I have no proof. I am going to let you write the math exam at lunch time today. Just so you know, if you ever need to talk, come and find me, OK?"

"Thank you, teacher. I will be here at lunch time. I want you to know how much I appreciate this."

On the way home, Lacey told Lloyd about her conversation with the math teacher.

"Do you think I should have told her about life at the Petries'?" she asked Lloyd.

Annie, who was sitting right across the aisle from Lacey and Lloyd, yelped, "Good God, no! We would all pay dearly if Mrs. Petrie found out. You know she would find out, Lacey, because Social Services would do an investigation. They would find nothing untoward, and we would all suffer. You can't tell anyone! Look what happened with the Schmidts. Absolutely nothing, that's what! They still have foster kids, and you can just bet that he is fooling around in the girls' bedroom still. What makes you think anything different would happen with Mrs. Petrie?"

"Annie's right, Lace," Lloyd said dismally. "Unfortunately, Annie's right."

He glanced across the aisle at Annie. Lloyd felt like a 5 year old again, totally helpless and unable to formulate any type of solution.

Later, while doing the supper dishes, Lacey whispered to Lloyd, "I think this is the night that Annie is going to make her run for it, Lloyd."

"What makes you think that?"

"Annie was so upset when she heard about me being put in the fridge, that I think she has finally reached the end of her rope."

Lacey then proceeded to outline her plan to follow Annie to the highway, hide in the ditch so that she could get the licence plate number, and then call Mrs. Bronson.

Lloyd was flabbergasted. "Lacey, Annie is afraid of the dark. She is not going to run in the middle of the night. My guess is that she will make a run for it right after the school bus picks us up. I think she will hide. Mrs. Petrie will think she went to school. While Mrs. Petrie is busy with the baby, I think Annie will take off with the 1st driver who stops for her."

"That does seem more like what will happen, Lloyd," Lacey agreed, "but I will stay awake tonight, in case she does take off."

"No! Lloyd protested, more loudly than he meant to. "I will go and get the licence plate number. You stay here. Do everything normally. Don't make Mrs. Petrie suspicious.

"Mrs. Petrie is far more likely to notice you not getting on the school bus than she will me. I promise you, I will get that number. Then you can call Mrs. Bronson if you like, but you are NOT following Annie."

They finished the dishes in silence. Before they left the kitchen, Lloyd spoke up once more. "Lacey, I love your idea, you know that. It's just I couldn't bear it if something went wrong and you got hurt. Promise me you won't try to follow.

"After I get the plate number, I'll run and put it in the Mailbox. Then, when it's safe, and not before then, you can retrieve the paper.

"Once you have the information, go to school as usual. Susanna will let you call Mrs. Bronson from her phone."

Lacey said, "I love Susanna, Lloyd, but can we really trust her? Seems as if we can't trust anyone except ourselves."

Lloyd gave his sister a hug. "Lacey, I trust Susanna with my life. You should too."

The next morning all 4 waited for the school bus. Mrs. Petrie was busy with the newborn, so, for once, she wasn't snooping outside, trying to overhear their conversations.

As soon as they saw the bus coming, Annie stood off to the side.

While Lester and Lacey were stepping on to the bus, Lloyd looked around. Annie was gone.

With an apology to the bus driver, Lloyd quickly said that he felt unwell, he had been fighting the flu for several days, and he would not be going to school today. As the bus driver closed the school bus doors, Lloyd waved at Lacey, who was watching through the window. As soon as the bus was on its way down the road, he turned and raced down the ditch.

He could see Annie standing by the side of the highway. He ducked deeper in the ditch, staying out of sight. Regardless of his efforts, Annie spotted him. After telling her that he was going to get the plate number instead of Lacey, Annie said, "OK, Lloyd, thank you. But you just stay out of sight. I don't want anything to screw up my getting a ride away from this place. Mrs. Petrie might come out of the house at any time now. I can't spend another minute in that house, Lloyd. I just can't."

"I understand completely. Don't worry, Annie," Lloyd said. "I've got your back. Even if the old bag does come out of the house and sees you, I won't let her stop you!"

"Duck, Lloyd!" Annie screamed the words before she could stop herself. In a quieter voice she said, "I hear a vehicle coming!"

Sure enough, a vehicle pulled up alongside Annie and stopped. The driver reached over and opened the passenger side door.

"Where ya going, little lady?" he asked.

"Anywhere but here," Annie said bitterly. "I'll get off when you reach where you're going."

"Well then, missy, hop right on in. I'm goin' all the way to Vancouver, so settle in, it'll be a long ride."

Lloyd couldn't see the driver, but as the truck slowly pulled away from the shoulder of the road, Lloyd scribbled on a piece of paper he had taken from his backpack:

Alberta Plate # LUVKIDZ
One ton truck – solid shell on back, no windows
Side lettering black and green – ZO'S HAULING
Bright orange, pumpkin orange

After looking around to make sure Mrs. Petrie wasn't around, Lloyd took off running.

Arriving at the Mailbox, he sat on the flat rock, trying to catch his breath and piece his thoughts together. He copied the information from the 1st piece of paper on to a 2nd piece. He then stuffed the copy in his pocket, leaving his original paper as far back in the Mailbox as he could in order to protect it, but also positioned so Lacey could find it.

When he reached the Petrie place, he quietly entered the mud room and tiptoed to his bedroom. Lacey was waiting for him, full of questions.

"Sshhh!" Lloyd whispered. "I'll tell you everything on the school bus tomorrow. In the meantime, say nothing, absolutely nothing, get it? We want to give Annie as many hours to get away as we can."

"Got it!" Lacey stage-whispered. "I won't say nothin'."

"Anything!" Lloyd corrected.

"Huh?" Lacey queried.

"Anything," Lloyd repeated. "You won't say anything."

"Where is the old broad anyway?" Lloyd whispered.

"Getting the newborn ready. Social Services is coming to get her. She has been adopted, lucky baby."

As soon as Lloyd put away his backpack, he and Lacey went to the kitchen and set the table for supper.

Mrs. Petrie was busy with the baby and Social Services for quite some time. Hopefully, Annie would be miles away before Mrs. Petrie realized that Annie had not returned on the school bus with the other kids.

By the time Mrs. Petrie was finished with the social worker, Lloyd had supper ready. Mrs. Petrie looked surprised when she entered the kitchen. She even thanked Lloyd for his efforts.

Both kids rapidly started to talk, trying to delay the inevitable, that being Mrs. Petrie noticing that Annie was missing.

Calling Lester and the twins to the table, Mrs. Petrie started to dish up her food. Suddenly, she pushed away from the table, in such a fury that the chair tumbled over backwards.

"WHERE IS SHE?" she roared in her most terrible voice. **"NOBODY EATS UNTIL YOU TELL ME WHERE ANNIE IS!"**

Lloyd stood up before he spoke, giving himself a height advantage. "We don't know exactly where she is," he said truthfully. "We just know, when we waited for the bus this morning, she was with us. When we got on the school bus, we didn't pay attention to Annie. We just sat with our friends. We never noticed that she wasn't on the bus, and we didn't notice that she wasn't in school. We have none of the same classes. I'm sorry, Mrs. Petrie, but that's the whole truth of it."

Behind his back, Lloyd uncrossed his fingers.

"I DO NOT BELIEVE YOU!" The dragon enunciated every letter in every word, speaking in slow motion. She took a deep breath before continuing. "Perhaps I should put the twins in the fridge until you decide to tell me what is going on. What do you think of that idea?" She glared around the table.

Lacey swallowed hard. Her stomach hurt. She said nothing, just stared down at her empty plate.

Lloyd stared at Mrs. Petrie, not flinching despite the crazed look in her eyes. "You will **NOT** punish those twins for something they didn't do! Over my dead body! Do you hear me?"

"Now, I told you already. We don't know where Annie is. Try and punish any one of the kids in this house for something they have no control over, and Mr. Petrie will hear about it before he even reaches the door. **GET IT?** If you don't believe me, go ahead and try it, but you will regret it, I promise you."

"Now, I cooked this supper, and we are all going to eat it." With that, Lloyd sat down. "Pass the potatoes, please, Mrs. Petrie," he said calmly.

Shaking with impotent fury, Mrs. Petrie rose from the table and stomped out of the house on to the veranda, where she sat silent for the rest of the evening.

She listened to the kitchen clean-up noises. She watched as the twins came outside and tried to weed the flower beds. Without their beloved Annie to show them what to do, they soon gave up and went to play in the sandbox.

When she was finished with her kitchen chores and dusting, Lacey came out and helped the twins put away their toys. She accompanied them into the house and gave them their baths, read them a bedtime story. She then sat with them until they fell asleep.

Once her homework was done, Lacey got ready for bed. Lying awake in the darkness, she prayed that Annie was somewhere warm and safe. She prayed that they would hear from her soon. It was so quiet. Alone and frightened, Lacey cried herself to sleep.

On the school bus the next morning, Lloyd filled in Lacey and Lester on the previous day's events. He told them that Susanna had promised to bring her phone to school today so that Lacey could call Mrs. Bronson.

"You did bring her card, didn't you, Lace?" he anxiously asked.

"I always carry it, Lloyd."

The school bus driver stopped at the school to let off the students. Susanna was anxiously pacing back and forth in front of the school bus parking area. Spotting Lloyd and Lacey, she ran over to them.

"Is she gone? What happened? Did you bring Mrs. Bronson's number? Oh, my goodness, I can't believe the things that go on. Do you want to try and phone now? Do you want to try and phone at lunch time? What?" She finally calmed down enough to allow someone else to speak.

Lloyd said, "I think this is the best time to call. There's an hour time difference between the B.C. Social Services offices and here. It should be easy enough to call Mrs. Bronson's cell number."

Susanna asked Lacey to give her the card and she dialled Mrs. Bronson's number into her phone. As soon as it rang, she handed it to Lacey.

On the 3rd ring, Mrs. Bronson's voice came on the line. "Evelyn Bronson speaking. Who is this?"

"It's Lacey Jordan, Mrs. Bronson. I'm so glad that you answered your phone." At this point Lacey choked up, unable to continue. She stood there shaking. Susanna put her arm around the younger girl, squeezing her shoulder.

Lloyd reached over and took the phone from Lacey's hand. He spoke with Mrs. Bronson, telling her almost everything. Out of an abundance of caution, something held him back from reading the licence plate information to her that he had managed to obtain. He stopped speaking.

For a full minute, there was silence on the line.

At last, Mrs. Bronson spoke. "Are you sure about your story, Lloyd? It seems hard to believe that Mrs. Petrie is as evil as you say. She always seems so pleasant and competent whenever I have had any dealings with her. Now, I know that foster care is not the same as your own home, but locking children in an old fridge? Really?" This last word was spoken with incredulity. It was completely clear to Lloyd. Evelyn Bronson did not believe him.

For several seconds he could not speak. Finally, he resentfully said, "Forget it, Mrs. Bronson. Just forget it. You promised Lacey help if ever she should need it. But now that we all need help, you weasel out of it. You should know us by now. We don't make up stories. We don't call unless we really need help. It is a joke, the foster care system, just a joke. Have a nice life!" Trembling, he handed the phone back to Susanna.

"What now?" Susanna asked.

"I don't know." Lloyd's voice quavered. "The police weren't any help when either Charley or Amelia disappeared. Oh, they made a feeble attempt for a pathetically short time, but when it came right down to it, there was no help from the police or Social Services. Nobody gave a crap about a missing teenager, especially someone with no family to push them into further action. Now Mrs. Bronson doesn't believe us, I'm completely at a loss. All I know is, Mrs. Petrie can't be allowed to hurt anyone, ever again."

Susanna let his words sink in. Finally, she asked, "Lloyd, would you consider letting my dad help? He seems to be settling down since Mom died. Not only would he be helping you guys, he would be helping himself."

Lloyd turned and spotted Lester, waiting on the fringe of the group.

"Lester," Lloyd asked, "Do you think you will be OK if you go back to the Petrie's after school? Lacey and I will go with Susanna and speak with her dad."

Lester nodded.

Lloyd instructed him firmly. "Whatever happens, don't let Mrs. Petrie bully you. And for heaven's sake, don't let her punish the twins. You are bigger than she is. Think you can handle it? I promise, we will be there with help as soon as it is humanly possible."

Lester swallowed. "I'll be OK, Lloyd. Go do what you have to do. I won't let her harm the twins. Hopefully, you'll be back tonight with the help we all need. I ain't scared." He then turned and went into the school, shoulders straight, head held high. The new responsibility seemed to strengthen him.

Watching him, Lloyd breathed a sigh of relief. He had faith in Lester. He would keep things under some sort of control until help could arrive.

In the meantime, Susanna shut off her phone.

"I just spoke with Dad," she said. "He will pick the 3 of us up after school. Hang in there, guys. Dad will know what to do." Susanna walked in to the school, waved at Lloyd and Lacey, followed by a thumbs-up.

The day dragged on and on. Lloyd, Lacey, and Susanna, could not concentrate on their school work.

Lacey's teacher handed back her math exam. Lacey peeked at the corner where her final mark was written in red. Even the fact that she got 93%, on an exam that was worth 20% of her final mark, failed to cheer her up.

At lunch time, she chose to sit by herself in a corner of the playground. She tried to eat, but her stomach ached so much she could only make a half-hearted attempt.

At long last, the final bell rang. Quickly collecting their backpacks, the 3 of them hurried out to the parking lot to meet Henry Greschner.

Henry was waiting. As the kids climbed into his truck, Lacey thought that maybe, for once, something in their life would finally take a turn for the better.

"Hey, kids!" he greeted them. "I thought we might just stop at Mountain Goat Lake on our way home and have us a wiener roast. I brought all the fixings. It's a good place to talk about things. Good place to figure things out."

"Oh, and just so you know, I called Mrs. Petrie and told her the current plan is that you'll be home tomorrow on the school bus. I said if there was any change, I would let her know."

"You did?" Lacey just had to ask, "What did she have to say about that?"

"Well," Henry said with a quiet chuckle, "I'm pretty sure it was one of the few times in her life she was at a loss for words. I didn't ask her, I just plain out told her."

"I also told her that she better leave her foster kids alone. I said I would be keeping an ear out for any more shenanigans. I told her that if I heard anything more about a fridge or a paddle, being kept home from school as punishment in order for kids to do her housework, or any other form of unwarranted punishment, I would report her to the police and make dang sure that she couldn't take in any more foster kids."

Catching the look Lacey gave Susanna out of the corner of his eye, Henry cautioned, "Now don't go getting mad at Susanna. I pretty much bribed her into telling me. Even though I am not your foster parent any more, I truly care about the 2 of you, and what happens to you."

"Wow!" was all Lacey could think of to say. Inwardly she shuddered. There would be hell to pay when they got back to the Petrie place, no doubt about it! She was pretty positive that Mrs. Petrie could not give up her Dr. Jekyll/Mr. Hyde routine any time soon. She was a sick woman.

"Holy crap!" Lloyd said.

"You go, Dad!" said Susanna.

As he pulled into the parking area at the lake, Lacey could feel the tension easing between her shoulder blades. As soon as the truck stopped, she jumped out and ran to the water. She quickly leaned over and ceremoniously dipped her hands into the cold lake. "Hello, Mountain Goat Lake," she whispered. "Oh, how I've missed you!"

"So, Uncle Henry," Lloyd asked, "How are you doing? I can only imagine how tough it is, and how lonely you and Susanna must be, with Aunt Harriet gone. Lacey and I miss her somethin' fierce, and we aren't even living here."

Henry Greschner was silent. Finally, with a shuddering breath, he said, "Well, Lloyd, I sure can't lie about it. It's been the toughest time in my life. For a while, I just wanted to lay down and die myself. But after a pretty severe pity party, I took a look at my girl here." He glanced over at Susanna. "I knew that I couldn't do anything rash. My daughter needed me to be strong. So, now, I just take one day at a time. My woodworking helps, and coming down here to Mountain Goat Lake helps. Every day the pain dulls a little. Thanks for asking."

He stood up abruptly. "Well, what say we get a fire going and roast these hot dogs? Don't know about you, but I'm hungry. Then, while we're eating, we'll try and figure out what to do about Annie and about your foster care situation."

Once they had their fill, Henry looked at Lloyd and Lacey. "So, better tell me what's up."

Lloyd filled Uncle Henry in on all the happenings since they left the Greschner foster home, including the fact that Charlie, Amelia, and now Annie, had all run away and had not been seen or heard from since. He recounted that neither the police nor Social Services had made much of an effort to try and locate the missing girls.

He also told him that the Schmidts were still looking after foster kids, even though George Schmidt had molested Charlie before she finally ran away.

Lloyd told him about the Savards practically starving their wards, while they ate like kings. Again, Social Services either ignored it, or didn't believe the complaints that came from the children.

He conceded that their time on the Bourke farm had been a learning experience. Lloyd had learned a lot about farm chores, but he remained bitter about having to relocate to a new foster home yet again when the Bourkes took in an adult farm worker. He bitterly told Uncle Henry that the Bourkes could have made room for all of them, if they really wanted to.

Ending up with the Petrie fiasco, he wondered aloud why no one would believe kids when they tried to let others know of their predicament.

Henry had listened without interrupting. When Lloyd finally stopped speaking, he said, "Well, you kids have been through the wringer, haven't you?"

"First thing needs to be done, is try and determine the fate of those 3 missing girls. I have a friend who lives near Vancouver. He's a retired detective. I'll give him the details and have him do some snooping around."

"Now, Lloyd, tell me about this vehicle that picked the girls up."

"Actually," Lloyd said, "Lacey saw it the first 2 times. When it stopped for Charley, Lacey didn't pay much mind. After it stopped for Amelia, she later realized that the same vehicle had stopped for both girls."

Lloyd then went on to tell Uncle Henry about the morning Annie ran away, how he had followed her and hid in the ditch. When the truck stopped, he told him about getting the details and writing them down. Reaching into his jeans pocket, he handed the copy to Uncle Henry.

"Hmmm. Who else did you give this information to?"

"No one," Lloyd said quietly. "I was going to give it to Mr. Silverman or Mrs. Bronson, but something stopped me. I think it was the fact that they pretty much ignored everything we have ever told them. Susanna, Lacey, and I, all agreed that it would probably be better to give the paper to you."

Uncle Henry looked at Lloyd. "This piece of paper you gave me has 'COPY' printed at the top. Where's the original?"

Lloyd looked over at Lacey, who had opened her mouth to say something. He gave an imperceptible shake of his head. She closed her mouth.

"I put it in a safe place. I was afraid that Mrs. Petrie might find it. She snoops in all our things when we're not around."

Henry looked at the paper again. "Tell me something, if you can. Did all 3 of the girls run away on the same day of the week? That is, was it a Tuesday, a Friday? I'm asking, because I think it would be a lot easier to track down this truck, if we knew the delivery schedule."

Lacey spoke up. "I know," she said. "It was a Thursday, all 3 times."

Lloyd looked over at his sister, surprised. "How do you know that, Lace?"

"I've been keeping a journal," she said. "Mrs. Bourke gave it to me in the elm tree one day. She said it helps a person to keep track of what's important in life, by writing down things, both good and bad. She said it would be something for just me, and it would make me feel better, more secure. So I did. And it does."

"I didn't have the journal when Charley and Amelia ran away, of course, but I missed them both so much that I remembered the days as clearly as if I had written them down. Once I got the journal, I wrote the days in there."

"Well, Miss Lacey, you're not just another hat rack, are you? That, my dear, is very helpful!" Uncle Henry smiled at her.

"Uncle Henry," Lacey began, "why do you think that the foster parents and the police didn't make much of an effort to search for them?"

"Well, I don't know about Charley, because she was only 14 years old. But the other 2 were 16, nearly done school. I guess maybe everyone figured, wrongly of course, that those 2 girls were nearly grown and could look after themselves. Tell me, did Charley look older than 14, do you think?"

Lacey shrugged her shoulders, she didn't know.

"I can answer that," Lloyd said. "She looked older. Poor Charley suffered a lot at the hands of Mr. G. It aged her. She looked the same age as Amelia and Annie. They all looked like they could be older."

"I remember Mr. G sneering at her one day at the supper table. He told her that she should fix herself up, that she looked like she 'had been ridden hard and put away wet', whatever that means. Anyway, he made her cry."

"All right," Henry Greschner said. "I will call my detective friend first thing in the morning, after you kids go to school."

"In the meantime, Lacey, do you have Mrs. Bronson's card? I think it is time someone other than you 2 has a little chat with her about your foster care situation."

"Now, I want you to quit worrying. Just for the time being. Leave it to me.

"How about we head on home and have dessert? Susanna learned to make a mean cherry pie from her mama, and I just happen to know that there is a fresh one in the fridge. When she asked me to help you, she baked it special."

Vastly relieved of their burdensome responsibility, for the remainder of the evening they simply enjoyed each other's company.

As they waited for the school bus the next morning, Henry told them to have a great day and not to worry about anything. He would take it from here. They saw him head on back to the house, his cell phone already held to his ear.

Feeling like the weight of the world had shifted off of their shoulders, they got on the bus, determined not to worry about what was sure to happen when they got back to the Petrie house after school.

To their great relief, when they got off the bus, they noticed that Mr. Petrie was home early from his business trip. He greeted them in a most friendly way, even asking about their day.

Mrs. Petrie was nowhere to be seen, and the kids didn't bother to ask where she was, they simply didn't care.

After 10 days, Lloyd and Lacey still didn't know how Uncle Henry was making out. When Lloyd asked Susanna if she knew anything, she did not.

Mrs. Petrie prepared meals, but other than that, she said nothing to any of the children, she ignored them completely.

At least there was no implementation of any of the discipline methods she had at her disposal. The fridge still sat menacingly in the corner of the garage, the paddle still hung on the wall in the mud room, smooth side out to avoid anyone asking about the ridged side.

Every morning they waited at the breakfast table with bated breath, anticipating that perhaps Mr. Petrie would be leaving on another business trip, resuming normal breathing only when he stood up to leave, saying, "See you this afternoon, everyone. I'm off to the office."

More days passed. After another 10 days, there was still no word.

Lloyd could wait no longer. He would take matters into his own hands. Wednesday evening, he snuck out of the house and went to the Mailbox. Once he arrived, he double-checked that the original information was still there. He left another piece of paper in the hiding place, right beside the vehicle information.

Thursday morning, Lloyd held back while Lester and Lacey got on the bus. As usual, they were busy chatting with friends and didn't notice when he waved the driver on and then ran towards the ditch where Annie had last been seen.

Not long after the school bus was out of view, a vehicle came up the road. Lloyd held out his thumb and the truck stopped.

The driver's face was hidden by a 5-gallon cowboy hat. His hair was long, sticking out from beneath the hat, further obscuring his face.

"Going somewhere, fella?" the driver asked in an intentionally deep voice.

"Yes, how far are you going?" Lloyd asked.

"Vancouver."

"Great! That's where I'm going also. Thanks for stopping."

Lloyd threw his backpack in and then climbed into the cab of the one-ton, pumpkin orange truck, with a shell covering the truck box, with black and green lettering that read 'ZO'S Hauling' on the side.

Without even a glance at the driver, Lloyd breathed, "I'm ready."

"Well, then," said the driver in his normal voice, "Let's roll!"

Neither Lacey nor anyone else would see Lloyd again for many years.

Chapter 8
Where Is Lloyd?

When the bell rang, Lacey gathered her things together and strolled out the school doors and over to her bus. Her school day had been very busy. She was tired. Climbing on to the bus, she immediately walked to the back and sat by herself. She leaned against the window and shut her eyes.

The driver's voice awakened her. He was yelling the full length of the vehicle, "Hey, Miss Lacey Jordan! It's your stop. Come on now, get off, I haven't got all night."

Half asleep, she stumbled towards the front. As she climbed down the steps, she thanked the driver for waking her. Waving goodbye, she began to walk to the back of the house.

She didn't see Lloyd get off, but she figured he must have gone into the house already.

Before she even had her coat hung up, Mrs. Petrie grabbed Lacey by her hair.

She screeched, "Where is your lazy good-for-nothing brother? I need him to help me with some chores. Where is he?"

Her face contorted into a mass of wrinkled rage, she shook Lacey, hard. "I asked you a simple question girl!" She shook her again with one hand, and pulled her hair with the other, harder this time.

Cringing, Lacey edged closer to the woman, trying to loosen Mrs. Petrie's grip and thus avoid the pain from her hair being pulled. She winced, cried loudly, "I don't know Mrs. Petrie! I thought he came into the house ahead of me. I fell asleep on the bus and didn't see him get off. The bus driver woke me up. Honest to God, I truly do not know where Lloyd is."

Shoving Lacey out of her way, Mrs. Petrie charged up the stairs and flung open the boys' bedroom door. "Lester!" she hissed in her truly awful voice, "Have you seen that good-for-nothing?"

Without waiting for Lester's response, she turned and charged towards the bathroom.

Hammering on the door with both fists, she gave an ear-piercing yell, followed by her saliva spraying everywhere as she barked, "Lloyd, if you're in there, you damn well better get out here! I have something for you to do."

Waiting for the briefest of moments, she tried the doorknob. The door swung inwards, revealing – nothing! The bathroom was empty. By this time the woman was apoplectic. Her face contorted, her complexion darkened to an almost burgundy hue. She literally shook with fury.

For just the briefest of moments, Lacey gleefully thought the woman might have a stroke, but then she felt guilty. Later that evening, she would wonder why she felt guilty. That terrible, awful woman would never change.

Mrs. Petrie grabbed Lester by the ear, marching him out of the boys' room and down the stairs, shoving him beside Lacey.

Lacey's teeth were chattering as she stared at the furious foster mother.

"Why don't you believe us, Mrs. Petrie?" Lester asked quietly. "We told you we don't know where Lloyd is. That's the truth. If you won't believe us, there is nothing more we can say."

Taking a deep breath, Elsie Petrie tried unsuccessfully to calm down.

Her voice vibrating, she told Lester and Lacey to go out and search for Lloyd. There would be no supper for any of the foster children until Lloyd was found.

She stomped to the fridge, grabbed a couple bottles of beer, and then stomped out to the veranda. She threw herself into a chair.

Opening one of the beer bottles, she drained it in a few swallows. She immediately reached for the 2nd bottle, muttering angrily to herself as she did so. She hollered at Lester to bring her a couple more bottles, and to then get the hell on his way.

Lacey and Lester just stood, rooted in place.

"Well, you idiot children, what are you waiting for? Get searching!"

Lacey turned to Lester and whispered, so Mrs. Petrie couldn't hear. "Lester, would you go to speak with Martha Schmidt? Maybe Lloyd was there."

"Okay," Lester said, "but where will you look?"

"I have an idea," Lacey said. "I'll let you know if and when I find anything. Now we better run. The twins will be crying for their supper soon. We need to search and get back as quickly as we can. I don't trust Mrs. Petrie to be alone with Peter and Paula for long. She might put them in the fridge, or beat them with the paddle until we get back. We need to hurry."

Lester took off running, not looking back.

Lacey began running, heading for the Mailbox. All the way there, she prayed that Lloyd had left her a message in their secret spot.

Out of breath, trembling with anxiety, Lacey reached and sat down on the flat rock. Her chest heaving, she tried to catch her breath. She also tried to collect her courage. She thought to herself, *What if there is nothing there? Then what?*

In a matter of minutes, she stood up and walked on shaky limbs towards the tree stump. She reached in. With her 1st try, her fingers felt nothing. Her heart sank. Breathing deeply, she reached in again, deeper this time. Not only did she withdraw the piece of paper with the truck details on it, her fingers closed around a 2nd piece! She held on to both papers tightly as she returned to the rock and sat down once again.

Lacey glanced briefly at the 1st piece of paper. It contained the details of 'the pumpkin truck' as she had come to think of it. With trembling hands, she unfolded the 2nd piece. She read:

LACEY

By the time you read this note, I will hopefully be in Vancouver. I just can't sit around waiting for empty promises to do something. I know Uncle Henry is doing the best he can, but nothing is happening. He has so much on his plate now. I don't feel it is fair to depend on him when I can actively search for our missing foster siblings. Who knows! Maybe I will even find Dad and Mom while I'm searching. Pray that I do.

In the meantime, I intend to wait for your 'pumpkin truck' and hitch a ride. I am pretty sure the answers we are looking for are connected to that truck and its driver.

Now, please don't get mad at me but I have had to let Susanna know about our Mailbox. I will be too far away to put notes in it for you, and I have both Susanna's mailing address and Uncle Henry's cell phone number. If she has news that she can't tell you about at school (in case someone overhears your conversations), she will get the information to you via the Mailbox.

Don't worry about me. I can look after myself. I just hope and pray that Mrs. Petrie doesn't take the news of my running out on all of you kids.

Lacey, you're the best sister a guy could ever have. Stay strong. Pray for me. Pray I find the answers we need.

LLOYD

She couldn't breathe. Clutching the note to her chest, she cried until she couldn't squeeze out another tear.

Finally, exhausted and anxious, terrified, really, she put the note in her pocket. Reluctantly, but resolutely, Lacey began to walk back to the Petries'.

The time it took for her to return to the house transformed Lacey. She could physically feel her tears drying up. She could physically feel herself growing hard, and cold, and bitter. She vowed that if anything happened to her brother, she would never rest until he was avenged.

Mama's ideas about raising kids was a joke, she thought. *Mama always told us that kindness and courtesy towards both friend and foe were the most important things in life. She said that the ability to forgive was a blessing.* She read Lloyd and Lacey Bible stories, and told them that God was always there for them. All they needed to do was ask and He would help them.

Lacey thought, *Hmmpf! Fine way He had of showing it. Can't see where He helped Mama when she couldn't make ends meet. Fine way of showing it when Mama abandoned her kids. Fine way of showing it by the foster homes she and Lloyd had been placed in!*

She kicked a fair-sized rock in frustration, painfully stubbing her toe in the process.

Well, if the ability to forgive was such a blessing, if her mama's idea of teaching her children the values of kindness, courtesy, and forgiveness, was to abandon her children, then Lacey decided that it simply wasn't within her ability to believe those lessons any longer. She thought it was all crap. Her mama didn't have a clue what she was talking about, and she sure as heck didn't have a clue about raising kids!

Kicking pebbles along the way, she grew more and more determined that life for her was going to get better. She was sick and tired of being pushed around, sick and tired of bad things always happening to her. She didn't know how, but she was going to change her life.

So intent on her thoughts, she was momentarily startled when the Petrie house suddenly loomed in front of her. She could see Mrs. Petrie standing in the back yard. Lester and the twins stood stiffly by her side.

Lacey clenched her jaw. Throwing her shoulders back, she marched purposefully towards the house. However, despite her new resolve, she was worried. She worried not for herself, but for Lester, and little Peter and Paula. Mrs. Petrie might not punish Lacey, but that wouldn't stop her from taking out her wrath on the other foster kids.

"Well?" Mrs. Petrie glared at Lacey. "Did you find him?"

"No, of course not," Lacey said sullenly. "Do you think I'm a miracle worker or something? Lloyd ran away. He ran to get out of this screwy foster care system. He ran away from you, Mrs. Petrie. He ran, and he's never coming back."

Curiously mute, the foster mother turned and went into the house, slamming the screen door behind her.

Deciding not to tell Lester about Lloyd's note, she just said that she couldn't find any sign of him.

Mrs. Petrie had prepared no supper. She sat on the front veranda, a bottle of beer in her hand, 2 more bottles waiting on the small table beside her.

The twins were hungry, grouchy and irritable. Lacey told everyone to sit at the table while she made grilled cheese sandwiches.

After they ate, Lacey asked Lester to clean up the kitchen so she could get the little ones ready for bed.

All night, Lacey lay awake, worried nearly to death about Lloyd. *Where is he?* she wondered. *Please God,* she prayed, *keep my brother safe.* Miserable, she didn't catch the discrepancy between her new-found bitterness towards God, and her prayer.

Sometime in the middle of the night, she got up and hand-printed 2 copies of each of Lloyd's notes. She would give one copy of each to Susanna at school. She hoped that Uncle Henry would know what to do from here. She would also call Mrs. Bronson, read her the notes, and then ask Susanna to mail a copy of the notes to Evelyn Bronson. Hopefully, someone would know what to do next.

When her alarm rang, Lacey got out of bed. She was ready for school and at the breakfast table, not long before Lester. The twins appeared in their pyjamas, sleepily holding on to each other's hand.

Mrs. Petrie sat at the table, drinking a coffee. She made no sign that she was going to get breakfast, so Lacey got up and poured cereal into 5 bowls, added milk and placed a bowl in front of each person, including Mrs. Petrie.

Lacey tried to choke down her cereal, but it stuck in her throat.

Looking at Mrs. Petrie, she said, "Mrs. Petrie, the bus will soon be here. We haven't got a lunch. We need you to give us some money so we can eat at the cafeteria today. It's Friday, so we don't have to worry about school lunches for a couple of days but I will make sure they are ready on Monday."

When Elsie Petrie didn't acknowledge her, Lacey went to get her purse. It hung in the closet on the same coat hanger as Mrs. Petrie's coat. Beginning to get angry, because the bus was due to arrive any minute, she slammed the purse down on the table. Startled, Elsie grabbed it, reached in and handed Lacey 2 $10 bills.

Lacey snarled at her foster parent, "If I come home from school and find that you have laid a hand on either of those twins, or you haven't taken care of them properly while Lester and I were at school, I will be talking to Mr. Petrie. You can bet your life on that! **AND** I will get hold of Social Services and let them know again about your punishment methods. **AND** I will call the police. I will make such a stink that they will believe me this time."

"I know you think I'm just a kid and that nobody will pay any attention to me. Want to try me? My brother is gone because of you. **Believe you me** *(a favourite expression of her mother's, and unconsciously uttered, even in the same tone of voice!)* when I tell you that if it comes down to it, they **WILL** believe me! I'll make sure of it." Removing her hands from her hips, Lacey said, "Now, I'm going to school!"

She turned and gave each of the twins a quick hug. She handed Lester one of the $10 bills. At the door, she called calmly over her shoulder, "By the way, Mrs. Petrie, your husband called last night – while you were sitting on the veranda having your beer. He said not to bother you, but to tell you that he'll be home today."

Lester sat beside Lacey on the bus.

"Holy crap!" he exclaimed admiringly. "You really gave it to that old battle axe! The amazing part is you could tell she believes you! How old did you say you are? I'm impressed!"

"It's nothing Lester," Lacey said wearily. "I'm just so worried about Lloyd, afraid that if he doesn't come back, or if we don't hear from him soon, something terrible will have happened to him. I'm so sick of feeling helpless."

"When Charley, Amelia, and Annie, disappeared, I was even younger and more helpless. All I could do was worry and fret. Everybody just assumed the girls were okay after they ran away. We don't know that, and it haunts me. The search for each of them was so short, so half-hearted, but I couldn't do anything. I dream about them, a lot."

"For all I know, Lloyd is the only family I have in this world. My dad's a crook and a jailbird. Heaven only knows what my mom is up to. So, if something happens to Lloyd, I will really be alone."

A solitary, large tear rolled down her cheek and she batted it away angrily.

Lester reached over and awkwardly patted Lacey on her hand. "But remember, Lacey," he said, "Lloyd didn't run away from you, he's following a lead on the missing girls. There is a difference. Also, Lloyd's tough. It would take someone a lot bigger and a lot stronger than him to botch up his search efforts. I think we need to stay positive. Negative thoughts need to be thrown out with the twins' bathwater, don't you think?"

A tiny, quivering smile shadowed its way across Lacey's face. "Thanks, Lester. I know, I really do, but it's a lot easier said than done. I will promise you, though, that I'll try my very best to stay positive. No avoidable negative thoughts."

Changing the subject only slightly, she turned and looked at Lester. "I'm going to talk to Mr. Petrie at the supper table tonight. Are you ready for it? Will you back me up, no matter what I say? Because I need to get out of this foster home. Everyone does."

"Mrs. Petrie should rot in hell for the terrible things she has done to the kids in her care. You think you've seen her upset before? She's going to be even more upset at supper time after I say what I need to say."

Lester stared at Lacey. "Of course, Lace," he said quietly. "I'll agree with you tonight, no matter what you say."

The school day seemed interminable. Lacey spent most of the day in a stupor, trying to formulate what she needed to say to the Petries rather than listening to her teachers, her thoughts alternating between sheer determination and sheer terror. She only hoped the sheer determination side of her won out!

When she and Lester finally got home from school, the twins were playing quietly in the sand box beside the house. Mrs. Petrie was sitting on the veranda, telephone in one hand, bottle of beer in the other. There was no sign of Mr. Petrie yet.

Rather than going straight to her room, Lacey stood behind the front door, out of sight of the veranda, but where she could clearly hear Mrs. Petrie's side of the telephone conversation.

She heard the woman say, "Martha, I just called to ask you a question about Charlotte. They never found her. Folks say it was because the search didn't get going when she first disappeared. The reason I am asking this, is one of my fosters took off running. Now I really don't care about this kid. He's 17 so he will be gone from the system soon anyway."

"Figured I just won't report his running to the Social Services people until I absolutely have to. They'll just keep sending the monthly cheque, know what I'm saying?"

There was silence as Elsie Petrie listened. Then she said, "It worked, huh? How many cheques did you get before you called them? (Listens.) Only 3? (Listens once again.) Yeah, she was only 14, you say, so there would be more concern for a kid of that age than for, say, a 17-year-old. They'd get pretty suspicious if you didn't report a kid of that age missing. (Listens.) You're saying they kept paying you even after you reported her missing? Oh, you reported her missing, the police did their lazy ass search, then you called Social Services and said she came back on her own. But she never came back, did she? Aah, it took a while for them to do a home visit, and they then found out that she was still gone!"

"They make you pay the money back? They tried, but wasn't worth their while to sue you? Hmm. I'm surprised they didn't yank the rest of the kids from you. (Listens.) Yeah, I agree. They're so terribly short of foster parents that they just gave you a warning but didn't yank the other kids. But, they're keeping a closer eye on you and Mr. G."

"Well, thanks, Martha! I better get going. The old man's going to be home in time for supper, and the bus just dropped off the kids. Thanks for the advice. Makes sense to me and, as you know, with the little bit of money we get paid for looking after foster kids, if we can continue collecting, why not? We're not hurting anyone, as far as I can see. Talk to you soon!"

Mrs. Petrie hung up, immediately dialled another number.

This conversation basically went the same direction as her conversation with Martha Schmidt, only this time, she was speaking with Bertha Savard, about Amelia. From what Lacey could discern from the one-sided conversation she overheard, Mrs. Savard collected 6 cheques between the time she called Social Services to report that Amelia had returned to the foster home, and when they actually checked up on the Savards!

Incredible, thought Lacey. *What a screwed-up system, affecting so many helpless kids. No wonder there were so many nutty people in the world.* Any of the foster kids that Lacey had met had absolutely zero chance of growing up 'normal'.

Realizing that Mrs. Petrie was getting ready to come in to the house, Lacey backed up quickly and raced to her room. Looking out her bedroom window, she heard Mr. Petrie's vehicle pull up into the driveway. Her heart pounding, she finalized her thoughts before going downstairs to set the table for supper.

Peter Petrie appeared and placed 2 large pizza boxes on the counter, before grabbing 4 bottles of beer and joining his wife on the veranda. Lacey set the oven to 'warm' and placed the pizzas in the oven until cocktail hour was over.

The Petries finished their drinks and then came in to the house and sat down at the table. Lacey called Lester and the twins, and then dished up the pizza onto each plate.

Supper was eaten in silence. When they were nearly finished, Mr. Petrie asked how the past week had gone in his absence. Mrs. Petrie placed the point of her high heel shoe on Lacey's foot and pressed down, hard! Lacey gasped, but said nothing, she just smiled at her foster mother, and then insolently winked at her!

Elsie Petrie smiled brightly, fakely. "Just fine, darling," she simpered. "Everything went wonderfully."

Before she could tell another lie, Lacey interrupted. "Your wife's full of dog crap, Mr. Petrie. You have no idea of the terrible things she does when you are not around. My brother Lloyd couldn't take it anymore. He's run off."

Before she could lose her nerve, Lacey continued. "I heard Mrs. Petrie on the phone today, first with Mrs. Schmidt and then with Mrs. Savard, talking about their missing foster kids, Charley, and Amelia. How they both falsely reported to Social Services that the girls had returned from running away. They never came back, then or now! They lied so their government cheques would keep on coming, in spite of the fact that they weren't looking after those girls any more."

Mrs. Petrie tried to interrupt. Lacey turned towards her and savagely hissed, "Shut up! I'm not done!"

Turning back to Mr. Petrie, tears coursing down her face and plopping onto the table, she continued. "Mr. Petrie, have you ever really looked at the black refrigerator in the back corner of your garage? Yes? No?" She waited briefly before speaking once again.

"I suggest we take a trip out there right now. We need to show you something that every one of us kids have experienced. Come with us!"

By this time, Mrs. Petrie looked like she tottered vicariously on the immediate, inner edge of a stroke! She didn't get up from the table with the rest of them. Shaking visibly, she simply sat still, awaiting their return and her impending fate.

Peter Petrie stared in horrified silence as Lacey demonstrated. She folded herself into the fridge, motioning to Lester to fasten the chain. Before he could do so, Mr. Petrie sprang forward. "Don't bother," he croaked. "I get it!"

"Follow us," Lacey said, "we have something more to show you. They headed for the mud room at the back of the house, where the offensive double-sided paddle hung ominously on the wall."

"Have a real close look at this paddle, Mr. Petrie, both sides. The smooth side hurts enough, but the other side leaves welts, and it hurts beyond what you can even begin to imagine. Your wife, the evil old witch, makes everyone stand in the living room and watch while she makes the target of her beating pull down their pants and lay over the footstool. Humiliates them beyond belief. She wallops that poor, pathetic, innocent kid with all of her adult strength. She even jumps up into the air so the paddle will hit with greater force!"

Mr. Petrie looked like he might pass out. "Why didn't you say something?" he croaked. "Why in Heaven's name didn't you say something?"

Lester answered for Lacey. "Because, Mr. Petrie, your evil, nasty, ugly bitch of a wife told us that if we ever said anything, she would take it out on Peter and Paula. Those little people don't deserve that. If Mrs. Petrie hit them with that paddle with the strength she has shown when she hits the bigger kids, she would kill them."

Mr. Petrie sank to the floor. He pulled his knees up to his chin, placed his face down on top of them. Sobbing audibly, he could only whisper incoherently. He rocked back and forth, repeating incessantly, "I didn't know! Honest to God, I did not know!"

"Yeah, well, so you didn't know," Lacey said woodenly. "More to the point, though, what are you going to do about it, now that you do know?"

"I don't know what to do," he said piteously. "I just don't know what to do!"

Lacey said, contemptuously, "I know, and I'm not even an adult. Hell, thanks to people like your wife, I've never even been a kid!"

"How about calling Social Services and getting us all placed in new foster homes, for starters," Lester offered.

"I can do that," Mr. Petrie said. Standing up shakily, he turned and headed towards the kitchen table.

Elsie held her hand out towards her husband, beseechingly. Peter slapped her hand away. Without even a further glance, he walked over to the telephone.

"I need to speak with the social worker that looks after the foster children placed in our home," he said into the receiver. "My name is Peter Petrie, and my wife is Elsie Petrie. Yes, it is urgent, please call her cell phone!"

"Peter!" Elsie Petrie wailed. "Don't do that! I can explain!"

He ignored her, simply stood waiting for his call to transfer. He spoke tersely to the person on the other end of the line. "We have an emergency situation here, ma'am. We have 4 foster kids placed in our home, in my wife's care. I need you to come to our house. Yes, **NOW!** These kids need to be moved immediately. I want you to ensure that no other children are ever again placed in our care, **EVER!** And I want you to bring a police officer with you. Charges need to be laid against Elsie Petrie. No, it cannot wait. I don't give a tinker's damn that it is already 8 o'clock at night. This is an emergency."

"And, by the way, tell the police officer that is coming with you, that there's yet another missing teenager."

"Now, please, hurry!" (The 'please' an afterthought, but he figured this was one time where there might be more benefit from getting flies with sugar, rather than with vinegar.)

He hung up. He walked over to his wife, who was still sitting at the table, mewling like a frightened kitten. Only she wasn't a kitten. She was a vicious, man-eating tiger. He could barely stomach standing beside her.

Mr. Petrie stared at his wife. Pure, unadulterated hatred spewed from his eyes. "Don't you move, woman." he spat bitterly, "Don't you fucking move, or I will tie you to this chair."

With an abrupt change of tone and demeanour, Peter Petrie turned to the children. "Best you get your things packed, kids. Lacey, if you wouldn't mind, can you help the twins? No matter what, you won't be spending another night in this Hansel and Gretel house, even if I have to take you to a hotel until you can be placed somewhere else."

As if a single person, all 4 children surrounded Mr. Petrie, hugging him fiercely.

"We believe you, Mr. Petrie," Lacey said softly, "We believe that you didn't know what was going on. The only successful thing that Mrs. Petrie did? She made us all believe that we had to convince you that things were just fine, whenever you came home. When you left? Wasn't your fault. Your wife's a great actress in your presence."

Peter laughed, a bitter, dry sound from his parched throat. "My ex-wife, you mean. I don't want to lay eyes on that evil person ever again. Now, please get packed. I'm doing the same."

They all left the room at once, leaving Elsie Petrie sitting ashen faced, ghostly white, unable to move or to speak, unable to explain herself. Even to herself.

Chapter 9
Stumpy and Hilda Somers

It was nearly 11 p.m. by the time a Social Services worker showed up at the Petries' house. She was accompanied by 2 R.C.M.P. officers.

Before they rang the doorbell, one of the officers took out his phone and dialled the Petries' number. Peter Petrie answered the phone. He assured the officer that it would be safe for them to come in. He opened the front door, inviting them into the house.

Elsie Petrie still sat motionless, her cheeks raw and flaming red from her bitter, salty tears that had not stopped flowing since the confrontation at the supper table.

Mr. Petrie gave a concise recounting of the evening's events to the policemen and the social worker.

When he was finished, the officers walked over to Mrs. Petrie. "Stand up, please, ma'am," one of the officers said. "You are coming with us." She just sat rooted to her chair, staring uncomprehendingly at her husband. He stood as far away from her as possible.

Finally, she spoke in a broken voice. "Peter, what is wrong with you? Why are you doing this to me? They can't arrest me for simple discipline measures! You are rarely around, you don't know how difficult these children are when you aren't at home. They had to be disciplined, don't you see? Don't make me go away. Don't let them take me away!"

"We can give the little monsters back to Social Services and you and I can continue with our life. We were happy, before the foster brats, we... "

"Shut up, Elsie," her husband interrupted her. His voice was ice as he spoke quietly. "There is no longer any you and me. You and I are no more. In fact, I hope you rot for what you have done."

"I'm no better than you, because I was negligent. I should have paid more attention. There had to be signs, no matter how subtle, no matter how skilled these children were at hiding your crimes. I should have known. At the very least, I should have let the children know that they could tell me anything, anything at all! I let them all down."

He turned to the officers. "Get her out of my sight! I will come to the detachment tomorrow and write out a statement. Do you want statements from the 2 older children, as well?"

"Yes, sir," the younger police officer said. "We need statements from them."

Peter Petrie then told them that Lloyd Jordan, one of their teenage wards, was missing. The officer said that if it was okay with Mr. Petrie, he could file a separate statement at the detachment when he came in the next day.

"OK, Mrs. Petrie," the older officer said. "Come with us now. You will spend tonight in a holding cell at the detachment. It's unusual to house a female prisoner overnight, but I checked. There are no other prisoners at the detachment tonight, and our female guard is willing to have you stay there."

"I want a lawyer!" Elsie Petrie whined, testy and terrified at the same time. "You can't question me without a lawyer!"

"No intention of it, ma'am," the older officer said. "If you have a lawyer, you can phone him or her from the detachment. If you don't have a lawyer, we will give you a list and you can pick a lawyer from there to call."

It took both policemen to lift the distraught woman out of her chair and lead her out to the R.C.M.P. cruiser.

Mr. Petrie turned to the social worker. "What now?" he wearily asked.

"Well, sir," she replied. "We have arranged for another foster home for Lester and the twins. The couple are prepared to take them in tonight, no matter how late we arrive. They live about an hour east of here. They are wonderful people. Unfortunately, Lester will have to change schools."

The woman turned to Lacey. "I am just waiting for a telephone call back from Hilda Somers. Mrs. Somers has agreed to take you as soon as she is able to contact her husband, Stumpy, who is out of town on farming business. He will be back tomorrow and if he is agreeable, (and I am quite sure he will be), then I can take you there tomorrow, right after school."

"There are 2 very good things about this placement, Lacey," she continued. "Mr. and Mrs. Somers just live 2 kilometres down the road. That means you will not only be able to continue at your present school, you will get there on the same school bus."

"They don't have any other foster children. Although they have housed foster children for many, many years, they decided recently that they needed to semi-retire from fostering. However, being the kindly people that they are, they couldn't give up being foster parents all at once. Even though they are no longer young, they have applied to Social Services to foster just one child, preferably a teenager."

She smiled at Lacey. "You, Miss Lacey, qualify on both counts!"

The worker turned once again to Mr. Petrie. "Are you okay with Lacey spending the night here? I can meet you at the detachment tomorrow morning. I will bring Lester with me so he can complete his statement."

"Of course, Lacey can stay," Mr. Petrie said. "Lester can also, if it makes it easier for you in the morning. You wouldn't have to drive all the way to the detachment."

"That's a kind offer, Peter," she said. "I thought about that, but I think the twins would benefit from having at least one familiar face around, as they adjust to their new placement."

Mr. Petrie nodded with complete understanding. He walked over to Lester and shook his hand. "I am so sorry, Lester, that I let you all down. As I said, I should have seen something, anything."

"Just so you know, the very first thing that gets done tomorrow morning – I'm taking the door off that old fridge, chopping that offending chain into many pieces. Then, Lacey and I are going to throw that sucker in the county landfill."

"Goodbye, Lester, you've been a model foster child. Behave yourself at your new foster home, and concentrate on your studies. The best way for you to forget the horrors you've endured here is to get an education and live the rest of your life being a better person than Mrs. Petrie was."

Lacey stepped up to Lester and gave him a hug, whispering in his ear as she did so, "I'll miss you, Lester. Keep an eye on those twins for me! Hopefully, we'll see each other again someday. Good luck!" She stepped back, tears glistening in her eyes, a lump choking off her airway. Following Lester and the social worker outside, Lacey stood on the veranda and waved at the vehicle until it was gone from her sight.

Just as she was going to say goodnight to Mr. Petrie, the phone rang.

When Peter hung up the phone, he turned to Lacey and told her that Stumpy Somers was delighted to hear they were taking in a teenage girl as their newest foster child. They would be expecting her tomorrow after school, and were very much looking forward to meeting her.

Lacey mumbled an exhausted "Good night, Mr. Petrie" before dragging her feet up the stairs to her room. Once she crawled into bed, she lay awake in the dark for a very long time.

Oh, Lloyd, where are you? she thought. *What kind of things are you finding out? Are you lost, hurt, in danger? Have you found Charley? Amelia? Annie? Don't forget to check the Mailbox and leave me a note from time to time, even if it is through Susanna.*
I miss you, Lloyd. Things just go from bad to worse it seems. Tomorrow, I go to yet another foster home and you won't know where to find me. I intend to call Mrs. Bronson and give her my new address and phone number so, when you try to find me, she will have something to tell you.

Lacey sat down at her little makeshift desk and wrote a letter to Lloyd. She would put it in the Mailbox in the morning, so Lloyd would be able to find her when he came back. Feeling only marginally better, but satisfied that she at least had the letter completed, she crawled into bed. Completely drained, beyond exhausted, Lacey tossed and turned in her bed, unable to sleep.

After what seemed like hours, Lacey finally fell into a fitful sleep. Lonely, tears of frustration and uncertainty puddled and glowed on her cheeks, highlighted by the silvery light of the moon outside her open bedroom window.

After all the disturbing events of the night before, both Mr. Petrie and Lacey slept late. They didn't hear the honk of the school bus horn when Lester and

Lacey weren't waiting at the end of the driveway. They didn't hear the frustrated roar of the school bus engine as the driver finally left without his charges.

At 9 o'clock, Lacey finally dragged herself out of bed and into the shower. Holding the sheet of paper containing the letter to Lloyd tightly gripped in her hand, she quietly tiptoed down the stairs. She left a note on the kitchen table that simply said she was out for a run and would be back soon – in time to make them some breakfast. She let herself out the back door, making sure to hang on to the door so it wouldn't make a sound as it shut. She then took off, running as fast as she could in the direction of the Mailbox.

When Lacey arrived at the flat rock, she was huffing and puffing for air. She lowered herself on to the rock and lay on her belly until she caught her breath. For a few minutes more, she lay there, staring over the edge, mesmerized by the view of the water flowing lazily along the ravine below her.

Once she was able to breathe normally again, she went to the Mailbox and reached inside. Knowing there would be no word from Lloyd, but disappointed nonetheless, her fingers blindly, unsuccessfully, searched for a note, a letter, anything! Nothing.

Lacey reached into her pocket and took out the folded-up letter to Lloyd. She put it inside the tree trunk, out of sight, out of the weather, but in a spot where she knew Lloyd or Susanna could retrieve it.

Looking up at the sky, Lacey uttered a silent prayer. For the safety of the missing girls, for Lloyd's safe return, for her own safety as she moved to yet another new foster home. She prayed for her parents, even though she knew deep in her heart that they were either dead or didn't care a whit about either of their children. Prayed out, she turned and began to run back to the Petrie house.

Out of breath once again, she quietly let herself in. The smell of toast and bacon wafted enticingly in the air. Stepping into the kitchen, she found Mr. Petrie sitting at the table, patiently waiting for Lacey.

"Good walk, Lacey?" he asked.

"Yes, thank you, I did. I just needed some fresh air and solitude after last night. I hope I didn't worry you."

"No, my dear, you did not. You have a level head on your shoulders for someone so young. Thanks for leaving the note though. Now, wash up, breakfast is ready. It's keeping warm in the oven."

When Lacey returned to the kitchen a few minutes later, Mr. Petrie was sitting at the table, a lengthy missive in front of him.

She took the 2 plates out of the oven and placed them on the table. She then sat silently and waited for Mr. Petrie before she began to eat her meal.

After a couple more minutes, Mr. Petrie scrawled his signature across the bottom of the last page, moved everything out of the way.

Looking at Lacey, he explained that he had decided to write out his statement while he waited for her. It would save time at the police detachment.

"Hardest thing I've ever had to do," he told her. "We've been married for nearly 25 years. I knew she could be kind of cranky, but I never had any inkling that she was downright ugly mean! It's criminal, what she put you kids through."

"What do you think will happen to her?" Lacey asked.

"Not sure, but figure she'll either face criminal charges or they'll send her to a mental institution to get her head read. Time will tell, I guess, but my choice would be to lock her up in a psychiatric ward, which is where she belongs. Throw away the key. But," he sighed, "it's not in my hands, is it? Only one thing is for damn sure. She won't be moving back in with me!"

Lacey began to clear the table.

Peter Petrie pushed his chair away, stood up, and announced, "While you are clearing away the breakfast dishes, I'll load up that old fridge and we'll drop it off at the dump on our way to the police station."

Lacey quietly pointed out to him that perhaps he shouldn't do away with the fridge quite yet. They might need it as evidence if Mrs. Petrie had to go to trial.

Mr. Petrie smacked himself in the forehead. "Oh, good Lord! Of course! I was just so anxious to get it out of the place I didn't think! Thanks, Lacey!"

"Well, I'll just take that wooden paddle and put it in the fridge. When you are done in the kitchen, we might as well hit the road, what do you say?"

Lacey nodded.

She asked Mr. Petrie if he would call the school and tell them why she wasn't in class today. He immediately went over to the phone and made the call.

"Mr. Petrie," Lacey said hesitantly, "I don't feel comfortable giving a report to the police about Mrs. Petrie's actions."

"Why not?"

She smiled, a bitter, sad grimace rather than a full-out smile.

"My brother Lloyd and I tried to let Social Services know about one particularly terrible foster home we lived in. We were just totally ignored. The next foster home wasn't much (or any) better than the one before. We had one terrific home, but Susanna's mother died. We had another one that was just OK, but the rest were crap. So, I doubt very much that the police will believe me this time, either! So, my reason? It is because foster care people don't give a crap about foster kids. No matter how I try, I haven't had any luck having adults believe me."

"Mrs. Bronson, a child care worker in B.C., gave me her business card and her cell phone number. She told me to call any time, whenever I needed to. That was a laugh! We got nowhere with her either. Oh, she sounded great, said she would have Alberta Social Services look into it. Nothing happened!" She continued bitterly, "But I'm going to have to trust that if I call her and give her my new foster home information, she will give it to Lloyd, when he calls her to find out where I am."

Peter Petrie looked earnestly at Lacey. "I believe you, Lacey, and I'll make sure the police believe you too. I took pictures of that old fridge with the chain around it, and I brought the dreadful paddle in the truck, all ready to show the police. You will have to give them a written, sworn statement, meaning that you swear that what you write down is the absolute truth."

135

"Now, kiddo, get your jacket. Let's get this over with. Then we'll come back here and wait for the social worker to come get you and take you to your next home. I'll wait for you in the truck."

As Lacey gathered her things together, she looked at the table. Mr. Petrie's statement was still there. She picked it up and took it with her out to the vehicle.

"You forgot your statement," she said as she climbed in. "I brought it with me. Here."

"Oh, man!" Mr. Petrie groaned. "I guess this mess has me more upset than I realized. Thanks for bringing the statement, Lacey. Now let's see if I can get us to the detachment in one piece."

He backed out of the driveway. They made the trip in silence, he dwelling on the end of his marriage, Lacey on whether or not she could convince the police that the abuse really and truly happened.

The clerk at the main desk in the police station asked them the nature of their visit. After Mr. Petrie explained, she directed them to an interview room, and then asked if she could bring them something to drink. Both Mr. Petrie and Lacey declined. They sat silently, waiting.

After about 15 minutes, the clerk poked her head into the room, explaining that the officers would be here in about another 15 minutes. This time, Mr. Petrie asked for a cup of coffee. Lacey asked for a Coke. Both beverages arrived very quickly.

A light tap on the door signalled the arrival of the 2 officers who had been at the Petrie home the evening before.

"I'm sorry," Mr. Petrie said, "but I don't remember your names. As you can well imagine, this whole mess has me somewhat addled."

"Certainly understandable, sir," said the older officer. "I'm Sergeant Fred Gablehaus, this is Constable Parker Sutton."

Glancing through papers from the file folder the sergeant had in front of him, he read silently for a few moments. Looking up, he said quietly, "Now, Mr. Petrie, tell me about the events of last night."

Peter Petrie held out his written statement. "I have it all here, sir," he said. "I thought it might save some time today, writing it out beforehand."

"Thank you, Mr. Petrie," Sergeant Gablehaus said. "It will save time but humour me please, for right now, just tell me in your own words, what happened last night."

Mr. Petrie took a deep breath and recited the events as he recalled them.

When he was through, Constable Sutton patted Lacey gently on her arm. "Your turn," he said. "Just tell us in your own words what happened last night, and what has happened to you during the time you've been staying at the Petrie's place.

"Bear in mind that you can only tell us what happened to you, what you saw, what you heard or saw happening to another child in the Petrie's care. You can't tell us about anything that someone else told you happened. You must have seen or heard it for yourself. Understand?"

Lacey nodded. She took a deep, steadying breath, and then recalled in complete detail the things that went on during the time that she and her brother had been in the Petries' foster care.

At one point, Constable Sutton interrupted her. "Where is your brother, Lacey? I don't recall meeting him last night. Why isn't he here, giving his statement?" Peter Petrie answered for Lacey.

He said, "That is the 2nd reason why we're here today, sir. I told you last night. Lloyd Jordan ran away. We are here to file a missing person's report, as well as deal with this other stuff."

"Okay, then, first things first. Have you anything more to add, Miss Jordan?" Constable Sutton asked.

"No sir, just that I want you to know that I'm telling the truth! I don't lie."

Sergeant Gablehaus replaced the papers in the file folder, including Mr. Petrie's hand-written statement.

He handed Lacey a pad of paper and a pen.

"We need you to write down everything you told us on this pad of paper, please. Just write it like you told it. You don't have to be eloquent or fancy, just completely truthful. When you are finished with that statement, we will come back and deal with your missing brother."

"Mr. Petrie, please wait out in the front lobby until she is done."

"Actually, your wife is still in cells here. She has a court appearance tomorrow morning. After that, she will likely be transferred to a holding facility for women. If you would like to see her, this is a good time."

"Not interested," Mr. Petrie said. "She has done enough damage. I don't care to speak with her or see her, either now, or ever again. Thanks, though," he added sardonically.

"No problem, just wondering if you wanted to see her," the Sergeant said.

By this time, Lacey was busy writing and barely noticed when the men left the room.

It took her more than an hour to hand-write her statement, but when she was finished, she was satisfied that it was as truthful and as complete as she could offer it.

The young constable came back into the room. Lacey handed him her statement.

"Now what?" she asked him.

"Well, Sergeant Gablehaus will be back in shortly with Mr. Petrie. We'll fill out a missing person report on your brother. While we are doing that, our office clerk will type out your statement and Mr. Petrie's statement. You will have to read your statement over, once it is typed and if everything is in order, you will sign it."

"What about Mrs. Petrie?" she asked.

"She will appear in court tomorrow morning. She will either plead guilty or not guilty, or her counsel, if she has counsel, will request an adjournment. If she doesn't have counsel yet, the judge may grant an adjournment to allow her time to obtain a lawyer."

"The Crown Prosecutor may request a psychiatric assessment. If so, the judge might very well send her to Alberta Hospital to get a psychiatric report done. If that is the case, she will have to stay in hospital until the assessment is complete and then appear in court again. If no psych assessment is ordered, unless she is granted bail, she will stay in remand at Ft. Saskatchewan, if there is room, until her next court appearance."

"If she is remanded to Ft. Saskatchewan, any court appearance prior to a trial would likely be held by closed circuit television (CCTV). In other words, she very likely would not have to appear here in Northern Alberta until her actual trial."

"Oh." Lacey watched the officer from the corner of her eye. She could think of nothing to say to him. She did, however, think that he was really very nice, and also very hot!

"How old are you, Lacey?" the constable suddenly asked.

Lacey crossed her fingers under the table. "I'm 14," she fibbed.

"Really! I thought you were older than that."

"I feel a lot older," she replied. "My brother and I have been through a lot of stuff. I was 9 and Lloyd was 13 when our mother just walked away and left us on our own. Our dad was in prison for embezzlement. Don't know where either of them are now. Dad could be back in prison, for all we know."

For the briefest of moments, Lacey debated whether or not to continue, then she blurted out, "Just so you know, the foster care system really sucks. In my opinion, there is no way to improve it either."

"Really? Why's that, Lacey?" Constable Sutton asked.

"Because," she responded acridly, "not a single person believes kids when they try to tell an adult how bad things really are. They just don't. So, kids have to remain in an abusive home until they're either old enough that they can no longer be in foster care, or they run away before then."

"Even when they run away, there is only a minimal search for them before they are given up on. My 3 friends and my brother could all be dead for anyone knows, or even cares."

Despite her best efforts she could not control the bitter tears that ravelled down her cheeks.

Uncomfortable, not knowing how to respond, Constable Sutton stood up.

"Just going to get us a cold drink, Lacey," he said. "Coke?"

"Sure, that'd be fine."

Waiting for him to return, she reached into her jacket pocket for a tissue. Deep at the bottom her fingers encountered a card. Withdrawing it, she realized that it was Evelyn Bronson's card with her cell number on it.

Constable Sutton returned with the beverages.

Lacey gave him a calculating look before asking, "Do you think that it would be OK if I used a phone to call my British Columbia social worker? She left me her card and said that if ever I needed anything, to call her."

"I'm sure it will be fine, Lacey. You'll just have to wait and call once we are done here, OK?"

Lacey nodded.

Before the silence could become uncomfortable, the door opened. Sergeant Gablehaus and Mr. Petrie entered the room.

Mr. Petrie sat down beside Lacey. The sergeant handed a typed statement to each of them and requested that they read it very carefully. If they detected any errors or needed to change anything, they should speak up. Once they reviewed the documents, they would sign them in front of Sergeant Gablehaus.

During the silence that ensued while they were reading, Lacey could feel the eyes of Constable Sutton on her. She blushed slightly, but continued reviewing her statement.

Several minutes passed before both Lacey and Mr. Petrie looked up, reading completed. The typed statements were signed, witnessed by Sergeant Gablehaus, and handed to Constable Sutton. He left the room to give the file to the front desk clerk.

When he returned, attention was focused on a new file, that of the missing Lloyd.

Sergeant Gablehaus asked Lacey to recount in as much detail as possible, the events on the day that Lloyd ran away.

She said that he hadn't run away. He had left the foster home to look for the missing 3 girls.

Sergeant Gablehaus interrupted her briefly, asking for the names of the missing girls.

Lacey told him, "Charlotte, we called her Charley. She was at George and Martha Schmidt's foster home with Lloyd and me. The 2nd girl was Amelia. That was at Simon and Bertha Savard's place. The 3rd girl, Annie, at Mr. and Mrs. Petrie's."

"Do you know their last names, and their ages?" Sergeant Gablehaus asked, not unkindly.

"Yes, sir. Charley Ford. She was 14. Amelia Anderson was 16. Annie Barkley was 16 also."

"And your brother, Lloyd? What's his full name, and how old was he?"

My brother's full name is Braden Lloyd Jordan, but he's called Lloyd. He's 17."

She explained how she had unexpectedly recalled details of the truck that had picked up each of the girls on the 3 separate occasions. She gave them the details of the 'pumpkin truck' that Lloyd had written down when he had watched Annie climb in. She handed the paper to the sergeant.

Sergeant Gablehaus looked directly at Lacey. "Your brother's been gone long enough. Why didn't you report him missing sooner?"

"I knew that it would take him some time to track down the girls. He promised to keep in touch. I just figured he is still looking for them. I did ask Mrs. Petrie whether or not we should report him missing. She said no, that he had 'made his bed, now he should lay in it'."

"Besides," Lacey continued, with an apologetic glance towards Mr. Petrie, "I heard her talking on the telephone with Martha Schmidt. I heard her tell Mrs.

Schmidt that Lloyd could look after himself. She said she didn't intend to report him missing because she would keep collecting money for his care if she didn't report it."

Lacey did not tell the sergeant that Uncle Henry was supposed to be looking for him, with the help of his friend in British Columbia.

"Okay," Sergeant Gablehaus said, "We'll get a bulletin out on Lloyd right away. In fact, I think it might be prudent to re-post the bulletins regarding the 3 missing girls as well."

"We will not, however, be posting the details of the 'pumpkin truck' as you call it. That is a clarifying detail that shouldn't be made public yet. We will do a search of that vehicle and that licence plate and see if the results will lead us anywhere. Please keep that information to yourselves until I advise you otherwise.

"I can promise you, Miss Lacey Jordan, that we will actively search for your brother and the 3 girls. Constable Sutton, here, will keep Mr. Petrie advised. I'm sure he will, in turn, let you know what is going on."

Lacey wasn't sure if the Sergeant meant Mr. Petrie or Constable Sutton would let her know. She hoped he meant Parker Sutton!

Getting up from the conference table, Sergeant Gablehaus thanked them for coming in, and left the room. Peter Petrie followed him out.

Lacey held back, looking shyly at Constable Sutton. "Thanks, Constable Sutton," she said. "I appreciate you telling me about what Mrs. Petrie will be going through."

"Nice to meet you, Lacey," Cst. Parker Sutton said. "I'd sure like to see you again someday, after you are a bit older!"

He grinned, shook her hand, holding it a little longer than necessary. "I can promise you one thing, Lacey. No matter what, I won't give up on finding your brother or those missing girls."

Mr. Petrie was standing in the front office, in earnest conversation with the sergeant. Lacey stood at a respectful distance, waiting for him.

After several minutes, he shook Sergeant Gablehaus's hand. Turning to Lacey, he said, "OK, kiddo, let's go."

She suddenly remembered that she needed to phone Mrs. Bronson. Approaching Sergeant Gablehaus, she asked him if she could use a telephone. She explained to him who she was calling, and why.

He took her to a tiny office, just off the front entry. "Take your time, Lacey," he said. "I'll leave you be. See you again."

Mr. Petrie motioned to her that he would wait in the truck and left the detachment.

Evelyn Bronson answered on the 3rd ring. She seemed harried, in a hurry. Lacey ignored the sense of urgency emanating from the other end of the line. She filled Mrs. Bronson in on all of the events. The conversation took a long time. Shortly after it began, Mrs. Bronson shed her coat, listening carefully to everything that Lacey was telling her.

"Dear God!" she kept saying. "What in Heaven's name?"

When Lacey concluded by telling Mrs. Bronson that she was going to yet another foster home, Mrs. Bronson told her that she was going to immediately contact Alberta Social Services to report the abuse of the system by Mrs. Petrie. She promised to contact Lacey at Stumpy and Hilda Somers' place to see how she was doing, and to give her any information she might find out about Lloyd.

"Thanks for calling, Lacey," Evelyn Bronson said. "I'm sorry I wasn't able to help you."

"Do you think Jayson Silverman might be able to help?" Lacey asked. It seemed to her that men got more breaks in the world than women or girls. It was a long shot, but somehow Lacey thought he might know something more than Mrs. Bronson did.

There was silence on the line. Then Mrs. Bronson said, "Jayson is no longer with Social Services, Lacey."

"What!!" Lacey croaked. "Where is he? Lloyd didn't know that. Mr. Silverman gave him his card and told him to call if he needed help. You'd think he would have at least let Lloyd know that he was leaving!"

"He left very unexpectedly, Lacey. I really don't know any details. Just, I showed up for work one morning, went to his office to talk about a file, and he was gone!"

Lacey was silent. "Well, I did tell Lloyd that if I got moved to a new foster home before he got back, that I would leave word with you. He has your phone number as well as Mr. Silverman's. Please, Mrs. Bronson, if Lloyd calls you, give him Mr. and Mrs. Somers' telephone number. I'm sure he will be calling very soon with news. I just know it!"

"You know I will, Lacey," Evelyn Bronson said firmly. "Good luck at your new foster home. I promise, I'll let you know immediately if I find out anything of consequence.

"You take care now, Miss Lacey." Evelyn choked tearfully as she hung up her phone.

Lacey left the detachment and climbed up into Mr. Petrie's truck.

"Think we should stop for a bite to eat before we go home," Mr. Petrie said. "I'm getting a trifle peckish, how about you? There's a gas station restaurant down the road that serves a mean burger."

"I could eat something," Lacey said.

"Did you get hold of your B.C. social worker?" he asked.

Lacey snorted bitterly and then told him about her conversation with Mrs. Bronson.

"Can you believe it?" she asked. "Mr. Silverman just took off without a word to anyone, not even Mrs. Bronson, his co-worker! Poor Lloyd, now he has no one to ask for help."

"Well, at least I gave him Mrs. Bronson's phone number. She promised me she would call if she hears from him. I said, 'You mean **WHEN** Mrs. Bronson, not **IF**.'"

Lacey sat quietly during the remainder of the short drive to the restaurant. She didn't feel hungry, but she ordered a burger and a milk shake. They were delicious and, despite her despair, Lacey ate and drank every bit of her lunch.

By the time they reached the Petrie house, the social worker was already there, waiting in her car.

Mr. Petrie looked at Lacey, "You're packed and ready to go?"

"Yes," Lacey replied. "I'll just go get my things."

Mr. Petrie went over to speak to the woman while Lacey gathered up her few belongings and then went out to the vehicle.

She turned to Mr. Petrie. "Thanks, Mr. Petrie, for helping me these past 2 days. I sure wish you had been around more, but I totally understand that 'work is work'. That's what my mother used to say when I would ask her why my dad was rarely at home."

"I'm sorry you now have to live all alone. Take care, and hopefully I will see you again before too long."

Peter Petrie stood in the driveway, gazing vacantly at the departing vehicle long after it vanished from his sight. He then turned and shuffled into the house, where he immediately began to pack up all his wife's clothes. He didn't want any reminder of that hideous woman anywhere.

Lacey was too frustrated to care about what her new foster home would be like. All she wanted was to hear from Lloyd. She wanted him to call with great news, namely that he had found the missing 3 girls. She wanted him to call and say he was coming back, or at least to call and say he was OK.

The social worker seemed to understand Lacey's need to just be. She didn't disturb her with a bunch of useless questions. In fact, she simply drove in silence, saying nothing at all.

The Somers' farm was only a couple of kilometres past the Petrie house. About 300 metres from the main road, the farmhouse looked very inviting. It was a large bungalow, with nice, clean, white siding, black trim, and black shingles on the roof. A spacious screened-in veranda encircled 3 sides of the house. Multiple sets of comfortable looking padded lawn furniture were positioned on all sides of the veranda. Despite some misgivings, Lacey found herself wanting to pick and choose the direction she wanted to face if she was relaxing on that peaceful veranda.

A vegetable garden grew around the back of the house. A hedge of Saskatoon bushes surrounded the garden. The outbuildings included a small barn, a machine shed, and a chicken house. A triple-car garage was attached to the house.

Stumpy and Hilda Somers rose as one from the loveseat beside the front door, both smiling broadly.

In spite of her gloomy thoughts, and the events of the past, Lacey found herself responding positively to the friendly looking couple.

Approaching the veranda, Mr. and Mrs. Somers met her half-way.

Hilda Somers asked if she could give her a hug. Lacey, not used to being asked about anything, shrugged her shoulders in a non-committal gesture. After a brief, friendly hug, Lacey decided that Mrs. Somers' hug was just the medicine she needed!

Stumpy Somers put one hand on her shoulder while he shook her hand energetically with his other. His eyes twinkled as he introduced himself.

"Well, Miss Lacey Jordan, it is such a pleasure to meet you. We assure you, we are delighted to have you stay with us, just delighted. I'm Stumpy, and this here's the love of my life, Hilda. We sure hope that you will like it here."

"Just so you know, you will be treated as a grown-up person, not some little kid. If there is anything you want to know, or tell us about, don't be bashful. You can say or ask anything of us, as long as you are polite and don't take the Lord's name in vain. We're not church-going folk, but just look around at the beauty surrounding our little farm here. You can't look at that view and tell me that some higher power greater than lowly man didn't design this part of the world!"

Hilda Somers put her hand on her husband's arm. "Stumpy, give the gal a break. There's lots of time to wear her ears out with your jawing. Why don't you get her things out of the car so that the lady can get on the road again."

She turned to Lacey and gently suggested that Lacey say goodbye to the lady who had delivered her to the farm. She said she would then show Lacey around the house.

Lacey walked over to the car. "Can you do me a favour?" she asked the woman.

"Certainly, anything, Lacey."

Lacey gave her a piece of paper on which she had written Evelyn Bronson's name, address, work phone number, and her cell number.

Before she could explain, the social worker smiled at her. "Yes, don't worry, if I find out anything, anything at all, I will let you know, and I will let Mrs. Bronson know. I have worked with Evelyn on other files. I greatly admire her and will be pleased to be able to put our brains together to see if we can come up with some solutions regarding your brother and the missing girls."

"Here is my card if you need to get in touch with me." Handing a business card to Lacey, she then said, "Well, I had better get on the road again, but one thing I must tell you. These are great people, Lacey. I have never placed a foster kid in this home who wasn't happy here. They have looked after more fosters than a schoolhouse full of children, so I know whereof I speak!"

With a wink and a wave, the woman got into her car and drove away.

Lacey glanced down at the card in her hand. The social worker's name was Victoria Linfield. Lacey sincerely hoped that she wouldn't have to contact her for any reason. She did, however, place her card in the same jacket pocket as Evelyn Bronson's card.

Mr. Somers had already disappeared with Lacey's meager belongings. Mrs. Somers was waiting patiently to give Lacey the tour.

The aroma of fresh baking tantalized them as they entered the front door. Lacey felt her mouth begin to water.

The inside of the home was as warm and inviting as the outside. The kitchen counter was full of freshly baked bread, buns, and cinnamon buns.

Bright and cheery, each room in the house contained large windows. The Somers' bedroom was located at the far end of the house. There were 3 large bedrooms, each with its own separate bathroom, located at the opposite end. Each bedroom had a door that opened on to the veranda. Lacey couldn't help herself. She began to think that this might be a really good foster home. She wasn't however, naïve enough to believe it completely. After all, she had thought that each of the previous fosters were good places. How wrong she had been, most of the time!

She turned to Mrs. Somers. "Which room is mine?"

"Whichever you choose, my dear," Hilda said. "You are our only foster child. Take your pick."

Lacey chose the room furthest away from the Somers' bedroom, even though any bedroom of the 3 was far enough away to be totally private.

The room she chose was lovely, decorated in warm and inviting colours. There was a double bed, a large dresser, a desk with a proper adjustable chair, and a large bookcase filled with books. Beside the bookcase there was a comfortable rocking chair and footstool, just the perfect spot to cozy up in the chair, under the colourful afghan that lay across its back.

The bathroom was roomy. A combination shower/soaker tub filled one end. There was lots of shelving for makeup, and a nice deep sink. There was even a linen closet filled with matching towels.

Mrs. Somers observed Lacey. "Think this will suit you, Lacey?" she asked.

"Oh yes, ma'am, it will more than suit. Thank you."

Lacey stared at Hilda Somers for a minute. "What shall I call you, ma'am?" she asked Hilda.

"Whatever you're comfortable with. Our previous foster children always called us Mr. Stumpy and Mrs. Hilda. How does that sound?"

"Sounds fine, ma'am," Lacey said.

"Sounds fine, Mrs. Hilda," Hilda gently corrected Lacey. "Now, why don't you get unpacked while I get supper started. When you are done, come on back to the kitchen."

"You know, Lacey, I already know about your background and that your brother is missing. I hope you will be happy here, and I truly hope that your brother shows up soon. When he does, he is most welcome to stay here as well. Stumpy and I will pray for him to come back safely to you."

"Now, I will leave you to get settled. See you in the kitchen." Hilda Somers turned and left the room, closing the door gently behind her.

It didn't take Lacey long to get unpacked. She was getting used to being shuffled from home to home like some bag of wilting groceries. She pretty much had the unpacking routine down to a fine art.

She left her room and looked in each of the other 2 bedrooms. Satisfied that she had picked her favourite, she slowly continued her walk towards the kitchen.

The living room looked nice. A big-screen television was mounted to the wall at one end of the room. A pair of easy chairs and a sofa sat opposite the TV. The room looked well used and comfortable. Lots of books and movies filled a wooden cabinet below the TV. Lacey noted that each and every book was not perfectly aligned. *Good sign,* she thought.

The laundry room door was open. She noticed that another door opened from the back of the laundry room into the garage. She couldn't help herself, she checked both the laundry room and the garage. Nowhere did she spot either an old fridge or a wooden paddle. There was a large stand up freezer in the garage. Shaking, holding her breath, she opened the door and looked in. It was full. Nothing in there but shelves filled with frozen meat, garden vegetables, and baking. Deep breath. *Another good sign,* Lacey thought.

Walking slowly, the only other rooms she noticed were a den containing a large desk, matching filing cabinets, and a bookcase, and a powder room, just off the kitchen.

Reaching the spacious kitchen, Lacey asked Mrs. Hilda if she could help her. Mrs. Hilda asked if she would like to set the table. "Just check out the cupboards and make yourself acquainted with the location of things," she told Lacey.

"I don't want you to think I'm snooping," Lacey said.

"Lands sakes, girl, it's not snooping! You live here now. Our home is your home. You just look away to your heart's content. There's nothing here you can't see."

In a few minutes, Mr. Stumpy came into the kitchen. Without asking her, he took 2 bottles of Coke out of the fridge and handed a bottle to Lacey. "Bad habit of mine," he said. "Shouldn't drink the stuff, but I gave up drinking booze 20 years ago. Gave up a bad habit for another, I suppose."

Mrs. Hilda teasingly offered, "That's not the only bad habit you've got, old man!" Winking at Lacey, she continued, "But, there is nothing so bad that I'm giving you away. We're stuck with each other 'til death do us part'. Can't say that I find that idea unwelcome."

The meal was delicious. Even more delicious was the cheerful banter that occurred during the entire meal. The Somers filled each other in on the happenings of their day. They included Lacey in their conversation, asking questions, but not pushing her to reveal anything about herself that she was not ready to.

Used to eating meals in silence, or at least having to listen to bitter, acrimonious insults hurled at the foster children, Lacey adjusted to the new meal routine in record time – probably under 2 minutes!

After eating all her meal and TWO giant, fresh-baked cinnamon buns, Lacey rose and began to clear the table.

"Not tonight, gal!" Stumpy protested. "I expect you have some homework to finish after the upheaval of the past couple days. Time enough for you to help with chores in a day or so. You go on, now, and get your homework done. Just come on into the living room and say goodnight before you go to bed."

"I'm telling you again, Miss Lacey, we are very happy to have you in our home, and we sure do hope you will be happy here."

Lacey went to her room and got her school supplies set up on the desk. Finishing her homework and doing a bit of studying, she then eagerly sat in the rocker beside the bookcase, a novel in her hand.

About an hour later, having heard nothing from Lacey's room, Stumpy and Hilda peeked in. Lacey was sound asleep in the rocker. Hilda went to wake her, Stumpy said, "Nah, just leave her be, my luv, just leave her be."

When Lacey's alarm rang the next morning she was still asleep in the rocking chair. She jumped to her feet, wondering for a minute where she was.

Good grief! she thought, *I slept through the entire night in my new home in a rocking chair!* She hurriedly went into her bathroom. A short time later, showered and dressed, backpack ready to go, she walked into the kitchen, where Stumpy and Hilda were already at the breakfast table.

Murmuring an apology, Lacey slipped into her chair. Her breakfast sat in front of her.

"Sleep well, my dear?" asked Hilda.

"Yes, ma'am – Mrs. Hilda," Lacey said. "Haven't slept through the night like that since my brother left." Glancing at the kitchen clock, she jumped up. "The school bus will be here any second I expect. I better get outside."

"You've still got a few minutes. I called the school when we found out you were coming, and they checked the school bus schedule. Don't have to kill yourself rushing outside."

"By the way, here is your lunch. Mr. Stumpy made it for you, so Heaven only knows what unhealthy stuff is in there, but I'm sure it will be delicious!"

"After today, though, you can make your own lunch. That way, you will have a lunch that you know you like." Mrs. Hilda handed her a very full lunch bag.

On impulse, Lacey gave Mrs. Hilda a brief hug. Turning to Mr. Stumpy, she simply touched his arm and said, "Thank you, Mr. Stumpy, for making my lunch and being so kind." Her eyes glistened as she turned toward the door. Hearing the bus coming down the road, she quickly ran to the end of the drive.

Between classes, Lacey spotted Susanna. She rushed over to her.

"Hey, Susanna! Any word?" She held her breath, waiting for Susanna to answer.

"Nothing, Lacey. Nothing at all."

"Really? Well, what about Uncle Henry's friend? Has he been able to figure anything out?"

Susanna shook her head sadly. "Dad's friend had a serious stroke. He will be OK, but not for a long time. They have moved him to a rehabilitation centre where he can have physiotherapy every day. Unfortunately, his speech is affected, and both hands are badly crippled up. He can't even write."

Lacey was quiet for a moment, then she said, "Of course, I'm very sorry for your dad's friend, but I'm also bitterly disappointed for us. I don't mean to be ungrateful, but darn it, Susanna, just DAMN!" Frustrated, unbidden tears once again. Lacey was beginning to think she was the world's biggest crybaby.

Susanna nodded, as worried and broken-hearted as her friend. She gave Lacey a quick hug, told her she would sit with her at lunch so she could hear all about her new foster home, and then ran off to her next class.

Lacey walked through the rest of the morning in a daze. Why hadn't Lloyd contacted someone? Mrs. Bronson promised Lacey she would call her as soon as she heard, Uncle Henry's friend could be of no further assistance. (*If he ever was of any assistance to begin with*, Lacey thought uncharitably).

With a shake of her head, she decided that she would get off the bus early after school and check out the Mailbox once again.

At noon, she and Susanna sat under a big tree and ate their lunch. Susanna asked Lacey lots of questions about her new foster home, and also about Mrs. Petrie.

Lacey told her all about it, including the fact that Mrs. Petrie had been arrested. She recounted going to the police station to fill out forms. She also told her about the hot young constable, turning an endearing red whenever she mentioned Constable Parker Sutton. She mentioned him often! Susanna didn't fail to take note of her friend's obvious attraction.

"Wow!" Susanna commented when she could squeeze in her observations. "You have had an eventful couple of days! I am really, really happy that you have finally got into such a great foster home, Lacey."

"Well, it's only been such a short time that I'm still holding my breath," Lacey said quietly, "but so far, it is awesome!"

"Mrs. Hilda said I can have friends stay over any time I want, and I want you to be my 1st friend to have a sleep-over with. What a change, hey? I'm really anxious to show you my new room. It's not as nice as my room at your place, but it's a close 2nd!"

"I'm going to get off the bus early on my way back to the Somers' place and check out the Mailbox. If there is anything there, I'll call you as soon as I get back to the farm."

"Sounds great, Lace." Susanna said, "Maybe Lloyd will phone this weekend. We just have to hope and pray that he'll call and that he's OK. We should watch the news on TV tonight and tomorrow, because I imagine the police will have something on the air about Lloyd's disappearance."

"Yup!" Lacey perked up briefly. "They're also going to redo the bulletins about Charley, Amelia, and Annie. You know, I just can't help but feel, that even after all this time, those girls are OK. If anyone can help them, Lloyd can. We just can't lose faith and quit believing that everything is OK."

Both girls frowned intently with new-found resolve as they headed back to class.

It was quite a bit further from the Mailbox to the Somers' place, but Lacey nonetheless stepped off the school bus at the same stop as she used to when she lived with the Schmidt's. She quickly made her way toward the secret place.

When she found nothing in the Mailbox, she sat down on the flat rock and cried bitterly.

Talking to herself all the way home, she tried to convince herself that Lloyd was OK, that he was just too far away to leave a message in the Mailbox. But, if he was OK, why didn't he phone Susanna, or at least call Mrs. Bronson? It was becoming increasingly difficult to keep a positive, upbeat attitude.

Feeling lonely and gloomy, she walked slowly. She just didn't have the 'oomph' to run or even walk quickly. By the time she got to the farm, Mr. Stumpy and Mrs. Hilda were waiting on the veranda, worried beyond belief.

Only when the 2 adults simultaneously hugged her until she thought she would be squashed to death in the group hug, did she realize just how late it was.

Lacey was very contrite. She apologized sincerely for being so late. She wasn't used to having people worry about her. It made her feel happy and sad at the same time.

On an unexpected but sudden impulse, she decided she was going to trust these 2 kind people. If they were that worried about their new foster kid, then she believed they truly did miss her and worry that something terrible had happened to her.

Lacey sat down beside them on the veranda.

Apologizing again, she explained where she had been and why. She didn't tell them the exact location of the secret Mailbox because she could not, she and Lloyd had made a pact. However, she did feel that she owed them the explanation.

Mr. Stumpy cleared his throat. "Lacey," he began gruffly, "you worried us near to death! We worried that something might have happened to you like it did to the other 3 missing foster girls. My missus was beside herself."

Hilda swatted him playfully. "Watch your tongue, old man. You were more worried than I was!"

"Come on, you 2, supper's keeping warm in the oven. It's 8 o'clock already. Let's eat." Lacey was suddenly starving.

Partway through the meal, Stumpy told Lacey that if she wanted to check out her Mailbox any time, he would drive her to where she wanted to get off, and then he would wait in the truck while she went to check. She wouldn't have to hurry, he would wait however long she took.

Lacey stared at the kindly old man. "You'd do that for me?"

"Of course. You are part of this family now, Lacey. You need something? You just ask either one of us. Simple as that."

Overcome with emotion, all Lacey could say was, "WOW!"

Too late to watch the news. The 3 of them decided that they would make sure to watch it the next night. Hopefully, the wide-spread television news would bring some word of Lloyd and the girls.

The next night, the news reported both Lloyd's recent disappearance, as well as blurbs about each of Charley, Amelia, and Annie.

Too insecure yet to completely trust her new foster parents, Lacey couldn't bring herself to ask Mr. Stumpy to drive her so she could check the Mailbox. After an entire week of hearing nothing, he approached Lacey himself. He suggested that every Sunday morning they drive to Lacey's drop-off spot so she could go and check the Mailbox.

"Don't you go to church?" Lacey momentarily forgot that Mr. Stumpy viewed the farm as his church.

He said, "I can worship the Lord anyplace, Lacey. Don't need no building to find Him. I can talk to God in the truck as well as anywhere else. I try to read the Bible on Sundays. That works in any place I choose to read it, even in the cab of my truck."

Lacey simply swallowed the giant boulder that threatened to choke her. "Thanks, Mr. Stumpy," she whispered.

True to his word, Stumpy faithfully drove Lacey back to a location near the Schmidt place. She would just as faithfully race to the Mailbox. Always, she came back to the pickup truck crushed, and empty handed.

Days turned to weeks, weeks turned to months. Lacey turned 14, then 15.

Lacey and Susanna remained close friends, despite their difference in ages. Susanna went to university, but wrote and phoned Lacey often.

Lacey continued to study hard, making excellent marks in school.

Some days she was devastated, worried, other days furious that nothing had ever turned up and that Lloyd had not contacted somebody, anybody that could get word to Lacey. Still, she never completely lost hope.

After spending 30 days in Alberta Hospital waiting for a psychological report to be prepared, Mrs. Petrie had been found fit to stand trial.

She was charged with numerous charges. They included fraud (for collecting cheques despite the missing Annie and then Lloyd), assault (for using the fearsome, infamous paddle), unlawful confinement (for locking the children in the refrigerator). There were other charges, as well, but Lacey could not remember what they were.

Eventually, Mrs. Petrie's counsel and the Crown reached a deal. In return for a guilty plea, many of the charges were dropped. She did plead guilty to the fraud, unlawful confinement, and assault charges.

Sentenced to 18 months in prison, Elsie Petrie served 12 months in the Ft. Saskatchewan Prison for Women. She was then released, having served 2/3rds of her sentence.

The judge ordered that never again was she to care for foster children. She had to pay back all of the money she received from Social Services while Annie and Lloyd were not physically in her care.

She and Mr. Petrie divorced. Their place was sold. No one knew where either of the Petries went. No one seemed to care.

149

Chapter 10
Emerging from the Depths of Despair

For Stumpy and Hilda, the time passed quickly. For Lacey? Not so much.

Her 14th birthday arrived not long after she moved in with the Somers.

Before she knew it, she was 15 and still no word from Lloyd. Nothing about the missing girls.

Susanna was now in her 2nd year of university. Busy with her studies and campus friends, she didn't communicate much with Lacey.

Other than acquaintances at school, Lacey kept pretty much to herself. Her only regular activity was her weekly trip to the Mailbox. Of course, there was never anything in that old tree stump.

Shortly after Lacey had turned 14, Stumpy and Hilda went through all the hoops, regulations and home studies required by the government. They obtained, firstly, a Temporary Guardianship Order, and then, after some delays, they finally secured permanent guardianship of Lacey. This made her very happy for a time. She felt at last that she belonged somewhere in this wide (but so far mostly ugly) world. The Somers were very dear to her. She was grateful for all they did for her, but especially that.

Although Stumpy and Hilda did their best to raise her spirits, she was sinking further and further into a deep depression. Black thoughts occupied most of her waking hours. Nightmares interrupted her sleep. She was exhausted all the time. She lost weight, which she could ill afford to lose. Moody and irritable, she spent a lot of time in her bedroom.

One Saturday afternoon, the doorbell rang. Lacey was in her bedroom. She ignored the bell for a few minutes. When the bell rang again and there was no sign of either Stumpy or Hilda, she went to answer the door.

"Oh, my gosh!" she yelped. "What are you doing here? Have you found my brother?"

"Aren't you going to ask me in, Lacey?" Parker Sutton asked, with a grin.

"Oh! Of course, please come in. Whatever are you doing here? It's so great to see you! I thought about you from time to time, but I figured you would have been transferred to some other detachment by now. Or maybe you have and are just passing through? Oh, my gosh constable, it's so great to see you!"

Sensing that she was repeating herself, she finally closed her mouth long enough for Parker to answer her.

Teasingly imitating her rapid-fire staccato, he fired answers back at her. "First off, Lacey, I'm here to see you. Secondly, I am at the same detachment.

The RCMP doesn't transfer members as often as they used to. I asked to stay here. Thirdly, it is now Sergeant Sutton. Fourthly, I'm not just passing through. I know your 16th birthday is coming up. I wanted to wait to see you until you were fully 16, but I couldn't get you out of my head. So, here I am, Miss Lacey, ready or not. How the heck are you anyway? Whew, I don't know how you can talk so fast, so much, and still have breath left over!"

Lacey stared at him unabashedly. Out of uniform he was just as handsome as in his uniform, maybe even more so. Although he was 12 years older than Lacey, he looked not a day over 17. She couldn't help herself, she continued to stare at him while he waited with a twinkle in his eye and a huge ear-to-ear grin on his face.

Finally, a throat-clearing noise behind her brought Lacey back to earth.

Grabbing Parker by the hand, she turned excitedly and dragged him towards the kitchen.

Stumpy and Hilda sat at the table, waiting patiently to be introduced.

"Mr. Stumpy, this is Sergeant Parker Sutton. Parker, this is my permanent guardian and my rock, Stumpy Somers."

Turning towards Hilda, Lacey put her arm around her and squeezed her gently. "And last, but not least, this lovely woman," she said with deep affection, "is my other permanent guardian, Hilda Somers. Hilda, this is Sergeant Parker Sutton. I met him at the RCMP detachment the night that Mrs. Petrie was arrested."

Stumpy rose from the table and shook Parker's hand firmly. "Glad to meet you, son," Stumpy said, in his most warm and welcoming voice.

Hilda approached Parker and gave him a brief hug. "Lovely to meet you, sergeant," she said. "Please, have a seat. I just baked some cinnamon buns fresh this morning. You look like the kind of guy who could eat 2 or 3 of them. Coffee?" Not waiting for his answer, she busied herself at the kitchen counter. In no time at all she had plates, cups and cutlery on the table, followed momentarily by the most delicious looking buns Parker had ever seen.

Grinning at Lacey, he asked, "Did you make these, Lace?"

"Not these ones," Stumpy interjected. "These were made by my lovely wife. But I can tell you unequivocally, young man, that Lacey bakes a close 2nd, she really does. Now, dig in!"

For several minutes the only sounds in that homey kitchen were the sounds of chewing, swallowing and reaching for more.

After finishing his 3rd cinnamon bun, Parker leaned back with a contented sigh. "Ma'am, those were the best danged buns I have ever eaten in my entire life. Thanks so much!"

Lacey could hold back no longer. "Did you bring any news?" she asked anxiously. "You must have learned something by now. It's been going on 3 years. Nobody has heard anything. What did you learn about the truck? You had the licence plate number and the information on the sign on the side of the truck. Something must have turned up!"

Parker reached over and held her hand, not letting go as he spoke to all 3 of them.

"We followed up, regularly. A motor vehicle search of the truck revealed that the owner of the company, ZO'S HAULING, is a numbered company, registered in the Province of Alberta. The company delivers goods between Alberta and British Columbia every Thursday. They've done that since the month before the 1st girl, Amelia Anderson, was picked up."

"We tried to determine the name of the truck driver on each of the dates that the girls disappeared, and on the night that Lloyd left. They were all picked up by the same truck. I was sure that the driver would be the same person in each case. He was. Unfortunately, he no longer works for ZO'S HAULING. We have been unable to track him down. He left the company shortly after Lloyd was picked up. There has been no sign of him since. He seems to have disappeared into thin air. I'm pretty sure he has changed his name. It's very suspicious, but he has done an excellent job of disappearing."

"No sign of the girls, or of Lloyd either. They haven't shown up in any hospital records, no certificates of death have been issued in either province. That's one good thing."

"These cases have become cold cases, but I have kept all 4 files open at the detachment. I refuse to give up on them. Somebody is going to slip up somewhere, sometime, and when it happens, we will be ready."

"I'm so sorry, Lacey. I know this is not the news you were hoping I could provide. I just want you to know that I will never give up, never."

Sensing how terribly disappointed she was, he still held on to her hand.

Turning to Mrs. Hilda, Parker asked if she and her husband would allow him to take Lacey to dinner and a movie. He said he realized the nearest movies theatre was over an hour's drive away from the Somers' place, but they would have an early dinner, see an early movie, and he would have her back home by whatever curfew they imposed.

Impressed by his earnestness, Stumpy and Hilda exchanged glances before Stumpy said, "If you can't trust a sergeant, you can't trust anybody. When you live in the country you are fully aware of the distances between home and a movie theater. No curfew, but we would appreciate you having an early dinner and seeing an early movie, having her home at a reasonable time."

Lacey looked at the 3 of them. "What if I don't want to go on a date with Sergeant Sutton?" she asked in a dark tone of voice.

Three faces stared at her blankly, not comprehending where she was headed with the statement.

Lacey sighed dramatically, before she laughed impishly and said, "Sergeant Parker Sutton, I would be delighted to go to dinner and a movie with you. Can you give me time to shower and get ready?"

Parker just looked at her, grinning.

Stumpy said to Parker, "Women! They're always in a rush when it suits 'em, but they love to keep a man waiting. If you like, you and I can go outside and have a look around the farm while Miss Lacey primps and crimps."

"Sounds just fine, Mr. Somers. I'd like that."

"Stumpy, I'm just Stumpy, Parker. Come on then, let's leave the ladies be. I figure by the time we come back inside in an hour or so, Lacey should be ready."

For the first time in a very long time, Lacey looked forward to something. Singing along to the radio, she prepared for their date.

When the Somers obtained permanent guardianship of Lacey, both Hilda and Stumpy had asked that she call them simply Hilda and Stumpy rather than Mrs. Hilda and Mr. Stumpy. Lacey would have called them anything they wished, she was so happy to be an official part of their family.

Lacey was ready before the men were back at the house.

Anxiously, she asked Hilda, "Do I look all right? Am I over-dressed, under-dressed? What do you think? Honestly now!"

"My dear, you look stunning. The sergeant is wearing dressy jeans and a nice dress shirt under a sweater. You're wearing dressy jeans with a very pretty blouse. That means to me that you are perfectly dressed. Now, for heaven's sake, relax until they get back in here. You are going to have a lovely time. The lad certainly is interested in you. I don't know of any other young men who would wait nearly 2 years to ask a gal out, unless he was definitely, completely interested!"

"Ah! I hear them in the kitchen now, Miss Lacey. Let's go see what they have to say for themselves."

"Well, well," Stumpy teased. "Look who just made a liar out of me. All dressed up and ready to go!"

Lacey blushed, saying to Parker, "Ready?"

"Sure am," he said. "Let's hit the road, shall we?"

Lacey gave Stumpy and Hilda each a big hug before turning to follow Parker out the front door.

Later, after the young people had driven away, Hilda held tight to Stumpy's hand.

"Maybe this is the start of Lacey finding her way out of the doldrums, Stumpy," Hilda said. "Let's pray that it's so. That girl has had enough sadness to last her for a lifetime."

That was the beginning. Lacey and Parker spent every possible minute they could together.

Sergeant Sutton's job kept him busy, but Lacey was also busy with her school activities. She was an Honour student and was determined to keep her marks up. She didn't want to give Hilda and Stumpy any excuse to curtail the relationship.

As happy as she felt whenever she was with Parker, Lacey's mind was never far from Lloyd and the missing girls. She was intelligent enough to realize that the chance of all 4 being found alive was getting more and more remote, but she still had so much faith in Lloyd. She would not give up, ever. As clever as she was, her heart almost always overruled her brain.

Parker was very patient with Lacey. He fully realized not only the trauma she had suffered when her friends and her brother disappeared, but that Lloyd was her only sibling. To have their father put in prison and her mother abandon them! He really couldn't imagine the pain and repercussions that such events in young peoples' lives could cause. So, when she talked about it incessantly, he didn't mind. He just tried to find activities for them to do that would take her mind off Lloyd, if only for an hour or so.

Stumpy and Hilda enjoyed hearing about their adventures. When Lacey mentioned one day that she would like to take Parker to Island Lake (otherwise nicknamed Mountain Goat Lake), Stumpy went out and bought a brand spanking new canoe, as well as a carrier to mount on the top of Parker's vehicle. When Lacey protested that the purchase of the craft was too expensive, Stumpy gruffly said, "I'll be the judge of that, young lady. You young people just enjoy the gift."

Lacey and Parker spent many hours swimming, canoeing, and having picnics at Mountain Goat Lake, watching the deer and studying the beautiful, majestic Trumpeter swans that called the lake home, year after year. Occasionally, they even spotted a black bear fishing on the far side of the water. Although the bear stared at them curiously, it didn't perceive any threat.

'Live and let live' appeared to be a shared motto between the people and the swans, as well as any other wildlife. Lacey and Parker never tried to interfere with any of them. If the young couple were swimming, they swam a good distance away from the Trumpeters, so as not to disturb the beautiful birds. If they were canoeing, they would keep well away from the nesting area. Often, they would stop paddling and just observe the Trumpeter swans from a non-threatening distance.

Sometimes, they would drive up the hill and visit with Uncle Henry. Henry was doing much better, although he missed his daughter so much it was painful. He had begun to see a lady whose husband had died about the same time as Aunt Harriet. Although he protested to Lacey that they were 'simply friends', Lacey could tell that the woman meant more to Uncle Henry than that. She fervently hoped that something permanent would grow from the friendship.

Because Lacey was doing so well in school, she had managed to fit several Grade XII courses in with her Grade XI studies. At the end of June, she would have only 4 more courses to take before she had enough credits to graduate. She would finish all 4 courses at the end of the 1st semester, which started in September, and ended in February. Her plan was to then find a job and work until university started the following September.

Although she had not yet decided fully what she wanted to take at university, she was leaning heavily towards a degree in social work. Lacey had never doubted that she would further her education, nor that her high marks would earn her enough scholarship funds to pay for at least most of the cost. If not, she would get a part-time job while she was going to school.

Stumpy had already told her that they had money saved for her future schooling and that she was not to 'worry her pretty little head' over any possible lack of funds. He said she would make better grades if she didn't have to work.

Several times, when Parker was working, Lacey took Stumpy and Hilda to Mountain Goat Lake. The elderly couple loved it there. They were proud of the knowledge Lacey had regarding the lake and its inhabitants, delighted that she shared her knowledge with them.

The 3 of them spent hours in the canoe, Stumpy steering from the rear. He told Lacey that he used to canoe a lot, but hadn't for quite a long time.

Lacey sat at the front of the vessel and paddled. The paddling was more strenuous than at the back. Stumpy was no spring chicken, and she wanted to spare him as much strain as possible. She noticed that he hadn't lost his paddling skills, and was very adept at steering the canoe.

Hilda sat in the middle and enjoyed the view. Their first time out, she commented that she felt pretty lazy, letting the other 2 do the physical work. Lacey told her that she prepared the picnics, which were always plentiful and beautifully prepared – that was her job. She told Hilda to just sit back and enjoy the lake. Hilda happily complied.

They went up the hill and had tea with Uncle Henry. Uncle Henry proudly showed off his latest woodworking project. Stumpy and Hilda were suitably impressed.

"He seems very nice," Hilda said, the first time she met him.

"He is," Lacey said. "If every foster parent was as great as Uncle Henry and Aunt Harriet were, and you 2 are, nobody would ever run away. There would be no foster children getting screwed up because the foster homes would all be good ones."

"They really need to screen the prospects more carefully." A single tear slid down her cheek, ran down her neck. "Then the girls and Lloyd would never have disappeared."

The day she turned 16, Parker took her to the lake. Stopping the canoe a respectful distance from the Trumpeter who was sitting on the nest, Parker reached into his pocket. Handing her a small, beautifully wrapped box, he said quietly, "Happy Birthday, my love."

Lacey looked at the box, and then at Parker. "You didn't have to get me anything," she protested, but she was already unwrapping the present. Inside was a lovely diamond engagement ring! She looked over at Parker, her mouth hanging wide open in a very unladylike manner. Before she could speak, Parker asked, "Lacy, you are the love of my life. I want nothing more than to make you happy. You have had little happiness in your life, and I want to bring you enough to make up for what you didn't have, plus extra to last our lifetimes. Will you marry me?"

Lacey nearly tipped the canoe as she rapidly leaned over and kissed him. "Oh yes, Parker, oh yes!"

Back on the shore, they loaded up the canoe. Lacey wanted to go right home and show Stumpy and Lacey her beautiful ring. She needed them to share her happiness.

After fastening down the canoe, she ran around to the other side of the vehicle, nearly knocking Parker off his feet as she jumped into his arms. "The only thing that could have made this engagement occasion any better would have been if you had got down on one knee, Parker!" She giggled as she waited for his response.

"I thought about it, Lace," he quipped, "I really did. But if I had done that in the middle of the lake I would have tipped the canoe and frightened Mama Trumpeter right off her eggs! However, here, give me the ring back."

"Nooooo!" came her anguished cry. She put her hand behind her back.

"Just for a minute, Lacey, I have to put the ring on your finger, otherwise, it's bad luck."

"Really? All-righty then!" She handed the ring back to Parker and waited.

Right there, on the sharpest, roughest, thickest pieces of gravel for miles around, he knelt down and took Lacey's left hand in his. "Miss Lacey Colleen Jordan, will you be my wife and my best friend for the rest of our lives?"

Crying happy tears, Lacey said she would.

"Want to stop and tell your Uncle Henry?" he asked.

"Next trip," she said dreamily. "I want to tell Stumpy and Hilda first. Then I want to call Susanna. Uncle Henry is next." She turned to Parker and brushed his cheek with her lips.

When they arrived at the farm, Stumpy was sitting on the veranda, reading *The Western Producer* but still keeping an eye on things around the farm. When Lacey practically leaped out of the vehicle, Stumpy stood up and opened the screen door. "Better come out here, Hildy, my love," he called. "I think you better hurry! Something's up with our girl."

Before Lacey could reach the veranda, Hilda was at the screen door. Hands on her hips, she called, "Whoa, girly, slow down! You're gonna break something!"

Lacey stood with her hands behind her back, waiting for Parker to reach the veranda. Then she casually (sort of!) began telling Stumpy and Hilda about the beauty of the lake. She waved her hands as she was speaking, waiting for them to notice. However, the Somers were too busy watching her happy face to notice anything else.

Finally, Lacey said in an exasperated tone, "Notice anything different about me?"

"Well," Stumpy drawled. "You seem mighty perky today, that's different."

"Very humorous," she drawled. "Hilarious, Stumpy, you're a hoot!"

By this time, Hilda had spied the sparkler. Taking a moment to compose herself, she walked over to Lacey and picked up her left hand.

"That's a might pretty piece of bling. Birthday present, I presume?"

Stumpy sat down, hard!

"Isn't it wonderful?" Lacey looked from one foster parent to the other. When there was only silence, she broke it. "Aren't you happy for us? What's wrong? I thought for sure you would be as happy as we are!"

"Sweetheart, of course we're happy for you. We want what you want, and that is for you to be happy." Hilda reached over and gave Lacey a hug.

Stumpy turned his head away and made a great show of cleaning his eyeglasses, hoping that no one would notice his damp eyes.

Lacey grew increasingly irritated. "**BUT**?" she drawled, "I detect a big **BUT** here!"

Hilda said, "You know what, everyone, let's take this to the kitchen table. Conversations always flow more calmly at the table. Everything is better with tea and home baking." She turned and headed for the kitchen.

Sensing Lacey's irritation, Parker held her back, kissed her gently, whispered in her ear, "It's OK, Lacey, give them a few minutes to get used to the idea. They love you and want what's best for you. I imagine this is a shock to them. You're only 16. I'm sure they thought you would be around at least until you left for university. They can feel the beginning of huge hole in the special place in their hearts where you now fit. Give them a minute, hon, just give them a minute."

Lacey held back for a couple of minutes, getting her disappointment under control.

She knew Parker was right. She knew it, but she was nevertheless disappointed, bitterly. She had been so sure that Stumpy and Hilda would have been as excited for her as she, herself, was. Their thrilled reactions, or rather lack thereof, were hard for Lacey to accept.

As she simmered down and thought more clearly, though, she began to appreciate that if she was in their shoes, she would be very concerned also. Emotions still tottering, but now leaning more toward elation than disappointment, she resolutely squared her shoulders and headed in the direction of the kitchen.

She sat down and immediately opened her mouth to defend herself. Stumpy stopped her. He put his hand gently on her arm. "Just wait, girly, for Hildy to get the tea ready. Take some deep breaths in the meantime. And don't look so scared! We ain't gonna bite and we sure as heck aren't going to interfere with your happiness. We just need to discuss some things that maybe you 2 haven't thought about, beyond the excitement of getting engaged."

"Everyone," he said, nodding at Parker to indicate that he was included, "everyone will get a chance to speak."

He then stood up and went to help Hilda. Carrying some plates to the table, he looked straight at Lacey and winked.

After what seemed to Lacey like an hour, everyone was seated, sipping tea and reaching for scones, butter, cheese or jam. She sipped her tea, but couldn't force herself to eat anything at the moment.

"You know, Parker," Hilda said, "we've never asked you much about yourself. We know you are a fair bit older than our Lacey girl, but exactly how old are you?"

"I'm 28, Ms. Hilda," he replied honestly. "I know that is a huge gap, but Lacey is very mature for her age. She has been through so much in her young life. I love her, and I just want to be there for her through thick and thin, try to take away some of the bad memories, help her make new, positive ones. I want her to be my best friend as well as my wife. I just want what's best for her."

"I also want to become an official part of your family. I know you are fond of me already, and I love the 2 of you to pieces, but I need – well, let me put it this way, both my parents are deceased. I have no siblings. My parents were only children, so the only family I have in this world is me."

Hilda paused for a minute before she spoke once more. "Well, my dear, you know we've grown very, very fond of you in the past months. In fact, we love you like you were our own son. Loving you or not is not now, nor ever will be, the issue."

"Have you considered this scenario? When you get to be as old as Stumpy and me, Lacey is still going to be a relatively young woman. Do you think that would be fair to her? I mean, you could be in a wheelchair, or have some form of dementia, or just be plumb wore out, or Heaven knows what else."

She turned to Lacey, and asked, "See where I'm going here, Lacey? You need to think about these things."

Lacey said, "Hilda, Stumpy, I know the age difference is a biggie. My feelings for Parker are larger than that. I look at the 2 of you and I think, that's what I want for Parker and me. I want a marriage as strong and faithful as yours is."

"Yes," she continued, "when Parker gets old, he very well might be disabled, and I might have to become his aide, as well as his wife and best friend. On the other hand, it could be me who becomes ill, and he would have to look after me. Ill health doesn't discriminate strictly on age. Anyway, isn't that what love is all about? You 2 know that better than anyone else I have ever met. Well, except for Uncle Henry and Aunt Harriet. You are both healthy. Don't you think your love and devotion to each other has played a large part in keeping you both alive and well? I sure do. You 2 are my inspiration, my mentors. I want Parker and me to be just like you. I know the road won't always be a bed of roses. You forget the places I've lived and the ugly things I've seen. I'm determined not to live like any of those people. I might only be 16, but I have lived an entire lifetime in the years since Dad went to gaol and Mama left us, an entire lifetime since the girls and Lloyd disappeared. It has made me grow up fast! I'm ready for whatever comes along. I really am."

"Parker has a successful career with the R.C.M.P. He's already a Sergeant and who knows how high up the ladder he might climb? The thing is, he won't be able to stay at that small detachment forever if he wants to advance. No doubt about it, he'll have to move, probably sooner rather than later. I will be heartsick to leave the 2 of you, but I need to be with Parker!"

"Stumpy," she beseeched, "you must understand what I'm trying to say. I know Hilda does. Please, won't you give your consent, and wish us happiness?"

Stumpy silently looked over at his wife, his eyes shimmering with moisture. "What do you think, my Hildy, help me out here."

Hilda immediately rose out of her chair and stood behind her husband. Kissing the top of his head, she simply looked at both Lacey and Parker, unexpectedly unable to say anything.

Finally, she took a deep breath and said, "Congratulations you 2, be happy, work hard, live long."

Clearing his throat, Stumpy declared, "just one thing. Lacey, you are going to finish your Grade XII before you get married. You have to prove to us that you can graduate with at least as good grades as you have always earned."

Hilda broke in. "What about university? Don't you think that is important?

"You know, I've always regretted not furthering my education. If I had it to do over again, I would have still married Stumpy, but I would have found a way to earn at least a college degree. There were no post-education correspondence courses when I was young and of course living here, we were too far away from a college or university for me to attend without leaving home. I wasn't about to leave Stumpy to run the farm all alone."

"Now, I'm not saying I continually mourn over my loss, not at all, but if I had it to do over, is all I'm saying."

"I understand, Hilda," Lacey said quietly. "But I have thought about it, a great deal."

"It won't be long before Parker gets transferred to a larger center where, hopefully, I can continue my education. I'll still be young enough to enroll in a university or college then. For now, I will be happy becoming the best wife and friend to Parker that I can possibly be."

Parker looked at Lacey proudly. "Believe me, Stumpy, Hilda, I will be so proud of her if she chooses to do that. I will do everything I can to encourage her. I won't block even a single step of her way."

"Well, then," Stumpy declared, "More coffee Hildy."

Let the celebration begin!"

Chapter 11
Looking for Love

Mr. and Mrs. Parker Sutton

Neither Lacey nor Parker wanted a big, formal wedding. With Lacey's parents gone who knows where, and Parker's parents deceased, they decided that a small, informal ceremony at their beloved Mountain Goat Lake would be in order. Uncle Henry offered his place for a celebration bar-be-que following the ceremony. His offer was gratefully accepted.

The guest list was tiny. Only Uncle Henry and his friend Cora Stuart, (who was, by now, much more than 'just a friend'), Susanna (bridesmaid), Fred Gablehaus (best man), Stumpy and Hilda, Mr. Petrie, and Evelyn Bronson.

Although Lacey wanted to invite Jayson Silverman and her friend Lester, nobody knew how to contact either of them. Other than a brief "hello" when he would play in the odd basketball tournaments between his new school and his old one, nothing had been heard from Lester since he was removed from the Petrie foster home. Mrs. Bronson had been unable to track down Jayson Silverman since the day he left the Family and Social Services offices.

Because February in Northern Alberta can be bitterly cold and snowy, and they wanted to get married at the lake, Lacey and Parker set their wedding date for the long weekend in May. Not only would Lacey be finished with her final exams by the end of February, she should have all her marks back long before the wedding.

The one downer in the wedding plans was the harsh reality that Lloyd was still missing.

Christmas came and went. Lacey tried hard to be upbeat but she missed her brother more than ever. She put on a brave face and somehow got through all the festivities without spoiling the holidays for Parker, Stumpy and Hilda.

After the Christmas break, Lacey buckled down. As she had promised Stumpy she would, she studied hard for her final exams.

In March, they mailed the few wedding invitations they needed for the small wedding. Lacey took Parker with her to the Mailbox and left an invitation addressed to her brother inside the old stump. Stumpy continued to take Lacey to check the Mailbox.

Every week, she prayed that there would be a positive response from Lloyd in the Mailbox. Better yet, she prayed that he would show up at the door. Mrs. Bronson had the address and telephone number of Stumpy and Hilda. Lloyd had left with Mrs. Bronson's card and Jayson Silverman's card in his backpack. There was no reason that Lloyd couldn't track his sister down.

Every time she checked the Mailbox, the wedding invitation to Lloyd lay stark and alone, its position unchanged from where Lacey had placed it.

The middle of May, Lacey received her final marks in the mail. She had passed her Grade XII exams 1st in her class. Stumpy and Hilda were very proud of her.

Hilda took Lacey to the nearest city, approximately an hour and a half away, to shop for a wedding dress. Because the wedding was going to be small and informal, Lacey looked until she found a very simple, but beautiful, 2-piece long skirt and blouse made of very soft and flowing beige cotton. A combination of embroidery and lace, in a darker shade of beige, around the neck, sleeves, and hem of the blouse, as well as the bottom of the skirt, completed the ensemble. It was perfect for a wedding by the side of the lake. Better still, she would be able to wear it on many occasions. She and Hilda stayed overnight in a hotel. They went to a movie in the afternoon, and then had a lovely dinner in the hotel restaurant. It was a fun get-away, but both Hilda and Lacey missed Stumpy and were anxious to get home the following day.

As much to keep busy as to earn a bit of spending money, Lacey got a job at the service station that was about 3 blocks from the Schmidt's house. She started the day after she came back from the shopping trip, planning to work full time until the wedding.

There was not a lot of choice in rental accommodation in the little town where Parker worked. However, he and Lacey looked every weekend that Parker wasn't on duty. It took a couple of months before they found a cute little 2-bedroom house to rent. It had a fenced-in back yard. They decided that once they were married and moved in, they would get a dog.

The town was small enough that you could pretty much walk wherever you needed to go. One day, while Parker was doing some overdue paperwork at the detachment, Lacey wandered the main street. She stopped in at a cute little gift shop, a coffee shop, and the main grocery store, to speak with the owner/manager of each place. On the spot, all 3 establishments offered her a job. She just needed to decide which job she wanted. All 3 managers were willing to wait for her to start until after the wedding. Lacey promised to let them know her choice as soon as possible.

Lloyd and Lacey's Mailbox was at least a half an hour drive away. Parker suggested that, depending on their work schedules, she drive to Stumpy and Hilda's once a week. That way, she could have a visit with Hilda, and then go with Stumpy and check the Mailbox.

Lacey was excited to receive Evelyn Bronson's RSVP back in the mail, saying she would be delighted to attend. Hilda called Evelyn and invited her to stay with them when she came to the wedding. She happily accepted.

The Justice of the Peace that served their area agreed to perform the ceremony at the lake.

Susanna arrived home 2 days before the wedding. She quickly arranged for flowers and other decorations. When she was finished decorating the covered veranda where the reception would be held, it looked like something out of a magazine.

The evening before the wedding, Hilda prepared a roast beef dinner. Lacey and Parker, Susanna, Fred Gablehaus, and Evelyn Bronson, enjoyed a lovely evening. No one mentioned Lloyd.

The morning of the wedding dawned cool but clear. The forecast was for a sunny day, a balmy plus 20 degrees Celsius with no precipitation and no wind. Lacey saw this as a good omen because the Victoria Day weekend in May in Northern Alberta often saw snow! People planned all winter to go camping on that weekend. Often the weather was bad and the campers sat miserably around their campfires, wet and frozen.

By 3:45 in the afternoon, everyone was assembled by the side of the lake. Folding chairs had been set up. Susanna and Hilda had arranged beautiful, large potted plants on either side of a wooden arbour Uncle Henry had designed and built, as a wedding gift for the young couple. Lacey and Parker would be able to move the structure to the back yard of their new home and plant vines at the base of it. The vines would climb the latticed sides of the arbour. A free-standing bench sat between the sides. A padded cushion fit the top of the bench, and completed the lovely work of art.

The short ceremony, performed by the Justice of the Peace, was over in 15 minutes. Lacey had been unable to stop herself. She kept looking for Lloyd. Once, Parker even had to poke her gently with his elbow to remind her that it was her turn to answer the JP. She squeezed Parker's hand apologetically, and concentrated fully on the few remaining minutes of the wedding ceremony.

Uncle Henry, Cora, and Susanna, had outdone themselves. Lanterns glowed softly along the roof line of the veranda. There was enough food for 10 times the number of people who were there. Beautiful music carried softly throughout the area from excellent-quality Bose speakers.

At the conclusion of the meal and a few short speeches, Uncle Henry invited everyone to come to his workshop for a few minutes. When they got there, Stumpy and Hilda were grinning, unable to hide their excitement. Taking both Lacey and Parker by the hand, they stopped in front of a very large area, completely covered with a tarp. Motioning for the newlyweds to remove the tarp, everyone clapped in awe as they looked at a fabulous bedroom suite. Stumpy and Hilda had commissioned Uncle Henry to build it. It was their wedding gift to Lacey and Parker.

Despite the *'No Gifts Please, Your Presence is our Present'* that appeared on the wedding invitations, everyone had brought a gift.

Once the gifts were all opened, Lacey, overwhelmed, managed to croak out a thank you before she burst into tears. The guests attributed the tears to happiness and too much excitement. They carried on with their partying, ignoring her tears and including her in the festivities as if she was not a soggy mess.

Finally, Parker whispered to her that perhaps they should be the first ones to leave. It was late and Uncle Henry was looking pretty tired. Susanna overheard. She hugged both of her friends and told them that Uncle Henry would be delivering their gifts, including the arbour and the bedroom suite, to their new home in a few days.

Teary-eyed once more, Lacey thanked Susanna. Susanna would be unable to see their new home this trip because she was taking some university courses during the summer, but she promised to keep in touch. She tactfully didn't mention Lloyd or the missing girls.

The young couple made the rounds of the remaining guests, thanking them for coming, thanking them for the wedding gifts, and saying goodbye.

When they reached Uncle Henry, he squeezed Lacey so tightly she squeaked! "I have some news for you, Mr. and Mrs. Sutton." He turned toward Cora and pulled her closer to him. "Cora and I are going to be married the July 1st long weekend. We want you to be sure to mark that date on your calendars. It wouldn't be the same if you couldn't share in our happiness."

Lacey clapped her hands and excitedly called out, "Oh! Everyone, listen, wonderful news! Uncle Henry and Cora are getting married!"

As soon as the noisy excitement from the announcement subsided, Parker and Lacey waved goodbye, got into their vehicle and drove away.

They were spending the night in a motel close to the detachment. Parker had to work the next day. Lacey intended to clean their rental house. When Monday came, she was going back to speak with the managers of the 3 places that had offered her a job. She would make up her mind before then and hopefully start work immediately.

Monday didn't work out. Uncle Henry brought the arbour and the new bedroom suite in his large grain truck. Because Parker was working, and the furniture was too heavy for Henry and Lacey to unload by themselves, they had to wait until Parker came home from work in order to unload it.

It was nearly 6 o'clock when Parker came home. With all 3 of them unloading, they finally finished an hour later. It was too late to start cooking supper. Besides, Lacey hadn't had time to stock the pantry cupboard yet. Henry, Parker and Lacey went to the hotel restaurant and ate. Right after, Uncle Henry had to get home. Cora would be waiting, He didn't want her to worry.

Parker looked around the small house. Each of the tiny rooms held packing boxes full of things, mostly Parker's from his previous rental apartment.

He looked over at Lacey. "Mind if I don't help you unpack this stuff tonight, hon?" he asked. "It was a nutso day at the office and I'm wiped. Let's just assemble and make up the bed and turn in early, okay?"

Lacey was a little disappointed, but agreed. Just before they went to sleep, she told Parker that she was going job hunting in the morning. She wanted to start work as soon as possible.

"No rush, Lacey," Parker mumbled, half asleep. "Take your time, something will show up soon enough. Just get us settled and then worry about working."

The phone rang at 3 a.m. Lacey leaped out of bed, wide awake, her heart in her throat, wondering where she was.

"I'm on call, Lacey." Parker said. "We'll just keep the phone next to my side of the bed. Then, when it rings, you don't need to answer it. You'll get used to it, I promise. Now, I have to go to the detachment. Just go back to sleep." As quickly as that, he was gone, leaving Lacey wide awake. She lay there for quite some time. Finally, she got up and started unpacking the kitchen boxes. By the time Parker came home at around 5:30, Lacey had the kitchen organized and was starting on the bathroom.

Parker gave her a hug and a kiss, whispered, "Looks nice. See you in a few hours, I'm exhausted." He fell onto the bed, fully clothed and started to snore.

At 7a.m. the phone rang again. Another call out. She sat up. "I'll make you some toast and coffee."

"No time," Parker said, "Gotta go. See you when I see you!"

By noon, Lacey had the entire house unpacked and organized. She decided she would buy groceries in the afternoon, and go job hunting the following day.

She made a nice supper and then sat waiting for Parker to come home. By the time he arrived, everything was dried out from keeping warm in the oven, but Parker sat down and ate, praising his new wife for her culinary talents.

"It's so nice to come home to you, Lacey," he said. "Sure beats coming home to an empty apartment, making myself a bite to eat, and then falling asleep in my chair watching television."

"Parker," Lacey began tentatively, "is this the way it always is?"

"What do you mean, hon?" he asked, his mind on the television set. "What do you mean by that?"

"I guess I mean, aren't there other members at the detachment that can take some of the night calls? Why do you have to take all of them?"

Parker looked at her. "I'm the Sergeant, Lacey. I need to be on scene. I'm not the only one who goes out on a call, but the constables are pretty green in this little town. They need to be trained. I need to make sure everything goes as smooth as can be. If I want to get a promotion, I need to do more than my share." He turned back to the TV. As far as he was concerned, that appeared to be the end of the matter.

"Oh!" was all Lacey said. She thought to herself that she better find herself a job real soon or she would likely die of boredom.

The next day she retraced her steps, calling in at all 3 stores. After speaking with the managers once again, she promised she would let them know the next day which job she would prefer. Thinking about it while she waited for Parker to come home for supper, she decided that the grocery store might not be the most fun, but it was certainly the busiest, of the 3 jobs. She was pretty sure she needed to be busy enough that she would come home tired. With the hours Parker was keeping, she wouldn't see much of him. She needed a distraction. She couldn't just sit around waiting for Parker every day.

The manager of the grocery store was delighted to hire Lacey. However, he didn't want her to start for another 2 weeks. They agreed on the starting date.

Lacey walked home and stared at her spotless little house, wondering what she was going to do with herself for the next 2 weeks.

She picked up the phone and called Hilda.

"Lacey! So nice to hear from you. Stumpy and I were just talking about you 2, wondering if you are all settled in yet."

Lacey, feeling guilty for not calling sooner, said, "We are pretty well set up. I have a new job at the grocery store but I don't start for 2 weeks."

"Why I'm calling, though, is to ask you both to come for supper next Sunday. Parker finally has a day off. Please say you'll come. This visit is long overdue."

"We'd be delighted, dear! Of course, we'll come. Stumpy wants us to bring dessert. How about I bring a flapper pie?"

"That would be great! In the meantime, though, I really need to get back to the Mailbox to see if Lloyd has been in touch. Stumpy, what's a good day for you? I have the car all week because Parker drives a patrol car."

"Any day, Lacey, any day at all. How about tomorrow?"

Oddly, Lacey felt close to tears. How she loved those 2!

"I was hoping you'd say that, Stumpy. See you tomorrow morning. Probably late morning, if that is fine with you?"

"Perfect," Stumpy enthused. "We've missed you, gal. Hilda says you will stay for lunch. She won't hear of anything less."

At supper that evening, Lacey told Parker about her conversation with Stumpy and Hilda, and told him that they would be coming for supper on Sunday.

"That's nice, hon!" Parker said. "I miss those 2 great people, and I'm sure you miss them even more than I do. Looking forward to the visit."

"Oh yeah, I almost forgot. The manager of the grocery store has hired me. I start in 2 weeks."

Parker stared at her. "What's the rush? I thought you were going to get the house settled before you went to work. We're not starving, you know. You don't need to go to work right away, or ever work, for that matter. We can easily live on my salary. We won't be rich, but we'll be comfortable."

Lacey gaped at her husband, her mouth hanging open.

"What!" she squawked, in a much louder voice than she intended. "Are you telling me you don't want me working?"

She held up her hand to stop him before he could say anything. "You want me to get this tiny house organized? Look around you, Parker. Open every single cupboard door and closet door. Look in every drawer. Look in the basement, for God's sake! It's not a finished basement, but I have scrubbed every inch of that place. There is nothing left to be done here in the way of organizing, absolutely nothing. Even the yard is raked. I bought paint for the fence. That's my project for this coming week. Once that fence is painted I have nothing to do with my time other than everyday household chores."

Pausing for breath, Lacey leaned back, waiting for Parker to say something, anything. He just gazed at her, his eyes puzzled and hurt.

"I thought you would be excited, hon," Parker finally said. "You know how many women would be thrilled to not have to work?"

"Those are **OLD** women, Parker! If I was 40-something, yeah, I would probably be excited. But, I'm only 16, and I need to have something to do besides wait for you to come home every day. At least if I'm working, I won't worry that some psycho is going to shoot you in the head while you are rushing around trying to save the country. At least if I have a job, I will have people to speak with. You are either working or sleeping."

"Know what, Parker? I sit here and I wonder every day how you found the time to date me before we got married. You worked shifts, yes, but we still saw each other several times a week. I just don't get it. Instead of getting off shift and sleeping till morning, you drove to see me. We spent time at the lake, we did stuff, Parker. We did stuff together. It's as if you put this wedding ring on my finger and then forgot all about me. I feel like I'm just a convenience for you, that you truly don't even know I'm here, except when it comes to having supper on the table."

"I wasn't the Sergeant then, Lacey," Parker began patiently. "The demands on my time were less. Anyway, we see each other every day now. I appreciate what you have done with our home, Lacey, I do."

"Maybe you could take some college courses by correspondence? That would fill up your time. Or, what about volunteer work? Small towns always need volunteers."

He stared at her, waiting, clearly expecting her to agree with him and tell him she would not take the job.

"You don't have a clue, Parker. Have you ever looked at those women who are volunteering? Like, have you really looked at them? Like, they're all white-haired grandmothers with no education and nothing better to do with their time. I really don't mean to be rude, because I know they are very necessary and, like, do wonderful jobs organizing things and seeing they come to fruition. But Parker, like, I'm 16! Give me a break."

Lacey couldn't help but listen to herself. She had always hated the slang word 'like'. She rarely used it, so she must be super upset! Embarrassed, but still annoyed, she kept quiet for a minute.

"I'm going to work at the grocery store in 2 weeks," she said sullenly. "Like it or lump it, I'm going to work."

Her lip jutting out like a petulant child, she pushed her chair back from the table and began to clear away the dishes.

"I guess this isn't the best time to talk about having kids, then?" Parker asked quietly.

Lacey's response? A thunderous black look that spoke more clearly than words ever could. It gave new meaning to the expression 'if looks could kill!'

They spent the rest of the evening in front of the television. Staring blankly, comprehending little of what they were watching, Lacey finally got up, muttering, "I'm going to bed. Good night Parker."

When Parker came to bed, Lacey lay on her side as far away from him as she could. She heard him sigh and roll over towards her. He put his arm around her, forcing her to lie closer.

"I know you're not sleeping, Lace," he softly said. "I just want to say I'm sorry. I guess we have a lot of things to talk about that we never thought of before we got married. I was just so in love with you, and you certainly seemed to reciprocate the feelings."

Lacey turned towards her husband. She placed her hand on his cheek. It was wet. Feeling like a piece of dog crap, she hugged Parker tightly.

"I'm sorry, too, Parker. I guess marriage is more of an adjustment than either of us thought, huh?"

Prepared to discuss the problems of newlyweds the world over, Parker not so rudely interrupted her with a lingering, passionate kiss. The phone, for once, was silent.

After their love making, they fell asleep, snuggled together in one small portion of the giant king sized bed. The phone didn't ring the entire night. For the moment, there was peace between the 2 of them.

When morning arrived and the alarm rang, Lacey went into the kitchen while Parker was in the shower. She made bacon and eggs. She realized that it was a peace offering of sorts, but it felt good to be sitting across the table from her husband, watching him enjoy the breakfast she had prepared before he headed off to work.

"Great breakfast, hon," Parker said when he finished eating. "What are your plans for today?"

"I'm going to drive to Stumpy and Hilda's," Lacey said. "Stumpy and I are going to check the Mailbox in case there is some word from Lloyd. I'm going to stay for lunch, but I'll be home before you get off work."

"That's a good idea, Lacey. Have a nice day, OK? I'll see you tonight."

"Parker," Lacey spoke hesitatingly. "Is there anything new on Lloyd or the missing girls? You haven't mentioned them since just before the wedding. Surely something has come up by now."

"Nope, nothing, my love." Parker looked at his wife, his eyes dark with pity.

"Lacey, you know I will tell you immediately if and when something shows up. You also know, I'm sure, that the longer we hear nothing, the worse the news will probably be. Think of it this way, 'no news is good news'. Maybe that will make the waiting to hear something a little less difficult. I can promise you, without a word of a lie, that I am checking often. As well, the people in British Columbia that I have investigating these disappearances are excellent at giving me interim reports."

"Give my love to Stumpy and Hilda. Tell them I'm really looking forward to seeing them on Sunday. Have a great day, OK?"

Lacey threw her arms around Parker, kissing him hard. "I love you, Parker. Keep safe, my luv," she whispered. "I don't know what I would do if something happened to you!"

"Doing my best!" Parker grinned at his new, very young wife. "Doing my best!"

He turned and waved before he began the short walk to the detachment.

Much more cheerful, Lacey finished cleaning the kitchen and then headed towards the shower.

Excited about seeing her foster parents, she showed up at the farm mid-morning rather than late morning. Both of the people that she had come to love most in the world came running to greet her. In the midst of the group hug, she tried to apologize for coming earlier than planned.

"Who cares about that, girl?" Stumpy said gruffly. "You're welcome here anytime, anyplace, any hour, day or night. Parker too! Just because you 2 are hitched, don't mean our door is locked."

"Now, let's have a coffee with Hildy, and then you and I will head to the Mailbox."

Smiling broadly, the 3 sat at the kitchen table, eating fresh cinnamon buns and drinking coffee.

After about 15 minutes, sensing that Lacey was getting antsy, Stumpy rose. "Let's check out that Mailbox, gal," he said. "Hildy, see you in an hour or so. Our girl will be ready for lunch by then!" He kissed his wife warmly and they were off.

Respecting Lacey's privacy, Stumpy sat on the flat rock while he waited for her to check the tree stump.

For perhaps the 100th time, Lacey told herself that Lloyd wouldn't mind that she had told Stumpy about the Mailbox, and showed it to him. She was sure that he would appreciate the fact that Lacey wasn't all alone with Lloyd gone, and realize that she desperately needed support.

She stood in front of the tree stump. A part of her wanted to lean over and feel inside immediately. Another part of her decided to prolong the agony. At last, she knelt in front of the stump. Reaching in and towards the back, she momentarily got excited when she didn't feel the wedding invitation. After further rummaging around in the hollow, her fingers touched the envelope. It had simply fallen down and settled deeper into the tree stump.

Lacey was bitterly disappointed yet again.

Returning to the flat rock, she could not hold back the hot tears burning the back of her eyelids. She leaned against Stumpy and cried her eyes out. Stumpy just held on to her and let her cry.

"Stumpy, I just can't understand it. Lloyd is a smart and careful brother. He wouldn't take any unnecessary chances when he left to track down the missing girls, I know he wouldn't! So wherever can he be? What's holding him back from returning to me?"

In both mental and physical agony, she leaned forward, rested her head on her knees. Her hands pressed tightly against her painful belly.

Stumpy reached into his back pocket and withdrew his handkerchief. He handed it to Lacey. In her distress, she was unaware that her nose was running like a tap. Almost choking with grief, she blew her nose.

"That's a great deal of disappointment for a young girl," Stumpy soothed. "I just don't know what to tell you. There are so many looking for him and for the 3 young girls."

"What does Parker say about it?"

"Not much!" Lacey sounded more bitter than ever before.

"He says he has people working on it, but I'm not so sure about that. Something must have turned up. People don't just disappear into thin air. It isn't as if there was absolutely no clue. My description of the truck was very precise. Including Lloyd, that truck went by and picked up hitchhikers 4 times! How is it that there are no witnesses? Surely somebody, somewhere, saw something! There just has to be more that can be done in order to find them. There has to be."

She leaned her head on Stumpy's shoulder. He patted her back while he thought about whether or not to broach another subject with his girl.

Finally, he turned Lacey towards him so that he could look directly into her eyes. He wanted to be sure she was listening. "Lacey, this is a terrible dilemma I know, but I can't help thinking that you have more problems than the missing youngsters. Do you want to talk about them?"

"Marriage isn't the blissful scenario that I thought it would be, Stumpy," she said simply. "It's hard work!"

Stumpy couldn't help himself. He laughed!

"Not funny!" Lacey couldn't believe that Stumpy was taking her so lightly. "You and Hilda make it look so easy. You love and respect each other every single minute of every single day. That's how I thought it would be with Parker and me, but it's not! He doesn't want me to work, even though I have found a job and I start in a couple of weeks. He actually mentioned having children! My gosh, Stumpy, I'm 16! I'm still a kid myself. I don't want kids yet, maybe never! I just want to work. Eventually I want to go back to school, but until we live in a city that has a university or a college nearby, I just want to work. I want Parker to find Lloyd and the girls."

"I want us to have the kind of loving relationship that you 2 have. That's not so much to ask, is it?"

"Another thing. Parker is a workaholic. He can't trust the constables to take some of the night calls. He says he needs to be there to train the young guys. Really? Every single time? He's never home. While he's gone, I have nothing to do but worry about where he is, what he's doing, if he's going to come home in one piece or if he will get killed or injured on the job!"

"He tells me I worry too much. Well, I have nothing else to do!" She whined pitifully, feeling very sorry for herself.

Although Stumpy was not one to interfere in anybody's business but his own, he felt he had to speak. "Lacey, listen to me very carefully. It's important. I hear what you are saying, but you need to listen carefully to yourself. You need to really hear yourself, question yourself. Is it really worth fighting about?"

"What I am hearing at the beginning of nearly every one of your sentences is, 'I want! I want! I want!'"

"You both need to realize that there are 2 of you now. You're married. Marriage is a partnership. You should be discussing what you both want, not just what you want. There are compromises to be made in a marriage. It's not 'all

169

about me' any more. There are 2 people at the beginning. Hopefully, that number 2 will grow as babies come along. It will never be just 'all about me' again. Get used to it."

"It's not a bad thing, mind you. It's wonderful to have a partner to meander through life with, to share the good as well as the not so good. You'll find, eventually, that it's so much better than just 'all about me'. I promise you, Lacey, that it's much, much better."

"Hilda and I, we didn't always have the relationship we have now. We had to work at it, work hard every single day we were together. We still do, always will. Marriage is team work."

"It took a long time before we both realized that in order for each of us to be happy, we had to learn that there is always 'give and take' in a great relationship. We had to learn to sometimes put the other person first."

"My greatest pleasure in this life is doing things for my Hildy that I know make her happy. Sometimes it's as simple as getting her a cup of tea when she's feeling down, without her asking."

"Don't worry, Lacey, you're very bright. You'll get it."

"What you really need to do before anything else is to learn to talk to each other, be willing to compromise when things aren't going entirely your way. I mean talk to each other. That includes listening, really listening, to what your partner is saying. It means not only listening but hearing what the other person is trying to tell you."

"Communication is 99.99 % of a good marriage, but it takes 150% effort from each of you, 24 hours a day, 7 days a week, 365 a year – 366 in a Leap year." He grinned at Lacey, taking careful note that she did indeed seem to be listening intently, truly hearing the meaning of his words.

"Neither the husband nor the wife will ever get their own way all the time, maybe not most of the time. You have to learn to accept that, deal with it, talk about it. You've got to accept that things won't always go your way. Parker needs to get his way sometimes too. Hear him out. What is he really trying to tell you?

"Now, my girl, I'm not saying that it's never just about you. I'm really saying that you need to think about each other as well as yourselves. It's about making each other happy. It's about working at it every day. Before you know it, it's no longer work, it's pleasure, making both your lives comfortable. That, my darling Lacey, is marriage!"

"Pick your battles carefully. Nothing is worth going to bed angry over. Not one single, solitary thing. There's a reason the expression 'never go to bed angry' is so important. Heck no, it's not important, it's vital!"

"You're very young, my Lacey girl, and I am getting the distinct impression that you and your young man didn't talk about much before you tied the knot, and it certainly appears that you don't converse much now either. Oh sure, you yack at each other about non-essential things. That's not communication, that's avoidance."

"Hilda will tell you to go to the library and get some self-help materials to read. I'm telling you also, do it! There is no shame in admitting that things can be changed and made better. Heck, I did my share of reading and learning also. It's a tough thing for a young person to do, admit they might be wrong. Don't let pride stand in the way of a great relationship. Swallow it and move on."

Glancing at his watch, Stumpy decided that enough was enough. He stood up stiffly, hauling Lacey to her feet.

"Come on, kiddo," he said. "Hildy will have our lunch ready and she'll be wondering where the heck we've disappeared to. Let's go on back to the farm. We can talk some more while we eat."

After lunch, Lacey helped Hilda tidy the kitchen. She then decided that she needed to go home so she could prepare a nice supper for Parker. Hopefully, he would be home in time to eat it for once.

She hugged Stumpy hard and whispered in his ear, "Thanks for the listening ear, Stumpy. I feel a lot better having vented to you."

"Good to hear, Miss Lacey, any time!"

"See you Sunday!" Lacey called as she backed down the drive. "Parker and I are really looking forward to your visit!"

"Hildy, my love," Stumpy said thoughtfully as they watched Lacey drive away, "I'm afraid we failed to prepare our young miss for the trials and tribulations of learning to be married. And Sergeant Parker Sutton certainly did not warn her of the difficulties she would encounter being married to a Mountie!"

"Now, now, my darling Stumpy, don't be too hard on our Sergeant. I doubt if he knew himself how hard it would be for Lacey to be married to a Mountie. Or, for that matter, for Parker to be married to someone who is not a policeman."

After Lacey had gone, Stumpy and Hilda sat side by side on the veranda. A cup of coffee in his hand, Stumpy recounted his conversation with Lacey while they were at the Mailbox.

"Oh, my, Hildy, I just hope I got through to her. I think the whole world should be as happy as you and I are."

Kissing her husband on his prickly cheek, Hilda snuggled closer. "Stumpy, you're a good man. I think you helped Lacey today more than you know. Thank you. From what you told me, you accomplished an excellent intervention."

"Thanks, oh my prejudiced one!" Stumpy grinned. "I covered a lot of territory with our girl this afternoon, my love. I just hope she heard it. The rest is up to both of those youngsters. They've got a lot to learn and a long way to go."

Driving home, Lacey thought hard about what Stumpy had told her. It seemed to her that it was just common sense, but she appreciated his input. She resolved to make an honest effort to follow his advice.

She tried. She really tried, however, it was extremely difficult to initiate a conversation with someone who was so tired that he fell asleep watching the news on television night after night. She wondered what was wrong with her. She certainly didn't remember Parker being this tired when they were dating.

The 2 weeks until her job commencement passed very slowly for Lacey. She tried every evening to talk with Parker about important, meaningful things.

The evening before she was to start her new job, she reminded Parker that she would be starting work at the grocery store the next morning.

"That's nice, hon," he muttered, turning up the television volume as he spoke.

Lacey got up off the couch and slammed out of the house.

She wished for the 100th time that they had a dog that she could walk. Every time she brought it up, Parker said, "Yeah, yeah, as soon as I get some time we'll look for your dog."

Increasing her pace in an effort to wear off her boiling temper, she soon was jogging down the sidewalk.

Finally worn out, she stopped to catch her breath. Sitting on a park bench, she was soon approached by another jogger, a woman she did not know.

"You're Lacey Sutton, are you not?" the woman asked. "I'm Jillian Hamilton. I'm a constable with the R.C.M.P. Your husband is my sergeant."

Lacey looked at the woman with curiosity. "It's very nice to meet you, Jillian." She sat in shy silence, waiting for the older woman to speak again. Soon she did.

"I've seen you out jogging, but never had the chance to introduce myself, until now. I'm wondering if you would like to stop at the little café and have a coffee. My treat."

"I'd like that," Lacey replied. "Race you!" She was off before her new friend could even stand up.

Although Lacey was 10 years younger than Jillian, Constable Hamilton was in excellent physical form. She easily caught up with Lacey. They jogged companionably the short distance remaining to the coffee shop.

The evening was still sunny and warm and they chose to sit outside at one of the small bistro tables and drink their coffee.

"So, Lacey, how do you like our little town so far?"

"I'll like it much better once I'm working. I start tomorrow at the grocery store. It has been pretty lonely these past couple of weeks. Parker is working all the time. When he's not at work, he's sleeping in front of the TV set."

"Hmmm, sounds to me, young Lacey, as if you have a case of the 'OMG my life as a cop's wife isn't what I envisioned,' and 'what have I got myself into!'"

She stopped and looked at her new friend. "Am I right, Lacey?" she asked gently.

Tears brimmed in Lacey's eyes but did not spill over. Swallowing hard, she asked, "How did you know?"

Jillian grinned. "Because, my young friend, I've been in your shoes. Well, actually my ex-husband was in your shoes. It didn't take him long to figure out he didn't want to be married to a police constable. He couldn't take the evenings alone, waiting and worrying. He wanted a family, I wanted a career. I chose a career." She shrugged her shoulders.

"How long were you married?" Lacey questioned.

"Not long enough to work things out," Jillian responded. "We got married when I was 21. Divorced 2 years later. I've been on my own for the last 3 years."

"Doesn't the R.C.M.P. have some kind of seminars, or at least information, for non-member spouses? You know, some information explaining… " Here Lacey heard herself whining and she stopped before continuing, "Sorry, Jillian. I don't mean to complain, it's just I am finding it really difficult engaging Parker in any type of meaningful conversations. He is so tired all of the time."

Jillian remained quiet for a minute or so, contemplating on whether or not to be frank with this young bride. "Well, your husband is definitely career-oriented. Just like me."

"To answer your question about information or seminars for non-member spouses, I haven't heard of any. In fact, when my own marriage was floundering I asked my sergeant (not Parker, a previous sergeant), that very same thing."

"His response was quick and brutally honest. He told me, "I'm neither concerned nor interested in the families of my officers. You want to be a cop? You work your relationship problems out for yourself. You want to let your spouse raise kids, mostly by himself because you're working day and night? That's up to you, but don't come crying to me when you can't manage your career and your home life.""

Lacey gasped. "Where is that sergeant now?"

"Don't know, don't care," Jillian responded morosely. "He was divorced, had 2 kids that he never saw. Threw his entire self into his job. I imagine he has climbed the corporate ladder quite a few rungs by now, but I am pretty sure he lives a very lonely life. That is, unless he woke up and smelled the coffee. Somehow, though, I can't see it."

"Anyway, Lacey, I better get back. I have an early start in the morning."

"One little piece of advice though, before I go, if you don't mind. Never let Parker leave for work, dayshift or nightshift, without kissing him goodbye, telling him you love him, telling him to be safe. His job is dangerous, no doubt about it, but give him something to come home for. Ask him about his day. He'll tell you what he can. Don't let him come home to a grumpy, whiney, clinging vine. The terrible things he deals with on a daily basis are bad enough. He needs you to appreciate him. He needs to see a smiling, friendly face. Good luck with your new job."

"And don't worry, if you keep yourself busy enough, you and Parker will work things out. You've only been married for what? A month or 2? Your fun is just beginning. One little tip though. Don't give up on trying to get Parker to communicate. Eventually he'll figure it out. He might surprise you. I certainly hope so."

With a cheery wave, Jillian left Lacey sitting on the café's patio with a lot to think about.

The next morning Parker sat at the kitchen table, reading the newspaper. Lacey walked into the room, a smile pasted on her face. "Morning, my love," she said, as she planted a smooch on top of his head. "How did you sleep?"

Parker looked up, startled. Setting aside the paper, he smiled back. "I slept well, hon. Thanks for asking."

Finishing his coffee, he stood and looked at his wife apologetically. "Sorry I have to run. I'll see you tonight." He started towards the door, looked back. "Oh yes, and good luck with your first day on the job. Have a good one!"

Before he could rush off, Lacey rose from the table, took her husband by both hands and said quietly, "I love you, Parker. Be safe today." She hugged him and gave him a kiss goodbye.

Parker hugged her back. "Thanks, Lacey! I will have a good day. See you tonight." He then opened the door, leaving Lacey at the table thinking that maybe, just maybe, there was hope for them yet.

Things went well for the next month. Lacey was busy getting used to her new job. Parker was busy day and night with his sergeant's duties.

Lacey didn't really mind that Parker was too tired at the end of the day for serious conversations. She was exhausted as well. Although she was training for the cashier position she was originally hired to do, standing all day took some getting used to, even at the tender age of 16. Also, part of everyone's job was to ensure the shelves were fully stocked and dusted. Trying to make a good impression with her boss and new co-workers, she often lifted more heavy items than was good for her.

She volunteered for extra shifts. Her co-workers were quite happy to have her fill in for them, especially on the weekends.

Although conversations between Lacey and Parker often seemed to be limited to "How was your day?", "Good, thanks!" and "Good night, have a good sleep!", every morning or evening just before Parker left for work, Lacey kissed and hugged him warmly, told him she loved him, and to keep safe. She never once forgot that particular bit of advice she had received from Jillian.

On a rare day off, Lacey woke up and realized that it had been almost 2 months since she had last checked the Mailbox. Horrified, she turned to Parker. He had worked the night shift and had just fallen sound asleep.

"Parker, Parker, wake up!" She shook his shoulder with a ferocity that had him leaping out of bed, yelling anxiously, "Where's the fire? Did you hear a shot? Shoot the tires!"

"Don't be dumb," Lacey said. "Get back into bed. I'm sorry I woke you, but I just realized that I need to take the truck and go to the Mailbox today. It's been nearly 2 months since I checked it. What if there's something in there?"

Suddenly she heard a soft snore and realized that she was talking to the wall. She quietly got out of bed and went into the kitchen to call Stumpy and Hilda.

Hilda answered the phone.

"Well, sweetie, we have been wondering about how things are going over there!|

"You say you want to come out this morning? That would be wonderful.

"Is Parker coming with you? Oh, he is working nights. Well, as much as we would love to see him, we certainly understand that he needs his sleep."

"I'll make us a nice lunch."

"Yes, I'll tell Stumpy."

"Of course, he will want to go with you! See you soon. Drive safe!"

Hilda hung up the phone and rushed over to the counter to punch down her bread dough which threatened to overflow the bowl and slide onto the counter. She then went looking for Stumpy.

He was very happy that Lacey was coming. He would definitely accompany her to the Mailbox.

When Lacey arrived at the farm, she ran into the kitchen and warmly hugged Hilda. Hilda smelled delicious, like warm bread just out of the oven, like melted butter, cinnamon and raisins. Hilda smelled like home. She could have stood there, smelling the delicious aromas forever.

However, anxious to get to the Mailbox, she soon grabbed Stumpy by the hand, hauling him through the door before he could even say hello!

"See you soon, Hildy, my love!" Stumpy bellowed in an exaggerated tone that falsely indicated how hard done by he was. "That's if our girl, here, doesn't pull my arm right out of its socket!"

Chuckling all the way to Lacey's truck, he climbed in and buckled up for the ride.

Stopping the truck just off the road in a farmer's field entrance, the 2 of them walked the rest of the way. The mid-summer sun was already hot, comforting on their shoulders.

Birds chirped loudly as they happily dug for worms in the wheat field. A slight breeze rustled the developing heads on each stalk. Not yet ripe, of course, the pale green colour spread into the distance as far as their eyes could see. Come autumn, the pale green would turn to a rich, warm, golden colour.

Sometimes, if you were lucky, when the wheat had grown tall and strong, you would see a black bear in the distance, popping his small head up above the wheat, his curious nose sniffing the air for any strange or threatening smells, his beady black eyes scanning the landscape for danger. The bear would have no interest in humans as long as they kept their distance. Bears didn't bother humans with the strange scent, if the humans didn't bother the black bears with the stinky scent.

Other than the merry chirping of the birds, the countryside was so quiet, so peaceful. The sky was clear. Not even a wisp of cloud dared to blemish the azure hue in any direction.

Just before they reached the flat rock, Stumpy grasped her hand, pointing with his other one.

Standing deceptively close enough that Lacey felt almost certain she could reach out and touch him, stood a very large bull elk.

Holding their breath, Stumpy and Lacey stood motionless, admiring the magnificent animal.

The bull stared back. For a good 5 minutes, the 3 gazed admiringly at each other.

Finally, the giant turned and casually walked slowly and gracefully away, his majestic head swaying as he balanced his heavy rack of antlers. Stumpy counted 8 by 8 points – a truly imposing specimen.

"How incredible, Stumpy," Lacey breathed once the elk was a good distance away. "And it was as if he just knew we would cause him no harm. Did you see how close he was to us? Doesn't it appear that he must have a massive headache from carrying that large rack of antlers around? I'm just so happy it's not hunting season. With that many points on his rack he must be fairly old, right? It would be a shame to hunt him after he has lived this long. That's what I think, anyway."

Stumpy let her prattle on. His breathing was getting raspy from the walk. He gratefully slid down on to the flat rock to wait for Lacey while she went and checked the stump.

A shrill scream penetrated Stumpy's eardrums, and he not very gracefully rose from his supine position on the flat rock, hurrying towards Lacey.

"Stay there, Stumpy! Sit down! I'm coming to you."

Reaching Stumpy, Lacey shrilled, "There's an envelope in the Mailbox!"

Shaking from head to toe, she sat down beside him.

In her hand was a letter-sized envelope. Nothing was written on the paper, no addressee, no address, just a plain white envelope.

"It's got to be from Lloyd, Stumpy," Lacey whispered. "I can't, I just can't. Will you open it, please?"

Stumpy took it from Lacey's trembling hands and messily tore it open.

"Read it first, Stumpy and then read it to me."

Stumpy scanned the single sheet of paper and then gave a deep sigh.

"What is it? Isn't it from Lloyd?" Lacey asked anxiously. "Stumpy?"

Stumpy gave Lacey's arm a soft pat. "No, not from Lloyd, but nice news nevertheless. Want me to read it to you, or do you want to read it for yourself?"

"You read it," Lacey said. She wasn't all that interested in a note that wasn't from Lloyd, but so as not to appear ungrateful, she listened while Stumpy read,

Hi there Mr. & Mrs. Sutton!
I tried to call you last weekend, but there was no answer and your voice mailbox was full. I was only here for the weekend. Dad and Cora got married. It was the tiniest wedding, just the groom, the bride, myself, Cora's son, and the Justice of the Peace in attendance. The 5 of us then had dinner at the hotel dining room. Then I had to leave right away as I had exams on Monday. So sorry to have missed you, but thought you would like to know about Dad and Cora!

Dad has still not heard anything from either Lloyd or the private investigator that is supposed to be tracking him down. I think he must have more lasting damage than was first thought. Dad has tried several times to get hold of him but to no avail. His phone is now disconnected. Perhaps he died.

Anyway, sorry again to have missed you. Hope all is well. See you at Christmas.
Love,
Susanna
XOXOXOX

"Well," Stumpy said. "That contained news, didn't it?"

Lacey agreed. She was so sorry to have missed seeing her friend Susanna. She was happy for Uncle Henry, she really was. She tried to appear cheerful, but she failed. Miserable, her heart and mind were elsewhere.

Without speaking, Lacey and Stumpy walked back to the truck. They stopped for a moment at the spot where the bull elk had stood, but he was long gone.

When Stumpy and Lacey reached the farm house, Hilda was sitting on the veranda, patiently waiting. One look at Lacey's face told her all she needed to know. She didn't ask how the trip went. Standing up, she simply said, "Come on in you 2, lunch is ready. While you wash up I'll get it on the table." Without another word, she walked back to the kitchen and proceeded to set out the lunch.

When they were finished, Stumpy discreetly left the kitchen, saying he had to check on something in the barn.

Lacey said goodbye to Stumpy. She said she was leaving right away and would see him another time. She thanked him for accompanying her to the Mailbox.

"You're not leaving yet, my girl. You dry. I'll wash," ordered Hilda.

Hilda took a closer look at her former ward. She didn't like what she saw. Lacey looked thinner, tired, drawn, and very unhappy. She was riddled with nerves. The slightest noise made her jump.

"I'm worried about you, gal," Hilda said quietly. "You look terrible for an almost-new bride and a young woman with a new job that she tells everyone she likes. What's up? You know you can tell me and Stumpy anything. It will go no further without your say so."

Lacey abruptly sat down at the table and put her head in her hands. Hilda just let her be. She knew she would speak up when she was ready.

After several minutes, Lacey handed Hilda the note from Susanna.

"I was unhappy when I got here, yes, Hilda," Lacey began. "But now that Susanna has nothing more to tell me about Lloyd and the investigation into the girls' disappearance, I feel just like a chunk of me fell into the creek and a piece of heavy driftwood is holding that piece of me under the water."

"I've kept bugging Parker nearly every day for news. I don't think the R.C.M.P. are doing anything anymore. It really makes me wonder how many more disappearances have happened where the victim was never found. How can the families survive?"

"When I try to get Parker to talk with me about my concerns, or at least listen while I vent my concerns, he just gets annoyed. He either turns the television up or goes to bed. I don't blame him for getting mad, but I feel like if he doesn't listen to me or make a harder effort, I will go insane!"

"Why don't people get told before they are married about how hard it really is to be so closely connected to another person, to have that first love rush continue? Why is it such hard work?"

Hilda simply put her arm around Lacey and smiled. "Because, my young one, young people know it all and won't listen if someone tries to clue them in. Anything worthwhile is worth working for. When you have to work for something, it becomes more precious, more valuable to the person who has worked so hard. There are very few people in this world who can tell you without exaggerating, that their 'perfect' marriage is without bumps in the road. If they tell you that, they are either lying or they don't give 2 hoots about their spouse or partner. They don't care enough, or even at all, to make any effort to correct a problem."

"They probably don't have a missing brother and 3 missing friends either," Lacey muttered inaudibly.

"Sorry? Lacey, I didn't hear that."

"Nothing," she churlishly growled. "Not important."

Stumpy came back into the kitchen just as Hilda sat down across from Lacey. Catching a glimpse of him out of the corner of her eye, she surreptitiously waggled a finger at him to come forward and help her out. He did. In accord, they reached for Lacey's hands.

"Lacey," Hilda began, "you know how much we love you."

"I know you think that you can tell us anything and we will be on your side no matter what. We have already told you that we are willing to hear anything and everything you have to say. We mean that from the bottom of our hearts."

"But, honey, you have to know that even if we are on your side, we are going to tell you what we honestly think. If you want to do something that we feel will hurt you more than you are hurting already, we are not going to go along with your idea."

"That's what love is, Lacey – keeping your best interests always in the forefront of our thoughts."

"Now, it is not always going to be what you want to hear." Hilda stopped and looked at Stumpy beseechingly, reaching for his other hand. He grasped it firmly.

Looking Lacey straight in the eye, he began. "My girl, we know that what you want is different than what you are going to get. The mountain is steep. You're at the very bottom. You have such a long way to go, Lacey. If we concur with what I'm pretty sure you are asking, we'd be doing you no favours."

"Correct me if I'm wrong, but you want to move back here with us, am I right?" He waited for Lacey to answer.

Shamefaced, she nodded.

"I think you know," he said in the most caring of tones, "that we can't agree to that."

"Lacey, your marriage is only beginning. A scant 2 months isn't even enough time to know what kind of toothpaste Parker likes best. And for sure, he can't read your mind. You gals make us guys feel pretty inadequate a lot of the time."

"You are so very young… "

Lacey opened her mouth to protest but thought better of it. She snapped it shut and waited for Stumpy to continue.

"I know, or at least I think I do, that the longer Lloyd and the girls are missing, the more desperate you are getting. I can't begin to imagine the pain that is causing you.

"But, my girl, you have a husband who loves you very much. He must feel helpless, not knowing what to do to ease your pain."

"Help him to help you. Tell him what you need. Tell him how you are feeling. He can't help what he can't know. The only way things will improve is if you let him into your mind and your heart. Like I just said, help him to help you."

Lacey was silent but not sullen. Stumpy and Hilda could see that she was thinking hard about what they were saying.

"Lacey, do you get what we are trying to tell you?"

"I do, Stumpy, I really do, but it is so terribly hard." Her lower lip trembled as she gulped down a sob.

"Nobody ever promised you a rose garden, my girl," Stumpy said as he patted her shoulder clumsily.

"You're an intelligent person, so think about this – maybe you need to speak to a doctor about helping you deal with the helplessness you're feeling when it comes to Lloyd and the girls. It's a gigantic burden you're carrying on your skinny shoulders. As much as we want to help you, we are not trained to ease such a heavy load."

"Will you at least think about it?"

Lacey nodded. "Of course, I'll think about it, Stumpy." She glanced at the clock. "Oh, my gosh, I better get home. I'm sorry to have been such a Gloomy Gus."

"You know I appreciate your advice always. I have a lot to think about now, don't I?"

Lacey stood up. Hugging both her foster parents tightly, she then stood tall, squared her shoulders and spoke loudly and resolutely. "I can climb this mountain!"

She then drove home, determined to have a long chat with Parker either at dinner or right after.

Chapter 12
All the Wrong Places

Adam Draper

Although Lacey's intention was to be intractable, the best laid plans… as the saying goes, are often doomed to fail, particularly with young people.

She tried, she really did, but as more time passed, the more determined she became. If Parker and the entire Royal Canadian Mounted Police couldn't find Lloyd and the missing girls, she would just have to do it by herself.

She set a deadline. If she had heard nothing by the middle of June, she would set forth on her mission.

For an entire 2 months, she asked for and received every Thursday as her day off. By either the Grace of God or pure dumb luck, Parker was working days every one of those Thursdays. Lacey need not explain her actions to her husband. Despite stoic efforts by each, communication between them was poor to middling at best.

Thursday mornings, she told Parker, she was spending the day with Stumpy and Hilda. That was not a lie, she eventually turned up at their door. Before that, though, she parked in Peter Petrie's driveway and waited for the pumpkin truck.

Although Mr. Petrie still owned the place, he did not stay there. Lacey backed up the driveway and parked in front of the garage. She felt perfectly safe surveilling from that position. She did not need to be very close to the main road. Her eyesight was excellent. The truck was brightly coloured.

At 10 o'clock every Thursday morning, like clockwork, the same truck rambled past the Petrie place. Same truck, same licence plate number as Lloyd had written down such a long time ago. Alberta plate number LUVKIDZ. One-ton truck – solid shell on back, no windows. Side lettering black and green – ZO'S HAULING. Bright orange, pumpkin orange.

As soon as the truck went by, Lacey started up her truck and headed for Stumpy and Hilda's farm.

Every Thursday, Lacey and Stumpy took a sojourn to the Mailbox. There had been nothing in the stump since the note from Susanna. Despite the disappointment, every time she checked, she enjoyed the time with Stumpy. He was a very knowledgeable man, a good conversationalist, non-judgmental. The countryside was beautiful and peaceful. She could feel the tension in her shoulders loosening as they meandered to and from the Mailbox. She looked forward to those Thursday treks.

She did not, of course, tell him about her impending plans. He might not be judgmental about most things, but he certainly would not approve of his beloved young foster daughter putting herself in harm's way!

Hilda asked Lacey every week how things were going. Every week Lacey's answer was the same, "Just fine, thanks! I love my job. I'm keeping busy. Parker is just fine, thanks for asking. He sends his love."

Parker and Lacey's 1st wedding anniversary came and went. Parker had made plans to take Lacey out for a nice dinner, but at the last minute? An urgent call. Once again, the best laid plans!

He apologized for not buying her a gift, flowers or a card. He had simply been too busy. He was sorry. Lacey lied and said it didn't matter, but it did.

The first weekend in June, Parker actually had a day off. Although he was exhausted, he agreed to go with Lacey, Stumpy, and Hilda, to Mountain Goat Lake.

Hilda packed a lunch. Lacey helped her while the guys loaded the 2 canoes on top of and into the back of Parker's truck. The women would have been willing to bet that it couldn't be done, but the fellows proved them wrong. Stumpy had bought himself a new canoe and was anxious to try it out. He said that if he had to carry it on top of his head all the way to the lake, he would do it.

Despite his fatigue, Parker enjoyed the day. The sun was warm, the sky was clear. The Trumpeters honked softly as if welcoming their people back to this little piece of paradise that the swans returned to each and every year.

"Oh, Lacey," Parker said as he trailed his hand in the chilly lake, "Thanks for talking me into this trip. We really need to do this more often. It's been a great day."

Hilda surprised Lacey with an early birthday cake, complete with 17 candles. It was delicious, and meant more to Lacey than she could adequately express.

Lulled by full bellies and warm sun, all 4 agreed to forego a visit to Uncle Henry and Cora this time. It was time to go home.

Dropping Stumpy and Hilda off at their door, and before Lacey could speak, Parker regretfully declined Hilda's offer to go in for coffee. He had some paperwork to finish up before he went to work the next morning. "Thanks anyway."

Parker asked Lacey if she could drive home. He couldn't keep his eyes open. Lacey readily agreed. Parker was asleep before she backed out of the driveway and on to the road.

Once home, Parker shut himself into the spare bedroom, which doubled as an office, and completed his paperwork. He then crawled into bed, forgetting to say goodnight to Lacey, who was sitting in front of the television.

She went to the fridge and checked Parker's schedule which was attached to the side. Perfect! He was working days on Thursday. She decided that even if it was not quite the middle of the month, Thursday was **'D' day.** ('D' for departure).

She made herself a note to call Hilda on Wednesday evening and apologize for the fact that she would not be there the next day to check the Mailbox. She would tell them she had to work.

Today was Sunday. Counting today, there were only '4 more sleeps' until the search for Lloyd would begin.

Checking on her husband to ensure he was sound asleep, Lacey went into the small office and typed up a letter to Parker. She would place it on his pillow on Thursday morning, after he had left for work.

She would have to leave the truck in Mr. Petrie's driveway. Parker would have to find a way to pick it up. She was pretty sure Jillian Hamilton would be only too happy to assist Parker in any way she could. The few times Parker had anything to talk to Lacey about, it usually included Jillian as part of the conversation! Funny, Lacey thought to herself, maybe I should be jealous, but I'm not. I don't care what happens here at home while I'm gone. When I come back, it will be with Lloyd and the girls in tow. She would find them or die trying.

Having finished her letter, she leaned back in her chair and tried to envision Parker's thoughts as he read it. She had written:

My dearest Parker,
By the time you get this letter I will be well on my way to finding Lloyd and the girls. I must ask you this: PLEASE DO NOT TRY TO FIND ME. This is something I have to do. No one else seems to be trying anything at all. I cannot just sit for the rest of my life and not make any effort to find my brother.

I know you and everyone else thinks they are all dead. Don't you think if my own brother died I would have felt it in my heart? I have no such feelings. I know he is alive! I just know it!

If I have any inkling that things are going awry, I will get in touch with you. Please, do not worry about me. I know what I am doing. As I said, it is something I HAVE to do. This may take me quite some time, but I will succeed. Please show Stumpy and Hilda this letter and tell them not to worry. I know what I have to do. Give them my love, as I now give my love to you.
Love always, LACEY (P.S. The truck is in the Petrie's driveway)

The week dragged on. Between trying to pack her things and keep them hidden in case Parker should notice (although there was not much chance of that!) and going to work every morning with her secret plan weighing her down, Lacey was a nervous wreck.

Wednesday afternoon, at the end of her shift, Lacey went to her boss's office. He had already left for the day. She wrestled with whether or not to call him, decided against it. She put a short note on his desk that said only:

So sorry, a family emergency has arisen. I have to go to Vancouver. Will keep in touch, Lacey.

Wednesday night she lay in bed, wide awake. Parker had been called back to work. She fervently hoped and prayed that he would not be out all night and then not go in to work Thursday morning.

At 11 p.m. she heard the back door open. When Parker came to bed, Lacey, pretending to be asleep, kept her breathing steady. Parker sighed, rolled over, and was almost instantly asleep.

By 6 a.m., Parker was dressed and ready to leave. Lacey got up. Dizzy with both fatigue and nerves, she steadied herself before going in to the kitchen.

"You're up early, Parker. What time did you get home last night?"

"Not too late. Have to get in early though. I didn't do the paperwork after the call out. I was too pooped."

He planted a kiss on her cheek and turned to leave.

"Hey!" Lacey said, "What kind of a kiss is that?" She reached up and put both arms around his neck. Squeezing him fiercely, she whispered in his ear, "Have a good day, Parker. Keep safe. I love you!"

Looking surprised but pleased, he patted Lacey on her shoulder. "I will, I will keep safe, and I love you too. Now, I have to run."

Lacey remained in the kitchen, unexpected tears leaking from her eyes. She mentally shook herself, then hurried into the bathroom and got ready to leave.

She found herself parked in the Petrie driveway with time to spare. Taking several deep breaths to calm herself, she got out, locked the truck, hid the key in the usual agreed-upon spot, grabbed her backpack, and walked down the driveway to the edge of the highway.

She didn't have long to wait. Right on time, the pumpkin orange one-ton approached. Lacey held out her thumb and the truck slowed down, pulled over and stopped.

The driver reached across the cab and opened the door. "Howdy ma'am," he drawled. "Where ya heading?"

"Vancouver?" Lacey responded. "Yes, that's where I'm heading, to Vancouver."

"Just so happens that's where I'm going also. I have a schedule to keep so hop on in and let's boogie on down the road!"

Despite her nervous stomach, Lacey had to smile at the corny sense of humour the driver seemed to exude.

Once she was settled and her seat belt fastened, she slipped her backpack off of her shoulders and put it on the floor in front of her feet.

"You can throw that in the back if you like," said the driver.

"It's fine here," Lacey said quickly, "there's stuff in here I might need. It's not in my way. Thanks!"

"Well now, I must admit you're mighty pretty company. Name's Adam, by the way, Adam Draper."

"I'm Lacey," she said.

"No last name?" Adam queried.

"Just Lacey," she mumbled. "I'm just Lacey."

"Well, 'Miss Just Lacey', it's a pleasure to make your acquaintance. Sit back and enjoy the ride. It's a long way to where we're going so sleep, talk, heck even sing if you want. You'll find I'm easy to please."

Out of the corner of her eye, Lacey observed Adam Draper. She tried (without much success) to appear neither too inquisitive nor downright snoopy.

Although it was hard to tell with him seated, she guessed that he was probably approximately 2 metres tall. He had very long legs. He wore a scuffed pair of black and tan leather cowboy boots. The heels were so worn down they were almost non-existent. Over a black T-shirt he had on an unbuttoned, black and grey plaid shirt, with the sleeves rolled up to his elbows.

His dark black hair and his dark, almost-black eyes suited his rugged face. He had the most amazing white teeth. For as black as his hair was, his complexion was very pale. Smooth skinned, no wrinkles. It appeared to Lacey that he wasn't out in the sun much, if at all.

His hands fascinated her. Large, rough-skinned and callused, they had seen hard work.

She guessed he was probably somewhere in his mid to late 20's. VERY easy on her eyes!

For the first half hour they rode in complete silence.

Finally, Lacey broke it. She asked him, "So, Mr. Draper, how long have you been a truck driver?"

Adam grinned. "Mr. Draper was my dad, and Mr. Draper was my Gramps, too. If you don't mind, please, just call me Adam."

He continued, "Well, Miss Lacey, I can't say as I am a truck driver, really. I'm just filling in for a buddy of mine. This is his regular route but he's got himself in a little pickle and had to take some time off. I've just finished college and am taking some time off from work for a little R & R. At the moment money's a little tight. The pay for the fill-in position is excellent, and so, as you can imagine, I'm very happy to drive his truck for him while he's away."

He didn't say the name of his pickled friend and Lacey thought it inappropriate to ask. Not that it would have made any difference, she was pretty sure she wouldn't have known him anyway.

Sitting on her hands, fingers crossed, she lied. "My brother is a truck driver. He drives a truck something like this one in the Vancouver area. He loves his job. Just thought you might know him, both of you driving the same class of trucks and all."

Adam threw Lacey a sharp glance. "Be pretty remarkable if I did know him. As I told you, I'm not really a truck driver, just filling in for a friend."

"Yes, I recall you saying that."

Changing the subject slightly, before she changed her mind and told this stranger Lloyd's name, she continued her gentle probing. "What do you normally do for a living, Mr. – Adam?"

Adam glanced over at Lacey, seeming to think about whether or not he should tell her what he really did for a living. Finally, he grinned and said, "I'm a butcher. My dad owns a butcher shop in southern Alberta. Been working under his callused old thumbs for most of my life."

"Interesting. I've never known a butcher. What sort of training did it entail, for you to become a butcher?"

Again, Adam glanced over at his passenger. "Really? You're really interested in how to become a butcher?"

Lacey couldn't help it. She giggled.

"Well, to be truthful, I'm not so much interested in finding out how I can become a butcher, but I'm more interested in finding out about your training. That truly does interest me."

"Aah!" Adam sighed. "I see."

He let out a deep breath that sounded almost like a sigh.

"My grandfather opened the family butcher shop way back in 1950. Been in the family ever since. Gramps has been gone now for over 10 years."

"Dad learned the trade from Gramps. He learned it well and the shop has continued to thrive."

"I, in turn, apprenticed to my dad. He figured that learning from him was education enough. But the more time passed, the more I hankered for some further education in the art of butchering. I decided to go to Olds College this past year and get my certificate. Figured if butchering was going to be my life-long career I might as well learn all I could."

"My dad's a stubborn old cuss. Said if I was going to 'desert' him for an entire year, I could just pay my own way. I asked him if he would still have me in his shop when I was done. You know what he said?"

"No, what?"

"He said, if I didn't learn any highfalutin, fancy smanchy manners in that there Olds College, I could come back."

Adam laughed, then said, "I really don't know about any manners I learned, but I went to school, passed with the highest marks in my class and will soon continue to be standing on my feet in all kinds of temps, depending on whether or not I'm in the cooler or on the sales floor, for 8 hours or more a day, just as I have been since I was a teenager first working the counter in the shop."

"You sound as if you are unhappy there," Lacey said.

"Nah, I'm content there. My dad wants to retire at the end of the year, then the shop will be all mine, to do with as I wish. Most days, we get along pretty good, just some days he is having a hard time turning over the reins."

"I won't be changing much. 'If it ain't broke, don't fix it,' is pretty much my motto."

"But I like to push my dad's buttons and let him think that nothing in the shop will be the same once he's out of there. Make him think that, the minute the door slams shut behind him, I will be taking my meat saws and demolishing the joint."

"Sounds like you really love your father," Lacey said wistfully.

"Yeah, I guess I really do," Adam replied. "There's just my dad and me now. My mother died 2 years ago, so I guess my dad is having a hard time retiring. He's never had time for any hobbies and I keep trying to encourage him to find something to do outside the butcher shop."

They drove along in companionable silence for a while.

Crossing the border into British Columbia, they continued until they reached a very small town, more likely a hamlet than a town. Adam pulled into a service station/restaurant and parked the truck beside the building.

"Are you hungry?" he asked Lacey.

"Not yet," she said.

"Well, I'm going to grab a quick snack. If you need the washroom it's over that way." He waved his arm towards the general vicinity.

"I'm OK," Lacey said. "If you don't mind, I'm just going to lay back and rest my eyes. Don't hurry on my account. If I can't sleep, I have a book in my backpack."

"Suit yourself," he said and sauntered off towards the restaurant.

When she first climbed into the truck, Lacey had spotted a manifest lying on the seat between the driver and the passenger. Glancing out the window to ensure that Adam Draper was not coming back, she quickly grabbed a pen and a piece of paper out of her backpack.

Looking outside once more to make sure Adam was not returning, she quickly flipped the manifest open to the last page. As quickly as she could she copied the information down. It included a name, phone number, address, and directions to get to the address. She really hoped that when Adam made his delivery to that address, she was still in the truck. If not, she had the details. She would just have to find it for herself. She also really hoped that she could read her own writing, she had scribbled everything down so fast!

Just as she finished writing the last few words of the directions, she looked up. Adam was advancing, he was nearly at the driver's door!

Lacey slammed the manifest shut and tried to put it back exactly as she had found it. She had her backpack open and was stuffing her notes inside when Adam opened the door.

Trying not to look flustered but failing miserably, she brightly asked, "So how was the food at this place?"

"Fine, just like any other roadside café," he said. "Here, I brought you a sandwich just in case you decided you were hungry. And a coffee. It's black, but there's a creamer and some sugar packs in the bag with your sandwich."

He appeared not to notice her flustered expression. Perhaps he thought she had fallen asleep and just woke up. She could only hope!

"Thank you, Adam," she said quietly. "That's very nice of you. What do I owe you?"

Now he did look at her. "Nothing," he said. "You can buy us something the next time we stop."

"That's a deal," she said. The smell of the coffee made her realize just how long it had been since breakfast time. Opening the paper bag, she pulled out the ham and cheese on whole wheat sandwich and began to devour it. It tasted delicious and for the few minutes it took her to practically swallow it whole, there was silence in the truck.

Finished, she leaned back in her seat.

"Thanks again, Adam. It's been a lot longer since breakfast than I thought. It was delicious."

"You're welcome, Lacey. Most welcome."

A few minutes passed. Adam kept glancing over at his young passenger. Finally, he said, "OK, Miss Lacey, I've told you my life story. What's the scoop on yours?"

"I have a pretty good idea that you're running away from something. Don't see many pretty young girls hitching along the stretch of road where I picked you up. No cop's gonna pull me over for kidnapping a minor, is he?"

Lacey stared unabashedly at Adam for several long minutes, saying not a word, weighing the wisdom of telling this almost-a-stranger everything or perhaps more wisely, telling this almost-a-stranger absolutely nothing.

Perhaps it was a total lack of wisdom, perhaps lack of maturity, perhaps simple desperation, but Lacey suddenly decided to let loose.

Once she started talking, she couldn't stop. She talked, and talked, and talked. Adam didn't interrupt her once, just let her speak.

She began at the beginning, when her father went to prison, when her mother walked out and left Lacey and her brother alone. She spoke about the visit to the prison and about the succession of foster homes. She spoke about the disappearance of the 3 girls, and about Lloyd going off to try to find them. Not coming back. She told him about Parker, about how, despite being an R.C.M.P. sergeant with a lot of connections, he was unable to find out anything. She spoke about her failing marriage, and finally, she spoke about how she was going to find her brother and the 3 missing girls or die trying.

The one thing she did NOT tell Adam, fortunately, was names. Names of the people she was searching for, names of her parents, names of her brother or her husband. Something deep within her cautioned Lacey that it was important, no, it was absolutely vital, that she keep this information to herself. Not knowing why, she kept silent in that regard.

When she finally quit talking, she was exhausted. Her cheeks were wet. She didn't realize she had been crying.

Adam stayed quiet. When he next glanced over at Lacey, she had already drifted into a fitful, light sleep. He reached forward and turned the radio on to an easy listening station. He hoped that she would sleep for a few hours at least.

When she awakened an hour or so later, she asked Adam where his 1st delivery was. He told her it was in Hope, British Columbia. He explained that Hope was a small place, located at the beginning of the infamous Coquihalla Highway and the end of the tortuous Hope-Princeton Highway.

As far as Adam knew, Hope's main claim to fame was that the town of Hope was a filming site for the 1982 movie, *First Blood*, starring Sylvester Stallone as Rambo. In that movie, Hope's main street was 'blown up'.

"Interesting," Lacey said. She then asked him if he would be stopping at any other place between Hope and Vancouver. He said no, he would be going straight through to Vancouver once he stopped in Hope.

"How far is it from Hope to Vancouver?" she queried.

Reaching into the console beside him, he pulled out a map of British Columbia and suggested she have a look.

"The distance from Hope to Vancouver is 152 kilometres," she told him.

"And the distance to Harrison Hot Springs from Hope is 40 kilometres. I have a friend who lives there," Lacey lied. "Will it be possible for you to drop me off there? She will drive me to Vancouver after we visit for a couple of days."

"Sure, no problem," Adam responded. "It will be nearly midnight when we get there, though. Do you know where you're going?"

"My friend told me to get dropped off at an open service station and call her. She will come and pick me up."

"That's OK, then. There's only one service station that will be open when we get there. I know where it is, and it's an easy on and off the highway."

"I could drop you off at your friend's house, but this old wreck of a truck is kind of noisy to be driving into a residential neighbourhood at midnight. Your friend's neighbours would probably be mighty put out if we woke them up at that time of night."

"I do have to make my delivery in Hope, though. Hope you don't mind waiting. It won't take very long."

Lacey gave him a tremulous smile. "And what would you do if I said that I did mind waiting?"

Adam appeared to be the king of sharp looks. He glared over at her, realized she was kidding. He grinned sheepishly. "Guess you're kind of stuck with me unless you want to hitchhike at 11 o'clock at night, huh?"

They pulled into Hope around 10 p.m. Spotting a burger place, Adam realized that they had not eaten anything since lunch. He pulled over and parked. Looking over at Lacey, he said, "We better have a bite here. I'm getting mighty peckish, how about you?"

She laughed.

"What's funny?" Adam asked.

"Sorry, Adam, I wasn't laughing at you. It's just that one of my foster parents always used to say that when he got hungry. So, yes, I'm getting mighty peckish also. Let's eat!"

"And by the way, I'm buying. You bought my lunch."

After eating their excellent burgers and fries, Lacey jogged around the small building several times. She then did some stretches before she climbed into the truck once more.

Leaning her head back against the headrest, she nonchalantly looked around, pretending great interest in the scenery. She was, in fact, taking careful note of where they were going. She did, of course, have the directions she had copied, however, she always found it much easier to find a place if you had a trial run, so to speak.

It wasn't too far. Adam drove north of the highway for perhaps 4 blocks. The road ended and a fenced mobile home park was situated at the bottom of a large hill. She took a wild guess and estimated there might be as many as 20 or 30 mobile homes in the park, most of them close together. The postage stamp sized lots barely offered enough space to park one vehicle without encroaching on the street.

Adam drove to the furthest street, made a right-hand turn and drove a couple of short blocks.

Although the tired looking mobile home was technically still in the park, it perched alone in a mixed clump of tall trees, both evergreen and deciduous. The trim badly needed repainting.

Odd, she thought to herself as she peered through the darkness, *there aren't any steps.* The blinds on the windows were all drawn so she couldn't tell whether or not anyone was in the trailer. It looked neglected. More than neglected, it looked completely abandoned.

There was, however, a fairly new looking dark SUV parked where the steps should be. It was too dark to see the exact make and colour of the vehicle, or to read the plate number.

"I won't be more than a few minutes, Lacey," Adam said. "I just have to get the parcel out of the back of the truck."

Lacey pretended to be half asleep. "Take your time, Adam," she said softly, "I'll just snooze until you get back."

When Adam was finished fumbling around in the back, she heard him lock the canopy. He walked by her side of the vehicle. She noticed that he was carrying a black leather bag. It made her think of a doctor's bag, (the kind they used to carry when medical practitioners still made house calls). She thought it rather strange that he was delivering an unwrapped package. Wouldn't the insurance company have a fit if they saw how casually the parcels were handled, how easily the cargo could be damaged.

She saw Adam glance in at her as he passed. She leaned her head back, pretending to sleep.

He stopped in front of the SUV and leaned down. She couldn't see what he was doing. In a few seconds, he reappeared. He had a ladder. Leaning it against the trailer wall, Adam climbed up about 3 or 4 rungs, stepped on to the porch, walked over to the door, and knocked. It sounded like a coded knock. She heard a tap-tap-tap, then a pause, then 3 more taps, then 2 loud bangs as he pounded his fist twice on the door. Adam then waited.

In short order, the door opened, but only slightly. There was a soft glow from a lamp or a flashlight, she wasn't sure which. She couldn't see who answered the door. She couldn't even tell if it was a man, a woman, or a child. Adam stepped into the mobile home. The door closed swiftly.

Lacey glanced at the clock on the dash. It read 10:50.

Praying that she wouldn't be caught, she quickly got out of the truck, shut the door so the interior light wouldn't attract attention. She rushed over to the SUV. There was just enough moonlight that she could tell it was a dark grey Jeep Cherokee, B.C. plate #DMW123. She practically flew the couple of metres back to the truck. Once inside, she grabbed her pen and paper from her backpack, then wrote the information on the same page as the directions to the mobile home park.

Lacey kept watching the clock as the minutes crawled by, 11:10, 11:25, 11:45.

A blood-curdling scream filled the air! Lacey jumped, looking wildly around in all directions. Even in the cab of the truck, the decibel level of that scream was enough to wake the dead. Waiting a minute and looking down the road towards the other mobile homes, she was sure the neighbours must have heard the noise, even from 2 blocks away. No lights turned on. Nobody came.

Finally, at 12:15, Adam came out. Perching on the ladder was rather awkward as he still had the black bag in his hand. He climbed down without incident, returned the ladder to its previous resting place. Cautiously looking around, Adam returned to the vehicle and climbed in, muttering, "Sorry about the delay. It took longer than I thought it would." He threw the black bag behind his seat.

"Have to get diesel," he said. "There's an all-night place just up the road."

In a matter of minutes, he pulled up to the full-service diesel pump. "I normally pump my own diesel," he said, "but I need to visit the washroom, probably for several minutes. I'll be back as soon as I can. Ask them to fill it up and check the oil, please, Lacey."

"Are you okay, Adam?" Lacey asked.

"I will be. Back as soon as I can."

As soon as he was out of her sight, Lacey reached back and grabbed the leather bag. With one eye looking out the window she opened the bag, looked in and emitted a croak! Bile rose up, burning her throat. She swallowed hard, grabbed her cell phone and snapped a picture. She then hurriedly closed the bag and put it back.

Her body shook and her teeth chattered as she stared at the picture on her screen which clearly showed the contents of the bag. Inside was a lethal-looking meat saw. The saw sat on a too-small piece of paper towel. Several other lethal looking, butchering-type tools rested at the bottom of the case. On top of the saw, sat a small Ziploc sandwich bag. Inside the sandwich bag was a thumb, fresh blood coating both the thumb and the inside of the bag!

Retching, gagging, feeling like she was going to choke, Lacey forced herself not to vomit.

She suddenly remembered to look out the window. She spotted Adam near a pop machine. Quickly turning off her cell, she hid it in the bottom of her pack. Still shaking, she sat on her hands, hoping Adam would not notice how upset she was.

Whistling as he got in the vehicle, he handed Lacey a can of Coke and a chocolate bar.

"Thanks, Adam. Mind if I save it for later?"

"It's yours, Lacey, do with it what you will."

It seemed like forever before they got to Harrison Hot Springs. The 40 kilometre drive might as well have been 40,000.

Adam pulled into the service station. "Are you sure you don't want me to drive you to your friend's house? We're later than I intended getting here."

"No!" Lacey said, half hysterical. She forced herself to settle down. "I mean," she continued more calmly, "my friend said no matter what time it was, she will come and get me. You go on your way. Thanks so much for picking me up and bringing me all the way here. You have no idea how much I appreciate your kindness."

"You're most welcome. It was nice to have such good company on the long drive. Maybe we will run into one another again some time?" He handed her his business card, which advertised the butcher shop. "Call me any time, OK, Lacey? Good luck finding your brother."

Lacey stumbled when she got out. Catching herself, she leaned against the truck. Standing upright, she managed a sickly smile as she waved at Adam. With a tiny toot of the horn, he waved back and headed out on to the highway once more.

Watching until the pumpkin truck vanished from her sight, Lacey was unsteady on her feet, she stumbled clumsily towards the service station's bathroom.

Unable to get the horrifying image from her mind, she leaned over the toilet and threw up until there was nothing left in her stomach. She got the dry heaves and sat down on the toilet seat, bent over and clutched her stomach until they stopped.

I have to get myself together, she thought when she was finally able to leave the stall. Her face looking back at her in the mirror looked dreadful. Her complexion was a greenish-white. She hadn't brushed her hair since morning. Her clothing was rumpled. She looked sick, frightened, and disgusting.

Of course, she didn't have a friend who lived in Harrison Hot Springs. She would have to find someplace to sleep tonight, if sleep was even possible. In the morning, she would have a shower, do her hair, change her clothes, and then hitchhike back to Hope. What she was going to do when she got back there, she didn't have a clue. She would have to figure that out in the morning, or whenever inspiration struck.

Leaving the restroom, she went in to the service station. She asked the cashier where the nearest motel was. He gave her directions to a small motel only 2 blocks away.

It was the middle of the night. Lacey was alone in a strange town, walking down a strange street toward a strange motel. Nervous, she developed a crick in her neck from rubber-necking as she walked. Fortunately, there were no other pedestrians, and the only vehicular traffic was on the highway – the opposite direction from the motel.

Standing outside the motel office, she prayed there was a vacancy. She went inside and rang the bell that stood on the desk. After about 4 rings, a tall, skinny fellow came out of the back. She could hear the television blaring in the background.

Fortunately, there was a room available and Lacey gratefully reached for the key.

Inside the tiny, very old room, she looked around. It was definitely old and tiny, but spotless. *Thank heavens for small mercies*, she thought. Double-checking the lock and chain on the door, she sank down on the bed, fully clothed.

She was sure that she wouldn't be able to sleep, that she would see the sawed-off thumb in her mind's eye the entire night. Lacey lay down and in less than a minute was sound asleep.

Several hours later, she awoke with a start. The clock read 5 a.m. Bleary eyed and groggy, she went to the bathroom. This time when she reached the bed she undressed and crawled back in.

The next time she awoke it was 9 o'clock! She dragged herself out of bed. There was a coffee machine on the dresser. She set it up and left it working its magic while she had her shower.

Feeling much better, she came out of the bathroom and poured herself a cup, dumping in a lot of sugar. She needed the boost.

She then phoned the office and inquired whether or not there was a Greyhound bus that stopped in Harrison Hot Springs heading east. She was told that the bus would stop at the service station just off the highway in one hour. It stopped at another service station just on the edge of Hope before continuing on to Alberta. Thanking the man, she then grabbed her purse and went into the restaurant just off the lobby of the motel for breakfast.

She arrived at the service station with a half hour to spare. She bought a coffee and a magazine and then sat down on a bench outside to wait.

Riding the bus in the daylight was much different than travelling at night, but Lacey was oblivious to the scenery passing by.

She gazed thoughtfully out of the bus window, trying to formulate some kind of a plan. She knew she should ask the police for help, she knew she should call Parker and let him know she was OK. She knew she should tell him what she had found. But honestly? She didn't want to talk to Parker. She didn't want to listen to him telling her that she needed to come home. As a matter of fact, she wasn't sure she ever wanted to go home. She just did not know.

She had remembered to bring Susanna's telephone number. Lacey thought she would give her a call once she had a plan and knew where she would be staying. If Susanna had her car with her at the university, maybe she could come and see Lacey.

Just the thought of talking to her friend made Lacey feel more settled. She opened her magazine and no sooner started to look at it, when the bus driver announced the stop at the service station just outside of Hope.

She quickly gathered her things and stepped off the bus. She was going to go in to the station and ask about accommodations in Hope, but she spied a bulletin board nailed to the side of the building.

She glanced at the numerous pieces of paper pinned to the board and suddenly one particular paper caught her eye. There it was!

ROOM FOR RENT. NON-SMOKING FEMALE. ONE BEDROOM WITH BATH.

WITH KITCHEN PRIVILEGES – $450 PER MONTH. WITH BOARD, $550.'

The notice included an address and a telephone number. Lacey quickly took the notice off of the board, pulled out her cell and dialled the number.

The woman who answered the phone sounded elderly. She told Lacey that no, she hadn't rented the room yet. She wanted to know how old Lacey was. Lacey lied, said she was 22. She prayed the woman wouldn't ask her if she had a job. She lucked out. The woman on the other end of the line didn't ask that question. She did tell Lacey, though, that she would stand for no noise, no parties, and she expected her to keep her room neat and clean.

"Well, young woman, you might as well come on over and see my place. Where are you now?"

Lacey told her.

"Well, young woman," she repeated herself, "you're about a half-hour walk to my place. Need directions?"

Lacey looked at the address, which somehow looked vaguely familiar. "Ummm," she began …

The old lady interrupted her. "It's the '*MOBILE HOMES ARE BEAUTIFUL*' mobile home park."

Lacey couldn't believe it! The same trailer park? Unbelievable!

"It's fine, ma'am," she said. "I know exactly where you are. See you in about a half hour."

Now, Lacey thought excitedly, *the only thing that could be better is if my bedroom window looks in the direction of that old mobile home we were at last night!* She couldn't wait to get to the park. The name of it made her smile – *MOBILE HOMES ARE BEAUTIFUL.* That would explain the neatness and tidiness of the park. Probably all seniors.

She hurried off in the general direction – towards the north end of Hope. She was pretty sure the old lady would frown upon her being later than she was expected to arrive.

Twenty minutes later, Lacey arrived at the mobile home park and searched for trailer 2. As luck would have it, the mobile home was on the opposite side of the road to the dilapidated structure she was at the night before. She stood at the side of the mobile home. By looking very carefully down the road, Lacey could just make out the outline of the old wreck. Although she couldn't see the door, she could see the parking pad. If someone drove to that address, she would be able to see the vehicle. Now, she just had to hope that the window in her room looked out in that direction.

Lacey felt that things were beginning to fall into place. Straightening her shoulders, she went to the front door of mobile home 2 and rang the bell.

Almost before the doorbell stopped ringing, the door was opened. A tiny old lady stood there. "Are you her?" she barked at Lacey. "Did I talk to you?"

"Yes, ma'am," Lacey said politely. "You talked to me a half hour ago and I came right here. My name is Lacey Sutton. May I please see the room?"

"Yeah, yeah, hold on to your britches. Come on in. Don't just stand there, young woman, come on in and keep the flies out." The feisty senior stared at Lacey suspiciously. "You don't look like you're 22, but then I don't look like I'm 83 either, I suppose."

Lacey followed the elderly lady down the hallway. Stopping at the 1st bedroom on the left, the lady opened the door and stood aside so Lacey could enter the bedroom. The room was a surprisingly good size. She hadn't been in many mobile homes and had envisioned a tiny little room. An adjoining door led to a full bathroom. She turned to the owner and asked, "Do we share this bathroom?"

The lady said, "You only have to share this bathroom if either of us has visitors. I have my own bathroom attached to my room at the end of the hall. There is a 3rd bedroom on the other side of this bathroom, but it is not adjoining. Matter of fact, I have it set up as a home office. I like to pay my bills, balance my bank account and such in there. I also have a television, an easy chair, and a wall full of books. I always watch television with a set of headphones on, so you won't find that the television or my phonograph music will bother you any. My hearing is good, but it is better with headphones. Shuts out any other noises and I can concentrate better."

"Well, young woman, what do you think? Want to rent the room?"

She waited for Lacey to respond.

"Please," Lacey said. "When is it available?"

"It's available as soon as you set that there backpack of yours down in the room. Of course, I will need rent for this month and an extra month's rent as a damage deposit. Do you want board or just room with kitchen privileges?"

Once again, she waited for Lacey to respond.

"How about I pay you for room and board, ma'am?" Lacey queried. "But if I am working and my hours don't coincide with your meal times, would it be all right if I made myself something to eat when I got home from work?"

"Not a problem, so long as you don't leave a mess in the kitchen and I don't have visitors at the time. As you can see, the kitchen and front room are almost like a single room."

"OK," Lacey said. "Will you take a cheque or would you prefer that I go find a bank and get you the cash?"

"Cheque will be fine. I know where to find you if your cheque bounces," she cackled.

"Great!" Lacey exclaimed. "I don't believe you have told me your name, though, ma'am. I have it to put on the cheque?"

"Oh, silly me. I am sorry. I'm Stella French."

"Thank you, Mrs. French, I'm sure I will be happy here," Lacey said in a somewhat dubious, somewhat hopeful tone of voice.

"Here you are, my cheque for $1,100.00, $550.00 for the one month damage deposit and $550.00 for the 1st month's rent."

"Thank you, young woman. What did you say your name was again? Oh. Never mind, silly me, it's on your cheque. Lacey Sutton. Well, Miss Lacey

Sutton, welcome to my humble abode. Here's your key. Don't lose it or I'll have to charge you for a new one."

"Now, I'm a very private woman. Don't expect me to entertain you. As far as I'm concerned, you're just a paycheque to me. I won't be holding your hand or babysitting you. Understand?"

"Yes, ma'am," Lacey said. "Just one more question, please. Where is Buy-Low Foods from here? I have a job interview in an hour. Can I walk there?"

Stella French said, "You can walk pretty much anywhere you like. Hope's a small town."

She then gave Lacey directions to the store.

"If my old legs were to walk it, it would take at least a half an hour. Your young legs can probably get there in about 10 or 15 minutes. Good luck with your interview, my dear."

"Now, I must go to my office. I have things to do. Besides, *'The Young and the Restless'* is going to be on my television set in a matter of minutes. Never missed a day of that story since it came on television. If you need a snack before you go, there's fruit and yogurt in the fridge. Just make yourself at home." She scuttled off to her little den without a backward glance.

Lacey went in to her new room. There were venetian blinds on the window. She adjusted the slats so she could see out but no one could see into her room. She had as perfect a view of the old trailer as was possible, through the trees and the distance it was from the main part of the mobile home park.

She quickly unpacked her meagre belongings from her pack. The room had a single bed, and a small desk.

The good-sized closet had a California Closets insert and would be super easy to organize. There were 4 drawers on the right-hand side, a short hanging rod with a shoe rack below it, and a hanging rod for full-length clothing. A shelf above the rods completed the space.

Once Lacey was organized, she sat down at her desk and turned on her cellphone. Her mailbox was full, filled with messages from Parker. He sounded more pissed off than frantic in the first several messages. He sounded frightened in the next bunch. In the last message, he sounded downright terrified. Regretfully, Lacey deleted every message. She would call Parker if and when she had something concrete to tell him. In the meantime, she would leave her phone turned off. She didn't want him tracking her down. All she needed was to have a policeman show up at Stella French's door looking for Lacey!

She couldn't delay any longer. With a large shudder, she flicked her screen to the picture of the black leather bag and its contents. Yup! It was still a bloody thumb. Nothing had changed in that regard. Her ears still echoed with the terrifying scream she heard just before Adam exited the trailer.

She would keep a close watch for vehicles coming and going from the old trailer. Once she had a pretty good idea of what vehicle or vehicles parked there, what days, and for how long at any one time, she would figure out what to do next.

Right now, she had to go and find herself a job.

As of right now, everyone who had searched for the missing girls and for Lloyd had been searching in all the wrong places. Lacey prayed fervently that she was in the right place.

She wondered who that thumb belonged to. *Did it belong to Charlotte, also known as Charley? Did it belong to Amelia? Maybe to Annie? Or, dear Lord, no,* Lacey prayed, *don't let it belong to Lloyd.* She immediately felt guilty for even wishing something so terrible on anyone.

She studied the picture more carefully. From the picture, one really couldn't tell either the actual size of the thumb or the gender. All you could see was a very jagged edge, and a short-cut, clean fingernail. No nail polish. It could belong to one of the girls, or to Lloyd, or to none of them. Perhaps this was something different all together? Although Lacey wouldn't wish such a terrible event to happen to any living person, she guiltily hoped and prayed it didn't belong to anyone she knew.

The last thing on her mind as she got ready to leave the mobile home, was Adam Draper. She had been so instantly drawn to him. He had seemed like a really, truly nice guy. She wondered how much money he had received for chopping off and taking away one small thumb.

Feeling sick and disgusted, she left the mobile home and went to Buy-Low in search of a job. Her funds were limited and she was pretty sure she would be in Hope for quite a length of time before she found Lloyd and the missing girls.

Optimistic by nature, despite her trials and tribulations since she was 9 years old, Lacey just knew she would find them. She just knew it!

Chapter 13
No Good Life

Evan Smithson

Lacey applied for a job at Buy-Low foods. After she completed filling out the application form, she waited for the manager of the store to come in and interview her.

She looked around as she waited. The store was immaculately clean, the shelves fully stocked. The meat and the produce looked fresh and inviting. The deli contained a large number of choices. The baking in the bakery section looked almost home-made. It looked delicious! Lacey made herself a mental note to pick something up to take to her landlady as a special treat.

A man walked into the office where Lacey was waiting. He looked to be in his mid-to-late 50's. Short, maybe 165 centimetres, and rotund. What little hair he had on his head was white and curly. His eyes twinkled behind his glasses. He smelled like a smoker.

The man walked over to Lacey. She stood up as he approached with his hand out. She took his hand and hers was heartily pumped.

He introduced himself as Evan Smithson, the Manager. "But you can call me Smithy, everyone does."

Sitting down at his cluttered desk, he picked up her job application.

"I see you worked at a grocery store in Alberta. Before that you graduated from high school. What made you get a job rather than get a further education? Your marks were well above average."

Lacey felt embarrassed but she replied honestly. "I intended to go to university, and my foster parents urged me to go. Stumpy, he's my foster father, had even saved up money for my tuition. I had a terrible time convincing him that I wanted to save up my own money for my education, that it wasn't fair that he should have to spend his life savings on an education for someone who isn't even his biological daughter."

She stared at the manager intently before she said, "However, before I had to worry much about anything, I got married."

"I see," said Evan Smithson. "Do you have any children?"

"No, sir, I do not. I would like children someday, but I'm only 17. I have a lot of years before I need to worry about raising children."

The manager sat listening. He did not interrupt her. Finally, to break what was beginning to be an uncomfortable silence, she continued. "My husband is a sergeant with the R.C.M.P. in Alberta. We aren't separated, exactly, but we aren't together at the moment either."

"If I hire you, will you walk out on me in a few days, a few weeks, maybe a month or 2? Go back to your husband?"

"No, Mr. Smithson, I can promise you that I won't walk out on you without the required amount of time to give notice. At this moment, I can honestly tell you that I can't see myself going anywhere else for quite some time."

Lacey decided then and there that she would not be telling this man or anyone else the real reason that she was now living in Hope.

She sat still and watched him as he re-read her job application. Thoughtfully, he set it down again. He stared intently at Lacey for a moment before saying, "OK, young lady, I'll take a chance on you. I'm a pretty good judge of character and something tells me you will be an asset to our team. However, if I was to call your former place of employment, would that manager recommend you?"

"I am pretty sure he would, sir, however, he doesn't know that I have moved here. He wasn't in his office when I had to leave, so I just left him a note. I'm not proud of leaving that way, but an emergency came up and I had to leave immediately. Nobody knows I am here, sir, including Parker."

"Parker?" Mr. Smithson queried.

"My husband, sir."

"When can you start?"

Heaving a huge sigh of relief, Lacey said, "I can start immediately, sir."

Standing up, she suddenly remembered. "I really hate to ask this, sir, before I have even formally started my job, but could I have Thursday as a regularly scheduled day off?"

"I don't mind working every other day or night of the week or the weekends, but I have to go somewhere every Thursday."

Mr. Smithson looked at Lacey and then grinned broadly. "Tell you what, young lady, call me 'Smithy' the same as everyone else does, and it's a deal. Thursdays are not the most popular requests for days off that I receive, so it's not a problem."

"Now, how about you start tomorrow morning at 8 o'clock. If you stop at the deli counter on your way out, Mrs. Brown will get you a uniform to take home. Be wearing it when you come in tomorrow."

"Welcome to our team, Lacey. I think you will like it here. We have a very small turnover of staff here. You are lucky that there was an opening. I look forward to a long and happy working relationship with you."

When she got back to the mobile home, Stella French was making supper. Something smelled delicious! Lacey handed Mrs. French the fresh strawberries and a sponge cake she had picked up at the deli as a special treat.

"Thanks, Lacey!" Stella said. "That's real nice of you. How did your job interview go?"

Lacey said, "It went just fine. You are now looking at an apprentice cashier at Buy-Low foods. The manager, Evan Smithson, seems like a real nice guy. He says the turnover rate of staff there is very low. I'm lucky they needed a cashier."

"I start tomorrow morning at 8 o'clock."

Stella handed Lacey a small knife and a colander, together with the basket of berries. Lacey began cleaning and hulling the strawberries.

"I know Evan Smithson," Stella said. "You're perfectly correct, he is a real nice guy. You could have a lot worse for a boss, that's for darn sure. His wife, Lucy, and I play bridge in the same bridge club on Tuesday nights."

The table was already set, so Lacey went to her room to get ready for supper. She hung up her uniform so it wouldn't wrinkle and then went back to the kitchen.

After supper, Lacey offered to clean up so that Stella could watch the news on television. She gratefully accepted the offer and toddled off down the hall.

Lacey sat on her bed and stared out the window towards the old trailer. It wasn't dark yet, but dusk was falling. Eerie shadows surrounded the place. There was no sign of life, and no vehicle in the driveway.

Before she could change her mind, Lacey quickly put on her jacket, grabbed her key and rapidly walked down the road towards the wrecky old joint. She decided on the spur of the moment to christen the old junk heap 'Freedom'. Maybe an optimistic name like that would bring Lacey good luck and she would find Charley, Amelia, Annie, and Lloyd there.

Taking care to remain out of sight of the road, Lacey quietly walked around Freedom. She stopped frequently and listened. Only a few songbirds trilled in the treetops, one last song before dark. Far in the distance, a lonely dog barked.

She reached the front end of the trailer just as a vehicle turned in, right towards her. For a split second, she remained stationary, a deer in the headlights. Gathering her wits about her, she leaped back, sat down in the tall dry grass. Held her breath.

Had the driver seen her? Her heart was pounding so hard that she couldn't hear herself think above the thumping.

Lacey lay down flat on her stomach. She was so busy thinking about and hoping that there were no rats rustling around, that she almost screamed. She always was an expert at scaring herself half to death!

The grass and the weeds were tall enough that she could peek out between some of the fronds without being seen. It must have been eons since Freedom's yard had seen any tender loving care (TLC), if ever.

She continued to peer through the leafage. The trouble was, all she could see was a pair of feet. It looked like men's feet to her. It was too dusky to see the type of shoes, but if those feet belonged to a woman – *poor thing*, was all Lacey could think. Large and wide, probably at the very least, a size 12.

She was afraid to lift her head high enough to get a look at the driver of the vehicle.

She checked her watch. 8 p.m. on the dot. She wanted to see how long that person stayed in Freedom before he left again. IF he left again.

As soon as the trailer door closed, Lacey raced back home. Frightened and excited both, she unlocked the door and quickly went into her room. She sat there in the dim light, staring out at Freedom. She hadn't got a look at the licence plate, but she was almost positive that it was the same vehicle that was parked there on Thursday, when Adam entered and then came outside with the thumb.

Boy, am I a terrible judge of character or what, Lacey thought to herself. *Parker turned out to be such a different man than the way he revealed himself to me when we were dating. I thought he was a talker and that we could and would talk about everything, big or small, unimportant or vital stuff. Yikes, I was dead wrong!*

She continued to think. *Adam seemed like a super guy. I felt like I could tell him anything, in fact, I did tell him things, way too many things. Thank heaven I didn't give him any names. But he seemed to listen, really listen to me. I wasn't used to that. I was flattered that a guy so much older than me would treat me with such respect, give me so much attention. I could have fallen for him easily on the trip to B.C. He was so nice and so thoughtful. That is until 'the butcher' slashed off a thumb!*

Lacey was so busy having a conversation with herself about the guys in her life that she very nearly missed the departure of the vehicle at Freedom. She missed seeing him come out of the door and get in to the vehicle. From her vantage point looking out her own bedroom window, she still didn't know whether or not there were any lights on inside the dreadful old trailer.

The driver took a left at the corner and then stopped at the side of the road, under the streetlight. He appeared to be calling someone on a cellphone.

It was definitely a male, but Lacey couldn't begin to venture a guess about his appearance. He was too far away. In a couple of minutes, he drove on down the road.

Try as she might, Lacey could not make out the complete plate number. She got part of it – W123. She saw that it was a dark Jeep Cherokee. Pulling her notebook out of her backpack, she checked the number. The last four digits of the plate number she had recorded in her notebook were W123. She now knew that it was the same vehicle as the one she saw on Thursday.

Although she wanted to race down the road and bang on the door with the coded knock she had made a note of, she thought better of it. She would watch every night for 2 weeks and record any and all comings and goings at Freedom. Why 2 weeks? No specific reason other than that Lacey wanted to make sure the delivery vehicle driver stuck to the same timeline, and the jeep driver did as well. She did not want to attempt entry into Freedom only to be caught by either one!

Unable to settle down, she looked at the clock and decided it wasn't too late to phone Susanna. She had tried to call her several times since she came to Hope. She had left her a detailed message the last time she called. She had told Susanna that she was living in Hope and working at the Buy-Low grocery store. Maybe now was a good time to try again. She had a lot to tell her.

Susanna answered on the 1st ring. "Lacey!" she screamed into the phone. "Oh my gosh, Lacey, thank heaven you called me. I lost your number and... I got your message... I was just about to phone the grocery store and try to get your number when I got your message! But now here you are, phoning me before I could call you!" She paused for breath, giving Lacey time to say hello.

Before Lacey could say another word, Susanna said, "Lacey you have to go back home…

Lacey interrupted her. "Not yet, Susanna, I can't go home yet. Listen to all the stuff I have to tell you."

Susanna practically screamed into the phone. "Lacey, listen to me! It's urgent!"

Lacey couldn't imagine any news more urgent than what she had to tell Susanna, but she stopped, took a deep breath. "Okay, Susanna, what can possibly be that urgent?"

Susanna said quietly, "It's Stumpy, Lacey. It's really bad. He's in the hospital and asking to see you.

"Dad called and told me that Hilda has bought you a plane ticket. You are flying WestJet from Abbotsford tomorrow. It's about an hour from Hope to the airport in Abbotsford. Your ticket will be at the check-in counter. She also arranged a car rental for you at the airport when you land. That's paid for also. For now, you just need to figure out how to get to Abbotsford."

"What's wrong with him, Susanna? What's wrong with Stumpy that I have to go back in such a rush?"

Susanna said softly, "I don't know, Lacey. But it must be serious for him to ask to see you ASAP. I'm going to hang up now and let you get ready to leave. You have my number. Call me when you know what's up, OK? Please! And just so you know, it's a miracle that you called tonight."

"Nobody has been able to get hold of you – you never answer your phone apparently! And then I lost your number, and then just in the nick of time you phone me!!! Oh, Lacey, thank you for phoning me!"

"Bye, Susanna," Lacey blurted out, and then hung up on her friend.

She quickly went to the room where her landlady was watching television and knocked on the door. She didn't wait for Stella French to open it. She stuck her head in and said apologetically, "Mrs. French, I'm sorry to bother you but… " Lacey started to cry.

In between sobs she was able to communicate what the problem was. She knew Stella would have Smithy's phone number, and probably knew the bus schedule from Hope to Abbotsford also.

"Lacey, don't worry about anything. You don't need a bus schedule. I will drive you to the Abbotsford airport in the morning. Don't worry, you won't miss the plane."

"Now let me go and look for Smithy's phone number. You'll need to call him immediately."

Lacey said, "I guess that will be the end of my new job. But, oh, Stella, I have to go and see Stumpy. He asked for me! He's real sick and I have to see him."

"Of course, of course you do, dear. Now, Smithy is a real fair guy. He'll understand. Just let me get you the number. You sit here in my comfy chair and I'll give you the number and then make you a nice cup of tea." Happy to be useful, she scuttled off down the hall and found the phone number.

Lacey sat and waited for Stella to come back. While she waited, she took several harsh, shuddering breaths in an attempt to calm herself before she had to speak with Smithy.

She needn't have worried about his reaction. When she explained who Stumpy was and what the problem was, he told her that, of course, she must go home. He would keep her job for her for as long as she had to be home. All he asked was for her to keep him apprised. This she promised she would do. Blubbering loudly, she thanked him, hung up and went to pack a bag.

True to her word, Stella French got Lacey to the airport in plenty of time. Hugging her landlady tightly, she thanked her profusely and promised to let her know what was going on and when she would be back again. She then turned and went through security.

The flight was uneventful and arrived right on time. She only had her carry-on bag and so didn't have to wait for her luggage.

When she got to the car rental kiosk, there stood Uncle Henry! He enclosed her in a terrific bear hug.

"Uncle Henry! What in the world are you doing here? I thought Hilda arranged for a rental for me! Oh, it's so good to see you, thank you for coming to pick me up."

"Couldn't let one of my favourite people drive all the way home and then to the hospital, now could I? When I knew you were coming for sure, I cancelled the car reservation. Now, let's go see Stumpy. Hilda has been at the hospital day and night. She will be mighty happy to see you, honey, as am I."

As they travelled the highway towards the hospital where Stumpy was admitted, Lacey filled Henry in on where she was staying and where she was working. She didn't fill him in on any details of her investigation. She just told him that she couldn't sit around and do nothing, that she was going to find Lloyd and the girls or die trying!

Uncle Henry was a very private man and he respected other people's privacy as well. Therefore, he did not ask Lacey about Parker. He figured if she had anything to say in that regard, she would say it.

He glanced over at his young passenger. She was sound asleep. He let her be.

Chapter 14
Stumpy

Uncle Henry had reached the hospital and parked the car. He leaned over and gently tapped Lacey on the shoulder. She half awoke with a start, but in a matter of seconds was wide awake and anxious to go in and find Stumpy. She grabbed her pack from the back seat, leaned over and gave Uncle Henry a hug, thanking him again for picking her up.

"Would you like me to wait for you, Lacey?" he asked.

"Thanks, but no thanks, Uncle Henry. I need to see what's going on with Stumpy. I see Hilda's vehicle parked just over there, so I'm sure I have a ride whenever I am ready."

"Okay, then. Say hi to Hilda from us, and tell Stumpy to get well soon."

He looked sternly at Lacey before he said, "Keep in touch my girl, we need to know what's up!"

Lacey stood at the main entrance, waving to Uncle Henry until he was out of sight. Taking a huge breath, she straightened her shoulders and entered the building.

"Can you please tell me the room number for Mr. Stumpy Somers?" she asked the attendant at the Information desk.

The very young woman, whose large name tag read '**Hi, I'm Madison**' looked at a list and then looked up at Lacey. "Mr. Somers is in the Intensive Care Unit. I'm sorry, miss, but you won't be able to see him. Immediate family only."

"I'm his daughter and he is asking for me." This was only a partial fib. Stumpy and Hilda were her permanent guardians, but she doubted if the young attendant would recognize her as family if she told her that, at least without a fuss.

As soon as the '**Hi, I'm Madison**' girl had given Lacey directions to the ICU, she practically ran in her hurry to see Stumpy.

Hilda sat slumped on a chair beside the closed door to Stumpy's room, her head in her hands. At first glance, Lacey thought she was dozing but when she quietly approached, Hilda raised her head and looked blankly at Lacey. Then, with a soft moan, she leaped up from the chair, still, at age 70, as spry as an acrobat in the circus. She grabbed Lacey and hugged her so tightly that Lacey struggled to breathe.

"Oh, Lacey! You came! You came! How did you get here? Did Susanna call you? Where have you been? Oh, I have a million questions, but they will have to wait until after the doctor comes out of Stumpy's room and speaks with us. He'll just be a minute he said."

Lacey sensed that Hilda was extremely worried and beyond exhausted. Grabbing another chair from outside the door of the next room, she pulled it over beside Hilda and sat down, never letting go of Hilda's hand.

Before she could say anything, the door opened and a doctor in a white lab coat came out. Seeing Lacey standing beside Hilda, he came over, shook her hand as he introduced himself.

"I don't know how much you know about what is going on," he said to Lacey. "Has Hilda filled you in?"

"No, sir, I have just arrived and we haven't had a chance to catch up. Please, can you tell me what's wrong with Stumpy?"

The doctor cast a worried glance over at Hilda and then he put his arm around her. *Not a good sign,* Lacey thought.

He looked from one woman to the other as he spoke. "Stumpy came in to our Emergency department 3 nights ago, exhibiting all of the symptoms of a severe heart attack. My preliminary examination confirmed that fact. However, some other symptoms were worrying me and so I ordered additional tests. The results have just come back."

He suggested to the women that perhaps they would like to sit down. Hilda sat, Lacey preferred to stand.

"The scans and the bloodwork indicate that Mr. Somers has indeed had a massive heart attack, but in addition, I am sorry to say, he has pancreatic cancer and malignant lesions on both lungs. His liver and kidneys are also cancerous. In other words, he is pretty much full of cancer."

"You can treat him, though, doctor, right?" Lacey implored the man. "He's healthy, healthier than I am. He might be old, but he has led an active life. Why, when he and I went walking, I struggled to keep up with him. You have to fix him, you just have to!"

Hilda sat calmly, waiting for the shock to lessen before she stood and put her arms around Lacey. She looked at the doctor and quietly asked, "How long, doc?"

Sadly, he said, "Hours maybe, a couple of days at the most. I'm so sorry, ladies, I'm so very sorry. Even if it wasn't so advanced, we wouldn't be able to operate because his heart is in no condition to withstand either the anaesthetic or the surgery."

"If you need me for anything, just ask the nurse at the desk over there. I hate to deliver such bad news and then run, but I have to be in the operating room right away."

Lacey took Hilda by the shoulders and shook her. Her face was right up against Hilda's face as she hissed, "What's wrong with you? You're just giving up? Stumpy deserves better than the, 'Oh, poor you, you have cancer and you're going to die' without even trying treatments to at least prolong his life if the cancer can't be cured. If Stumpy heard you now, he would be ashamed, Hilda. He would be ashamed!"

Hilda let her rant and rave until she ran out of steam.

Taking both Lacey's young, smooth hands between her own 2 old and wrinkled ones, she said, "Lacey, Stumpy knows. We talked about this possibility on our way to the hospital in the ambulance the other night. He has known for some time that he wasn't well. He went to see the doctor. He wouldn't let me go with him. He didn't tell me exactly word-for-word what the doc told him, but when he got back, we saw our lawyer, the very next day. We updated our wills. Stumpy told me he wanted no treatments of any kind if he had cancer. He said he was almost positive that he did have, as he put it, 'THE BIG C'. So, Lacey, on some level, Stumpy already knew."

"Now, young lady, pull yourself together as best you can and get in there and see Stumpy. He's been waiting for you, asking everyone coming and going in and out of his room if they know when you're coming. You're his pride and joy, gal, his pride and joy."

"Wipe your eyes and go on in. I'm going to get a coffee, but I'll be right here when you come out."

Lacey tremulously opened the door to Stumpy's room. It was dimly lit, most of the light emanating from numerous machines that hummed and thrummed, beeped and hissed, monitoring Stumpy's worn out carcass, protesting with loud beeps and warnings when something seemed amiss.

As she slowly and quietly approached the bed, Lacey was shocked to see the many tubes poking out of the man. He had an oxygen mask on. His arms were strapped to the bed. She supposed that it was to prevent him from pulling out anything attached to his body, accidentally (or on purpose).

She leaned over and kissed him on his weathered cheek. "Hi, Stumpy, it's Lacey. You wanted to see me?" She wanted to hold his hand but between needles, tubes and tape, she settled for holding one of his fingers instead.

He opened his eyes. Seeing Lacey sitting beside his bed he gave a shaky but wide grin. "You came! My girl, you made it. Thanks for coming!" Although he sounded excited, his voice was so faint that she had to lean over, her ear almost on his lips in her effort to hear.

His breath came in short, wheezy bursts, his voice raspy and worn.

"You're going to be fine Stumpy, you just rest now and get better," she said. "I'll just sit here beside you while you rest."

"Hilda?" he croaked.

"She just went to get a cup of coffee. She'll be right back."

Stumpy reached for her hand. "Good girl," he whispered as he patted it. Then, slightly stronger, "Don't forget, school money." Exhausted once again, he stopped.

Lacey stared at him. "What, don't even think about that! You have enough to do just concentrating on getting better without any of your usual deep thinking. Stop it, Stumpy, just stop it!"

"No!" His voice for that single word was strong, deep, and determined. "Money for school, remember!"

It took no imagination on Lacey's part to see that Stumpy was getting very much more agitated. She placated him as she said quietly, "OK, Stumpy, you have the money for me to go back to school. Thank you so much."

Reassured, he calmed down. Although he seemed to be more out of it than with it, after several minutes, he seemed to rally. "Know why, Stumpy?" he murmured.

"Are you going to finally tell me why you're called Stumpy?" Lacey smiled at him and squeezed his finger a little harder.

He beckoned her closer so he wouldn't have to try to torture his voice by speaking loudly. "Big baby," he mouthed. "Sturdy baby," he whispered, "strong, like a tree stump." He rested briefly, then he pointed at his chest, "Stumpy." Delighted that he managed to make himself both heard and understood, he smiled, patted Lacey's hand, and closed his eyes.

Lacey sat quietly, watching him. When she was certain that he was asleep, she tiptoed to the door. As promised, Hilda was seated in one of the chairs, waiting for Lacey to come out.

"He's asleep, Hilda. He looks so small and frail laying there in that bed. It hasn't been long since I last saw him. Only several weeks, right? How can a body disintegrate that fast?"

Taking a ragged breath, she reached for Hilda's hand. "Hilda, I'm sorry about what I said earlier. It was just such a shock, you know? I didn't mean what I said. You have done nothing for Stumpy to be ashamed of you for. Nothing, and I'm so sorry!" Tears coursed down her cheeks, stopping only when they pooled into a crease on her neck.

"It's OK, honey. I understand. The shock was horrific and you just lashed out at whoever was handiest. I'm a tough old hen, Lacey, I took it for what it was worth. Besides, honey, there is nothing you could say to me that would destroy our love for each other. You are as much our daughter as if I had given birth to you."

"So now, was Stumpy able to tell you what he needed to?"

Lacey tried to smile, but it was a desolate, hollow grimace. "He did, in a fashion. He told me to remember the money for school and he told me how he got Stumpy for a name! I'm so honoured, Hilda, just so honoured. You 2 are a gigantic part of my life, and I am so grateful to have you both."

They ceased to speak as a nurse went into his room to check on him. When she came out, she told them that he was still asleep, and they continued their conversation in soft and quiet tones.

"So, Miss Lacey, where have you been and what have you been doing? Oh, but first-off, have you spoken with Parker yet? The poor man is beside himself with worry, Lacey girl!"

"Now, I mean this in the kindest way, sweetie, but: SMARTEN UP! No matter what sort of troubles you are having, you can't solve them by running away. I thought I taught you better than that."

She stopped and sat, waiting for Lacey to tell her what was going on, if she would.

Lacey glanced at Hilda. She was shocked at her foster mother's appearance. The past couple of days had obviously tormented her. Lacey had never seen her look so old, wrinkled and drawn, so tired.

"Hilda, have you been home at all since Stumpy was brought in here? To sleep? To shower? To change clothes?"

The anguish on Hilda's face, the greasy lanks of hair hanging down onto her forehead, and the faint, sweaty odour, answered Lacey's questions without a spoken word from Hilda.

"Hang on a minute, I'll be right back," Lacey said. She got up and walked over to the nurses' desk, speaking urgently for a few minutes.

When she returned and sat down beside Hilda, she said, "Hilda I just spoke with the nurse. For the time being Stumpy is being kept comfortable. He is deeply asleep and the nurse said that he will likely sleep for at least 6 hours. They have medicated him for pain and given him something to make him sleep deeply."

"Let's do this – you and I will go home, sleep for a few hours, then shower, change our clothes, have a bite to eat. I need to check the Mailbox, and I would love it if you would come with me. It is past time that you get to see where Stumpy and I went on our hikes. On our way, there and back, I will tell you everything I have been doing the past few weeks. Then we will come back to the hospital and sit with Stumpy. Sound like a plan?"

Too drained to argue, Hilda simply nodded her head. She stood up and entered Stumpy's room to check on him. The nurse was right, he was deeply asleep. His face looked calm and peaceful in repose. Other than his ashen colouring, he looked almost well. Hilda kissed her fingertips and pressed them softly on Stumpy's lips.

While Hilda was in with Stumpy, Lacey filled the nurse in on what they proposed to do. She asked the nurse to please call if there was any change. She told the nurse they would try to be back at the hospital by lunchtime.

When Hilda came out of the room, Lacey placed an arm around her drooping shoulders and steered her towards the exit.

Lacey held out her hand for the keys and then helped Hilda into the vehicle.

On the half-hour drive to the farm, Hilda napped while Lacey tried to figure out just how their lives could have gone downhill in such a hurry. She thought about just how much to tell Hilda about her new life. Her most worrisome thoughts were about how to talk to Parker. They couldn't communicate when they were living together, how could she ever make him understand now?

When they got home, Lacey parked the vehicle in the garage so that no one driving by would know they were home. She knew the neighbours would mean well, but now was not the time for visiting. Both she and Hilda needed a rest and then get back to the hospital.

She helped Hilda into the house and led her to her bed. Hilda lay down fully clothed, rolled over, and was instantly asleep again. Lacey took Hilda's shoes off, covered her up with a spare quilt that was draped over the end of the bed, and quietly left the bedroom.

Within a few minutes, Lacey was also in her own bed. As tired as she was, she tossed and turned for what seemed like hours before finally falling into a fitful, dream-filled sleep.

At 7 o'clock, she was awakened by the smell of coffee and Hilda's infamous cinnamon buns. Entering the kitchen, she saw Hilda, freshly showered and dressed in clean clothes, sitting at the table, drinking a coffee.

"Why didn't you wake me, Hilda?" Lacey asked. "Now you'll have to wait for me."

"Not a problem, Lacey girl. Just go have your shower. After you've had a bite of breakfast we'll head out to your Mailbox. It's been more than a week since Stumpy checked it."

"OK, I'll hurry," Lacey said. "And I'll call the hospital before we leave for the Mailbox, get an update."

"I've already called," Hilda said. "The nurse said the doctor was there at 5 this morning. There was no change, and Stumpy was still sound asleep."

Lacey gave Hilda a hard squeeze. "I'll hurry," she said simply and went off to have a much-needed shower.

A half-hour later, warm sweaters, knitted caps and gloves were the order of the day. The sun had risen and was faintly warm on their upturned faces, but the slight breeze put a definite chill in the air. They walked briskly for the first half of the journey.

As they walked, Lacey filled Hilda in on the events in Lacey's current life. She had been unsure about how much to tell her, but once she started talking, she couldn't stop. She told her about her new landlady, her new boss, and she told her about Freedom and what she was doing, or rather trying to do, in order to gain access to the old trailer. She even told her about the thumb.

Hilda listened without comment. She knew that if she interrupted Lacey before she finished, then she wouldn't tell Hilda everything there was to tell.

They approached the part of the trail where Lacey and Stumpy had seen the beautiful bull elk. They stopped and looked, but saw no sign of either him or any other wild thing. Soon after, they reached the flat rock. They sat briefly, catching their breath, and enjoying the trickling sound of the water in the ravine below.

Lacey took Hilda over to the old tree stump, explaining the routine as she reached into the back of the opening. "Oh, my Lord, Hilda!" she squealed. "There's something in here!" Her teeth chattered and her hand shook so badly that she couldn't hang on to the envelope.

"Let's go back and sit on the flat rock," Hilda suggested. "Then you can see what you have in your hand."

Lacey raced back to the flat rock, threw herself down, and waited for Hilda to catch up.

She sat dead still, staring at the plain white envelope in her hand. Looking at Hilda, she said, "I'm afraid to see what this is, Hilda. I've been disappointed so many times before."

"Want me to open it?" Hilda asked. Lacey nodded and handed it over to her without saying anything.

"It's from Stumpy, Lacey." She handed the envelope and the sheet of paper back to Lacey, unread.

"Oh! I thought it might be from Lloyd." She swallowed hard before saying, "But something from Stumpy is the next best thing. Can you read it to me, please, Hilda?" She passed the paper back to her without waiting for an answer.

"Maybe I shouldn't read it, Lacey. Stumpy meant this for you."

Lacey asked, "Did you know about it?"

"Yes."

"Well, then, please read it to me. I want to listen. If I read it myself, I might miss something, and I want to cherish every single word that Stumpy has to say to me in that piece of paper. Do you understand what I'm saying, and why?"

Hilda nodded. She then reached into her jacket pocket and produced a pair of reading glasses. She cleared her throat, glanced at Lacey, and began to read,

My dearest Lacey girl, my daughter in my heart and soul. A relation by blood would make you no more of a daughter to me than you are right now.

When you read this, I will probably be dead, or at least darn close.

I don't want you to grieve for me, Lacey, although it comforts me to know that you might miss me just a little.

I've had a good life with a great woman. Please take care of my Hildy for me. She's a strong woman and will scoff and tell you that she can darned well take care of herself. You and I both know that she certainly is capable of that. However, Lacey, Hildy will be lonesome. No matter where you are or what you are doing, can you please just check on her from time to time – maybe phone her every Sunday or something like that so she doesn't worry her beautiful head about you?

Hildy and I changed our wills. When I die, everything goes to Hildy of course. But, when she dies, the farm and everything else, goes to you, Lacey. What you do with it will be up to you, but in the 'secret wish part of my heart', I hope that you and Parker will live there and raise a family there. That farmhouse contained a lot of love over the years, still does. Hopefully you will continue to fill it with love. No pressure! (Ha ha).

I have set aside funds to pay for your continuing education. If it is not university or college, it can be used for correspondence courses, or any type of education. You just need to let Hildy know when you need all or part of the money. She knows what to do.

I hope you won't be too disappointed when you reach into the old Mailbox and find a letter from me, rather than from Lloyd.

Lacey, if it is at all possible, I will be watching over you and my Hildy from Heaven. I have tried to live a good and decent life so I'm not worried that I won't go there. Take care my girl, live a good life, and be happy. Love always, your Stumpy

Lacey was speechless. A lump the size of a tennis ball seemed to be lodged in her throat. She silently reached out to Hilda. Hilda put the letter into her outstretched hand.

"What a wonderful letter, Hilda. I will keep it forever." Giving herself a mental shake she stood up, then bent over to assist Hilda in getting to her feet, although the truth be known, Hilda didn't need any help. It was Lacey who needed the assistance at the moment, she was so overcome.

They reached the spot which opened onto the large wheat field. Lacey gasped and held out her hand to stop Hilda. "Look!" she whispered, "the bull elk is back. Isn't he something?"

As the 2 women stood in absolute silence, utterly still, the skittish giant cautiously approached them, a step at a time. He seemed to recognize Lacey. Stopping several metres from her, he simply stood and looked at both of them. His large and shining eyes appeared to be trying to tell them something.

Too awed, and too afraid of scaring the magnificent creature away, Hilda and Lacey simply stood and stared back for what seemed like a very long time. Eventually, the bull seemed to bow to the ladies, then raised his head, gave a small snort, and turned around. In no hurry, he ambled quietly and slowly until he was about half-way between the edge of the field and the bush in the distance. He turned for one more look, trumpeted loudly, and took off running.

Still awestruck, Hilda put her arm around Lacey. "Wasn't that something!" she exclaimed. "It was almost like he was trying to tell us something."

In accord, they both gave out a gasp. "Stumpy!"

Hilda anxiously said, "Come on, Lacey, we have to hurry. I think Stumpy is dying!"

As quickly as they could, without tripping and falling on the uneven ground, they hurried home. Lacey ran into the house and grabbed both her purse and Hilda's and rushed into the garage. Hilda was already anxiously waiting in the truck.

Foolishly ignoring the speed limit as they headed for the hospital, Lacey made the normally 30-minute drive in 20 minutes. Fortunately, there was very little traffic on the highway.

Hilda was out of the vehicle and at the main entrance practically before they were parked. Lacey ran to catch up, put her arm around Hilda to slow her down.

"Easy, Hilda," Lacey whispered. "Catch your breath."

They reached the nurses' desk. No one was there, so they turned to open the door to Stumpy's room. Just as Hilda grabbed the doorknob, she was nearly knocked over by the opening door.

The doctor said, "Thank heavens! I have tried to call you. Your answering machine was full."

"Darn! We didn't check the messages yesterday when we got home," Hilda bemoaned. Afraid to ask, she simply stood and looked at the doctor, her eyes like those of a deer caught in the headlights of an oncoming disaster.

"He's much worse, Hilda. It's almost as if he is waiting for you 2 to come in and say your goodbyes. He wouldn't let me give him any painkillers this morning. He wants to be lucid when you see him."

Lacey stood back, allowing Hilda into the room first. Hilda sat down in the chair by Stumpy's side, holding tight to his hand, tears shimmering in her eyes.

Lacey continued to stand in the doorway. She somehow felt that she shouldn't be here, that this was Hilda's time with her husband. Perhaps recognizing her uncertainty, Stumpy and Hilda looked at Lacey and simultaneously called for her to come and sit on Stumpy's other side.

"Well, my darling," Hilda began, "Lacey and I went to the Mailbox this morning."

"Yes!" Lacey broke in. "I got your wonderful letter." Her lip trembled. She had a very difficult time keeping control of her emotions. Helplessly, she looked toward Hilda.

"You will never guess what!" Hilda exclaimed. "On our way back from the Mailbox, we stopped at the side of the wheat field. You'll never guess what happened!" She recounted the meeting with the bull elk, including their feelings that he was trying to tell them something.

"I know," Stumpy rasped. "I dreamed that. God's way…"

Unable to speak further, he lapsed into silence, closed his eyes.

Hilda finished for him. They had been married for so long, and in fact had, from the day they first met, finished each other's sentences, knew the other's thoughts.

"It was God's way of telling us that the bull elk represented you, Stumpy, my darling. It was God's way of letting Lacey and I, and you, say goodbye, in case we didn't make it back here in time."

Suddenly, the machines that seconds before had been humming, thrumming, beeping and hissing, stopped their comforting noises and began to scream and screech. Before the nurse could fly in through the door, every sound stopped, including Stumpy's tortured breathing. While listening to the story of the beloved bull elk that he and Lacey had seen the 1st time they had walked to the Mailbox, Stumpy had peacefully passed away, a gentle smile on his face.

Hilda leaned over and kissed him on the lips. "Goodbye, my love, be with God," she whispered reverently. "He will lead you Home."

She then leaned back in her chair, silent tears making her feel like she was in danger of drowning.

Chapter 15
Parker

Back at the farm, Lacey wandered around in a fog.

Hilda was handling Stumpy's death much better than Lacey. Perhaps it was because Hilda, at her age, had lost many people, both relatives and friends, who were close to her. Perhaps it was her deep and abiding faith. Probably it was a combination of the 2. Whatever the reason, as devastated as she was, Hilda knew she had her work cut out for her, helping Lacey deal with the loss.

For Lacey, Stumpy was only the 2nd person close to her heart who had died. The first was Harriet Greschner. Perhaps it was her youth that made her bitter. *It just wasn't fair*, Lacey kept thinking to herself, *that God would take 2 souls who were so loved and needed here on earth.*

Sitting at the kitchen table drinking coffee, neither Hilda nor Lacey were hungry. Looking over at Lacey, Hilda said quietly, "Don't you think you had better call Parker and let him know before he finds out from Joe Blow on the street? You haven't spoken with him at all, have you?"

"When did I have time?" Lacey snapped. Immediately realizing that her tone was very inappropriate, she apologized. "You're right, Hilda, I need to talk with him, but I need to do it face-to-face. If I get someone to come and sit with you, may I borrow the truck?"

"Yes, of course you can borrow the truck. I don't need someone to come and sit with me. I was prepared for this. Lacey. I am going to miss Stumpy like I would miss my left arm, my right leg, and my heart, but Lacey girl, we're all going to die. No one gets out of this world alive, as the saying goes. I have to go on. I only have one life."

Lacey said, "I understand that, but it doesn't make it any easier. I won't go and see Parker until we get the funeral planned."

"There isn't going to be any funeral," Hilda said. "Stumpy was absolutely adamant about that. He wanted to be cremated and then, when I die, we would like you to dispose of our ashes. As he told you, the farm will be yours after I'm gone. In the meantime, I will continue taking care of this old farm for as long as I can. When I can't, then, if you are ready to live here, put me in a nursing home. If you aren't ready to live here by then, well, I'll lease it out until you are ready."

Lacey had quit listening after the 'There isn't going to be any funeral' part. "Hilda! We have to have a service for Stumpy. We can't just do nothing!"

"We can and we will, Miss Lacey. That was Stumpy's last wish and I promised. I intend to honour his last request."

"Now, soon there will be lots of people starting to drop by, most of them bringing food. They'll want to sit and reminisce. We'll have more company than we can handle in a day or 2. That will be all the memorial there will be. So, young lady, go talk to your husband. Then, come back here and let me know what's up."

"What are you going to do while I'm talking with Parker, Hilda? You'll be here alone."

"Lacey, my girl, I'll be alone a lot longer than that once you've gone, either back to wherever you just came from, or back home to Parker. I'm a big girl. Sad as Stumpy's death is, it is what it is. I can handle it."

"Now, get yourself cleaned up, put some makeup on, and go see your hubby!"

"And, to answer your question, I'm going to soak in a nice, hot, bubble bath, and then try and get some more sleep. Haven't had much since Stumpy got sick. It's time."

Lacey sighed, "Well, I guess I can't put this off any longer, then. I'll get ready and go."

Halfway out of the driveway, Lacey thought she probably should have called Parker and told him she was coming. She decided against it. If she went back in the house, then she wouldn't come out, that she would just stay there. She knew that whether or not it was his day off, Parker would be at the detachment. If he wasn't at the house, she would call him from there, and let him know they needed to talk.

Arriving at the little house, their truck was in the driveway. Feeling awkward, she rang the doorbell. When there was no answer, she dug out her key from the bottom of her purse, and went inside.

Determined not to notice any clutter, dirt or dust, she went straight to the telephone and dialled the detachment. Just her stupid luck! Jillian Hamilton answered the phone.

"Hi, Jillian, this is Lacey Sutton calling. May I please speak with Parker?"

There was complete stunned silence on the other end, then Jillian said, in an acrid tone, "You've got a nerve! Disappear without a word, without a trace, and then, just out of the blue, you appear as if nothing ever happened. You don't deserve a good guy like Parker. I don't feel like letting him know you are calling, if you want the truth."

Lacey was in no mood to be told off by someone she barely knew, someone who had no business interfering between Lacey and Parker. She cut her off in the middle of her diatribe. "Jillian, it's important. Put Parker on the line. NOW!"

"And what if I don't?"

Lacey responded in an equally acrid tone, "Then I'll come over to the detachment and raise the biggest fuss you can imagine. I'll tell everyone there that I'm sorry to interrupt everyone's workday, but you were being a bitch and wouldn't transfer my call. Your choice, Jillian, what's it going to be?"

In less than 10 seconds, Parker was on the line. "Oh, my God! Lacey! Where are you?"

"I'm at our house, Parker. We need to talk. I see by the schedule that this is your day off. What are you doing at work? Never mind, I know. Anyway, seeing as it is your day off, can you come home? We need to talk," she repeated."

"I'll be right home," he said. "Please don't disappear on me before I get there."

While Lacey waited for Parker, she strolled through their little house. It was tidy, but dusty. The bed was made. In the bathroom, she pulled back the shower curtain to check the tub. "Oh, no!" she breathed. Hanging on the shower head to dry were an embroidered black bra and a skimpy pair of matching black panties. They weren't Lacey's.

She sat down on the toilet seat. She knew in her head that she didn't have the right to be upset. After all, she had walked out with no warning, leaving only a note behind. But, in her heart, her blood was boiling. The bugger! She hadn't been gone all that long! Already, she was being replaced?

She grabbed the offending underwear off of the shower head and stuffed them into her pocket. She couldn't decide if she would confront Parker with them or not. She needed to think.

Racing through the rest of the house, she opened cupboard and closet doors, looking for what? She didn't know. Finally, Lacey just sat down at the kitchen table and put her head in her hands. She pulled the underwear out of her pocket and placed it on the table.

In a matter of minutes, she heard the back door open. She looked over at the doorway. Parker stood there. He looked ghastly pale, with deep black circles under his bloodshot eyes.

"Hi, Lacey," he said quietly. "What brings you back home?"

Lacy sat up straight. "Why don't you sit down and tell me how you've been, Parker? We have a great deal to talk about."

As he sat, he spied the underwear. "What's that? Is that yours?" he asked.

She said, "Nope. Found it hanging on your shower head, though. Maybe **you** can tell **me** who it belongs to?"

"Lacey, it's not what it looks like. Last night, a few of the guys from work came over for pizza and a beer. Jillian invited herself. Nobody could think of a polite way to tell her it was a guys' night."

"Everyone stayed for a couple of hours and then left. That is, everyone except Jillian left. She'd had more than a few beers and was feeling pretty tipsy. I told her she needed to go home. She came on to me. I pushed her away, told her that I was still married."

"She, she got real pissy about it. She laughed in my face, called me the biggest dope around. Said no real man would just sit around and wait for a no-good wife who took off without a word. I told her to get out. She said she needed to use the washroom. I said OK, but I also told her to get the hell out as soon as she was done."

"She did leave. Smiled at me as she was leaving, even said she was sorry, that she'd had too much beer. I thought that was it."

"I went in to the office this morning without having a shower because I was going to go for a run and then shower afterwards. I didn't know those things were there. That's the God's honest truth, Lacey."

Lacey stared at him, searching his face for any signs that he was lying.

"I believe you," she said finally. "I know Jillian has a thing for you. Anyway, if you had done something with her, I guess I wouldn't have the right to be upset. You didn't know where I was, or when, or even **IF** I was coming back."

Parker looked miserable. "I guess you better tell me what's going on, Lacey. I've been worried sick, thinking and dreaming about all sorts of terrible things that could have happened to you."

"Now, here you are, driving Stumpy's truck. I have an awful premonition that you aren't staying, are you?"

Lacey reached over and took Parker's hand. He didn't push her away, although his hand lay limply in hers. *He wasn't going to make things easy for her,* she thought, and *who could blame him.*

"I came back because Stumpy got sick," she said.

"How did you know? Did you call there? What's wrong with Stumpy? Will he be okay?"

Tears leaked out of her eyes. "He's not okay, Parker. He died."

She got up and threw the distracting black undies in the garbage can under the kitchen sink.

"Any beer left?" she asked Parker. "It's a long story and my throat is already dry."

He got up and got 2 bottles of beer out of the fridge, opened them, sat back down. He said nothing, just waited for Lacey to begin.

Begin she did. She made up her mind on the spot that she would tell him every single thing, leave nothing out.

It took a long time to tell Parker about what had happened since she left. They sipped 3 beers each from the time she began with her hitching a ride in the pumpkin truck, and ended with Stumpy's passing.

When she finished, Parker stared at her, fascinated. "That's some story, Lacey."

"What?" Lacey said, "You don't believe me?"

"I absolutely believe you." Parker said. He sat quietly for a moment before asking, in a calm and matter-of-fact manner, "I guess you won't be staying here, then, will you?" He swallowed hard. Although he waited for Lacey to reply, he already knew the answer.

"You know I can't, Parker. I'm close to solving the mystery. I can't leave it in the middle. I have to finish what I started. You're a policeman. You of all people should understand that."

"Oh, I understand it all right, Lacey, I do. What I really understand the most, though, is that you have absolutely no idea, no clue, of the danger you will surely be in, of the danger you are most likely already in. These aren't petty criminals you're trying to find. If what you suspect turns out to be right, then they're kidnappers who will stop at nothing to continue to live the life they are living, and to execute whatever other criminal activities they're doing. If they'll chop off a thumb, imagine what else they would do? Without a moment's regret!"

He continued. "Have you even thought about what you might find in that old trailer, if you do gain access? How are you going to rescue any people in that place, without assistance from other sources? What are you going to do with anyone you find in there? You do realize, I hope, that they could be brainwashed. One of them might even be one of the kidnappers, an active participant in the kidnapping scheme? What if he was left with the girls to prevent any attempted escapes? Who knows what shape they'll be in. And, have you even remotely considered the possibility that it might not even be your missing friends and your brother that are in that trailer? You know, they might just be an ordinary family, living an ordinary life."

Lacey interrupted him. He needed to pause for breath anyway. She explained her plan to monitor the activities at the wreck of a trailer she had named Freedom for at least a 2-week period. Then she would try to gain access, to find out what was going on inside. She told him she had already begun her monitoring, but her plan was thwarted when she called Susanna and had to come home to see Stumpy.

"Not that I regret that. Not for a second," she said. "I got to see Stumpy and talk with him before he died. And I had a wonderful walk with Hilda. I showed her the Mailbox. That's when I found Stumpy's letter." She reached into her pocket and pulled it out. Handed it to Parker, who took a deep breath and read it, mostly to keep Lacey quiet for a minute or 2.

Handing the letter back to Lacey, he said calmly, "Nice letter. But honestly, the rate you're going, you'll be dead before Hilda anyway. We're likely never going to get the chance to live in that grand old farmhouse, Lacey, and wouldn't that be a shame? How sad would it be for Hilda to find out that her dream, and Stumpy's dream, to see you inherit their earthly possessions was destroyed by your impetuous and preventable actions?"

For once, Lacey had nothing to say. Parker just sat, also mute.

When Lacey couldn't stand the silence a moment longer, she remembered the bull elk, and told Parker that story. She ended by asking, "Don't you think that's a miracle, Parker? Hilda and I are both convinced that Stumpy sent the elk to us, to comfort us as he, Stumpy, lay dying. Do you think so?"

Parker's mouth hung open as he looked at his young wife. "For heaven's sake Lacey, don't you get it? This is a possible life and death situation we are talking about. You're telling me about Bambi's father instead of concentrating on real life danger!"

"Bambi was a deer," Lacey said in an insolent tone.

"WHAT!! Fine then, not Bambi's father. You know what I'm talking about, Lacey. Don't play ignorant. It doesn't suit you."

By this point in the conversation, Parker was so agitated that he got up from his chair and started to pace throughout the little house. He couldn't sit down. He couldn't convince his wife that she was in mortal danger. Worse yet, he didn't have an inkling about how to convince her.

"When's the funeral?" he asked, "I'll need to get the time off."

"No funeral, no service," Lacey said. "He didn't want anything. Hilda is honouring his last request."

"So then, what are you going to do?"

"Fly back to Abbotsford. My landlady will come and pick me up, take me back to Hope. I have to get back to work. It's a new job. I don't want to abuse my boss's generosity."

"I'll drive you to the airport, then. Do you leave tomorrow?"

"Yes," Lacey said, "at 1:30, but it's not necessary, Hilda can drive me."

"Hilda can come with us if she wants," Parker said. "I need to think things over. It's a lot of stuff you have unloaded on me."

He looked intently at Lacey before asking, "Are you staying here tonight?"

"No. I have to stay with Hilda. She is going to be very lonely when I leave. I need to spend my last evening with her. You understand, I hope, Parker?"

Parker threw his hands up in the air. "Yes, I guess I do," he said. "I'll come to the farm tomorrow morning. Hilda and I will then take you to the airport in time to catch your flight."

Lacey stood up. "OK, then, Parker. Thanks. I appreciate it, and I'm sure Hilda will appreciate your company on the way back to the farm after I have gone. See you tomorrow."

She left in a big hurry, before Parker could see her tears.

She arrived at the farm just as several vehicles were leaving. Recognizing most of the occupants, she waved at everyone as they left.

Parking the truck in the garage, Lacey sat in the vehicle for a while, trying to remember everything she and Parker had discussed.

Finally, she wiped her eyes, climbed out, and entered the house in search of Hilda.

Lacey found her foster mom sitting at the kitchen table, staring helplessly at what appeared to be enough food for a year-long camping trip to Alaska. The table groaned under a load of pies, cakes, cookies, banana loaves, casseroles, stews, salads. There were loaves of homemade bread and dozens of buns. There were trays of cheeses and cold meats of all kinds. There were crackers, pickles, fudge, and chocolates. There were even bottles of wine, whisky, and cases of beer.

Hilda looked drained. She looked blankly at her foster daughter. "What are we doing to do with all this stuff, Lacey?" she asked, clearly bewildered. "Everyone means well, but look at all this food!"

Lacey was already sorting and organizing. "We'll freeze what we can't eat now. You'll find it handy to have a freezer full of prepared food that you only have to defrost and reheat. And you won't have to bake bread or buns for a year!"

"Parker is coming in the morning," she said. "He suggested you might come along while he drives me to the airport. Seeing as he is kind of batching at the moment, you might consider giving him a doggy bag, or even 3 or 4 doggy bags for him to take home."

Hilda stood up and hugged Lacey. "Yes, of course! And yes, of course I'll come along to the airport. I know you have to get back to Hope, Lacey. A new job won't wait forever."

Her voice hitched before she could catch herself. She continued. "I'm going to miss you something awful, my Lacey girl. But I don't want you to fuss about me, you hear me? I'll get along just fine. I have a lot of friends and neighbours who will keep an eye out for me. You just go and do what you have to do. When you're done that, you come back home to me."

"Now, how about I make us some tea while you finish putting that food where it needs to go. We'll get ourselves a good night's sleep, and deal with everything else in its own good time."

Lacey put everything that could be frozen into the deep freeze except for a pot of chili, a dozen fresh buns and an apple pie. Dishing the food into bowls, she placed them on the now nearly empty table. Hilda sat and poured the tea. Neither woman thought they were hungry but once they started to eat, they cleaned up their bowls. They even had room for a slice of apple pie.

Hilda asked, "How did the visit with Parker go?"

"Okay," Lacey said. "Of course, he thinks what I am doing is ridiculously dangerous. He's thinking about stuff tonight and tomorrow when he picks us up, I'm sure he'll have more to say."

She then told Hilda about the black embroidered underwear and Parker's explanation.

Hilda laughed. "I hope you believed your husband, Miss Lacey," she said between giggles. "It's too funny not to be believable, don't you think?" She tittered once more and then finished her tea.

"Sure, I believe him," Lacey said. "I know Jillian, and I know she has a thing for Parker. He doesn't reciprocate her feelings in any way, shape or form. Although, you know, Hilda? If he did, I would have no one to blame but myself. I haven't been much of a wife to Parker. I have been just too obsessed with finding Lloyd and the missing girls."

"Well, Lacey," Hilda said, "you just make very sure that you don't attempt anything on your own without some backup plan. I couldn't stand to lose you so soon after Stumpy."

"Oh! Before I forget. I'll check your Mailbox for you every week, just like Stumpy did. If there is anything in there, I will phone you. Sound like a plan?"

"You know it is, Hilda. Thanks so much."

"Now, I think we should hit the hay, don't you? It's been a stressful few days, and we need some rest. See you in the morning." She kissed and hugged Hilda. Soon the only sounds in the old farmhouse were the sounds of not so subtle female snores.

The next morning, the women were up early. Lacey didn't have much packing to do. She was ready before breakfast. Hilda was standing at the stove preparing bacon, eggs, toast, and hash browns when Parker drove up.

He opened the door when he heard Hilda holler, "Come on in Parker, dear. You're just in time for breakfast. Pour yourself a coffee and fill mine up again, will you please?"

Happy to oblige, he first went over to Hilda, gave her a giant bear hug, murmuring, "So sorry about Stumpy, Hilda. He was a wonderful man. I'll miss him. Anything you need, you just call me, you hear me?"

Once they finished breakfast, Parker looked across the table at Lacey. "Lacey, I hope you will listen to me. You know that I think what you are trying to do, while admirable, is too dangerous for an untrained person to attempt. But, if you will make me a solemn promise, I will promise you something in return."

"And what's that, Parker?" she asked disinterestedly, her mind already back in Hope.

He interlaced his fingers with Lacey's. He wanted her to look at him so she could see for herself, and therefore believe, his sincerity when he made his suggestion.

"I know a great R.C.M.P. member. He was one of my instructors at Depot in Regina. He's now in charge of the Chilliwack Crime Prevention and Operational Support Unit. His name is Inspector Mason Oakley and he lives right in Chilliwack."

"Here's what I am proposing. You keep an eye on the trailer for a month. I don't think 2 weeks will give you a safe estimation of the traffic in and out of that place. Make careful written notes. Keep track of all vehicles coming and going, including licence plate numbers. Make careful notes of the times they arrive, and the times they leave. The more information you have, the easier it will be to convince Inspector Oakley that you are not some flake, that you know what you are doing. Get it?"

Parker did not wait for her to answer before he continued.

"In the meantime, I will talk to Mason, explain what you are doing. Once the month is up, you and he will have a meeting regarding the rescue of whomever is inside the wreck of a trailer that you call Freedom. I'll go with you to the meeting, introduce you, and I will do whatever Mason asks me to do, if anything."

"If things go according to plan, I'm pretty sure that Mason will set up a rescue. I suspect he will allow you to have a part in the planning, so long as you follow his orders. After all, you have a vested interest in the mission."

"Now, Lacey, I need you to promise me that you will not attempt to rescue these people on your own. When the time comes to carry out the operation, Chilliwack is only a half-hour drive to Hope, so no matter what is happening, **YOU HAVE TO WAIT** for the squad to arrive. I repeat, **NO MATTER WHAT IS HAPPENING, YOU HAVE TO WAIT!** Will you promise me that? If you don't promise, I'm not going to get Inspector Oakley involved."

Parker sat back in his chair, holding his breath as he waited for Lacey to respond.

"Okay, Parker, I promise."

"Thank you, Lacey. Your safety means everything to me, and your promise will hopefully keep you safe."

Parker turned towards Hilda and only half-jokingly said, "Hilda, if you think she is going to break her promise, beat her with a stick!"

"Sure, sure, Parker," Hilda said. "Of course, I'll have to find a stick that will reach all the way from my farm to Hope!"

"Okay, you 2, enough!!" Lacey grinned in spite of herself. "Come on, I have a plane to catch."

Chapter 16
The Lookout

The flight back to Abbotsford passed quickly. Lacey had called Stella French and given her the flight details. Stella was waiting for her when the plane landed.

On the drive home, Lacey filled Stella in on her trip.

Stella told Lacey how sorry she was for her loss. Her landlady was most impressed with the story of the giant bull elk.

She also told her that Evan Smithson didn't expect Lacey to come in to work until the next afternoon. He hoped that would give her enough time to rest up from the stress of her journey.

Once they got home, Stella told Lacey to get unpacked while she made them some lunch.

As Lacey was unpacking, she made a decision. A few minutes later, sitting at the table, having a lunch of tomato soup and grilled cheese sandwiches, Lacey told Stella the real reason she was in Hope.

When she finished, she said to Stella French, "Everything I tell you, Stella, and I mean everything, 100% of everything, has to remain completely secret between you and me. If you tell a single soul, my friends and my brother will have absolutely ZERO chance of getting rescued. They will be killed. These people are evil." She told Stella about the thumb and then continued.

"I decided to tell you about this, Stella, for 2 reasons. Reason #1 is, in the short time I have stayed here, I have come to realize that I can trust you. And reason #2 is that I really need your help in this."

Stella said calmly, "You can trust me, Lacey. My lips are zippered beginning this minute." She pantomimed zipping her lips before she said anything more. In any other circumstances, it would have been comical.

Lacey asked, "Do you think you can help me?"

"I'll do whatever I can, Lacey. What do you need me to do?"

Lacey outlined the importance of logging every single activity that went on at Freedom, stressing the importance of accurately logging the dates and times of any people coming and going from the trailer.

"I can do that, Lacey. On a nice day, I'll sit in the shade at the side of my home, watching and reading."

"Sounds good, Stella, but what if you get company? Can you visit and keep track of the vehicles coming and going? What if someone who is visiting you asks you what you are doing?"

Stella became rather huffy. "Certainly, I can visit and still keep track," she sputtered. "I may be old in years, Lacey, but my brain is still as bright as it was 20 years ago!"

"If my visitors ask what I'm doing, I'll say I'm doing a traffic study, a survey for the town of Hope. The residents of this area want their main roads paved, and the town needs to know if the cost will be worthwhile."

"Good plan, Stella. I can see that you will be a huge help to me. Thank you."

"Now, if you'll excuse me for just a minute, Parker gave me a couple of journals that we can use to keep our records. I'll dig them out of my backpack and we can review them and decide the best way to use them."

"Just leave the dishes," Lacey ordered. "I'll do them after we deal with those journals."

The 2 women spent the next couple of hours formulating a plan. They organized the journals so that as much information as possible could be recorded in an easily read manner. The main section was for recording complete descriptions of every vehicle they saw stopping at Freedom, as well as accurate descriptions of the drivers, and times that anyone went to the trailer, either on foot or by vehicle.

They also included a section to include, in the unlikely but hopeful event, a description of any occupants of Freedom who might be seen, either outside or through the window.

What Lacey was really interested in, was the coming and going of the pumpkin truck every Thursday. If the driver, or drivers, came the same time every Thursday, and stayed for the same amount of time, she was pretty sure she could go over to Freedom earlier in the day and try to gain access to the trailer. At the very least, she wanted to be able to see inside to determine how many people were in there, even if only from the doorway looking in. As well, she fervently hoped to be able to identify the occupants.

She made a very wise decision, she thought, not to tell Stella or Parker about that part of her plan.

It really wasn't breaking her promise to Parker, she justified to herself, as long as she knew it was a safe time period to check it out. She wouldn't try to do anything during a time when they determined someone was expected to arrive at Freedom. She definitely wouldn't try to take them from the trailer to Stella's place. She would call and wait for backup, once she knew what was what, and who was in there.

That same afternoon, the telephone rang. Stella answered the phone. "Lacey, this call is for you."

"Do you know who it is?" she whispered as she took the phone from Stella's hand.

Stella shook her head. She grabbed a piece of paper and a pen after observing Lacey's frantic hand motions towards the counter. Handing them to Lacey, she discreetly left the room.

"Hello, Lacey Sutton speaking. Who's calling, please?"

"Lacey, this is Mason Oakley," said a deep voice. "Parker called me earlier today and explained everything that is going on in Hope. Now, I would like to hear it in your own words, if you don't mind. Can you start by telling me what drew you to Hope from Alberta in the first place?"

Lace began her story, beginning with the disappearance of Charlotte (Charley) Ford from George and Martha Schmidt's house. She told him that Charley had run away, and why. She described the pumpkin truck, and gave him the details that Lloyd had written down.

Next, she told him about Amelia Anderson running away from Simon and Bertha Savard's, and why. She told the inspector that Amelia, too, had been picked up by the driver of the pumpkin truck.

She told him that Annie Barcley was the 3rd girl to disappear. She ran away from the home of Peter and Elsie Petrie. Again, she described the reason for Annie's running and said that Annie, also, was picked up by the ZO'S HAULING truck, otherwise referred to as the pumpkin truck. She also told him all the details of Mrs. Petrie's breakdown.

Finally, she told him about Lloyd.

She apologized, said that she should have perhaps started at the beginning, which was the reason that she and Lloyd were put in the foster care system in the 1st place. Lacey told him everything that had happened to her and her brother since their mother walked out so long ago.

Mason Oakley listened without a single interruption. When he was sure that Lacey was finished, he asked a few more questions.

He then asked her what she planned to do for the next month. She told him. She also explained that, while Lacey was at work, her landlady would keep an eye on the trailer. She explained about the journals, and what they planned to record in them.

"Sounds to me like you are pretty organized, Lacey. I would like to come and meet with you in person, if you don't mind. That way, I can get a look at the place Parker says you call 'FREEDOM', and make some plans of my own. I find I have better luck if I have physically seen a location before my team executes a mission."

"When would be a good time for you? Please, bear in mind that I would like to come as soon as possible."

Lacey said, "I don't work tomorrow until 1:30 in the afternoon. Would you like to come in the morning?"

Inspector Oakley agreed that they would meet the next morning at 10 o'clock. He said he would like Stella French to be present at their meeting, because she would be helping with the surveillance whenever Lacey was at work.

The next morning, promptly at 10 o'clock, the doorbell rang.

Standing in the doorway was the most handsome man Stella had ever seen, and at her advanced age, that was saying something!

Mason Oakley was tall, black, and drop-dead gorgeous. His curly salt-and-pepper hair was cropped close to his head. His eyes were so dark it was impossible to determine if they were black or dark brown. He looked at Stella so intensely that she was sure he could see right through to the back of her head. He told Stella (because she asked!) that he was 93 centimetres tall. When she told him to speak English, that she was far too old to convert from the Metric system to the Imperial system in her head, he threw back his head and gave the loudest, most charming, most contagious belly laugh that either woman had ever heard. When he stopped laughing, he told her that he was 6 feet, 4 inches tall and just in case she was interested, he weighed 210 pounds. Then he asked her if it would be OK if he came in. It wasn't like Stella to forget her manners. Blushing furiously, she stepped back and motioned him inside. She apologized for being rude. Then she said, "Well, Mr. Mason Oakley, I'm sure you are used to women falling all over you, and that includes me."

He laughed again, and told her that she was a breath of sunshine, and he appreciated her forthrightness.

Lacey picked her jaw up off the floor and held out her hand. "Hi, Superintendent, I mean Inspector Oakley. I'm Lacey, and it's nice to meet you."

With an amiable grin that flashed the world's whitest teeth, he told the ladies to call him Mason. He suggested they sit at the kitchen table and conduct their meeting.

He was impressed with the way they had set up their journals. In fact, he made a sketch of their columns. He reviewed their plan, made some suggestions of his own, and then suggested that he and Lacey take a walk down the street, passing Freedom as if they were just taking a pre-dinner stroll. He wanted to see how much cover there was so that when his team came prepared to rescue the inhabitants, they could remain hidden until the appropriate time.

Stella wanted to come as well, but Mason asked her to look out the window and watch for any activity. He also asked her to report to him when they got back how far her line of sight extended. He said he also wanted to see for himself how visible she might be looking out of a window towards Freedom. He said once they figured those 2 things out, he would like her to sit at her picnic table, pretending she was already watching and recording, so he could make sure she didn't look conspicuous. Stella felt very important, and rushed off to her den.

Lacey and Mason began their stroll. When they got directly opposite Freedom, Mason turned around casually, walking backwards beside Lacey. He then turned around again. When they were about 200 metres past the trailer, he turned again. Stella was sitting at the picnic table, a book in front of her, and a coffee cup in her hand. "Great!" Mason said to Lacey. "That will work!"

"Have you walked all around the trailer, Lacey?" Mason asked. "I'm just wondering if there is another door, or if the front door is the only door."

"I only looked from a distance," she answered. "As far as I can tell, there is only one door. But, it appears that the windows are all of a size big enough that someone could crawl out in case of a fire or some other reason they needed to escape."

Mason said, "Yes, I noticed that also. Too bad there wasn't a ladder at the back. It's quite a height for a shorter person to get out of the window without falling and hurting something."

Lacey responded. "There is a ladder under the front of the trailer. That's how people get up to the door. You probably noticed that there are no stairs. The driver of the pumpkin truck pulls out the ladder and climbs up to the landing by the door. When he leaves, he puts the ladder back under the front."

"Hmm, to intimidate?" Mason thought aloud. "Too dangerous to go to the front of the trailer and pull out the ladder and take it to the back. Tell you what, Lacey, I have a stepladder in the back of my vehicle. When it gets dark, I'll sneak back and put it under the trailer, at the back. That way, it will be easier to set up the ladder and help everyone out of the window when the time comes, if need be."

"That means you'll have to hang around for the rest of the day and well into the evening, Mason," said Lacey. "If you don't want to wait, I can do it after I get home from work tonight. It will be dark then. Can you just leave the stepladder with us?"

Mason looked intently at Lacey. "I would like to do that, Lacey, but only if you promise you won't try anything, other than putting that ladder under the trailer, and then getting the heck out of there."

Lacey promised.

When they got back to Stella's place, Mason praised Stella for her good work. Stella blushed a brilliant red. "It's good to feel useful," she told Mason. "I won't let you down, Mr. Oakley, I won't let you down."

He explained to her what Lacey was going to do with the stepladder he took out of his vehicle. Glancing at his watch, he said, "Well, ladies, I must be going. Keep in touch, and keep out of trouble. Remember, you have a whole team behind you now, so no heroics, get it?" He stared right at Lacey as he said it. She nodded meekly. "Got it, inspector!"

"Great!" Mason said. "Another thing. Make sure no one sees you dragging that stepladder down the road. If you see someone walking a dog, or a car driving down the road, wait until the coast is clear before you take it, OK?"

"I understand," Lacey said. "Thanks for all your help today, sir," she said. "We appreciate your input. We won't let you down. We'll keep in touch. In fact, I have your mobile phone number. I'll leave a message on it saying 'Small job complete.' That way, I won't wake up your family by calling late at night."

"Sounds good, "Mason said. "Talk to you again soon, ladies." He folded his tall self into his vehicle. With a brief wave, he was on his way.

As soon as he left, Lacey listened to her landlady rave about the handsome, delightful, Mason Oakley. As soon as she could politely interrupt, Lacey got ready for work.

Arriving at the grocery store, she went directly to the manager's office. Her boss was sitting at the desk. When she rapped on the door, he got up and gave her a hug. "Lacey! I'm so very sorry to hear about your foster dad. Are you doing OK?"

"I am, thanks, Smithy," Lacey said. "And I'm ready to come back to work. Where am I today?"

"Till #3. Have a good day, Lacey. Happy to see you back."

In the very brief period of time that Lacey had worked at Buy-Low, the rest of the staff had already decided that they liked Lacey very much. She always worked hard, did whatever anyone asked of her, without complaint, and was always willing to help any of her co-workers with anything they needed.

When she got to her till, there was a beautiful bouquet of flowers sitting beside her register, together with a sympathy card signed by every one of the staff. Lacey was astounded, tickled beyond measure. "Thank you, everyone!" she called across the store. "You all are too kind." Taking a deep breath to get her emotions under control, Lacey got to work.

The store was busy for her entire shift. When she finished work at 9:30 p.m., she grabbed her flowers and headed out the door. Although the evening was already dark, her route home was very well lit and on a main road. Having been taught by Parker to always be aware of her surroundings, day or night, she arrived home safely.

She went in and changed out of her uniform into a pair of black jeans, a black hoodie, black socks, and black boots. Hearing the television set blaring, she pulled up the hoodie to cover her hair, and crept silently down the hallway. When she got to the door she planned on scaring Stella, but decided against it. Stella might be just a young person in spirit and determination, but Lacey didn't want to be the one responsible for giving her a heart attack!

Stella laughed when she saw Lacey. "Heading for a new career as a cat burglar, are you?" she teased.

Lacey smiled ruefully. "Nah, it's just I don't want to be seen when I take the stepladder down and put it under Freedom's back side, Stella."

Stella smiled. "I know, my dear, just joshing you."

The stepladder was light. A little awkward to carry in an upright position, Lacey settled on laying it down on its side and then picking it up and carrying it under her right arm.

She sat down on the front step, listened, and looked around. An elderly gentleman, walking his miniature poodle, passed by Lacey without noticing her. He seemed to be in a hurry to get back to his modular home, but with a dog leash in one hand and his walking stick in the other, it was slow going.

Lacey sat quietly until the man was gone from her sight. No sign of life anywhere in the park. No dogs barked, no vehicles anywhere within either hearing or seeing distance.

She picked up the stepladder, balanced it carefully under her arm, and hurried down the street to Freedom. Just as she reached the end of the trailer, she heard a vehicle. She raced around to the back, shoved the stepladder far enough under that it was safely out of sight, and then dropped flat onto the ground, barely daring to breathe.

She lay prostrate in the grass for several minutes after she heard the car go in the other direction, just to make sure she wasn't seen. Finally, she got up, brushed the dead grass off her black clothing, and ran back to Stella's. She quickly called Mason's phone and left the agreed-upon message.

Her last waking thought was: *At last, something is going to be done. Hang on Lloyd! Hang on girls! We're coming!* She closed her eyes and was instantly asleep.

The following day, an unforeseen opportunity seemed to drop from the sky and land in Lacey's lap. They were having a quick staff meeting. Smithy needed a volunteer.

"The grocery delivery man called in sick today. I have an order that needs to be delivered this afternoon. If you take the delivery, you can keep the station wagon overnight, and bring it back when you come in to work tomorrow." He stopped and looked around, his gaze settling on Lacey.

"Lacey," he said, "this delivery is for a trailer just down the street from Stella's place. Maybe you would like to deliver it, being that it is so close to where you live?"

"Sure," Lacey said, "but I am working until 6 today. What time do they want the delivery?"

"By no later than 4. You can leave just before then and do the delivery. Don't bother coming back to work after that, just come in an hour earlier tomorrow morning."

"Okay, that's all everyone. Back to work. Have a good day out there," Smithy said.

Chapter 17
Inside 'Freedom'

Lacey could not believe her luck! She was actually going to get to see inside of Freedom when she delivered the groceries. She was so excited she had to keep biting her tongue so she would not blurt out some inappropriate piece of information. This was for her to know and no one else to find out.

All day she repeatedly thought, *I'm not breaking a promise to Parker or to Mason. This is work. It's my job. My boss gave me this task to do. It is not related to the missing girls or to Lloyd, it's work.*

Lacey was a bright girl, she knew she was fooling herself, but she couldn't help it. She was going to see inside Freedom at 4 o'clock.

For a very brief second, she thought about calling Parker and Mason. As quickly as the thought flittered through her brain it flew straight out the door. She would tell them after she saw inside the trailer. That would be soon enough.

The day was interminable. Lacey kept herself busy every minute, but each minute felt like an hour. Finally, it was time for her to cash out.

Smithy had loaded the station wagon for her. Handing her the keys, he said, "It's the oldest trailer in the park, off by itself at the edge of the trees. Know which one I mean?"

"I do, Smithy. This is a lot of groceries! How often do you deliver there?"

"Every other week," Smithy said. "I've never actually made the delivery myself, though, so I don't know how many people are in that trailer."

Closing the back door firmly, he said, "Whoops! I nearly forgot. When you get there, give 2 short honks of the horn. The trailer's ancient and the steps are rotten. They've ripped them out but not yet replaced them, so someone will come out and put up a ladder for you to bring the groceries up. Strange, but true! You'd think that would be the first thing that would get repaired, wouldn't you? Oh, well, to each their own, I guess. See you tomorrow morning. Don't worry about filling the tank. One of our regular delivery guys will look after that."

Lacey was afraid she was going to hyperventilate! She took a couple of minutes to do some deep breathing exercises, then carefully drove away from the store.

She reached Freedom, drove past a few feet, and then backed the station wagon up to where the landing steps should be. She gave the obligatory 2 short honks, got out of her vehicle, and opened the back door. She waited for a couple of minutes, then honked again.

A woman's voice called out from the window, "There's a ladder under the trailer, just by your car. Put it up and bring the grocery bags to the door."

Lacey thought, *that's kind of rude. Not even a 'please' or an 'if you don't mind!'* She thought, irreverently, *I wonder if that person has a piano tied to her butt or if she's just lazy?*

With a mental shrug, she pulled out the ladder. It was made of wood and nearly as rickety as the landing. She unloaded the station wagon, hefting the heavy bags up and on to the landing. She then climbed up the wobbly ladder, moved all the bags to the door, and waited.

"Just leave them there, I'll bring them in later," called the invisible woman.

"I'm sorry, ma'am, but I can't do that." Lacey made up the excuse on the spot. "My boss says I have to get the money from you to pay for these groceries, and you need to sign for them."

She did need to sign for them, but she could charge them to the store.

The invisible woman gave such a loud sigh that Lacey could hear it from outside.

"How much is the bill?"

Lacey grabbed her invoice book. Darn it! She couldn't read the name of the recipient. She called towards the window, "$250.25, ma'am," she said, "and the invoice is ready for you to sign."

"Okay," said the voice. "The door's unlocked. Just bring the bags in. Leave them on the kitchen table. I'll get the cash and be right there."

As Lacey set the bags inside, she took furtive glances at the contents. There was a lot of packaged chicken noodle soup, nearly a bag full. Kraft dinner, sugar-sweetened cereals, white bread, and peanut butter. There was a distinct lack of fresh vegetables, fruit and meat. A lot of canned stuff, by the weight of the bags.

Once she had all the groceries inside, she lifted the bags up onto the kitchen table. The table was actually in the living room, just to the left of the entrance into the kitchen.

Lacey looked around while she waited for the invisible woman to appear. The trailer, although very old, was spotless. Beside the door, a mat held 3 pairs of shoes, all women's, different sizes. One pair of red heels that looked vaguely familiar, but Lacey couldn't place them. Second pair, pink flip-flops. Third pair, spotlessly clean white runners. Above each pair of shoes, a jacket hung on a peg. Above the red heels, a navy trench coat, again looking vaguely familiar. Above the flip-flops, a pink rain coat. And above the runners, a denim jean jacket, trimmed with a pretty blue lace on the pockets. Larger than children's sizes.

Lacey reminded herself that the missing girls would be much older now. Charley would be 23! They wouldn't fit into kids' clothing anymore.

Nothing else in the room indicated how many people might be residing here. A large calendar attached to the side of the refrigerator had writing on every Thursday, but Lacey was too far away to read the inscriptions. She was too afraid to wander away from the door to have a closer look.

Suddenly, a short, stick-skinny figure appeared from down a hallway. Wearing a navy hoodie and jeans, the hood was pulled up. It was impossible to see the face of the person who was holding the rim of the hoodie across his/her entire face. Only wary eyes peeked out.

Peeking out from the hood, the voice of a female choked, "Lacey?" Then frantically, "Don't say anything, please, Lacey. Just say nothing. Here!" She handed a fistful of money towards Lacey, but nearly dropped it. She reached out her other hand to try to catch the bills. An exercise in futility because that hand was heavily bandaged. The bills and a quarter fell to the floor. Both Lacey and the unknown figure fell to the floor, scrambling for the cash.

Still on her knees, Lacey queried in a harsh whisper, "What happened to your hand, ma'am?" Then, louder, "How do you know me?"

"You look the same, just older. Now, shut up!" the person hissed vehemently, "you'll get me in awful trouble. Just take the money and go!"

"I can't go until I get a signature," Lacey told the frenzied person. "You can sign for it."

The terrified person said, "I can't write. My thumb is missing. If I try to use that hand, it will start to bleed again. Please, can't you sign it for me?"

"Just use your other hand. It doesn't matter if it's hard for you to write with that hand. It's just a signature, and most signatures aren't legible anyway."

Lacey ripped a blank page out of the invoice book and hurriedly wrote: "You know me, who are you?" She then wrote, "I live in that trailer you can see from this window. I can help you. Come and see me."

Grabbing the pen, the girl wrote, "Charley. Can't help me. Go!"

She scribbled on the signature line, and then backed up towards the hallway that she had earlier appeared out of. Keeping her eyes on Lacey, she mouthed softly, but ferociously, 'get out while you can!'

The invisible woman practically screamed from the back of the trailer, "You! Delivery person! If I have to come out there you will regret it. Now, you have your money, you have a signature. Go! I'm counting to 10 and you better be gone. Put the ladder back where you got it. One… Two… "

She was actually counting! And not slowly! Lacey stumbled backwards, knocking the navy coat off the wall. She didn't stop to pick it up.

She practically threw the heavy wooden ladder under the trailer. Gravel scrabbled under her tires as she hit the gas and zigzagged down the road, her heart pounding painfully in her chest.

Lacey decided against parking the station wagon at Stella's. She was too afraid that the invisible woman might decide to come out of Freedom and recognize it. She drove back to Buy-Low, hung the key on the appropriate peg in Smithy's office, and then ran all the way home.

Puffing heavily, she opened the door and went into her bedroom to change out of her uniform, into a pair of jeans and a T-shirt. She lay down on her bed, waiting for her breathing to return to normal.

Before she regained her composure, she heard a vehicle approach, slow down, and turn to the right. Leaping to her knees, she watched a dark jeep approach Freedom and stop. The driver honked twice. Almost immediately, a woman came out. A man got out of the jeep, held out his arms and lifted the woman down off the landing. They were, of course, too far away for Lacey to identify either person. They both climbed into the jeep and immediately drove off.

Lacey quickly filled in the events of the day in her journal. A quick check-back in the journal for the licence plate verified that it was the same jeep that had been at Freedom before today.

She then sat in the middle of her bed. Her head was in her hands. She was deep in thought. Something was really bugging her, but she couldn't, for the life of her, figure out what it was. Something vaguely familiar, but what?

She left the bedroom and went into the kitchen to set the table.

Hearing movement, Stella came out of her den. Spotting Lacey, she went to the kitchen and asked her how her first day back went.

When Lacey told her, Stella's eyes nearly popped out of their sockets.

"You actually went in that trailer! Lacey, how could you? You know the rules! Mason would have a conniption fit if he knew about it."

Lacey gave Stella her reasons as to why it wasn't a violation, in her own humble opinion, of her promise. Looking dubious, Stella just shook her head.

"But, Stella," Lacey said plaintively, "something is really bugging me and I can't figure out what. I sure hope I remember soon. It's driving me nuts."

After finishing the supper dishes, Lacey went into her room and dialled Parker's number. He was so happy to hear from her that she felt guiltier than ever. All she told him was that she was back in Hope, safe and sound. She was back at work, and happy to be there. She told him about the staff flowers and card.

"Did you talk to Mason yet?" Parker asked as soon as he could get a word in edgewise.

"Not only did I talk to him, Parker," Lacey excitedly said, "but he came here, and we had a face-to-face meeting!"

"We have a plan, Parker. Don't worry. Mason has given me his very strict rules to follow. You don't need to worry about me for a single second."

Although she knew it was unfair, she did not tell him that she had been inside the trailer. He was far enough away that the less he knew, the less he would worry. Well, that was Lacey's theory anyway.

After a few more minutes of idle chatter, Lacey said she was sorry to keep the call short, but she had to call Mason. She told Parker she would keep in touch.

Teasingly, she added, "Be sure to tell Jillian hello from me. Oh, by the way, did you return her undies?" Unable to stop herself, she giggled.

Parker sputtered, "Very funny! To answer your question, no, I didn't return that stuff. You threw it out, remember? The garbage man picked up the trash today, black undies and all."

Lacey was still laughing as she hung up.

Before she called Mason, Lacey had one more item on her agenda for the evening. She pulled on her black hoodie and called out to Stella as she was leaving, "Hey Stella! I'm just going for a run. Be back in a half hour!"

Pretty certain that the jeep had not returned, or else she would have heard it, Lacey ran at top speed towards Freedom. Going around to the far side, she planted herself outside the small, frosted, bathroom window. Picking up a few pebbles she tossed them at the window, and called out, "Charley!" No response. More pebbles tossed, harder this time. Again calling, "Charley!"

After the 3rd set of pebbles, a head appeared in the now open window. A terrified face looked out. Recognizing Lacey, Charley said, "Oh, dear Lord, Lacey! What are you doing here? They'll be back any minute now and if they catch you... you have no idea what you are dealing with here."

Lacey interrupted. "Charley, just be quiet and listen to me, OK? I'm going to get you out of there. Who else is living here with you? Is Lloyd there? How about Amelia and Annie? Hurry up and tell me before 'they', whoever 'they' are, return!" She stopped for breath.

Charley was so terrified she could barely respond.

"Lacey, there's me here, of course, and Amelia. They killed Annie." After saying aloud that their friend had been killed, Charley sobbed in earnest.

"Lacey, I'm so scared."

"Why haven't you tried to get away, Charley?"

"It's complicated, Lacey. They said that if we try and get away, they will kill one of us, or both of us, or amputate our foot. They mean it, too. My thumb is gone, and Amelia didn't even try to run away. She just dared to talk back to Papa and Mama. The threat of punishment is more frightening when you think it will be your foster sister who will suffer."

"Now go, Lacey! They will be back soon. You can't be here. If they see you, then something dreadful will happen. Just go!"

Lace felt like she had been kicked in the gut. "Charley, you can tell me about Annie's death, how that happened, later. Right now, I need to know, have you seen Lloyd?"

"No," said Charley heartbrokenly, "we haven't seen him since we left Alberta."

"Well, who else is in the trailer? I know there is a woman there. Is she the kidnapper? Hurry and tell me before the jeep comes back."

Silence.

"Charley!" Lacey was practically screaming at the girl. Well, she was hardly a girl at 23.

How much time has passed, Lacey thought sadly. The thought that struck her next cheered her up considerably. She thought, positively, *I am definitely closer than anyone else has been to solving the mystery. I have actually just found the missing girls!*

She opened her mouth to yell at Charley once more, when she heard a vehicle coming up the road!

"Charley, they're coming back! I'll talk to you again, soon."

Lacey bent over and carefully hurried to the far end of the trailer. She dropped onto her belly, flattened herself to the ground, and held her breath. The dead grass and weeds were tickling her nose. It took all of her concentration not to sneeze and give herself away.

Listening carefully for any clues, she lay motionless, barely breathing.

A vehicle stopped outside the trailer porch. A man's voice said, "Hang on a second. I'll get the ladder and give you a hand up."

A woman's voice answering. "Thank you (Lacey couldn't hear the name). You know, this jeep really needs a good cleaning, inside and out. Maybe I will drive you to work tomorrow, and then bring the jeep home and clean it up. What do you think?"

"We'll see." The man's voice again. "Right now, we better check on those girls. They've been alone for too long today. They better still be here, and they better have done their chores!"

"They'll be here. They are too afraid to try anything since you cut Charlotte's thumb off. The girls trying to run away will not happen. That is the least of our worries these days."

The man helped the woman up the creaky wooden ladder. Opening the door, the woman called out, "Hello? Children? Mama's home! Did you miss me?"

Lacey could barely hear the response, but she distinctly heard 2 separate female voices. It sounded very much like they were saying 'Hello Mama, hello.' Then, 'We're ready for our bedtime story now.'

She couldn't have heard correctly. The voices responding to the woman sounded like young children's voices.

What the heck was going on inside Freedom?

She lay in the grass until she was sure that no one was coming out of the old trailer. She then carefully and quietly got up and crept past Freedom. She took care to ensure that she was bent over beneath the level of the living room window. That window reached all the way to the floor.

Once she was safely out of sight and earshot, she ran as fast as she could back to Stella's.

A short while later, she was lying in bed, her thoughts still in a jumble. Trying to sort out the events of the day, and totally bewildered by everything that had occurred, she suddenly sat bolt upright in her bed.

Oh, my God, she thought, *where is my brother? What could have happened to Lloyd? He should have ended up here in Hope. He hitched a ride with the pumpkin truck, just like all of us did. He should be in that trailer with Charley and Amelia! Whatever happened to him?*

She looked at her alarm. Already past midnight. Too late to call Mason Oakley tonight. She would call him tomorrow, as soon as she got home from work.

Too distraught to sleep, Lacey lay in bed and cried for her lost brother. She cried for Charley and her lost thumb. Most of all, she cried for poor Annie, who was dead. She could only pray non-specifically for Amelia until Lacey could find out what shape she was in.

Although she felt somewhat better after prayers, Lacey still couldn't sleep. She got up and reviewed her journal entries. Satisfied that the notes were as complete as she could make them, she consoled herself with the thought that if something happened to her, at least Mason and his team would have a starting point to continue investigating further.

She had a restless, fitful night full of 'what ifs' and 'how cans' and 'whatevers'. In the short periods where she managed to doze off, she had wicked nightmares.

Finally, well before dawn, she gave up. Lacey got out of bed, turned off her alarm clock, and got ready to face the day.

When she got home from Buy-Low that afternoon, Stella asked her how her run was the night before.

"Run?" Lacey asked, "I didn't go for a run."

"I'm pretty sure that's what you hollered as you went out the door last evening, Lacey. Did I hear you incorrectly, then?"

Caught in a lie, Lacey knew she had to tell Stella the truth. First, she made Stella swear on her Bible AND pinky-swear, that she wouldn't repeat anything that Lacey was about to tell her. Stella held on to her Bible and swore. She then locked her little finger with Lacey's and pinky-swore.

When Lacey completed her tale of the previous evening's events, Stella sat in her chair at the table, her mouth open. "Dear Lord, Lacey!" Stella breathed. "You were very foolish. What if the couple in the jeep had caught you?"

"Stella, calm down! They didn't catch me. The good part is that now, I know for certain who is in that trailer, and I am going to call Mason immediately."

"But… Oh, Stella," Lacey added with a catch in her throat, "whatever has happened to Lloyd?"

Lacey tried to call Mason, but got no answer. She left a message on his answering machine, a complete one, leaving no details out. She assured him that from now on, all she and Stella would do, would be to continue to monitor the traffic to and from Freedom. She told him she would report to him again in a couple of days. If something happened before then, she would call him immediately.

She decided she shouldn't call Parker. She knew herself well. Lacey knew that if she heard his voice, she would have to tell him everything that had happened the night before. She didn't want to worry him needlessly. She didn't call.

She did, however, call Hilda. Hilda assured Lacey that she was doing as well as could be expected. She was keeping busy, the neighbours were being helpful, sometimes too much so. She missed Lacey and thanked her for calling.

Lacey did not tell her about being inside of Freedom. She simply told her about work, and the kindness exhibited by her boss and the rest of the staff members.

The next day, Smithy approached Lacey at her register. Waiting until she finished with her customer, he asked her to put up her closed sign and meet him in his office. When she entered a few minutes later, Smithy said he had a call from the same customer Lacey had delivered the groceries to the day before. "She has another order to be delivered there today, Lacey," Smithy said. "Would you like to take it on your way home from work? The woman told me you did an excellent job yesterday. She hopes you will deliver her order again, today."

Despite a warning voice at the back of her brain, Lacey said of course she would deliver the groceries. Smart enough to partially heed that warning voice, she asked Smithy for a piece of paper and a pen. Pulling Mason's card out of her pocket, she wrote his name, address, and his cell number, home number, and office number, on the paper. Without going into detail, she handed the information to Smithy.

"If I don't make it back before closing today, get hold of this man, Smithy. I'll tell you why when we have more time, but for now, please, just hang on to this information. Use it if you have to. I promise I will fill you in. I will take the groceries and deliver them at 4 o'clock, just like yesterday. I will then come back to the store. Wait until closing time before calling Mason Oakley. If I'm not here by then, tell him to hurry."

Her boss held the piece of paper in his hand. His gaze alternated between the paper and his employee.

"Lacey, either you tell me right now what is going on, or I will send someone else to deliver these groceries."

"But..." Lacey began, "I'll..."

"Your choice, Lacey. It's simple. Tell me or not."

"If I tell you, Smithy, you have to promise me that you will still let me deliver these groceries. I need to do this."

"That depends on what you tell me. If I can promise you, I will, Lacey. Now shoot!"

Trying not to make it seem dangerous, Lacey nevertheless told Smithy her life story. Thirty minutes later, she sat back in her chair and watched her boss's expression.

Finally he asked, "This Mason person, is he legit? By that I mean, does he have your back, no matter what?"

Lacey said quietly, "Parker found him. He was an instructor at Depot in Regina, when Parker took his R.C.M.P. training. He would trust Mason with his life, and therefore, so do I."

"Well, Lacey," Smithy said uncertainly, "I don't like it, but I'll go along with you. Promise me you won't take any unnecessary risks. Promise me you will put those groceries on the landing and then hightail your behind right back to this store."

"You got it, boss," Lacey said. "I'll be careful. But, Smithy, we need to rescue those girls. By 'we', I mean Mason Oakley and his team. Something weird is going on in that old trailer. I have nicknamed the trailer 'Freedom'. I feel this might be my last chance to help with freeing Charley and Amelia. We need to get those girls out of there. Then the wrecked old trailer's name of 'Freedom' will have real meaning."

Lacey stood up, thanked Smithy, and went back to her cash register. Smithy remained at his desk, mentally kicking himself for agreeing to something so potentially dangerous, so awful.

Smithy stood up, prepared to go out and tell Lacey he had changed his mind. He sat down again. A promise was a promise, he would wait until closing. In the meantime, he would pray that everything Lacey had told him was exaggerated, that she would be back at the store quickly after making the delivery.

God, he hoped so!

Chapter 18
Operation 'Freedom' – Mason Oakley

Lacey had a nearly impossible time concentrating on her cash register and her customers until it was time to make the delivery. Somehow, she was not sure just how, her register balanced.

She went in to Smithy's office and retrieved the key to the station wagon. Her boss was not at his desk, so she was able to leave the store without any interruptions.

The vehicle was already loaded with the groceries. As with the previous delivery, it appeared as if the bags were filled with mostly heavy cans.

Arriving at 'Freedom', Lacey once again backed up to the spot that should have housed the steps. This time, rather than honking 2 short honks, she simply climbed out of the wagon, got the ladder out from under the trailer, and set it up.

Lacey prayed under her breath as she lifted the heavy bags up on to the porch. Her stomach felt like she had eaten razor blades for lunch. Her hands were sweating so badly that she could barely pick up a bag without it sliding back onto the ground. She was breathing so quickly she felt dizzy.

She kept telling herself, silently, *take it easy, the ordeal is nearly over, and soon the girls will be free at last.* She tried to ignore the little devil on her shoulder that seemed to repeat over and over, "The best laid plans of mice and men… " Pretty difficult to ignore, when it feels like an army of mosquitoes are droning in your ear!

Once all of the grocery bags were beside the door, she gave 2 short knocks, and then waited for someone to answer.

The door opened. Charley stood there, gaping at Lacey. "What are you doing back here?" Charley whispered in a truly viscous tone. "I told you, it wasn't safe for you to be here!"

Suddenly, Charley put her hand over her mouth to stifle a scream. She was looking intently over Lacey's shoulder. She backed slowly into the trailer, leaving Lacey standing all alone at the doorway.

The hair on the back of Lacey's neck suddenly stood on end. She slowly, carefully, bent over to pick up a grocery bag. A man's voice came from directly behind her. "Hello, Lacey, long time no see."

She turned slowly around, prepared to throw the heavy bag at the man.

"I wouldn't do that if I were you," the man said.

The sun was in Lacey's eyes. She couldn't make out who was speaking.

"Get in the trailer, slowly," said the man. "I'll bring the rest of the groceries in."

"Well, if you're going to do that, sir," Lacey quavered, "I'll just leave."

Squinting into the sun, the figure of the man remained indistinct, almost surreal. She started to walk towards the ladder.

A growly, evil chuckle emanated from the man. "Oh no, you don't, young lady. Get in that trailer."

Frozen in place, Lacey could not move. Her feet simply refused to budge.

"**NOW!**" snapped the man. "Get in that trailer, **NOW!**"

Lacey backed slowly towards the door, nearly tripping on the groceries. She stopped only when her back pressed into the back of a chair. The chair moved, pushing against the table. Holding her hands in front of her, clasped tightly in a futile attempt to stop shaking, she waited for the man to come in.

Before he entered though, a woman's voice came from behind Lacey. She spun around, short of breath, choking in both fright and disbelief. Lacey stared, not believing what her eyes were telling her!

"Mrs. Bronson?" Lacey said. "Is that you? What are you doing here?"

The same growly, evil chuckle she had heard a minute ago, sounded again behind Lacey. She spun towards the sound.

"Jayson? Jayson Silverman? What's going on here? I'm really confused!"

Lacey positioned herself so that she could see Evelyn Bronson on her left, and Jayson Silverman on her right. Charley was nowhere to be seen.

Jason leered at Lacey. "No, no, no, Lacey! YOU don't get to ask the questions. YOU get to answer the questions."

"The first question is, what are YOU doing here?"

Trying hard not to show the pair how frightened she was, Lacey said simply, "I work for Buy-Low and I'm making a grocery delivery. Small world, isn't it?" She gave a sickly half-grin.

Jayson said, slowly, "Too bad you and Charley saw one another. If that wasn't the case, you could leave. Now, you will have to stay here with Evelyn, and become part of her little family."

Turning to Evelyn, Jayson said, "I really have to get back to work now, Evelyn. I'll lock the trailer from the outside. You should be all right until I get back from work. The girls can't get out. Anyhow, I'll be home before 10 o'clock. I'm driving the truck back to Alberta tonight. Adam's final fill-in was last Thursday."

Evelyn asked, "What happened to the regular driver, the man that Adam covered for? That man's been off for 3 months. Why isn't he back at work?"

Jayson shrugged his shoulders. "Guess the boss fired him. Don't know any details. I didn't ask. I just know I have to fill in."

"Well," Evelyn persisted, "Who's bringing the truck here from Alberta tonight?"

"Zach," Jayson said.

Evelyn suddenly fluttered like a nervous butterfly perched on a colourful flower.

"Zach? Is coming HERE? Tonight? Why didn't you say so?"

"For Pete's sake, Evelyn," Jayson said, "Relax."

He turned his attention back to Lacey. "Now, Miss Lacey, if you try to escape, the same thing will happen to you that happened to Charley, Amelia, and Annie."

"And just what might that be?" Lacey asked.

"Curious, are we?" Jayson studied Lacey, but his expression was a total blank. His eyes were flat. However, deep beneath the lack of expression, a flickering madness seemed to glow in the back of his eyes, far more ominous than the blankness. Lacey was on the verge of total panic, but she managed not to show it. That was very fortunate, because she could not turn her eyes away from Jayson Silverman's. She felt as if he had cast some sort of spell on her! Of course, that was ridiculous – or was it?

"Charley was cheeky," Jayson said. "She talked back to Mama Evelyn. Charley lost her thumb. I wanted to cut out her insolent tongue, but Mama Evelyn wouldn't allow it."

"Amelia wouldn't eat what was served to her. Amelia is now tied to her bed. She hasn't been given anything to eat other than stale bread and water. We are trying to teach her manners. If someone goes to the trouble of preparing a meal here, you eat it. She'll stay tied in that bed until she apologizes to Mama Evelyn."

Jayson turned to leave. He focused his expressionless eyes on Lacey. "Guess I won't have time to bring the bags in, after all, Miss Lacey. You do it. Remember, though, no tricks, or when I get back, you will be missing more than a thumb.

"Mama Evelyn, you're responsible to see that she doesn't get away. Understand me?"

Without another word, he turned on his heel, jumped easily off the porch, folded his tall, lanky frame into the small jeep, and roared off down the road.

With Jayson gone, Lacey relaxed somewhat. She didn't think Evelyn Bronson could be nearly as psychotic as Jayson. She wasn't afraid of Evelyn.

Evelyn was still fluttering about, talking aloud to herself.

Lacey just kept standing in place. Glancing into the kitchen she managed to read the time from a clock on the wall – 6:05 p.m. An hour past closing time for the day shift. The night staff would be working, Smithy should have gone home for supper.

"*Dear Lord,*" Lacey prayed silently, "*Please let Smithy have reached Mason. Please let Mason have super-hero plans in place. I have a feeling that things are going to get real ugly here before they get better.*"

Evelyn Bronson smiled at Lacey. "Sit down, Lacey," she said. "I just have to make myself pretty. (Nervous giggle) We're having company tonight. As soon as I'm done, I'll sit with you and we can catch up. Won't that be nice? Make yourself at home. If you would like to make a pot of tea, I'm sure Charley will tell you where the makings are. Back in a flash." And she was gone in a flash.

Lacey suddenly realized that she had neglected to let her landlady know what was going on. Before she could figure anything out, Charley returned to the living room. Lacey motioned her to come closer.

"Charley, I have to make a phone call. Can you make tea and bang things around in the kitchen, loud enough that it will cover my phone call? Please, trust me, everything is going to turn out. This will be the last day you will ever have to spend in this dung heap. Now hurry, before Mrs. Bronson comes out."

Charley went into the kitchen. The phone was sitting on the back end of the table. Lacey grabbed it and quickly dialled Stella's number.

Stella answered on the 1st ring. "Hello?"

Charley, seeing Lacey's nod, started making a lot of noise in the kitchen.

In a panicked whisper, Lacey raced through her message to her landlady.

"Stella, just be quiet and listen. It's Lacey! I only have a minute, but I need you to do something. It's happening! Mason and his rescue team should be along tonight. I need you to get hold of him. His mobile phone number is on my desk. Tell him that the pumpkin truck will be here by 10 o'clock tonight. Tell him there are 2 adult males, 1 older woman, myself, and 2 of the 3 missing girls here. One of the adult males is a total wacko and extremely dangerous. The other man is the owner of the pumpkin truck. Tell Mason not to approach until both the orange truck and the jeep are parked at Freedom."

Lacey heard Evelyn coming out from the back. "Gotta go!" She practically threw the receiver back into the cradle. She then slipped into the kitchen, pretending to help Charley with the tea preparations.

Evelyn Bronson had changed her dress, brushed her hair, put on makeup, and very high heels. She tottered as she tried to walk sexily in the shoes.

"How do I look, girls?" Evelyn simpered.

"You look bee-yoo-ti-full, Mama Evelyn," said Charley, in a very different voice from her real voice. She spoke in an exaggerated child's voice.

Lacey looked from Charley to Evelyn and back, stupefied.

"Well, Miss Lacey," Evelyn cooed, "how does your Mama Evelyn look?"

Lacey stared at the clownish woman in front of her. Her makeup was smeared as if it had been applied by a small child. Her lipstick started below her nose and ended at her chin, with her lips in between. She looked like a completely crazy clown!

Crossing her fingers behind her back, Lacey lied. "You look fine," she said crisply. "But, Mrs. Bronson, you aren't my mother."

Evelyn's demeanour did an abrupt turnaround. She grabbed Lacey by the arm and practically threw her on to the sofa. She stood in front of Lacey, hands on her hips, and snarled, "Get something straight right now. You chose to enter my love-filled home. 'She who enters here becomes mine.'"

This was not a quote Lacey had ever heard before. She decided that Evelyn had made it up.

Evelyn continued with her strange story. "Foster children are unwanted, abused, and ignored. But, not by me!" She banged her fist forcefully on the arm of the sofa, saying, "I wanted you for my daughter from the time I first met you when you were 9 years old. For years, I kept track of your whereabouts. I waited and waited for a chance to keep you with me. Now, my lovely young daughter, I have you!"

Highly agitated, Evelyn Bronson wrung her hands continuously. Tears poured out of her eyes, smearing her mascara. Her mouth was twisted and puckered, making her look more like a monster cartoon creature than ever. White foam encircled her mouth. "You're my daughter now, Lacey. I love you, and I will take good care of you. You're my little girl, just as Charley and Amelia are my little girls. They're your sisters."

By this time, Evelyn was sobbing heartbrokenly. "Now, as long as you behave, and obey the rules of this house, you will be safe. If you don't, then Jayson will deal with you. If you won't be my little girl, you won't be anybody else's little girl either."

As quickly as she had started to cry, she stopped. In a completely normal tone of voice, she went over to the table. "Time for tea, young ladies."

Lacey decided that in this case 'discretion was the better part of valour'. Instead of arguing with the lunatic, she would play along. She winked at Charley, discreetly. She then turned and faced Evelyn. Adopting a childish voice, she said, "I'm sorry, Mama Evelyn, I didn't know. If you tell me your rules, then I won't disobey you."

With an inward shudder, she reached over and hugged Evelyn. "I love you, Mama Evelyn," she said.

Evelyn planted a huge, sloppy, happy kiss, right on Lacey's mouth.

Straightening up, Lacey barely resisted the urge to scrub her lips with her hands. "Now, Charley made us some lovely tea. Shall we have some while you wait for your company, Mama Evelyn?"

Evelyn clapped her hands with glee. "Oh, what a good idea. But, Lacey, you're too little for real tea. You'll have milk in a tea cup and pretend that it's tea, just like Charley. Now, let's sit at the table, in case you spill." She tottered over to the table in her ludicrous 4-inch heels, tipping herself onto the chair at the head of the table.

Charley sat woodenly, pretending to sip her milk, even blowing on it before taking a sip in case it was too hot, as per Evelyn's admonition.

"Not so fast, darling, it's hot," Evelyn had said. What Mama Evelyn said was Gospel, in Charley's brainwashed mind.

For a few minutes, Lacey studied Evelyn intently. Finally, she adopted her child's voice once again. "Mama Evelyn, may I take some pretend tea and a cookie in to Amelia? She's probably very thirsty and hungry. I'm sure she can smell the delicious cookies from her room."

"**NO!**" Evelyn said sharply.

Lacey had speedily figured out that the best way to appease Evelyn was to call her 'Mama Evelyn'. She played this card for all it was worth.

"But, Mama Evelyn," Lacey protested, whining as a child might. "Amelia is your little daughter, too, and she loves her Mama Evelyn very much, as much as Charley and I love you, Mama Evelyn."

241

Evelyn smiled proudly before she said, "Well, OK, but only if you're quick about it. We can't let Jayson know we fed her. She is being punished, you know. Once punishment is pronounced, I am not allowed to change it."

"However!" Evelyn said, having an 'ah-ha' moment, "you don't yet know the rules. So, hurry up, before Jayson gets here. Give her only a half a cup of children's tea, and only one cookie."

"Are you coming with me?" Lacey asked the crazy woman.

"Oh no! I'm not allowed to feed her. She's being punished. Now, hurry, please, my little one, before Jayson comes back!"

Not wanting Evelyn to become any more upset, Lacey quickly poured a 1/2 cup of milk, took a single cookie, and headed off down the hall, calling back, "Don't worry, Mama Evelyn, I won't be long!"

As an afterthought, she returned to the living room. "Mama Evelyn, may Charley come with me? She can carry the tea and I'll carry the cookie. That way, it will be faster than if I go by myself."

"Okay, but hurry, my daughters, hurry hard!" She giggled. "Oh, my goodness, it sounds like I am skipping a curling team, doesn't it? Silly me, I meant, hurry up!"

Leaving Evelyn muttering and giggling to herself, the 2 girls raced towards Amelia's room. Lacey was thankful that the cup was only half full. Despite that fact, the milk sloshed nearly to the rim of the cup as she ran.

The door was closed. No sound came through it. It was as silent as a tomb in that hallway.

When Lacey opened the door, the first thing that assaulted her nostrils was the most noxious odour she had ever encountered. A combination of urine, vomit, blood, and an unknown substance, produced a distinctly toxic smell. Trying not to gasp, she approached Amelia and reached for her hand.

"Amelia, we have brought you some milk and a cookie. You will have to eat and drink very quickly though, or Evelyn will come looking for us."

"Worse than that," said Charley gloomily, "Jayson will come back, and then we'll all be dead."

Lacey looked at Charley. "That's a little much, don't you think, Charley?"

Charley simply held up her bandaged, thumbless hand.

"Point taken," Lacey said simply.

She then focused her full attention on Amelia.

The young woman lay on the bed, her hands chained to the headboard, her feet to the footboard of a single bed. A tall girl, about 178 centimetres, she looked like a scarecrow. Under a single sheet, her legs were drawn up towards her chest, making her appear extremely short. The rest of her body barely showed beneath the sheet. Amelia was emaciated. She couldn't weigh more than about 36 kilograms. Her colour was ashen, her breath shallow and sour. She was clearly starving. Her eyes bulged in her hollowed-out face.

Initial shock worn off, Lacey turned to Charley. "Charley, I'll hold her up. You give her small sips of the milk and a very tiny bite of cookie. She looks as if she might choke, so maybe just break off a very small piece. Feed her a piece of the cookie, then a small drink of milk."

Amelia thirstily drank the milk, but she couldn't swallow the cookie until Charley dipped it in the milk. She then sucked on the cookie until it melted. She could swallow it then, but barely.

"Help is coming, Amelia," Lacey said. "Help is coming. You just hang in there, you hear me? We are all going to get out of here tonight. You just hang on!" Lacey gently pushed Amelia's hair out of her eyes, fluffed her pillow, and straightened her sheet. Amelia was too weak to speak, but she perceptively tightened her fingers on Lacey's hand.

"Girls!" came a frightened voice from the living room. Evelyn repeated, "Girls!"

"Coming, Mama Evelyn!" Charley trilled in her child's voice. "Coming right now."

She turned to Lacey in a panic. "Where's the cup? We have to take the cup. If Jayson sees it in the bedroom he'll know we have fed Amelia and we're all done for. I've got to get it!"

Seconds later, she was back in the hall, cup and left over piece of cookie in hand.

"Close the door, Lacey. Everything has to be the exact same as before. Hurry!" She was so terror-stricken that Lacey could actually see Charley's pulse throbbing in her throat.

Back in the living room, Lacey took the dishes from their 'tea party' (to use the term loosely!) into the kitchen and washed them. She deliberately took her time, not wanting to interact with Evelyn any sooner than she had to.

Finished in the kitchen, she reluctantly entered the living room. After a minute, she started towards the hallway.

"Where are you going, Lacey?" Evelyn asked.

"Just to the bathroom, Mama Evelyn. Just to the bathroom."

"Leave the door open, that's one of the rules. The bathroom door must always stay open."

"Why? I can't get out through that tiny window. I can't go anywhere."

"It's a rule," said Evelyn, "The bathroom door has to stay open at all times."

"What if I take a shower and Jayson or someone else is here? Even then?" Lacey asked, already knowing the answer.

"Door stays open, it's a rule. Door stays open, it's a rule." Evelyn kept repeating the rule until Lacey was pretty sure she was going to scream! "OK, OK! I've got it! Door stays open. Mama Evelyn," (she choked on the 'Mama' part), "I've got it!" Inwardly, Lacey was thinking to herself, *Mrs. Bronson, will you please, just shut up?*

Before she went into the bathroom, she sneaked past and silently opened Amelia's bedroom door. Legs now straightened, her skeletal body barely registered beneath the flimsy, worn sheet. She appeared to be asleep.

Lacey tiptoed around the bed and tried to open the window. It was locked, but she was able to force the latch back. Unfortunately, she was not able to slide the window open. She had been completely prepared to climb out that window, drop down onto the ground and then run for help.

DAMN! she thought. *What's Plan B?*

Leaving the latch in the unlocked position, she fervently hoped that when Mason and his team came, they would try that window and be able to force it open!

Lacey was totally dependent upon Mason and his team's rescue. *That,* she thought, *will have to be Plan B.*

Slipping out of the bedroom, she stopped in the bathroom. When she was finished, she made a point of slamming the lid down. The old toilet flushed so loudly that the lid slamming didn't have the desired effect.

Evelyn Bronson called out, "Be sure to wash your hands, my dear!" Lacey rolled her eyes, turned on the taps and noisily proceeded to soap and rinse her hands, muttering under her breath the whole time.

Back in the living room, Evelyn patted the sofa cushion beside her. "Come here, dear," she said to Lacey. "Let's catch up. Now that you are one of my daughters, you have to tell me everything that has happened to you since we last met."

"This is so exciting, is it not? I always wanted children, and now I have 3 daughters. Poof! Instant children!"

"Oh, and children! If I have my way, and I usually get my way, you will soon have a daddy! Too bad you will already be asleep when he comes to visit tonight, or you could meet him."

Evelyn clapped her hands gleefully, much like a 4-year-old child would. Suddenly, she stared at the clock in the kitchen. She became agitated once again.

"Oh, girls, it's after 8 o'clock! Time for your pyjamas and a bedtime story. We are behind schedule. You'll have to hurry, so we have time for reading before Jayson gets home, and before company arrives."

"Of course, you won't see our company, because you will be in your little beds, all tucked in."

"Off you go now, and hurry!"

Lacey, stalling for time, asked Evelyn why, if the company was going to become their daddy, they couldn't stay up later, just for this once, and meet him.

"Rules are rules," Evelyn stated simply. "They can't be broken or changed. Jayson says so."

Lacey gawked at her 1st social worker. Evelyn caught her incredulous look. "What?" she asked sharply. "Why aren't you getting your pyjamas on, like you were told to?"

Lacey said, "I don't have any night clothes with me. I don't have anything with me, because, **I'm not staying here!** So, you just go on. Read to Charley, because I have to go now. I'm late."

Evelyn stood up, shoved Lacey down on to the sofa. Her voice reverberated throughout the entire trailer. She said, in a tone that did not invite a response, "You, Miss Lacey, are going nowhere. You're too little to be out after dark.

Besides, do you think I am going to let you go again, after not seeing you for such a long time? Sit there, and do not move!"

Although taller and probably stronger than Evelyn Bronson, Lacey was afraid to incite further madness. She sat down.

Evelyn was in the kitchen, muttering to herself as she searched in drawers and cupboards for whatever it was she was looking for.

While Evelyn was thus distracted, Lacey surreptitiously moved towards the outside door. Just as she turned the doorknob, the door was yanked open and she literally fell through the doorway, right into Jayson Silverman's arms!

She straightened herself, prepared to make a run for it. Jayson gripped her forcefully. Lacey winced in pain.

"What the hell is going on here?" he asked Lacey in his deadly calm voice. "Where do you think you're going?"

Badly frightened, Lacey stood still, said nothing. The only sound was the chattering of her teeth.

"I asked you a question!"

"N-n-n, no-nowhere, Jayson," Lacey stuttered. "I was just opening the door to let some fresh air in. Mama Evelyn is just going to read us our bedtime stories."

"Humph!" was Jayson's reply. "Then why aren't you in your pyjamas and ready for your story?"

Lacey became indignant rather than scared. Looney tunes or not, this was getting beyond ridiculous!

She couldn't help herself. Rising up to her full height, she looked Jayson straight in the eye. "Because," she said levelly, "you ignorant piece of dog poop, I don't belong here, and I am **not** spending the night here! You go sit down beside Mrs. Bats-in-the-Belfry and listen to her feeble-minded stories. I'm leaving!"

Jayson shoved Lacey inside the trailer, so hard that she stumbled and fell against the table. When she went to get up, he kicked her in the ribs, then stood with his foot on her stomach, pressing hard enough that she couldn't budge. She had struck her left eye on the corner of the table. It throbbed, already swollen, discoloured. A broken blood vessel turned the white part of her eye a solid blood red. It watered enough that her vision was obstructed. A cut on her right temple produced a stream of blood that flowed down towards her right eye.

Through a loud ringing in her ears, Lacey faintly heard Evelyn. "Let her up, Jayson. It's time for her story. You know you shouldn't intervene in my story time with my girls. Let her up, I say!"

With a snarl of disgust, he kicked Lacey again, even harder than the 1st time. His large, worn cowboy boot hit both her cheekbone and her nose. She heard a crack when Jayson's boot connected with bone. He then grabbed her by the hair and threw her towards the sofa. A handful of hair could be seen between his fisted fingers. She landed beside Evelyn with a sickening thud.

Evelyn put her arm around Lacey. Dizzy from the attack, Lacey tried not to vomit. Leaning against the sofa back, she could have cared less that she might be dripping blood onto the fabric.

Charley came out of her bedroom, dressed in Bugs Bunny pyjamas, with matching rabbit slippers. Even through her injured eyes, Lacey was able to see the absurdness of the outfit on a grown woman. Looking profoundly embarrassed, Charley took a seat on the other side of Evelyn and waited for the bedtime story.

Evelyn held in her hand one of a series of books, *'Uncle Arthur's Bedtime Stories'*. The books were very old. Lacey remembered her Grandma reading *Uncle Arthur's Bedtime Stories* to her, and telling her that when her Grandma was a little girl, her own mother had read them to Lacey's mama. As far as Lacey's fuzzy brain could comprehend, that made at least 3 generations or more of children listening to Uncle Arthur at bedtime.

Just as Evelyn began reading one of the short stories in the book, the signal knock sounded on the door. Evelyn was so busy reading she didn't even hear it.

Jayson went to the door and opened it. Through her still blurry vision, Lacey tried to see who it was. When she figured it out, she immediately stood up, steadied herself and then walked over to the man.

"Zach? Zach Olivier, is that you? What are you doing here? You mean to tell me that **YOU** kidnapped my friends? You're a kidnapper? You told me and Lloyd that you were never going to do anything again that would land you in prison. And what about Lloyd? Did you abduct him as well? Where is my brother? Oh, God, Zach, don't tell me that he's dead!"

Breathless, not waiting for Zach to answer, Lacey dizzily sank down onto a kitchen chair, her energy spent, her body throbbing from the physical, hard kicks Jayson had inflicted upon her.

Her mind was dangerously close to being shattered by the realization that, not only had Zach pretended to be their father's friend, and pretended to be their friend, too, he was a liar.

He had 'helped' them all right, Lacey thought bitterly. *Zach had been instrumental in getting Lacey and Lloyd into foster care.*

He also lied when he said he was never going to do anything illegal again that might land him in prison. But, now? Now, here he stands, a full-fledged kidnapper. *Short of murder,* she thought, *it doesn't get worse than that.*

A sickening thought entered her poor, battered psyche. *He probably was a murderer as well!* Lacey hadn't yet found out exactly what had happened to helpless Annie. She tried desperately to concentrate on her surroundings, but it was difficult. Not only was her vision still blurred, but she had a massive headache on top of it. She tried valiantly to pay attention, praying that Mason and his team were nearby.

Zach, himself, appeared dazed. Turning from Lacey to Jayson, he barked, "What the hell, Jayson? I thought I told you to clear the room, lock the girls in their rooms so they wouldn't see me when I came tonight. Can't you obey even the simplest instructions for once?" With a disgusted snort, Zach sat at the table, opposite Lacey.

"Who are you?" Zach asked in a much warmer tone of voice than when he was talking to Jayson.

Lacey told him, even though she knew he would have eventually figured it out for himself. Although she was now 18 instead of 9 she looked the same. Well, maybe a little more weathered and worn, but pretty much the same.

"Ah, hell, Lacey," Zach began. "I don't know what to tell you, where to start."

"First of all," she said, "I want to know what happened to Lloyd. What did you do with him? After you tell me that, I'll hear the rest of your pathetic life story."

Zach put his head in his hands, speechless, as he tried to figure out how to tell Lacey what she wanted to know.

Before he could formulate the words, however, there was a quiet tapping on the door.

Jayson looked over at Evelyn, who was still reading to Charley. "Evelyn, you expecting anybody else this evening?"

Evelyn simply waved him off with a hand gesture and kept on reading.

The tapping became hard knocking. Loud, insistent.

"Answer the damn door!" Zach ordered Jayson. "Don't let them see inside. And speak nice to whoever is there, but get rid of them, get it?"

"Got it," Jayson grumbled.

"Good, now hurry up. You need to get on the road."

Jayson turned the doorknob, ready to tell whoever was on the other side of the door to get lost.

As Jayson had done with Lacey, the door was yanked open violently.

"Mason!" Lacey screamed, almost hysterical with relief, "Come on in! All of you, come in!"

Mason and 3 team members shoved Jayson outside. They entered the trailer.

Jayson took off running towards the pumpkin truck, but another team member was waiting for him. Pushing him roughly to the ground, the officer, dressed all in black, cuffed Jayson's hands behind his back, then jerked him to his feet.

"Give me your name!" snarled the man.

"Screw you!" Jayson snarled back.

"Okay, buddy, have it your way," laughed the man in a distinctly 'unfunny' tone. He shoved Jayson up against the team van. Pulling a card out of one of the pockets in his uniform, he read Jayson his rights. Jayson was then unceremoniously pushed into and restrained in the centre section of the 12-passenger van.

A mesh screen divided the prisoner from the driver's and front seat passenger's section. Another full width mesh screen behind Jayson further isolated him from any non-prisoner passengers. There were, of course, no door handles on the inside doors of the prisoner section.

The CCPOSU van was black. On each side of it, the team name was painted in an easy-to-read fluorescent white paint. It read:

CHILLIWACK CRIME PREVENTION & OPERATIONAL SUPPORT UNIT

As agile as a cat, the team member effortlessly leaped up onto the porch, scorning the ladder which was set up right beside him. Just before he positioned himself on the outside of the door to the trailer, he turned and gave a gleeful grin and a saucy wave to Jayson, who was sputtering and screaming. He was securely locked inside the vehicle, helpless and furious.

Meanwhile, inside 'Freedom', Mason looked over at Lacey. "You OK, Lacey? Everyone OK in here?"

"No," she managed to choke out the words. "We need an ambulance for Amelia, if she's even still alive. Down the hall, second door on your left. Hurry, please."

Mason motioned for 2 of his officers to check on Amelia. Without even turning his, he reached behind and shoved Zach back down in his chair before he could make a run for it. "Quit even thinking about it," Mason said simply. "I have a man posted outside. He'll shoot if he has to."

Zach sighed audibly and slumped back in his chair.

Mason finally took a good look at the spectacle on the sofa. "Hallowe'en?" he asked. Then, noting just how close to collapsing Charley was, he retracted his question. "Rhetorical question, young lady. Don't mind me. Just trying to lighten the tension a bit."

Evelyn Bronson simply continued reading aloud, oblivious to the people around her.

Poor Charley's cheeks were as red as an over-ripe apple. She was deeply embarrassed to be sitting in front of these strangers in her bunny pyjamas and slippers, listening to a young child's bedtime story. She shuddered, constantly and uncontrollably. Tears washed down her cheeks. She was too traumatized to reach up to wipe them away.

In the background, Lacey could hear one of the officers calling for an ambulance, STAT.

"Lacey? Where is the 3rd girl?" Mason asked.

Choking on a sob, Lacey simply shook her head before she whispered one word, "Dead."

"I'm so sorry." Mason said.

Then, "Can you tell me about today, Lacey?" Mason spoke gently, caringly. "Don't worry, I won't yell at you tonight. Maybe tomorrow, but tonight, I think you realize just what sort of a mess you got yourself into. Right now, I just want you to tell me your version of what is going on here."

Sensing how desperately Lacey wanted to be sitting anywhere except next to Evelyn, Mason patted the kitchen chair beside him. She got up and sat down next to him, unconsciously leaning to the side at an awkward angle in order to stay as far away from Zach as possible.

While Zach (mistakenly, as it turned out) assumed that Mason was distracted by Lacey moving to the table, he rose quietly, started to make a move toward the door. Unruffled, still looking at Lacey, Mason stood up, grabbed Zach, shoved him back into the chair once again. This time he handcuffed Zach's hands around the table leg. Uncomfortable position. Zach couldn't sit up straight. Mason didn't care. "Should have listened to me," he told Zach. "Now you have to wait until we are done here."

"I know my rights!" Zach yelled loudly even though Mason was still standing right next to him. "You're going to be responsible for my damaged back! Let me sit up straight!"

Mason simply walked back to his chair at the end of the table and sat down, completely ignoring his irate prisoner. Tipping back his chair, Mason reached into a pocket for his notebook and pen. Before he could ask Lacey any questions, they heard the siren of the ambulance approaching. The Fraser Canyon Hospital was only a few blocks away. Fortunately, they had been immediately dispatched to 'Freedom' and arrived in very short order.

The next several minutes were blurry. Lacey sat still and watched as the EMT's were directed to Amelia's room. Transferring the frail girl carefully onto a stretcher, they carried her out to the waiting ambulance. Mason asked where they were taking her. "To the Fraser Canyon Hospital, sir," said one medic. "You can check on her condition in an official capacity tomorrow."

The 2nd attendant said, "Whoever called for an ambulance said you have a 2nd patient as well?"

Mason pointed at Charley, who had somehow, amidst all the chaos, managed to slip into her bedroom and change into jeans and a T-shirt. Evelyn hadn't even noticed. She just kept reading.

"Thumb's been hacked off. Looks pretty bad," Mason reported tersely.

"Come with us, then," said the ambulance medic. "You can ride up front in the ambulance with me if you like. Let's get that thumb taken care of, shall we?" Charley practically ran out the door, she was so happy to get away.

"One fast question," Mason said. "I don't recall, are there any psychiatric facilities associated with that hospital?"

The EMT reached into a small case hooked on to the end of the stretcher and handed Mason a brochure. Mason skimmed it. There appeared to be numerous psychiatric resources in the area.

"Thank you. This is very helpful." Mason tucked the brochure into his shirt pocket for later.

Mason and Lacey walked beside the stretcher, out to the waiting ambulance. He asked, "Can you tell me anything at all about (here, eyebrows raised, he looked at Lacey for assistance, who promptly said, 'Amelia Anderson'). "Yes, Amelia Anderson, her condition right now?"

The response was a shoulder shrug and a discreetly whispered, "It's bad," before they rushed to get the stretcher into the ambulance.

Mason patted Charley on her shoulder, and said, "See you tomorrow, Charley. Then, we'll see what happens next, OK?"

The young woman nodded shyly, said, "Thank you, sir," in a timid but grateful tone. She climbed in the front seat and the ambulance backed out of the drive, lights flashing, but siren silent, until it was out of the trailer park. Mason could hear the siren begin, once it reached the highway.

Mason stood in front of 'Freedom' and cast his gaze upon the starry heavens. A dark night, the sky was filled with hundreds of twinkling lights, interspersed with lights from airplanes bound for Vancouver. Quiet, peaceful. In direct contrast to the events of the past few hours. With a soft sigh, Mason granted himself the luxury of another minute. He feasted his eyes on the light show in the sky, his ears tuned to the only sound close by, that of a cool and gentle breeze, softly rustling unraked dry leaves that covered the ground around 'Freedom'. Any traffic noise from the highway was drowned out by the extraordinary intensity of Mason's ability to totally focus on his assignment. Giving himself a mental shake, he reluctantly re-entered the trailer.

Back inside, the 1st thing he noticed, was that Evelyn Bronson had finally quit reading. Instead, she was wringing her hands and sobbing softly. "My little girls, my little girls, where are you?"

Mason looked over at Lacey, who by this time was standing against the far wall, by the hallway entrance, as far away from both Evelyn and Zach as she possibly could get. She appeared shell-shocked. He hoped she would be able to answer his questions.

"Lacey?" he spoke carefully, softly. "Would you be able to make a pot of coffee while I speak with Mr. Olivier?" He added, "Please, I'm getting mighty dry."

Lacey said nothing, but she did head for the kitchen, sliding tight against the wall to avoid getting too close to Zach.

With another glance at the hapless woman sitting on the sofa, Mason decided that she wouldn't be going anywhere on her own, any time soon. He waited while Lacey made the coffee, saying nothing, but not taking his eyes off of Zach. Zach was clearly intimidated. He knew enough from Mason's demeanour to simply shut up and wait.

Lacey came back to the table and sat down.

"Do you want to start, Lacey, or shall we talk with Zach?" Mason waited for her response.

"Zach first. I need to know. Until I know, I can't concentrate enough to give you any useful information."

"Zach it is, then."

"Am I under arrest?" Zach asked.

"Not yet, Mr. Olivier," Mason said. "Just trying to get the facts straight. Hope you don't mind if I tape this interview." It was not a question, but Zach responded anyway, with an indifferent shrug of his shoulders.

"Mr. Olivier," Mason asked politely, "Tell me something. If I remove your handcuffs, will you sit still and answer my questions, without trying to walk out of here? It will be easier for you to drink coffee that way."

Zach: "OK."

Mason: "OK, what?"

Zach: "OK, sir, I won't try to leave."

Mason: "Thank you. Now then, 1st question. That delivery van outside, 'ZO'S HAULING'. Can I assume it belongs to you?"

Zach nodded in the affirmative.

Mason: "Yes? No? Speak up so the machine will record your answers, please."

Zach: "Yes, it's my delivery van."

Mason: "The name, 'ZO'S HAULING' – 'ZO' stands for Zachary Olivier? Or, is it Zacharias Olivier?"

Zach: "Just plain Zach."

Mason made a notation in his notebook.

Mason: "How long have you had that van?"

Zach: "9 years. I got it just after I was released from prison. I was bound and determined that I wasn't ever going back to gaol. My wife and 2 kids were long gone, so I needed a new, fresh start."

Mason: "When did you start kidnapping kids?"

Zach: "Never kidnapped any kids. They were hitchhiking. Every one of them, every single time, came into the van and travelled with the drivers of their own accord."

Mason: "So, they entered your van and travelled to B.C. with your drivers, **of their own accord**?"

Zach: "Yes."

Mason: "What about leaving? I presume they were brought here to Hope, to this wretched old mobile home, the mobile home that Lacey calls 'Freedom'. Were they free to leave, once they entered these premises?"

Zach sighed, made a zipping motion across his lips.

Mason: "Why'd you do it, Zach? Why did you keep 3 young girls here against their will?"

Zach: "I didn't do that."

Mason: "Well, if you didn't do it, who the heck did? These young girls have been missing for years! They were long ago presumed dead. If it wasn't for young Lacey, here, they would still be missing and presumed dead."

"Were you banking on that fact? The fact that everyone thought they were dead, and so, that would make it OK? Okay to just brainwash them, terrify them to the point that they wouldn't try to leave, even if they could? Come on, Zach! I'm not stupid, I've got it figured out! Open up!"

"Tell us what exactly happened and why. We need to understand."

"There's one girl dead already. We'll talk more about her in a minute."

"Now, we have another girl that's so close to dead, we don't even know if she'll make it through the night."

"And, we also have a young woman with her thumb hacked off so crudely, that Heaven only knows if she's going to be able to use that hand for any useful purpose!"

"Plus, we have a helpless, crying woman who is treating the girls as if they were her babies? What's that all about?"

"And plus, we still have a missing young man."

At this point, there was an audible sound of distress coming from Lacey. Her eyes glazed over. Her right hand covered her mouth, presumably to stop herself from screaming. Her left hand gripped her right hand in a clearly unsuccessful attempt to stop it from shaking.

Zach: "Which question do you want answered first?" He grinned creepily.

Mason: "Don't be a smartass, Mr. Olivier. Just tell us the story."

Zach: "Let's talk deal."

Mason: "How can we discuss a deal, Mr. Olivier, when you haven't yet been charged with anything, when you might not even be charged with anything? The best I can tell you is this: IF and WHEN the time comes, and IF I am satisfied with your story, I will suggest to the Chief Crown Prosecutor that they might, perhaps, consider a deal. That's the best I can offer you at this very moment."

Zach: "Well, can't blame a guy for trying, can you?"

With an impatient exhaling of breath, Mason leaned back in his chair. Even though the machine was still recording, he would continue writing pertinent facts in his notebook.

"Any time, SIR! We're waiting, ready to listen," Mason said.

Zach sat up straight, looked over at Lacey, looked her straight in the eye, and solemnly spoke.

"First of all, I need to apologize to you, Lacey. I know that you and Lloyd were disappointed in me when I had Social Services come and pick you up at the prison, way back when. That wasn't my fault. I was acting on the orders of your father. He wanted to be sure that you both were properly looked after. Your mother was gone, and Paul certainly couldn't look after you, with the amount of time he still had to serve. He really did mean well."

"You were both such clever kids. Young, but old for your actual age. You both had to grow up in a hell of a hurry. You actually figured out how to go and visit your dad. You were that smart! I was impressed. I was also very jealous. My kids wrote me off completely. You tried to maintain a relationship with your dad. Yup, I was jealous."

"Anyhow, once you were taken away, I went to Vancouver. After checking the 'Help Wanted' ads for several weeks, I knew that I couldn't get a decent paying job, or probably any job for that matter, because of my criminal record. So, I decided to go into business for myself."

"I had made a few contacts in prison. I called in a favour, and bought my delivery vehicle from a guy I met in prison. He sold it to me cheap, carried me until I was able to pay it off in full, no interest."

"Another former prison friend who owed me a favour, had a body shop. He put the decals on the doors of the truck, after painting it the bright orange colour that I wanted."

"In the beginning, I went through several drivers. It seemed as if I was always putting up ads around Vancouver, looking for drivers."

One day, Jayson Silverman responded to one of my ads. When he showed up for his interview, he looked vaguely familiar to me, but I didn't recognize him by name. He was polite and well spoken. I hired him on the spot. Didn't check any references. In fact, I didn't even ask for any. Just confirmed that he had a clean driver's licence and that it was the proper class of licence. I ignored the feeling that I knew him from somewhere. Never gave it another thought. As an ex-con, I gave people the benefit of the doubt without any 3rd degree questioning, or checking out stuff. Believe me, it's a tough row to hoe, if you have a criminal record. I was willing to give people the benefit of the doubt, without hesitation."

"Because the job entailed driving all night, I decided it would be cheaper to rent a trailer, for the drivers to sleep in after the long drive from Alberta to Vancouver. A lot less expensive than springing for a hotel."

"Jayson was a loyal employee, and a good driver. He was always willing to forego a day off and drive extra shifts. We only had the one long trip from Alberta to Vancouver – on Thursdays."

"To backtrack just a touch, when the 2 social workers picked you up at the prison, I was introduced to Jayson and the woman who was with him. But, I paid no attention to either one of them. I was just happy that they arrived promptly to pick you up."

"I was brought up in the system, too, Lacey. It stunk then, and it still stinks, but like I said before, there was no other choice, what with your folks being gone."

"Sorry, I digress. Something about that lady social worker continually nagged at me. Finally, I couldn't stand it anymore. She had handed me her card at the prison. I had stuck it in my jacket and forgot about it for quite a while. I gave her a call."

"She told me she had been waiting for me to either phone or drop in to her office. I said I didn't know why she thought I would call her. I didn't know myself why I actually did it."

"It was then she told me that her maiden name was Olivier!"

"Evelyn is my sister. We were put into separate foster homes as very young children. When I turned 18, I hightailed it away from that stinking system. Couldn't leave foster care behind me quick enough."

"For whatever early reasons, I never tried to find her. Not once. Selfish, I guess, at the time. Young and selfish. Later on, after I served my time, I figured she would be better off without having an ex-con someday show up at her door."

"Boy, was I wrong! Evelyn went through some terrible foster homes. I guess nearly every kid in the system does. Some adapt better than others, some never adapt at all."

"I think she became a social worker for exactly the right reason. To try and make it easier for the children who were in the system. I'm sure she did make a difference to a lot of the kids."

"She really did," Lacey said.

Zach carried on. "Of course, after we reconnected, we kept in touch. She was still working for Social Services. In fact, Lacey, she told me about you and Lloyd. She probably wasn't supposed to talk about you kids, being part of her work and all, but she let me know how you were doing from time to time. She really wanted to keep you as foster kids herself, but the powers that be wouldn't allow it."

"She was happy, for a while. She married an apparently really great guy, but he died not that long after he and Evelyn were married. They both wanted kids, but it never happened."

"Once her husband was dead, she was extremely lonely. Then, to make matters worse, Jayson Silverman left his job. Without a word to Evelyn, in fact, without a word to anyone. She considered him her best friend, her only friend. When he took off, she was devastated. She felt betrayed."

"Looking back, I think that was when she first began to crack, although I didn't notice anything at the time. Didn't see her consistently enough to notice, I guess."

"I was here, sitting right here at this table, when I came up with a brainwave. Evelyn should leave her job. Move to Hope and look after the trailer for me. I would pay her for her services. She just needed to keep the trailer neat and clean, and feed the drivers that stayed here while they were waiting for their next run. Not hard work. She had worked hard her whole life. A free place to live, what more could you want, right? I figured this was a dream job, perfect."

"The very same day that I brought up the idea, my sister gave her notice. She moved into this old trailer and cleaned it right up. She's a fantastic cook, and the drivers all loved the time they spent here."

"I was also here at the trailer the day she first saw Jayson. I thought they had each seen a ghost. They both turned so deathly pale!"

"After a couple of minutes, Evelyn walked over to Jayson and gave him a gigantic hug. Knowing how much they had to talk about, I volunteered to make Jayson's run back to Alberta for him. He was grateful, and so, off I went, leaving them alone to reminisce."

"Little did I know the twisted plans that soon bubbled and brewed in the minds of those 2 schemers!"

"One day, when I was visiting Evelyn, Jayson came in. Over a delicious dinner prepared by Evelyn, they hit me from all angles."

"Evelyn was first. She explained how she wanted children, that her life was not complete, that she could be the world's best mother. I said she was too old to have children and besides that, in order for that to happen, she needed a sperm donor. She just laughed. She said Jayson had a plan."

"Jayson explained. Nearly every month, on the 3rd Thursday, a young hitchhiker, most often a female, would stand waiting along the edge of the highway in northwestern Alberta. Jayson had never picked anyone up. He told me he figured these kids were runaways from bad foster homes. He said that he was positive that, if he picked up a hitchhiker, he could convince her to come in to the trailer when they arrived in Hope. His excuse would be that he was making a delivery, that the lady of the house would feed them coffee and pie before they continued on in to Vancouver. The fact that it was a woman he was making the delivery to, would make the young girl feel safe."

"He said he knew for a fact, that after a brief search, the police forgot about young runaways. After a time, nobody would ever suspect that the youngster was alive, and well, and living in Hope, B.C. Voila! There was no crime even suspected, and Evelyn would have her 1st child."

"By this time, there were visible cracks in Evelyn's tired mind. When the 1st girl arrived, Charlotte, Evelyn was ecstatic! She had her 1st daughter. When she found out that Charley didn't have a job, or any place to go, it was easy to convince her to stay with Evelyn 'just until she found something'."

"Charley might very well have remained, happy and content, except Evelyn started behaving very erratically. She called Charley her baby, made her dress in childish clothing, read her very young children's storybooks, fed her baby food."

"Evelyn was beside herself the day Charley announced that it was time for her to move on. Fortunately for Evelyn, very unfortunately for Charley, Jayson showed up, just as Charley was going to walk out the door. Jayson dragged her back in to the trailer. A horrific scene followed. Evelyn was hysterical at the thought that her 'baby' was leaving, Charley was in hysterics, bound and determined she was going to get out of there."

Finally, at his wit's end, Jayson threw Charley across the room. Dazed, she simply sat there.

When her head cleared, she promised that she would stay with Evelyn, that she would not leave.

"Jayson didn't trust Charley. Charley didn't trust Jayson. For a few months, they tippy-toed around each other. True to her word, Charley didn't try to leave."

"Even though Evelyn was becoming more unstable by the day, Charley loved my sister. She decided that if it made Evelyn feel better, she could pretend that she was Evelyn's baby. Who would it hurt?"

"The next young girl that Jayson brought here was Amelia. You've met Amelia. She was a handful from day 1. Tried to run more times than anyone could count. Finally, Evelyn and Jayson chained her to the bed. It was the only way to keep her here. She stopped eating. They force-fed her, but only to keep her alive. At long last, Amelia gave up. She promised not to run. She promised to be a 'good little girl'. Evelyn was happy. Jayson and I were both happy because Evelyn was happy. Amelia wasn't happy, but she pretended to be."

At this point, Zach stopped talking. He asked to use the washroom. Mason told him to go ahead. Mason didn't trust Zach, so he stood where he could see the closed bathroom door.

A few minutes later, Zach returned and asked for another cup of coffee. He drank thirstily, and then continued his nearly unbelievable story.

"The 3rd member of Evelyn's little family eventually arrived. Annie Barcley was already 16 years old. She steadfastly refused to be treated as a baby."

"Evelyn's plan was for the children in her little family, to be the ages she made up in her head as they arrived. In other words, even though Charley was truly the youngest and Annie was truly the eldest, in Evelyn's mind they were reversed. It didn't matter what, Annie was not going to be babied. Truth be told, Annie made it difficult, not just for herself, but for the other 2 girls, as well."

"Turned out that quiet, soft-spoken Jayson had a hidden evil streak. He did not hesitate to eke out severe discipline as required."

"One morning, Evelyn asked Amelia to go and tell Annie that breakfast was ready. When Amelia got to the bedroom, all she saw was Annie's rear end sticking in the window. With one last flip, Annie fell out the window and on to the ground. Winded, she lay there panting. As she lay there, Jayson drove up. Evelyn pointed to the far side of the trailer. As usual, she was hysterical, to the point that she couldn't think of anything to do on her own."

"Jayson followed the direction of Evelyn's finger. He ran to the far side of the trailer. Sure enough, there lay Annie, gasping for air. When she saw Jayson approaching, she panicked. Told him that she fell out of the window when she was trying to clean it. Of course, that made zero sense, but got to give her credit. She tried."

"That time, Jayson beat her with a stick until she couldn't even speak. For a time, there were no more incidents."

"The next time Annie tried to escape was her last. She marched out the door, it was mid-afternoon. Evelyn had fallen asleep on the sofa. Amelia was doing dishes. Charley was about to follow Annie, no matter where she went. It wasn't a day where any of the drivers were expected."

"Before she could reach the door, however, a ruckus outside made her run back to the relative safety of the sofa."

Lacey couldn't help herself. She interrupted, bitterly. "Zach, you make all these horrible incidents sound so everyday, so matter of fact. Like this is the way life is supposed to be. You make me sick!"

Zach ignored her. Looking directly at Mason, he persisted in finishing his accounting.

"Jayson stood on the porch, hanging on to Annie by her hair. She screamed and kicked at him, but the more she struggled, the harder he yanked on her hair. When she cursed and swore, he slapped her, hard. Annie was beyond caring."

"She yelled, 'Jayson, you shit-faced, fucking pig! You let me go or I'll scream so loud that the old geezers down the street will all come running!'"

"Jayson didn't say a word…"

Now it was Mason's turn to interrupt. "Were you there, Mr. Olivier?"

"Nope," Zach said. "I got this part from Jayson, himself."

"Hmmm," Mason hummed. "Continue, please."

"Well, like I said before, Jayson didn't say a word. He just stood there, grinning at Annie as she struggled. It was futile, but she was so worked up she didn't realize that. Suddenly, Jayson picked her up. It was as if she was no heavier than a puppy. He warned her to stop struggling and yelling or he would do something drastic. Her response was the same. She yelled, 'Jayson, you %!@** pig! You let me go or I'll scream so loud that the old geezers down the street will all come running!'"

"At this point, Annie managed to somehow, nobody knows for sure how, get loose from Jayson's arms. Before he even realized it, she kicked him in the balls so hard that he doubled over in pain. Annie tried to get by him, but he managed to reach out, pulled her legs right out from under her. She fell off the porch, hit her neck on the edge of it as she fell. Broke her neck. That was the end of Annie."

Once again, Mason interrupted. "Where's the body?"

Zach shrugged. "Don't know. I simply told Jayson that he made the mess, he needed to clean it up. Told him I didn't want to know what he did with the body, just get rid of it."

"May I continue?"

Sickened, Mason simply looked at him as if to say: *Do what you want, you sick bastard, you will anyway.*

"Well," Zach went on, "Evelyn nearly went off the deep end. She mourned the passing of Annie just as if Annie was her real child. For weeks, she wouldn't get dressed, she just sat on that sofa in a stupor."

"Finally I had enough. I told Evelyn that if she didn't come out of her funk, I was going to take Charley and Amelia and give them to somebody else, somebody who would take care of them, instead of being selfish and just ignoring them, every minute of every day. Told her that she had to smarten up before my next trip, or the girls would be leaving with me."

"I went there a week or so later, and everything was back to 'normal' around there. She was sitting on that sofa, with Charley on one side of her and Amelia on the other, reading them their bedtime story."

"The next thing that happened, Amelia is back to her trouble-making self. At supper one evening, I was there, she asked Evelyn to pass her the potatoes. My sister was either paying no attention, or simply didn't hear her. Next thing everyone knows, **Charley** gets up, walks over to Evelyn's chair, picks up the bowl of mashed potatoes, and dumps it right on Evelyn's head. Screams, '**You Crazy Bitch**! Amelia asked you to pass the potatoes!'"

"While this is going on, Amelia stands up, cheering and clapping, banging on the table, screaming, "Way to go, Charley, way to go! Rub it in her hair!"

"Evelyn fell apart, crying and rocking back and forth, whispering over and over again, 'I'm a terrible mother, I'm a terrible mother. Whatever did I do to deserve ungrateful babies like this?'"

"I'd had enough. I got up from the table and, taking a page out of Jayson's book, grabbed Amelia by the hair on her head, dragged her with me to the back of the trailer, where I keep a tool box. I took a set of chains out of that tool box, marched her to her bedroom, threw her on the bed, and then hollered for Charley to come in and give me a hand."

"Despite her kicking, screaming and biting, we finally got her restrained. I told her that until she learned to respect her mother, she wouldn't eat. Nothing but bread and water until she apologized. I told her the average human can live 3 weeks without food, but only 3 days without water. Told her if she wanted to live, she'd better shape up in the next 3 days or I'd cut off her water. Of course, I didn't really mean it. Told her that she'd better hope that Jayson didn't hear about this. He'd cut off more than that. She knew I wasn't as mean as Jayson, she knew I wouldn't let her die."

"When was that?" Mason asked, trying unsuccessfully to hide the disdain he felt for Zach.

"It was 19 days ago."

Feeling ill, Mason weakly uttered, "Finish your story."

"Well, I'm pretty sure Miss Charley, with the help of Miss Lacey, of course, fed Amelia some tidbits. I found cracker crumbs on the sheet in Amelia's room today. Can't say as I blame them. Again, though, they'd better pray that Jayson doesn't hear about it."

"Who cut off Charley's thumb?" Lacey asked.

Zach said, "I'm getting to that."

"Jayson showed up at the trailer, a couple days after Amelia was chained to the bed. He demanded to know what was going on, why Amelia was being punished. He was really irate. As far as he was concerned, punishment was his job and his alone. He calmed down somewhat when I spoke up and told him that, in light of her actions, I had dished out the punishment."

"Now, seeing as you're so big on proper procedure, you better let Charley tell you what happened, when you see her at the hospital tomorrow. I wasn't here at the time." Zach sat back in his chair, a smug look on his face.

"Lacey," Mason said quietly, "please go over and bring Evelyn back to the table. Sit her down between you and me. That way she can look at either of us and not have to face Zach directly."

Lacey walked over to the sofa, pried Evelyn's arms from around the bedtime story book she was holding.

"It's OK, Evelyn, I'll bring you right back to the sofa. You just need to tell Mason something."

Evelyn made a snivelling whimper, then stopped.

"Now, Evelyn, if you can, would you please tell me what happened to Charley's thumb? First of all, when did it happen?" Mason asked softly so as not to frighten the mentally unstable woman any more than she already was. "Just look at me, please. Don't look at Zach."

"Umm," Evelyn answered, "it was about 10 days or 2 weeks ago. All the days are the same in here. We don't have a television set to watch and the radio is rarely on. I sometimes forget to write things on the fridge calendar. But!" Here she brightened perceptibly, "It was last Thursday. I know that, because Jayson came!"

"And what happened when Jayson came?"

"He got really angry with Charley because Charley didn't stop Amelia from dumping the potatoes on my head."

"I see," Mason said. "Tell me, does Jayson get angry often?"

Evelyn looked down at her feet and whispered, "He never used to."

"But he does now?"

Evelyn nodded her head.

"Can you answer with your voice, please, Evelyn? This little machine (he pats his tape recorder) can't record anything if it can't hear you.

"Now, again, tell me. Does Jayson get angry often?"

Suddenly, Evelyn sat up straight and looked Mason right in the eye. "He never used to, but now, it seems that he is angry all the time. And when he gets angry, look out! Someone is going to suffer. Just like the night Charley lost her thumb. It was bad, oh, it was very bad!"

Here, Evelyn hugged herself and rocked back and forth in the chair. She was visibly shaking, and her voice quavered as she tried to answer Mason.

"Do you have any idea why that might be, Evelyn? Why Jason is angry all the time?"

"Ummm," Evelyn drawled, "I think it's because he thinks he is the boss of everyone in this trailer. But, when Zach comes, Zach is the real boss. Jayson knows it, and it pisses him off. It seems when he knows Zach is going to come here, that's when he is at his worst. It's as if he has to release all this rage, this wrath."

"I see," said Mason. He really was beginning to figure out this whole sordid mess. He believed what he saw, believed what he heard. He thought, *I understand what's going on here, but boy, if a stranger walked in and heard this story, that stranger would think he or she had stumbled on a tribe of deranged aliens!*

"Evelyn," Mason said in a gentle, but firm, voice, "Please, tell me about Charley's thumb."

"Hmmm, let me see," Evelyn drawled again. "It got started when Charley dumped the bowl of mashed potatoes on my head. It didn't hurt. Charley was just acting out because she's little, you see. She's just one of my baby girls. I told Jayson to pay no attention, that everything had calmed down, but NO! Jayson lost it totally."

"He pushed the dishes that were on the table where Charley was sitting off of the table and onto the floor. Broke most of them. Then, he grabbed Charley by her hair and slammed her head down on the table. He told her to keep her head down, not to move a muscle. He went into the kitchen drawer where the knives are kept and got, it looked like, a serrated bread knife." (Here, Evelyn choked. It was a minute before she could continue.)

Evelyn went on. "Jayson pulled his chair up right beside Charley. He told me to hold her hand down on the table, to not let her hand move. He told Charley if she moved, it would turn out a lot worse, that he would cut off her whole hand, instead of just her thumb."

"'Jayson said he wanted to 'cut out her insolent tongue'. I wouldn't let him. I would have killed Jayson before I would let him do something that debilitating to one of my babies."

"Charley just sat up straight in her chair, put her hand flat on the table and glared at Jayson. Once again, he told me to hold her hand tight so she couldn't move. Then he, then he... he took that bread knife and sawed off Charley's thumb, at the knuckle that is right below the thumbnail.

Lacey felt like she was going to be sick. Taking a deep, steadying breath, she managed to hold her gorge.

Evelyn said, in a totally unruffled voice, a monotone. "That knife must have been pretty dull, because he sawed for what seemed like a long time before he was able to detach the thumb from her hand. There was blood everywhere. Her little face was a terrible grey colour, and her breathing was raspy. But she never moved, no sir, she stared at Jayson the whole time, bit her lip right through so it was bleeding also, but she never moved. My baby girl was stoic. So brave!"

"I know this is hard, Evelyn, to tell me about this terrible thing that happened to your little girl. You're doing great. Now, what did Jayson do with Charley's thumb, once he finally sawed it off?" Mason kept his eyes focused on Evelyn's in order to keep her attention.

Evelyn said calmly, "He put it in a Ziploc baggy and put it in the freezer part of the fridge."

Mason asked, "Is it still there?"

At this point, Lacey cut in. "It's not there, Mason. Jayson gave the thumb to Adam Draper, who was filling in for one of the regular drivers."

Mason now asked Lacey, "How do you know Adam had the thumb?"

"Because Adam had thrown a leather bag into the back seat of the truck. While he went back into the trailer, I looked inside. When I saw the thumb in the Ziploc bag, I took a picture of it."

"Do you have any idea what Adam did with it?"

"No," Lacey said. "I have no idea."

Back to Evelyn. He asked her to resume.

"Not much more to say. When Adam got here, Jayson went to the freezer and gave Adam the bag with Charley's thumb in it. Then, both Adam and Jayson went on their way. I rinsed the stump of Charley's thumb in cold water, then took a clean towel and held it on tightly until the bleeding slowed down."

"Another thing, Evelyn," Mason said, "and then we'll all leave this place. Tell me about your little family."

The mad gleam appeared behind Evelyn's eyes once more.

"They are perfect!" she crowed. "I had 3 wonderful baby girls, and I was sooooo happy. Then, Annie got in the accident on the porch, and she died. I wanted to die with her, but Jayson said not to worry, that he would get me a replacement baby. That cheered me up. And the next thing you know, my newest baby girl, Lacey, showed up."

"Now I have my perfect family once again. My mother always told me that 3 is the perfect number of children for a woman to have. Any fewer aren't enough, any more just wrecks her body and her mind."

Grinning like the mental patient she was soon to become, Evelyn held out her arms to Lacey. Lacey ignored her. Evelyn sat back, looking hurt, bewildered.

Mason stood up, stretched. "Well, ladies, it's time to go. Lacey, we'll give you a ride home. Then we will take Evelyn to the hospital and have her admitted for a psych evaluation."

Lacey said, "I can walk. You can see where I live from here."

"You are getting a ride, and I will see you get safely into your home. Don't argue," Mason said.

"After we admit Evelyn to the hospital here, we're going to take Jayson back to cells in Chilliwack, until I speak with the Chief Crown about where he should be held, pending his 1st and subsequent court appearances."

"I am going to ask that he be held without bail. He is a danger to anyone and everyone, including himself. He needs a 24-hour suicide watch placed on him. Don't want this sicko to off himself before justice can be served."

Evelyn stood up. "I'm not coming with you. I have to stay here and wait for my baby girl. I have to stay here with my other baby girl, Lacey. She's too little to be left alone."

Lacey looked at Mason as if asking for permission to speak. Mason nodded affirmatively.

Lacey walked over to Evelyn and put her arms around the woman. "Mama Evelyn," she said in a compassionate voice, "I'm staying with a friend. You have to stay at the hospital, where your baby girl, Charley, is. You need to make sure her thumb is OK."

"Oh!" said Evelyn, "You're right! Thank you, Lacey, good idea."

"Now, here's your bedtime story book. You have your friend's mama read you a story before you go to sleep."

Evelyn then put her hands on her hips, looked at Mason. "Well," she said in a regal tone, "what are we waiting for? Let's go!"

Lacey, Evelyn, and Mason, were already walking out of the trailer when Zach's voice broadcast across the room. "Hey! What about me?"

Mason gave a wry laugh. "Oh right, what about you, Zach?"

"You haven't been formally charged with any offence, yet, but I'm guessing, that after further interrogation, you are going to be charged, at the very least, with being an accessory to kidnapping. You'll be held in cells until the R.C.M.P. decide what to do with you."

"It seems to me that the easiest thing is to take you to the detachment in Chilliwack, along with Jayson. Hold out your hands, so I can cuff you."

With one last glance around the old trailer, Mason pushed the lock button on the door.

Lacey breathed a sigh of relief. 'Freedom' was now truly that. Although the guilty parties were not free in the usual sense, everyone was indeed free of this wretched place.

Mason walked Lacey to the front door of Stella's place.

"Good work, Lacey," Mason said. "You ever consider joining a police force?"

Lacey stood in the doorway, mindful that Stella was waiting anxiously behind her.

Right now, though, she studied Mason. Fully 2 minutes passed before she spoke.

Her face was drained of all colour as she asked him, "Do you think it would help me find out what's happened to Lloyd?"

261

Epilogue

A man and 2 women, one of the women no longer young, stood at the edge of the water. The late morning sun glistened brightly on the gently dancing waves of the emerald green lake. Their craft waited expectantly, tied to the jetty.

The man helped both women settle comfortably in the canoe before he climbed in and picked up his paddle. They glided smoothly along on the cool water, headed for the small island that beckoned in the distance. Reaching the land, the man positioned the canoe alongside an old jetty. While his wife held the canoe steady against the jetty, the man helped the older lady out of the craft. He then turned to assist his wife, but she was already out. He reached in and removed a wicker picnic basket and 4 folding lawn chairs from the canoe.

It was beautiful on the shore of the island. A cool autumn breeze heralded the coming winter, but today the sun shone brilliantly and warmed their cheeks as they sat on the beach. The man pointed skyward. "Look," he softly said. "See them? There are only 5. One must have lost its love. Trumpeters mate for life, just like you and me." His wife smiled and patted his hand.

Some time passed. His wife fretted. She said worriedly, "He should be here by now. He promised he would be here."

"We can wait a little longer," her husband said. "We'll wait as long as we can."

They waited for 2 more hours. Finally, the man gently told both women that they would have to return the canoe to the rental agent. If they didn't leave now, it would be dark. They quickly packed up the remains of their picnic and returned to the jetty. He reloaded the canoe, then helped the women back into the craft.

Reaching the center of the small lake, the man stopped paddling. His wife leaned back and he put his arms around her. The older woman trailed her hand in the cool water, watching the ripples grow larger until they disappeared. All 3 quietly watched in the distance as a young deer drank from the water's edge, in the same spot they had sat only a few minutes ago. After one last look at the island, with tears wetly rippling down her cheeks, the elderly woman reached to the bottom of the canoe and brought up a wooden container. She kissed the box and then gently lowered it over the side of the canoe.

Utter silence. Not even a bird trilled. The 5 Trumpeter swans floated in place, their beauty reflected in the stillness of the water. Time stood still. Each lost in their own separate thoughts, they deeply appreciated the peace and the quiet. They fully realized that all too soon their busy lives would drown out their memory of this blissful silence.

"I'm sorry he didn't show," the man gently said. After several minutes more, the man picked up his paddle and continued rowing back from whence they had come.

CPSIA information can be obtained
at www.ICGtesting.com
Printed in the USA
LVHW081521091019
633690LV00006B/160/P